CHRISTIE HODGEN

BOY MEETS GIRL

A NOVEL

New Issues Poetry & Prose

Western Michigan University
Kalamazoo, Michigan 49008

First Edition, 2022.

ISBN-13: 978-1-936970-74-2

Library of Congress Cataloging-in-Publication Data:
Hodgen, Christie.
Boy Meets Girl/Christie Hodgen
Library of Congress Control Number: 2021943296

Editor: Nancy Eimers
Managing Editor: Kimberly Kolbe
Art Direction: Nick Kuder
Cover Design: Paul Sizer
Production Manager: Paul Sizer
The Design Center, Gwen Frostic School of Art
College of Fine Arts
Western Michigan University

This book is the winner of the Association of Writers & Writing
Programs (AWP) Award for the Novel. AWP is a national, nonprofit
organization dedicated to serving American letters, writers, and
programs of writing.

Go to www.awpwriter.org for more information.

CHRISTIE HODGEN

BOY MEETS GIRL

A NOVEL

NEW ISSUES

 WESTERN MICHIGAN UNIVERSITY

Also by Christie Hodgen

Elegies for the Brokenhearted
Hello, I Must Be Going
A Jeweler's Eye for Flaw

For Jude

"It's never very pleasant in the morning to open The New York Times.*"*
—W.H. Auden

I.

Boy meets girl, is the usual story. Boy meets girl and chases girl, catches girl, then loses girl.

Or sometimes the story goes: Boy meets girl, chases and catches girl, boy and girl get married and buy a house. Then the boy and girl have kids, a little boy and a little girl, and pay a photographer to take pictures of their family sitting in a field, everyone matching, wearing blue jeans and bright sweaters. Boy and girl make these pictures into holiday cards, and stuff them in envelopes, along with attendant narratives describing the progress of their household year-to-date—the little boy has started kindergarten, scored his first soccer goal; the little girl can sing the alphabet—then address and mail these envelopes to other boys and girls across the country, whereupon their images are received and opened and pinned to corkboards, or sealed to the surface of refrigerators with magnets, or dropped into recycling bins, or sometimes, in the case of spiteful recipients, jealous ones, lonely ones, the cards are tossed in fireplaces and set aflame.

Occasionally: Boy meets girl, gets married, has kids, takes and mails pictures, etc., then meets another girl. A girl he likes better. Eventually the first girl finds out about the second, and the boy loses them both. Or marries the second girl. Then meets a third.

Often: Boy meets boy. Or girl meets girl.

But the story is never: Boy meets girl, though not at the

right time—she is still in high school, and he is just out of college, trying to make his way in the world—and so there is not much thought of chasing and catching, it is just a friendship. Boy and girl go about their lives, settle in different cities. One of them falls in love with someone else, the other has a child. Through it all, they keep in touch, talking on the phone once or twice a week, working through the small dilemmas of their daily lives, and also the political and existential dramas unfolding in the background. Though they see each other in person every few months—and though, now and then, one or the other wonders what it would be like if things were different, if they were together—mostly it's just the boy and the girl and the phone for twenty-five years. This is never how the story goes. This isn't how it goes, the girl thinks— the girl in this particular example, the girl we are talking about— because it doesn't make for a very good story. It's too long, too agonizing, there's too much back and forth, too much will-they, won't-they. And the ending—well, don't even get the girl started. Because even when a story like this finally comes to the end, even then it's not over.

1992

Here is the girl in a sandwich shop in Manchester, New Hampshire, the night it all starts.

Her name is Sammy. Or at least this is what she tells people when she's behind the counter. As in: Hi, I'm Sammy, the girl who makes the sandwiches. A little joke, though a private one—no one has noticed, put it together. Not so much as a smirk, not once.

This night, Sammy is rushing to close the shop. She has wrapped up all of the food and stashed it in the refrigerator, has filled and started the dishwasher, has wiped down all of the surfaces behind the counter. She has turned all the chairs up onto tabletops and is nearly done mopping the floor when he walks in—the future 42nd President of the United States. A little bell clangs, and a gust of wind fills the shop, as if, at the sight of the southern governor who appeared on *60 Minutes* just the week before—the candidate whose campaign is ablaze with celebrity and scandal—the shop has recognized him, and gasped. Sammy doesn't look up right away, but even before she sees the governor she can sense him—there's a kind of static in the air. It's true what they say about him, Bill Clinton. That he carries with him his own climate, his own energy. That he's a force of nature.

She straightens up, settles the mop in its bucket, takes a moment to wipe her brow with the back of her wrist. She is seventeen that year, and in the habit of exaggerating the motions of her labor. With her every move she hopes to suggest to the world that she is a pitiable creature, a poor soul trapped in a life of meaningless toil. Lately she has been reading Dickens, studying his heroes—Pip, Oliver Twist, David Copperfield—and has fallen into the habit of thinking of herself as one of them. She goes so far as to narrate the long, boring expanse of her days in the voice of Dickens. *Whether I shall turn out to be the hero of my own life*, she often thinks, sitting at her desk at school. And going through the lunch line: *Please, sir?* She sees herself as a character destined for greatness, poised unawares on the brink of some grand adventure: at any moment some hero, some villain, will walk into Bobbi's Hollywood Café, and everything will change.

Now onto this stage walks Bill Clinton, and who better? When Sammy turns and sees him—when she sees that someone important actually *has* arrived—she flinches. Not just because the governor is, at that moment in time, the most notorious man in the country, perhaps the world. But also because he's just kind of startling. He's so tall, for one thing—he takes over the room just by standing in it. And he's vibrant, his complexion pink and robust, his eyes bright. He seems to have been painted in oils, while the rest of the world is sketched in charcoal.

Yet somehow equal to these things, balancing them out—and Sammy understands this immediately, she feels as if she knows him in an instant—is a sense of the ordinary, the sense that the governor is a regular person, in the way that other candidates aren't. He holds himself with ease—hands in his pockets, head cocked. He's dressed just like anyone else, dark pants and a white shirt, open at the collar. On his wrist is a clunky watch, cheap plastic, the same kind Sammy's history teacher wears.

"Kind of a late night for someone your age," the governor says, "isn't it?" There's that slow Southern drawl, in every way the opposite of Sammy's New England language, in which people call to each other quick and angry, like crows.

"I guess," she says. "No more than usual."

"I don't want to cause you trouble," he says, nodding toward the deli case behind her. "Looks like you're closing up."

"No, no," she says. "It's no trouble. I can make you anything."

"That's fine," he says. "I appreciate that."

While he considers the menu board, sort of amused by it, it seems—Sammy has drawn along its borders cartoon versions of the very animals offered in sandwich form, smiling pigs and chickens and cows, in their expressions a friendliness she hopes will give customers pause—she puts the mop back in its bucket, takes up her place behind the counter. Her hands are shaking. Nothing interesting has ever happened to her before and she's filled with the sense of it. To occupy herself she opens the deli case and starts uncovering everything she'd just covered over in cellophane. In the deli case are long black bins of cold salads, various meats suspended in mayonnaise—chicken, crab, and a mixed seafood salad that includes tiny squid. She can see one now, its tentacle turned upward as if to defend itself against the net that ensnared it.

"These are all of our salads," she says, "but we also have regular sandwiches, any kind of sandwich you can think of, just about."

"What's good?" he asks. "What's the local special?"

"Well," says Sammy. "We're sort of known for our chicken salad. That's what most people order. It has grapes and walnuts and celery, and people like it." The governor is staring into the deli case, solemnly, as if considering how to handle some kind of global crisis. "I think it's okay," she says. "But I don't usually have it. I tend to go for, well, usually I just have a cheese sandwich."

"I don't want you to have to clean the slicer," he says.

He is so thoughtful. Like he knows and understands, even

before she does, the consequences of whatever agreement they reach together, like he's calculated everything in advance—his craving for one thing versus another, weighed against the amount of work it will cost her to satisfy that craving, versus the amount she will begrudge him, as she cleans off extra equipment, washes extra dishes. Then again—and this must carry the governor a long way—there's the likelihood she won't mind, that she's happy to do it, that this little encounter with a presidential candidate is the most exciting thing that's ever happened to her, that she'll be telling this story over and over, every chance she gets, for the rest of her life. "It's really no trouble," she says. "I don't have anywhere to be, anyway."

"Nowhere to be?" he says, chuckles. "I doubt that."

Sammy shrugs. She wants to convey to the governor the small, sad nature of her existence. That the world thinks nothing of her, that no one loves her, no one values her. And worst of all, that at such a young age, she is already used to it.

But the governor doesn't bite, just keeps staring in the case. Sammy's eyes dart about, looking at him, at the case, out the front window. She keeps thinking there must be people with him, staffers and reporters on his heels. She's worried someone will come in and ruin everything.

"I'll try the chicken salad," he finally says.

"When in Rome."

Okay. She is going to make a chicken salad sandwich for a possible future president. She finds a spoon and sticks it into the chicken salad. When she pulls up the spoon there's a moist crackling sound. Only then, the spoon heavy with chicken, does she realize she has nothing to put it on. So she sets the spoon back down in the vat and turns away to find the bread. Then she realizes she hasn't yet asked the governor what kind of bread he wants. She goes ahead and asks him. She has her back to him at this point, embarrassed.

"What's it usually come on?" he says.

"Marble rye."

"Fine, then. Give me the usual, local all the way."

"Okay." She bends down and pulls a sleeve of bread from the refrigerator, untwists its tie, fishes two slices out and sets them on the cutting board. Ties up the bread again, shoves it in the refrigerator. Then she remembers the dressings. "You have your choice of lettuce, tomato," she says. "Some people like pickles."

"Gimme all of it," he says.

"Sure thing." She opens the fridge again and digs everything out. It takes her a minute to find the tomatoes, then lettuce, then pickles. They're right in front of her, but she can't recognize anything. She's not doing such a great job. This is the worst job she's ever done with an order.

Finally Sammy gathers everything she needs and starts putting together the sandwich. She's torn between wanting to work quickly, to impress the governor with her efficiency, and wanting the moment to last. She tries to think of something to say. She considers asking him if he's really the governor, but that doesn't seem right—she knows he is, and he knows she knows. She considers asking him about his plans for the country, but that doesn't seem right, either. They are on a certain stage, and on this stage their behavior is governed by the fact that Sammy makes sandwiches, and the governor is hungry. On this stage, it doesn't matter who he is—he could be Jesus Christ, and she wouldn't ask him anything more than what he wanted to eat. The rule here is: if the governor wants to talk, to tell her how he plans to save the world, he'll have to bring it up himself.

She is really dragging things out. All she has to do is deposit a clump of chicken salad on a piece of bread, spread it around, arrange a leaf of lettuce, a slice of tomato, a few pickles. She's doing all of this, taking as much time as possible, but it's still going so fast. In a few seconds, it will be over. Tomorrow she'll be telling Bobbi Woolworth, the shop's owner—a sixty-year old woman who has modeled herself, in every conceivable way, after Marilyn Monroe, and whose fading looks, and efforts to keep them up, sort of make Sammy understand the cult surrounding Monroe, understand how fully it depends on her image having been arrested in youth—what happened. "I made Bill Clinton a sandwich," Sammy will say. "And?" Bobbi will say, sort of breathless, patting her hair into place. "What was he like?" "And nothing," Sammy will say. "He ordered a chicken salad. That's pretty much it." Then Bobbi and Sammy will both stare at the vat of chicken salad in the case. Bobbi will take a spoon and scoop out a bite for herself, then hand the spoon to Sammy and, though she doesn't eat meat, she'll have a bite anyway, and they'll both stand there chewing, savoring the chicken salad that dwelled, briefly, next to the chicken salad eaten by a presidential candidate, and this will be, in many ways, the closest either of them will ever get to the White House, to any real power.

By this point the governor is walking around the shop, hands in his pockets, whistling. Not any particular tune, just a series of plaintive notes strung together. He's looking at the pictures on the wall, old black-and-white shots of celebrities— Cary Grant, Elizabeth Taylor, Paul Newman, Doris Day. There are, or course, several pictures of Marilyn on the wall, in various poses and moods. There's the famous one on the city grate, where she's pushing her dress down against the draft. One where she's wrapped in a white fur shawl, her head thrown back. A picture of her and Joe DiMaggio, newly married. The governor stands in front of the pictures, lost in them. He's far off, probably back in Arkansas, the swamp where he spent his youth, where he first went to the movies and fell in love and dreamed of escape. *He's gone,* Sammy thinks. *He isn't going to talk to me.*

But just when she's given up he turns away from the pictures—he is suddenly back in the room. He looks right at her, like she's the most important thing in the world. "How old are you?" he says. A bit of a smile.

"Seventeen," she says. "I can't vote yet. So there's no point in, you know, talking to me."

"Seventeen," he says. Shakes his head, laughs. Everything is so easy for him. Like he's got the entire range of human emotions in stock, ready to fire. Wistful, is what he's produced here. "What do you plan to do with yourself," he says, "when you finish high school?"

"College," she says. "I have a few applications out."

"What's your top choice?"

"Virginia."

"Good school," he says. "Good school."

"They have the best program," Sammy says, "for what I want to do. Which is literature. I want to study literature."

"Literature!" he says, laughs. "That's fine. That's a noble enterprise." His mouth is open more or less constantly, Sammy realizes, in a kind of bemusement.

"I think so. And plus, you know, the money. The money's pretty great." The governor laughs again. She has had success with this joke before—that year, people are always asking her what she plans to do with herself. "I'm waiting to hear," she tells him. "But I think I have a good chance at a scholarship. I'm at the top of my class, all A's." She doesn't know what's come over her. For some reason, she wants to communicate to the governor that she's not just a kid in an apron, that she has hidden depths, untapped potential. Her every word is a crumb strewn along a trail. She hopes to lead the governor through the tour of her life, to make him see it all: the little house she lives in with her father, its rotting cedar shakes, its sloping front porch. Just inside the door she will show him her father asleep on his recliner in the living room, the television running, the local news and its scenes of grim resignation—the reporters standing on the street corners on which people have been shot and killed, or outside the factories where workers have been laid off. Then they will move on, hand in hand, to the kitchen, its linoleum floor buckled and peeling, dishes stacked in the sink and on the countertop, their faces smeared with the remnants of family meals, which are sad affairs, spaghetti warmed from a can, baked beans covered in ketchup. Behind the refrigerator and in the cupboards, mousetraps, a dozen of them, some flipped over with mice—her father's constant and mortal enemies—dead beneath them, in saintly repose, their eyes closed, their front teeth curved over their bottom lips. Then they will move to the tiny bathroom with its hexagonal tile floor, a handful of tiles coming loose and going missing each year, its perpetually dripping bathtub faucet. Then they will move on to Sammy's bedroom, where the governor will regard the twin bed on which she lies awake at night listening to that dripping faucet, slow and steady, and the governor will understand, somehow, that this young girl lies awake at night thinking of the days of her life slipping away with the same agonizing regularity and slowness, and he will understand how through it all she has persevered, applied herself to her studies, how through some miracle similar to the one visited on him in his youth she is now on the verge of earning a scholarship to a prestigious institution, where she will study novels and poetry, where she will be the last knight volunteering to defend a dying empire. Sammy wants to communicate to Bill Clinton that she is smart, like he is, that she has ambitions, like he does, but also that her ambitions are of a finer nature, having nothing to do with personal or political gain, that they have to do instead with the spirit, with the soul...

"That's fine," the governor says. "That's a fine thing. I don't think I could do as well, if I were in school today."

"Oh," she says. "That's not what I hear."

She has broken the rules twice now, has violated the sandwich maker's code of conduct. She has been too familiar with the governor, suggested she was an intimate, made mention of his job and his legendary intelligence. She can't seem to stop herself.

"I'm sure you'll have your choice of schools," he says.

"Well, it all depends on whether I get a scholarship. My dad's just, he's just a janitor."

"That's hard work," the governor says. "That's a noble thing."

Sammy nods. An image of her father flashes through her head, pushing a wheeled trash can down the long halls of her high school. A familiar feeling rushes through her. The agony of wanting to stay with her father in this town, to ease his sadness. And in equal measure, a mad desire to flee.

Sammy wraps a pickle in foil, puts it in the bag along with the sandwich. Adds a bag of chips. Rolls down the top. Normally she would just hand the sandwich over the counter, but in this case she brings it out to the governor. She hopes to offer it to him formally, with best wishes, but coming out from behind the counter her foot catches the corner of the mop bucket and she trips, falls into him. "Whoops!" she says. He catches her at the elbow. His hand is warm, and soft, and moist. She sort of jumps away from him, like she's been shocked.

"Easy, now," he says.

"I'm so sorry," she says. She can feel herself blushing. She thrusts the bag at the governor with one hand and sort of waves with the other. "Here. Here you go."

"How much do I owe you?"

"Nothing," she answers. "Don't worry about it."

"Come on, now."

"No, really," she tells him. "It's store policy. If a candidate comes in we don't, we never charge a candidate. It's part of the city's, you know, it's part of our hospitality." This is complete bullshit. She is surprised how easily it comes. It occurs to her that maybe this is what it's like for everyone else—that talking is so easy because none of it's real.

"I appreciate that," the governor says. He's probably used to this. Poor people, Sammy is just beginning to understand, are always giving things away to rich people, to powerful people, in the hopes of proving something.

The governor takes his wallet out of his pocket and fishes out a bill, deposits it in the empty tip jar. It sort of floats there, suspended, its edges pressed against the side of the jar. Sammy can see Lincoln's face staring at her, solemnly. Looking at Lincoln, it occurs to her that the governor will be president soon—however unlikely it seems at the moment. At the moment, Clinton is in trouble and Paul Tsongas, the well-liked senator from Massachusetts with the sensible economic plan, is in the lead. There are Tsongas signs—*Tcitizens for Tsongas!*—all over Sammy's neighborhood, and his volunteers are everywhere, it seems. In fact, a small group of them, three boys just out of college, comes into Bobbi's every night for sandwiches, and Sammy has developed a bit of a rapport with them. They like to ask her questions as she's putting their orders together, wanting to know the local opinion on issues like education and nuclear power, military funding, acid rain. *It depends*, she says. Or, *I don't think anyone around here really cares about that.* She tends to act aloof, because that is what voters do in Manchester—they like to tease the candidates and their staff, waiting to see how much they'll promise, how deep a hole they will dig for themselves. But in truth, Sammy is charmed by these boys, and has come to think of herself, too, as a Tsongas supporter—at least she would vote for him if she were old enough.

In Sammy's mind, Tsongas is destined for the presidency and his young staff, the first boys she has ever really spoken to at any length, will be moving on to Washington. Often it has occurred to her that these very boys for whom she is assembling sandwiches, soon these boys will be running the country.

But none of that matters now, all of it fades to black, because Bill Clinton has arrived like an eclipse, and is casting the world in his shadow. There is nothing anyone can do to stop him. Standing before Bill Clinton, Sammy herself has instantly converted, has proven a traitor with little to no resistance. She has even contributed to his campaign, given it sustenance. She has not only witnessed, but believed.

"I really think you're going to be president," she says. It just flies out.

"I hope so," he says. "I'm sure trying."

"You will. I can feel it."

He's backing toward the door, now. "Good luck with your studies." He sounds hoarse, tired. "I hope you get that scholarship."

"We're both waiting to hear, I guess."

"Maybe we'll see each other down there in Virginia," he says. Winks.

"I hope so."

He pushes the door open and the cold rushes in again, the little bell clangs.

He's out the door but leans back in for a second. "What's your name?" he says.

"Sammy."

He smiles wide, as if pleased by her name. "Good to meet you, Sammy."

And that's it. He's gone.

Sammy stands there, staring out into the darkness. Then she

hears the crank of an engine. A set of boxy headlights flashes on. The governor's car turns and advances right for the shop, and for a second it seems like he will come driving through the window, but then he turns, and she sees the car in profile, some kind of overlong Buick or Oldsmobile. She sees the future president, the gleam of his hair, then the tail lights as he breaks at the end of the strip mall, then the car disappearing into traffic.

Sammy sits on the floor behind the counter and replays everything in her head. She thinks mostly about tripping over the bucket. Over and over she sees it, how she's bringing him his sandwich and her foot catches on the wheel of the mop bucket and she trips. *Whoops*, she says. Keeps saying. It plays like a bloopers reel, in slow motion, forward and then reverse. She can still feel the warmth of the governor's hand on her wrist.

Then she starts to imagine the governor back in his hotel room, taking his sandwich out of its bag. She realizes now that she piled more chicken salad onto the governor's bread than the bread could reasonably be expected to hold, and when the time comes, when the governor unwraps his sandwich and spreads out the paper over the hotel bedspread—this is happening even now, she thinks—she will be there with him, sort of, in his hotel room, or at least it might be said she is there in spirit, and when he goes to take a bite a clump of chicken will fall in his lap, and he'll be torn—grateful that Sammy has given him so much chicken but annoyed she overdid it. He'll wipe the mayonnaise from his pants with his thumb, lick it, wipe at the stain again, though it won't quite come out. This is the price of running for president, he'll think, that people take hold of you and leave their greasy prints behind. At that moment, it will probably occur to Bill Clinton that someone at the top of her class, and with the grades Sammy claimed to have, might have figured out the physics of a chicken salad sandwich in advance and avoided this blunder. There's no way she'll be getting that scholarship, he'll think. As he eats the sandwich his head will hang heavy with this bit of dramatic irony, which probably settles over him at the end of each day: all the people he meets, all the dreams and hopes they tell him about, all of this is unfounded. He must know, somewhere, that all of this belief is misplaced, that nothing will really get better. He must know this even as he promises to help. It must bother him, Sammy thinks. Or maybe it doesn't.

She sits and thinks about these things until her father pulls up in his rumbling Buick. Then she scrambles up and makes two sandwiches, faster than she's ever made them—a cheese sandwich for herself, and a chicken salad for her father. She makes two sandwiches every night and never pays for them, a bit of petty larceny she both does and does not feel bad about, but tonight she has given Bill Clinton a free sandwich, and now her father, and the vat of chicken salad looks suspiciously low. She takes a giant jar of mayonnaise out of the case and deposits a heaping spoonful onto the salad, mixes it around, tries to fluff it so the bin looks fuller. In the process, she finds one of Bobbi Woolworth's fake nails in the salad—a blood red nail with a diamond encrusted at the tip—which is not unusual: Bobbi is always losing her nails in the food. For a terrifying moment Sammy imagines the governor biting into one of Bobbi's fingernails, and adds to her list of possible horrors his discovery of the nail and his disgust, possibly even rage. But then again, she thinks, one lost nail per vat of chicken salad is probably the statistical limit, there couldn't possibly be two. Could there?

She gives up and covers the bin, wraps the sandwiches, puts everything away, dumps the mop water out, turns off the lights, pushes open the front door with her shoulder. Just then she sees the tip jar, Lincoln still suspended there, and goes and grabs the bill, stuffs it in her pocket, heads back out the door, the bell clanking again, locks it, all of this in a mad rush—she can't wait to get to the car and tell her father everything, to tell him he's eating from the same batch of chicken salad as a possible future president. *Made by the same hands*, she imagines saying, in the dramatic voice of the ubiquitous narrator of all movie trailers. She imagines turning her hands in front of him as if they were sacred, holy, but when she settles in next to him—when she sees him in his red plaid jacket, with matching hat, the slight twitch at the corner of his mouth that indicates: *I am happy to see you, you know I would smile if I could, please accept this slight tic as an indication of my fondness for you*—she can't say a word about it. It's always this way with him. There are times you can talk to him, and times you'd better not.

"Hey, Buddy," he says, his breath fogging in front of him.

"Hey," she says.

"Busy night?"

"Someone came in at the last minute. I had to clean everything up again. Sorry."

"Tough break," he says. He knows all about this. Kids are always throwing up on his floors, just after he's cleaned them.

On the drive home, they listen to a sports program on the radio, men calling in to obsess over the Red Sox even in the off-season, retirees calling from Bradenton, Florida, where the team spends its winters. "We're excited for the boys to be down here with us," an old man shouts, his voice thick with phlegm. "It's seventy degrees and we're ready for some baseball." The man starts convulsing in a cough and the host hangs up on him. "We're all ready," he says. "We're ready to win."

Snow has begun falling, coming down in swirling circles, flakes landing on the windshield and sticking for a moment, then melting away. Sammy's father turns on the wipers and they moan as they drag themselves over the glass. In a few hours, she thinks, it will be morning again and they will be back in the car driving to school. Her father will park the car next to the dumpster behind the music wing and then unlock the band room door, which is secured by a chain and padlock. They'll walk through the dark room, which smells of dust and spit, then out along the hallways. He'll turn the lights on and they will flicker to life. When they get to the cafeteria he'll unlock it, and Sammy will sit at a table and read and then at some point will place the book on the table and fall asleep on it. Some minutes later she'll wake to the sounds of kids coming through the halls, a dull roar, the slamming of lockers, she'll go to homeroom with ink smeared on her face, and the day will begin, the same day for three and a half years now.

When they pull into the driveway the house is dark but for the glow of the television, which is always running. Sammy and her father come through the door and stomp their feet, kick off their boots, hang their coats on the rack. Scratch the head of their basset hound, who has been waiting at the door for their arrival. Her father goes to the television and fiddles with the VCR, and soon *Wheel of Fortune* appears on screen. They sit on the couch together, the dog at their feet now, whining. Sammy passes her father his sandwich and he unwraps it, she unwraps hers. She has been bringing home sandwiches from Bobbi's for almost two years now, and they have done this so many times, their movements always the same, they have become like some kind of Catholic ritual. There is a solemnity to them, the handing over of the sandwich and the unwrapping, the moment of silence they observe before taking the first bite. And finally, the conveyance of the last morsel to the dog, like some sort of communion.

They sit through *Wheel of Fortune*, speeding through the commercials, then *Jeopardy!* They have been watching these shows for as long as Sammy can remember, taping and watching and then taping over them again, so many times the picture is faint and warbling, so that watching these shows has the same quality, visually, as recalling a dream. Though the shows are different they produce the same effect in Sammy—an uncertain and grasping feeling. The moments she spends in the space of not knowing—of trying to solve a puzzle or think of the right question—are an exquisite agony. "Got it," her father says, all through *Wheel*, always before Sammy and usually before the contestants. During *Jeopardy!* her father states the questions, often running the board. Sammy and her father keep a tally of the prize money he would have won if he had been standing behind one of the podiums. Occasionally they mention the things they would purchase with his winnings—a new car, a beach house. A whole arsenal of luxury custodial supplies. A gold handled mop, her father says. A motorized trash can.

After *Jeopardy!* they switch to live television and watch the news, and then finally David Letterman, for whom they've been waiting all night. The father's interest is in Dave's opening monologue, his sardonic take on the culture and politics of the day. But Sammy's interest is in the following bit of banter Dave has with his bandleader, Paul Shaffer. Dave will ask Paul a question and Paul—short, bald, wearing dark glasses and a weird velvet jacket with a glittery collar—sort of sneers into his microphone, offering something so lame Dave needn't even reply. Simply presenting his blank face to the audience gets them laughing. The banter between Dave and Paul is one of the great sources of anxiety in Sammy's life, a nightly interaction that seems always to be bordering on Paul's humiliation, though then again, Paul never seems to understand he's the butt of a joke. In Dave's cool handling of a strange character there is something of magnanimity, something of condescension, and Sammy recognizes this attitude from the way many people talk to her. She has recently come to understand that she is a bit of a strange character. That there are winners and losers in the world, and that the sands are always shifting. Between two people one person always knows what is going on—what the score is—and the other person doesn't. And the person who doesn't is the fool.

Lately, the fact that Sammy almost never knows what's going on has begun to trouble her. With the boys from the Tsongas campaign, for instance, she is often at a loss for words. They are always using words like *Malthusian* and *Cartesian*, talking of Mao and Guevara and Marx, and she struggles to understand what they're saying. *Dialectical materialism*, she heard one of them say once, and she'd scrambled to retain the phrase in her mind, repeating it over and over until she could write it down, then look it up. And even then, looking up each word separately in the dictionary, she didn't quite get it. She wonders if college will be like this, one long conversation whose meaning is lost on her.

Dave breaks to commercial and Sammy finally turns to her father, who is half asleep.

"I need to tell you something," she says.

"Okay." He doesn't turn toward her. Sleep is tugging at him, he is almost lost to it.

"I just met Bill Clinton."

He rolls his head toward her. His eyes are open, now. "Really?" he says.

"Really. I made him a sandwich. I talked to him for like, twenty minutes."

"Huh. How was it? What was he like?"

"Amazing," she says. "Oh my god, it was so, it was just like, it was *wonderful*."

He raises an eyebrow. Even the dog lifts his head.

"He's going to win. I'm telling you, this guy is, he's more than just another guy. There's something huge about him, it's like he's not even human, it's like he's a *superhero* or something."

Her father's expression is skeptical. A skepticism rooted, Sammy thinks, in Clinton's dodging the draft. And smoking without inhaling. Causing pain in his marriage.

"He's not a serious candidate," her father says. "He's just having his fifteen minutes. When it comes down to it, when people get in the booth, they're going to go for the statesman, the person with the actual ideas for how to make things better. They're going to turn away from the scandal."

"I think you're wrong," Sammy says. "I'm telling you right now there's something about this guy, he wins people over. I really think he's going to win."

She recounts everything with the governor, and the sandwich, in excruciating detail. Her father's face works through several expressions, most of them scornful, but for a few seconds she thinks she sees a glimmer of interest, of belief. When she gets to the part with the bucket he laughs, and she keeps going, right up to the part when Clinton leaves, but then comes in again to ask her name.

"You said your name was Sammy?" her father asks.

"Well," she says, "it just flew out." It is the first nickname she has ever had and she is attached to it—she's trying to make it stick.

But confessing this bit about the name seems to have been a mistake. Because she has done something stupid, and kind of embarrassing, nothing she's said has any merit.

"You're a good kid," her father says. "But you're still a kid. You don't know how these things go."

"I still think you're wrong," she tells him. This is the first time in her life she has ever felt like she might know what she's talking about, like she knows more than her father does. She is part of this, now—she has a secret knowledge.

"President Clinton. Don't say I didn't warn you."

1992

The following night.

The boy in question, Ben, is riding around Manchester in a 1978 Volkswagen Beetle, wondering how he came to be where he is. What chain of events, what series of wrong turns, has led him here? Why has he signed up to work twenty-hour days, and sleep on the couches and floors of campaign offices in this miserable, third-tier city? What exactly does he think will happen to his body, eating whatever food he can find—Pop Tarts, stale pizza, those hot dogs turning on rollers at 7-11s, left so long under heat lamps they have dehydrated? Why is he drinking so much lukewarm, and yet somehow burned coffee? Why is he doing this to himself?

Ben doesn't need to look far for the answer, for in the seat next to him, driving aggressively, swerving to pass other cars but never once to avoid a pothole, is Kurtz. His freshman roommate in college and best friend for the past five years. Kurtz is the answer, both the sum and square root of every one of Ben's problems.

Tonight, they are out on one of Kurtz's famous repo missions. Which means they are driving all over the city pulling up Bill Clinton's campaign signs. They are creeping through neighborhoods, plucking them from lawns, and then stuffing them in the Beetle. They do this until the Beetle is full and they need to find a dumpster. They have already filled two and are now casing a stretch of road, a seemingly endless expanse of strip malls, looking for a third. America the Beautiful, Ben thinks. Not for the first time. He is from New York and can't make sense of these little towns, their wide streets and squat, ugly buildings. All the stucco. The power lines. The vast parking lots filled with pickup trucks and minivans. He wonders if, in addition to existential crises, there are such things as aesthetic crises. If so, he is having one. The main side effect seems to be an anxious, crawling feeling. It's like the opposite of claustrophobia. He feels the need for great, towering structures around him. Massive, bustling crowds. Fleets of yellow taxis, all of them honking their horns.

Kurtz swerves into the parking lot of a Dairy Queen, loops behind the drive-thru and parks the Beetle next to the dumpster. When he opens the door, the car's horn starts honking—a pinched but somehow still unbearably loud bleating. Kurtz had bought the car—or rather, Ben had bought it for him—during their last week of college, from an aging hippie who had installed an alarm but never bothered to fix it when it went haywire. The alarm went off every time a door opened, and sounded for a full minute. "It's like, *possessed*, man," the hippie had said. He was an outrageous cliché, with long silver hair tied back in a leather string, a tie-dye shirt, cargo shorts, Birkenstocks. "It's possessed but it starts every single time, guaranteed, man." Ben had bought the car anyway—it was only five hundred dollars, and Kurtz needed it for his job with the campaign. "Consider it a graduation present," Ben had said. He'd felt good about helping Kurtz at the time, magnanimous. But now, listening to the horn sound yet again, he regrets it—it is only possibly to feel good about buying this car if you never have to ride in it, he decides. He feels a headache emerging between his eyes.

Kurtz leans into the back seat and wrestles out an armload of signs. He takes a few steps toward the dumpster and is about to hoist the signs over the top when an employee steps out from behind the dumpster, a cigarette hanging from his mouth. He is just a skinny, pimpled kid in a Dairy Queen uniform—a polo shirt and an apron, khakis, a visor—and yet in this situation he outranks Kurtz, the Harvard graduate and presidential campaign employee. "Take that shit somewhere else," the kid says.

"Right on, man," Kurtz says. "Sorry, dude."

So Kurtz comes back to the car and starts shoving signs in the back again. Boris—a young campaign volunteer Kurtz picked up somewhere along the line, who follows Kurtz around like a disciple, a Russian emigré whose accent drives Ben crazy, and who is always leaning forward in the car, sticking his head between Ben and Kurtz to offer opinions no one wants to hear—complains for the hundredth time. "I do not have any room for my legs!" he says. "I cannot put them down!"

"Well," Kurtz says, shoving in the last sign, "this is the price we pay for democracy."

Kurtz isn't back on the road even a minute before a cop car pulls up behind them and sounds its siren, turns on its spinning red lights—they are being pulled over. "Fuck!" Kurtz yells, his voice even higher than usual, launched into the frequency of panic. "Oh *fuck*." He slides the Beetle to the side of the road. Regards the officer in the rearview. "Was I speeding?" he appeals to Ben. "Did I blow a stop sign? Did I, like, *fail to yield* or some shit like that?"

"All of those things," Ben tells him. "Although not within the last few minutes."

The officer approaches the car, and Kurtz cranks down his window. "Can I help you, officer?" he says. His tone is obsequious, but his voice is wavering.

"I've seen you riding up and down this stretch of road," the officer says. He leans his forearm on the door, pokes his head into the window. His head is buzzed like a boy's but it is silver, Ben sees—he is probably their parents' age. This is good. Ben knows enough about the world to know you don't want to get pulled over by a new kid.

"Your view is obstructed, you know," the officer says.

"Yes, sir," says Kurtz.

"That's a hazard," says the officer. "Especially on a night like this." There is some sort of freezing mix coming down, which seems to be a permanent condition in Manchester. Tiny pellets of ice have already covered over the windshield.

"You boys from Massachusetts?" says the officer.

"Yes, sir," Kurtz says.

"They're from Harvard," Boris adds, leaning up front. Probably the worst thing he could have said to a police officer. Ben shoots Boris a withering glance, and he retreats back behind the signs.

"What are you doing with all these signs?" the officer asks. There is an awkward beat of silence. "You know we've been getting some complaints about people's signs going missing?"

"We know, Sir," Ben says. "We're with the Clinton campaign. We're putting signs up for people who called and asked for them." He holds up his notebook, which is almost always in his lap. He is constantly taking notes, hoping to write a book about the campaign. Within the last five minutes he has written: *Dairy Queen kid behind dumpster, red visor, pimpled neck.* He has also drawn a cartoon of Boris, who is easy to caricature, pale and skinny and sickly looking, with long dark hair parted on the side, and a creepy little moustache, like Gogol. A dialogue bubble rises from his mouth: *I cannot move my legs!!!*

There passes a brief moment during which the police officer regards Ben, then the notebook, then Ben again. All the officer would have to do is ask to see the notebook. To confirm there are, in fact, multiple names and addresses listed there, people wanting Clinton signs in their yards. The trick, Ben knows, is not to break, not to waver in the slightest. He holds the policeman's gaze. Turns up one corner of his mouth slightly, lifts one eyebrow—an expression of confused innocence he has honed over the years.

"Okay, boys," the police officer says. "Go unload those signs and then go on home." He slaps the Beetle's door, then walks off toward his car. "Drive safe."

"Yes, Sir," Kurtz calls after him. "Thank you, Sir."

Then they're back on the road, the officer following behind, until Kurtz turns off into a residential neighborhood. All the houses here are small and boxy, Ben notes, just two windows and a door, and they look to him like surprised, horrified faces.

Once they are clear from the trooper's range, Kurtz explodes. "Fuck!" he yells. Pounds the wheel. He leans on the horn—as if they need to hear it again. "We need to turn this shit around," he says. "This isn't working. Everything we touch, everything's turning to *shit!*" He lets out a little scream. The whole scene would be dramatic, if Ben weren't so used to it. All through college, Kurtz had exploded into little tantrums. Multiple times a day something pushed him over the edge—a headline in the paper, something he saw on television, the drunken chatter of other students walking beneath their window at night—and he flew into a rage. He objected to hundreds of categories of offenses, wide swaths of humanity and its behavior, but his essential problem was always the same: he could not manage to bend the world to his will.

In this case, Ben supposes, Kurtz has a point. He had spent his time at Harvard studying the American political system, charting its history and mastering its processes, and now, instead of writing speeches or crafting policy, as he'd imagined when he signed on to work with the campaign, he is sliding around Manchester's icy roads, trying to unload a carful of stolen campaign signs. Worse, his candidate isn't doing so well—or not as well as he should be. Tsongas is slipping in the polls to a draft-dodger, a pot smoker, a serial adulterer with a honky-tonk accent. None of it makes any sense.

Eight months ago, when Ben and Kurtz had thrown their

caps in the air at graduation, the world had seemed to be theirs for the taking: carpets would unfurl for them, doors would slide open. *Roll on, deep and dark blue ocean, roll*, Ben had written, in his farewell note to Kurtz—because a little Byron never killed anyone. *Ten thousand fleets sweep over thee in vain*. What he had wanted to express to Kurtz was the inevitability he felt, the power, the absolute certainty of their future victories. Everything they wanted would be theirs, everything they designed would be built. But here they were eight months later, and none of that was happening. Fleets were sweeping over them, so to speak, not so much in vain.

Ben stares out the window. It is an exercise he performs sometimes, an exercise his mother, a psychiatrist, taught him. He stares and tries to remove himself from his surroundings and regard them in an objective, detached manner. He does this whenever he needs to retrace his steps, find out where he went wrong. Was it deciding, last month, to join Kurtz on the campaign trail? Obviously, that had been a mistake. But even before that, he had faltered, he had cut short his year abroad and come home. And why? For what reason? Because he had missed Kurtz, he has to admit. Missed being around Kurtz's crazed ranting, his naked ambition. Or to be more exact, Ben had missed the purpose Kurtz had given his life, for if Ben weren't around to take care of Kurtz, what would become of him?

The real question is, Ben decides, how and when he had come to consider himself Kurtz's guardian. When did that happen? He thinks for a moment, but can't remember ever feeling any other way about Kurtz. Even when they first met, back at Harvard. He tries to recall it exactly. As if remembering those first moments will help him understand what afflicts him now.

That first day, Ben had arrived at the dorm around noon, with his parents. For over an hour he had suffered through his mother's ministrations. She had made up his bed with the Ralph

Lauren sheets and comforters she had bought, had hung up his clothes in the closet—an array of shirts to rival Gatsby's, along with two new suits, blue and black, and a tuxedo. She had unpacked the new bath towels, robe, and slippers she had found at Barney's. The shaving kit. The soaps and lotions, the toothbrushes and toothpaste. Ben had sat on his bed, sulking, flipping through a course catalog, while his father had circled the room, hands in his pockets, head down, quietly angry in the way he always was when Ben's mother was spoiling him. "Greta," he said. More than once. "That's enough. For God's sake, that's enough. Let's go."

When his mother had finally finished, she asked about lunch. But Ben's father had insisted they head back to the city. They went back and forth about it, five or six rounds, and Ben felt what he usually did around them: conflicted. It had been this way his whole childhood. His mother spoiling him. His father protesting. Ben's affections had gone back and forth between them over the years. He was grateful for his mother's attention, yet also felt she should stop treating him like a child, that he should be given a chance to make his own way.

His parents were still arguing when Ben sensed, from the corner of his eye, a presence lurking in the doorway. He looked up and saw Kurtz—a short, slight boy with a giant duffel bag slung over his shoulder. He looked like a caddy, like someone hired to carry a bag up three flights of stairs, to deliver it in advance of his master's arrival. He had a small, delicate build—he couldn't have been more than five-three—and dark eyes, pale skin. His lips were bright red, and wet-looking. His hair was cut short, except at the top—a dark wing swung down over his left eye. He was wearing a green and blue rugby shirt, khaki pants, boat shoes, the uniform they all wore in those days, the clothes that said to the world: I belong here. Though on Kurtz, something was off. His clothes were too big, and wrinkled. The collar of his shirt was frayed.

That first moment, Ben had caught Kurtz frozen in

uncertainty—he was standing in the doorway with his knuckle poised to knock, his mouth open. Maybe that's what it was. The hesitation Kurtz had displayed. The obvious effort he had made to fit in, to dress the part, and the slight way it had failed—all if it had stirred something in Ben.

"Hi," Ben had said. He stood up from the bed, and his parents stopped talking, turned to the door. "Three-fifteen?" Kurtz said, pointing to the number affixed to the wall beside the door frame.

"Three-fifteen," Ben said.

"Looks like we're roommates," Kurtz said. He stepped into the room, extended his hand to Ben's parents. "The Rosenbergs, I presume." He shook the parents' hands, then Ben's. Ben was over six feet tall, broadly built, and had the sensation, bending down to shake hands with Kurtz, that he was shaking hands with a child, going through a bit of mock formality, for sport. *This is how to properly greet a gentleman*, his mother had taught him, years back. They had practiced with the doorman of their building, an old-timer named Alfred who wore a black uniform with brass buttons. It was like that now, an exercise, an indulgence, except for this time, Ben was the adult.

"It's a pleasure to meet all of you," Kurtz said. He bowed slightly, in the direction of Ben's father.

"What a polite young man," Ben's father said. "Where are your parents?"

"Oh, I took the bus in," said Kurtz, in a casual manner he seemed to have rehearsed. "My mother had to work."

What happened next was something that took Ben completely by surprise. His father, who had never once prolonged a social encounter to Ben's knowledge, who only endured them when absolutely necessary, said, "We were just discussing lunch. I hope you'll let us take you out with us."

So they'd gone to lunch.

During the meal, Ben had watched the dynamics at the table, watched as the bond developed between his father—who had grown up poor and clawed his way into Harvard, then Harvard Med, and who had ultimately married an heiress—and Kurtz. Meanwhile, Ben's mother was sitting back in the booth, her eyes going from Kurtz to the father, back and forth, occasionally stopping to take stock of Ben's expression. She could see what was happening and was worried for her son. She tried to use one of the tactics she practiced with her patients, cutting in now and then with re-directions, attempts to turn the conversation. "Ben likes to play tennis," she offered, hoping Kurtz would bite. "Maybe you two could play." But Kurtz had foiled her efforts. "I never learned," he said. "I always had to help my mother after school, then I had another job in a butcher shop on the weekends."

Ben's father nodded in approval. He had worked two jobs all through high school and college, and hardly let a day go by without mentioning it. "That's good," he said. "It's good to have that kind of job when you're young."

"It was honest work," Kurtz said. "And who knows, I might end up back there. There's a good chance I'll flunk out by the end of the year." He said this casually, dipping a french fry in ketchup. "The only reason I got into Harvard was because Bobby Jr. wrote me a letter."

Kurtz looked up, wanting to calculate the impression he'd made. The expression on Ben's mother's face was somewhere in the neighborhood of astonished. "Bobby *Kennedy?*" she asked.

Kurtz had inflated this little balloon and let it go, watched it float for a moment. And then, for his next trick, pulled out a pin and popped it. "My mom," he explained, "is one of the cleaning ladies at the compound in Hyannisport."

Looking back, Ben decides this was the moment Kurtz had

joined the family—they had all come to an agreement just then, instantly and wordlessly, to adopt him. Here he was before them, Kurtz, a veritable Oliver Twist, the son of the Kennedy's cleaning woman. They were honor-bound to help him, to help make true his American dream. Ben's father seemed delighted, his mother amused. As for Ben, he felt as if he had just been given charge of a little brother.

Like all little brothers, Kurtz turned out to be two people— formal and solicitous around adults, and a sniveling mess in their absence. Within a matter of days Ben could tell that Kurtz had trouble controlling himself—not just casually, but in a clinical sense. It became clear that the composure Kurtz practiced in public spaces was a deliberate falsehood, a grueling compression of his true nature. Each afternoon Kurtz came back to their room from class and practically exploded. Words came tumbling out of him, so fast and loud Ben could hardly make sense of them. Kurtz would deliver to Ben, nearly word for word it seemed, the same lectures he'd attended that day, annotated with Kurtz's opinion of his professors and fellow students. *Fucking moron*, was one of his favorites. Or occasionally, *fucking genius*. Whenever Kurtz settled down to read, or write his papers, he stopped every few minutes to ask Ben's opinion: Was Thorsten Veblen's view of capitalism prescient, or overly pessimistic? Where exactly did things break down during the transubstantiation of Marx and Engels's ideas into reality? He couldn't go more than three minutes without drawing Ben into a dialogue. And he was always moving around, pacing, waving his arms, or throwing a rubber ball against the wall and catching it, over and over.

And this: Kurtz was a horrible slob. His clothes were strewn across the floor, he *slept* in his clothes, actually, and didn't shower or brush his teeth on any kind of predictable schedule.

He seemed to eat nothing but Twinkies and Ding Dongs, and left their wrappers everywhere. Ben had grown up on the Upper East Side, in a sprawling, four-bedroom apartment with a view of Central Park. His home was tended to by a maid, his clothes washed and pressed and hung as if by magic—he hardly thought of what happened to them when he took them off. There was always someone there who took care of those things, someone who did the grocery shopping and cooking, someone to guard the door, sign for mail, phone for cabs. His new life here, with Kurtz, felt like a stint on the set of a movie.

What kind of movie, he wasn't sure. Kurtz was the lead, certainly—he had all the lines. But was this a tragedy? A comedy? A mystery? There was something admirable about Kurtz, something suggesting he would rise to greatness, and yet something doomed, too. Nothing symbolized this tension better than the giant corkboard Kurtz bought and stationed on his desk, propped against the wall. On it, Kurtz had pinned the names of the classes he was taking, the professors and their positions in the university, the papers and books they'd published. By the end of his first semester, Kurtz had charted his course through all four years: which classes he would take with which professors, the internships and scholarships he would apply for, the clubs he would join. His notations spread across the whole board and then outward, on Post-it notes, onto the wall. Above all of these notes, at the peak of the pyramid he had created, Kurtz had pasted a drawing of the White House. It was a painstakingly crafted, though still kind of sad rendering. He had drawn the house on a piece of copy paper, cut it out, then drawn and cut out columns and windows and steps, and pasted them in place. Starting at the bottom, and working upwards, it was as if every person Kurtz met or hoped to meet, every book he read or planned to read, was a stone on a path, a path leading him to Washington. Looking over these notes,

Ben was reminded of the crime dramas he sometimes watched with his mother, stories in which FBI agents were tracking killers. These agents filled their corkboards with pictures and maps, and linked together every point of contact with red string. At some point in these shows, there was always a slowly-widening shot of the corkboard, the agent standing in front of it with his head in his hands, stumped. It was a shot meant to suggest the agent, himself, had gone mad—that the pursuit of his goal had destroyed him.

At the end of their first year, Ben went out and rented himself an apartment in an exclusive building in the city. His plan was to live alone, to free himself from Kurtz, to spend long hours in bed reading volumes of poetry, for it was only when he was alone, reading Yeats or Auden or Keats or Whitman, that he felt he could hear the sound of his own, true voice. But for some reason when he arrived back at the dorm, he presented the news to Kurtz as if it were a joint venture. "I signed a lease," he said. "It's a two bedroom. So, you know, if you need somewhere."

"Fuck, yes!" Kurtz had said. He had dropped down to the floor and performed the motions of the call to prayer. "I *love* you, man! You're like, my *savior*." It was understood already that Kurtz couldn't afford it. Ben would pay the rent.

At the time Ben couldn't say, to save his life, what bound him to Kurtz, who was so loud and disruptive, who cost him so much time and money, whose interests and desires so often overshadowed his own. But somewhere during the next three years there came a point when Ben wondered what he would do without Kurtz. Kurtz always knew what was going on. Who was giving a lecture, a concert. Who was throwing a party. Which teams Harvard was playing or racing, when and where. He knew which votes were coming up before the Supreme Court, on the senate floor, in the house, and he knew the names and numbers of key representatives to call with complaints, the location of protests and public forums and fundraisers. Kurtz was always pushing Ben out the door, to events he had often secured tickets for by standing in long lines Ben would have never deigned to stand in. "Let's go, let's go, let's go," Kurtz was always saying. "Get your rich, lazy ass in gear. We're going out." They had gone everywhere together. When Ben thought back to his time in college, he thought almost exclusively of Kurtz.

Nearing graduation, Kurtz had made plans to join the Tsongas campaign, and Ben had asked his parents to fund what he described to them as a gap year. His pitch had gone something like this: That he had so far spent his life in a bubble, first Manhattan, then Cambridge, and if he wanted to achieve greatness, true understanding, he first needed to see more of the world, needed to walk amongst its people. He still planned to go to medical school, he assured them. He still planned to follow his mother into psychiatry, albeit a different branch—his plan was to work in the public hospitals, helping the worst cases, the schizophrenics and homeless, the truly mad and desperate, the possessed. But if he was going to be a whole person, a person with the wisdom necessary to help other people, he needed to defer for a year, roam for a bit. And he needed some money to do it.

Ben's father had resisted but in the end, just as Ben predicted, his mother had pushed for it, gotten him what he wanted. He'd graduated, then spent the summer in Europe, riding the trains, arriving in cities with no particular plan, other than to avoid the places tourists went, the monuments and cathedrals and museums. All through college, he'd read novels about young men wandering the streets and dark alleys of Paris and London and Berlin and Dublin and Prague, starving men with nothing but the clothes on their backs, and he wanted to recreate that feeling. He went for days without showering or changing his clothes, slept in shelters and hostels, and sometimes even outside, in public parks, with his head on his backpack. He spent several hours each day sitting on benches in public squares, or at the tiny tables outside of cafes, scribbling in his Traveler's notebook, writing down what he'd seen and heard on the streets, in the pubs, on the trains. He kept hoping something would happen. That he'd bear witness to some extraordinary event: a shooting, a bombing, a cataclysmic storm, a blackout that paralyzed a whole city and drove its people to desperate acts. Maybe he'd witness a violent protest, the start of a short-lived coup. What he wanted to accomplish that year, more than anything else, was to write a novel. His heroes were Hugo, Rimbaud, Kafka, Keats, Crane: men trembling on the edge of madness, of starvation, of sickness and death, but who churned all their suffering into art. Next year he would board that dismal submarine, his eight-year tour of med school and residency, but this year he wanted to live. To produce, in a matter of months, the kind of tour-de-force that only brilliant young men can create.

He'd wandered all through the summer and into the fall, keeping to himself, observing little clusters of people, listening to their conversations from the next table at a pub, or from the seat behind them on a train, trying to find a story. But nothing good ever happened. He seldom struck up conversations with others and when he did, they went nowhere—he never found himself invited along to a party, or a camping trip, or a bullfight. It had been so easy, in college, to fall in with groups of strangers, to start the night in one location and wind up across town, in someone's basement, or on their rooftop. It had been easy, he realized, because of Kurtz. Kurtz, who would size up a room and inevitably walk up to its most interesting occupant. The person with the trust fund, the person with the bag of cocaine in his back pocket. It occurred to Ben that maybe the novel he was destined to write was a political saga. Maybe his hero had been right in front of him all along: Kurtz, son of the Kennedy's cleaning woman, a scrappy nobody who navigates the desperate chaos of a presidential campaign, and somehow comes out on top.

So he went home.

It took Ben a few days to get ahold of Kurtz, but when he finally did, Kurtz told him to come up to Manchester. That the Tsongas campaign was taking hold, was going to go all the way. "You're missing out, man," he'd said. "This is a revolution, we're riding this wave all the way to Washington, we're already picking out the curtains for the fucking Oval, man."

So he'd taken the train to Manchester and joined up with the Tsongas team. By that time the campaign was in the thick of the New Hampshire primary race, and the staff was in a state of frenzy. The moment Ben arrived he began scribbling notes in his journal, hoping to capture the chaos of it all. A dozen or so people were milling about headquarters, all of them talking, some on the phone, some to themselves, some hollering across the room to others. There were maybe ten desks set up, arranged at odd, seemingly random angles. People were seated at the desks, hunched over phones, or stuffing envelopes, or entering data— what kind of data, Ben wondered?—into computers. There were stacks of lawn signs everywhere, boxes of buttons and bumper stickers strewn about. Multiple TVs and radios were playing at the same time, tuned to different channels. There were fast food containers and Styrofoam cups on just about every desk, and in little piles on the floor. It was as if a large group of children had been left unsupervised for a period of weeks.

Even though the room was bustling, Ben could hear Kurtz above it all. He was standing in a corner distributing stacks of leaflets to a group of volunteers. "We need to plaster these fuckers all over this city," he was saying. "Get out there and carpet bomb this shit. Leave no windshield untouched! Leave no man, woman, or child in peace!"

Ben shadowed Kurtz for the next few weeks, riding all around Manchester and its surrounding towns. In theory, Kurtz's job was to recruit local volunteers and organize their efforts in the city's neighborhoods. But in practice Kurtz seemed to spend much of his time driving around in what looked to be an aimless pattern, stopping in at businesses and public spaces, leaving behind signs and stacks of brochures, or pulling into parking lots and sticking fliers underneath the windshield wipers of parked cars. And of course, the dubious practice of tearing out lawn signs in favor of opposing candidates. "We can't let this shit normalize," Kurtz was always saying. "People see a Clinton sign and start to think he's okay, like maybe he's actually a serious candidate, like maybe he's not just some traveling preacher throwing tent revivals and speaking in tongues and curing the lame with the touch of his giant fucking hands."

Three weeks in, Ben's main impression of the campaign, of politics in general, was that it was nothing short of a miracle, how people came to occupy the White House. In a matter of months, a fleet of people riding around Manchester in taped-together Volkswagens, eating whatever food they could find and sleeping on floors and couches, in a matter of months these people might be heading to Washington, suddenly transformed into the leaders of the free world.

So this is how it is for Ben the night he first speaks to Sammy. He and Kurtz and Boris have, after escaping the police officer, unloaded the last of the signs in a middle school parking lot, and quit for the night—they don't want to push their luck. They decide to stop for dinner at Kurtz's favorite dive, a little sandwich shop in a mostly abandoned strip mall. The bell clangs when they walk in, and Ben notices the same girl behind the counter—a tall, skinny girl who wears her dark hair parted in the center and pulled back in a low ponytail. There's something birdlike about her. Her nose is a bit too large, and beaklike, and her bones are too prominent, she's a bit too long in the neck and limbs. She looks like one of those tropical creatures who stand around in swamps, balancing motionless on one leg. Those birds who are technically capable of flight, but whose efforts to launch themselves are comically awkward.

They have sat in this café many nights before, sometimes for hours, and each night Kurtz has called the girl forth several times to quiz her. How does New Hampshire feel about our nation's trading practices with China? Is New Hampshire worried about health care? The national debt? Equal pay? Each time the girl has emerged from behind the counter reluctantly, bringing a mop along with her, as if she is in need of something to defend herself. Her answers to Kurtz's questions have been vague. "I'm not sure," she's said, of the local education system, taxes, abortion, drug use. "I think it sort of depends who you ask." She has answered every question as quickly as possible, then ducked back behind the counter. But still, Ben can tell she is interested in them. He has noticed her watching them, her head turning toward them as they work out their positions, wage their battles. Several times he has caught her looking, and she has flushed and turned away.

This particular night, Kurtz starts in on the girl right away. "Sammy! What's happening? How's the sandwich business? How's the high school business?" He is always asking her questions, but almost never gives her a chance to answer them. "What's the special today? What do you recommend? What's the freshest thing you have back there?"

"The roast beef," she says, "is fresh. Or you know, I mean, I just unwrapped it."

They order the roast beef, and she turns away to fix their sandwiches. They arrange themselves at one of the three tables, and Ben pulls back his chair so he can watch the girl as she works. She is curled in on herself, hunched over her work, like a student hoping to shield her test from someone attempting to cheat over her shoulder. It's as if the assembly of their sandwiches is a secret process she has sworn not to reveal.

Kurtz starts railing against Clinton, calling him a hillbilly pervert, a backwoods cousin-fucker. The girl emerges from behind the counter and sets their sandwiches in front of them. Then she lingers by their table, wiping her hands on her apron, nervous. She hovers for a long moment while Kurtz carries on. Finally, Ben holds his hand up in front of Kurtz, and brings his chatter to a stop.

"Can we help you?" he asks the girl. He tries to sound friendly, but doesn't quite manage it—there's an edge of sarcasm. His mother has been telling him for years to stop with the irony, the caustic wit—*Stop making that face or it will freeze like that*, is what she's been telling him—and now he has to admit she may have been right: it's almost impossible for him to say something plain. The girl's face registers a flicker of uncertainty. He worries he might have put her off.

"I think you might want to know something," the girl says, so quietly he can barely hear her. "I mean, I think I have some information that might help you."

"What's that?" says Kurtz, looking straight at her. A bit of a challenge. Like she couldn't possibly know something he didn't already.

"I met Bill Clinton the other night," she says.

"Really?" Kurtz says. Interested now. He leans toward her a bit.

"He came in for a sandwich. We talked for a while."

"Huh," Kurtz says. He seems at a loss.

"He's really," she says. Faltering. "I don't quite know how to explain it but he's really charming, I guess is the word."

"So I hear," says Ben.

"But it's different in person, is what I'm trying to say. It's really, there's something. Don't get me wrong, your guy is better, your guy is better on policy and makes more sense, you know, as a candidate, he's like the responsible decision and everything, I totally get that. But the thing is." She is still nervous, working her hands, but she louder now, more certain. "I mean, if you guys don't find a way to make your guy, like, *magnetic* or whatever, you guys are seriously *fucked*."

There follows an awkward silence. The girl is like a child who, in an effort to impress her elders, has floated a new word, not quite sure of its meaning. Her brow is creased with uncertainty.

Boris turns to Kurtz and says, "This is what I've been *telling you*. This fucking *country*! You have to consider who this country has vaulted into the stratosphere of its celebrity, you have to think in these terms: there is Elvis, there is Michael Jackson, there is Charles Lindburgh." He is ticking these names off on his fingers. "There is Jon Bon Jovi, all of them achieving power through their image, their *person*, the danger here is in the *person* of this candidate, his physical *person*."

"The celebrity thing starts to happen," says Kurtz, "it *seems* like it's going to happen, but then it doesn't happen. Politics is the last institution wherein celebrity goes down in the end. Reagan aside. Total fluke. We're still a nation of rational actors. We're not a bunch of screaming girls at a fucking Beatles concert, as a population."

"But maybe now," says Boris, "maybe now the fabric of your society is worn enough so that it can no longer contain this frenzy, this frenzy of screaming little girls."

They are in each other's faces. Hot and close. The girl stands awkwardly, unsure whether to stay or go. She looks disappointed. She had been hoping for a conversation but only seems to have sparked a debate.

"You think this country," yells Kurtz, "is going to elect some hillbilly from the middle of nowhere, who crawled out of a fucking *swamp*?"

"Why don't you ask her?" Boris says. Gesturing at the girl. "If you want to know what the country is thinking, why don't you ask the girl with the sandwiches standing right in front of you?"

Kurtz and Boris turn and regard the girl. "I'm just saying there was a bit of a star quality there, he really did kind of remind me a little of Elvis." She nods at Boris. Cringes.

Ben feels a desperate urge to help her. "I've been telling Kurtz the same thing," he says. "He doesn't listen." He is using his most resonant, theatrical voice. He wants the girl to know he is paying attention, taking her seriously.

"That's because," says Kurtz, "you know I love you but, you don't know shit about politics. You live in a fucking fantasy world. You can't listen to him," Kurtz says, addressing the girl, though she doesn't seem to realize it—she keeps casting her eyes about. Ben understands the problem. Kurtz's left eye doesn't track with his right—it is more or less permanently sunk in its socket—and the combination of this, along with his talking so much and so fast, gesticulating wildly and changing subjects so often, makes it impossible to be sure if he is looking at you or talking to you. "He's just along for the ride," says Kurtz, "just observing the campaign and scribbling it all down in his notebook. We're working our asses off trying to get someone elected and he's just kicking back smoking cigarettes and getting drunk and thinking of how all this plays out in a fucking *novel*."

Ben flushes with something—embarrassment, maybe anger. He doesn't want to be dismissed or belittled in front of this girl. Then he wonders why he cares—it's true, after all, he doesn't really give a shit about the campaign. He practices a trick his mother wrote about in the pop-psych book she is known for, *Materializing.*

The trick is to imagine whatever feeling you're currently having as an object. To give it a color and a shape, a texture, a weight. The feeling he has now is small but sharp. It looks like a virus under a microscope, round at the center but with a series of crazy spikes poking out. The feeling is a sort of sickly yellow-green color, and it glows. Then he moves on to the second stage of materializing, which is to imagine scooping the feeling up in your hand and examining it, then setting it down in such a way that emphasizes your power over it—you can handle it however you like. But this feeling seems to be immersed in some kind of fluid. When he moves to scoop it into his hand, it floats away.

"Rosenberg here grew up on the Upper East," Kurtz continues, "with like, a *limo driver* taking him to school in the morning, but now what he wants is the only thing money can't buy. He wants to get his hands dirty. All he cares about as far as this campaign goes is rolling around in the mud with all the lowlife back-alley minimum-wage service workers, present company excepted of course." He nods his head toward the girl. "You can't pay any attention to anything he says. Ask him a question about politics and he'll come back at you with a quote from, from..." Kurtz searches for a moment. "Fucking *Keats*, for Christ's sake, some tubercular piece of shit, some faggot spitting up blood onto his little poems."

"Everyone knows Keats was in love with a woman," says the girl. "Fanny Brawne." She fidgets, tucks a strand of hair behind her ear. "I mean," she continues, "I mean all you have to do is read one of his poems, just one single poem, and you'd know he wasn't a, you know, a faggot." She winces.

"Still to hear her tender-taken breath," Ben says. "And so live ever—or else swoon to death." The final lines of "Bright Star."

The girl nods. "Right," she says. "Exactly."

"Whatever," says Kurtz. "Like I care. I'm trying to change

the world and you're talking about poetry. Which is the exact problem with every poet in the world."

The girl flushes—not just her cheeks, but her neck and chest. She turns and walks back behind the counter. Ben watches her as she works, wrapping up the meat and cheese, carrying the knife and cutting board to the sink. Her movements are languid, now.

Kurtz and Boris have started an argument about Yitzhak Rabin. Ben stands and wanders away from the table, approaches the portraits on the wall, the framed headshots of Marilyn Monroe, James Dean, Cary Grant. Then Marilyn Monroe again, and again—with Arthur Miller, with Joe Dimaggio, with Kennedy. The girl is just ten feet away, behind the counter, and Ben can feel her watching him—he is good at sensing these things. He tosses off, without even turning to look at her: "How is it a high school girl from Manchester knows so much about John Keats?"

"Oh, I don't know," she says. "Doesn't everyone?"

She's trying for a joke, but he plays it straight. "I don't think so," he says, turning her way now. "Not in my experience." He keeps his hands in his pockets, his head down. He is making an effort to be sincere.

"Well, that's what I plan to study next year," she says. "I want to study poetry. At Virginia." She says all of this with her back turned, wiping down the countertop.

"UVA?" he says. "That's a pretty good school." Then he turns to Kurtz and says, sharply. "Guess where she's going next year."

"Sandwich college," Kurtz fires back. "Advanced Hoagies. Special Problems in Chicken Salad."

"Introduction to Slicing Equipment," adds Boris, snickering. "Intermediate Giant Pickles."

"Virginia," says Ben.

"Fuck that," Kurtz says to the girl. "You should go to

Harvard instead. Virginia is just a bunch of blue blood frat boys, a whole bunch of Ashley Wilkes-type shit down there, Jason Compson-style bullshit, a bunch of rapists with flasks in their pockets talking about *tradition*, though what they really mean is slavery, what they really mean is Jim Crow, and good luck taking two steps without tripping over a fucking confederate flag, or a redneck with a loaded rifle, they have open carry down there, so, you know, it was nice meeting you."

"But the architecture," says Ben, "I hear the architecture is amazing."

"And Jason Compson went to Harvard," adds the girl. She seems a bit excited, like a contestant on some sort of game show, one where the first person to spit out the right answer wins.

"Whatever," says Kurtz. "You two can sit around jerking off to literary references. I have a campaign to run here."

"He doesn't run the campaign, mind you," says Ben, "he only thinks he runs the campaign."

"Like I *don't*?" says Kurtz. "Name one person on this team worth more than me."

"Pete," says Boris. "I think that Pete guy is worth more than you."

"Are you fucking *kidding* me?" Kurtz shouts. "That worthless piece of shit?" Kurtz and Boris are off again. Ben lingers at the deli case for a while longer. He is suddenly tired of the campaign, listening to people argue and complain. He wants something different. Another feeling stirs in him—something like hunger, or boredom. It is easier to identify, a bright blue cube. He picks it up and grabs it, and an idea blooms in his mind, an experiment, a remedy: he asks the girl to come out with them.

2011

They are no longer young, the boy and the girl.

It's seven-thirty on a Friday night, and Ben is in bed already. Partly he is in bed so early because of his sciatica—one of the side effects of sitting all day, the pain shooting across his hip and down his thigh, through the knee and calf and all the way to his big toe. And partly, he is just tired. Tired of work, and tired also of the galas and openings and screenings and fundraisers to which he is always invited. He has been to so many of these events he can't remember them all, nor distinguish from one another the ones he does remember. What he wants now is a bit of comfort. Something familiar. So he sits in bed against a pile of pillows with containers of Chinese takeout surrounding him, a Scotch precariously balanced beside him on the mattress. He sits in bed and talks to Sammy, who is home, too, on a Friday night, though for entirely different reasons.

Tonight they are talking about Occupy Wall Street, because Sammy has been watching the news and wants to know what it's like up close, how it's playing in the city. It's basically a joke, Ben tells her. A joke that's gone on too long, a joke whose punch line, when and if it arrives, can't possibly justify the time it took in coming, the anxiety and then boredom it produced in its own making. "All these protestors," he says, "are like cousins from out of town, college dropouts trying to find themselves in the city, knocking on your door asking if they can sleep on your couch.

And at first you're kind of charmed by the gleam in their eyes, their flannel shirts and their fingerless gloves, their wool caps and their rucksacks. You look at them and remember yourself at the same age. So you take them in, you feed them, you listen to their complaints. You offer bits of encouragement and advice. Cookies, power bars. But then a few weeks go by, and every time you come home from work there they are, just *hanging out*, just bullshitting, taking up more and more space, their clothes sprawled on the floor, their folk music trembling in the air, and then they start asking if their friends can hang out, and soon enough you come home and your apartment's full of kids, you're choking on patchouli and incense and clove cigarettes." Ben laughs, here, amused with himself, impressed with the metaphor he's created, how far he's managed to stretch it. "Until one morning you're like: *All of you, get the fuck out.* And you start throwing their shit out the window."

"Okay," Sammy says. "But I guess I don't understand how this is affecting you, personally. How like, your personal couch is being slept on."

"My patients," Ben says, "is how. They're obsessed with Occupy. It's all we talk about the whole hour. They're having nightmares, tantrums, they're performing badly at work."

"Really?" she says. "Huh."

"They're in bad shape. All the drunks are off the wagon, the addicts are popping pills."

"Wow," she says, frowns.

"The maniacs are up all night ranting, the cutters are wielding their little knives, the bulimics are barfing into toilets."

"I get it," Sammy says. She is crouching before an open dishwasher, the phone settled between her left shoulder and ear. She is trying, while balancing the phone, to retrieve a bright green plastic straw, her daughter's favorite, that has fallen from the dishwasher's top rack onto its pan. She reaches into the machine's depths and—yes!—retrieves it. She is always trying to accomplish some bit of housework while talking to Ben. In this case, unloading the dishwasher just to load it again, clearing the counter and sink so that, finally, she can start making dinner. It is getting late, and her daughter is hungry. Sammy has put Ava in front of the television for a bit, so as to be free to make dinner and talk with Ben, but it won't last—any minute Ava will trudge into the kitchen, her arms folded, wanting something. Sammy is always working against the clock, frantic. Every minute of every day is like this, a strange tug of war between an eight-year-old, and the rest of life.

"All the depressives are on a ledge and the sex addicts, of course," Ben says now, "are fucking their brains out."

Sammy is surprised to hear that Occupy is taking a psychological toll on Ben's patients—Upper East Side millionaires down to nearly last man. She has been listening to Ben talk about these patients, most of whom he collected in the wake of the 2008 crash, for three years now, and nothing he's told her, in all that time, has suggested they might be paying attention to the lives and complaints of the common man. Ben's patients tend to come to him with the kinds of exquisite anxieties and frustrations born of closed societies: *I once had many more millions than I have now, and the loss of these extra millions, as compared with my neighbor's recent gain in millions, is a humiliation, a grief I bear, a wound whose ache drives me to drink, to sleep with prostitutes, to crush pills and snort them into my bloodstream.* Now, for some reason, they seem to be flustered by a bunch of hippies standing around ranting and tripping in Zuccotti Park. Everything Sammy has heard about the Occupiers—the tents they've pitched, their makeshift libraries and publications, their music, the smells rising from their improvised kitchens, their Quaker-inspired style of governance, in which no one person has more power than another—is a direct affront to the aesthetics and practices of capitalism, to the lives Ben's clients have built for themselves. But like everything else hurled from below toward the upper reaches of society, all the rotten tomatoes, the fist-sized rocks, Sammy had assumed the protests were too small, too weakly-launched, to make any sort of impact.

"You can't possibly imagine what I'm dealing with," Ben says. "I mean, people are really fucked up."

"I guess that's, I guess that's good?" Sammy says. "Like maybe it's the beginning of the kind of conversation the protestors want to have? Maybe, with your patients, all this anxiety is the first flicker of understanding that they're invested in a system that's, well it's problematic to say the least, right?" Her brain is racing. She imagines the edifices of greed and corruption cracking, then crumbling, imagines bags of money plied from the fists of the wealthy (Sammy imagines them as fat men in tuxedos with white mustaches, monocles, cigars jutting from their clenched teeth, basically the Monopoly man) and distributed to the poor, she imagines the end of poverty, the beginning of sustainable environmental practices, extravagant funding for education and universal healthcare, Americans remaking themselves after the example of, say, the Norwegians, taking up their style of living and dress, their understated architecture and minimalist furniture, their beautiful public spaces. She imagines the United States as a nation characterized by ingenuity, industriousness, responsible behavior. She imagines kids walking to school in lederhosen. She pictures Ava with her hair in braided pigtails, carrying a metal lunch pail and a pile of books tied together with a leather strap. Then she starts to wonder if the Norwegians wear lederhosen, or whether it's just the Germans . . .

"Maybe," she says, "all this angst is a positive development, maybe it's their conscience peeking through?"

"No, no," Ben says. "You don't get it. They're not wallowing in existential *pain*. They're pissed. They're full of rage."

"Oh," she says. Everything she just saw glimmering on the horizon, the triumph of socialism, the lederhosen, it all wavers and disappears.

"They're murderous. They want to open fire on the park. *Not* opening fire on the park is what's making them crazy. I have to talk them down."

"Oh," she says again. She's like a kid whose ice cream cone has just dropped on the pavement, due to nothing but her own clumsiness, her failure to make the appropriate calculations, to see things as they really are.

"They *despise* the protestors," says Ben. "The sound of them. The sight of them. The smell of their food, their hairy faces, their drumming circles. And the whining," he says. "What they hate most is the whining."

"Well, I'll give them that. Nobody likes whining."

Ben pokes at a container of noodles with his chopsticks. He is no longer hungry, but the noodles are glistening and delicious. He sucks one into his mouth, considers what to say next. He is always having to explain the world to Sammy, who is somehow still naïve, despite being a professor and parent. This has been his job and sometimes frustrating duty for as long as he has known her.

"It's easy to take stabs at these rich guys," Ben says, "but when you think about it, they're not entirely unsympathetic." He explains his theory: that he is working with a population whose city and way of life have been threatened in unprecedented ways. "Particularly the financial workers," he says, "who worked in the towers, I mean, some of them saw their colleagues plummet from the top floors." Then, he continues, just as things were getting better, the market collapsed, and they lost their money and jobs. For a while lots of them were suicidal or homicidal or both. And

61

now, finally, just after they recovered from this second blow, right when they're tapering off meds and their portfolios are recovering, now this bullshit. It's not so much the protest itself, he explains, as the fact that it's playing on still-tender wounds. His patients feel themselves to be under attack again, although this time in a completely unnecessary manner. These self-important kids coming along and making a canvas of Zuccotti Park, trotting out on its concrete face their art or revolution, or whatever the fuck they're calling it. "I don't really know," he says, "I'm too busy at work to follow the news."

"I think they're calling it a movement," Sammy says. "Technically."

Ben starts talking about one of his clients, one who's harboring very particular fantasies of homicide. He has vivid nightly dreams of dousing the protestors' tents with gasoline, then throwing a match. He has even begun visiting them on weekends, standing at the edge of the park for hours, watching. "It will all burn down," he keeps saying. "I'll watch the flames and laugh." This patient is Austrian, and when Ben imitates him, he uses the voice of Arnold Schwarzenegger.

"Wow," Sammy says. "That's, that's pretty fucked up."

"While they're out there jerking off," Ben says—Schwarzenegger says—"the rest of us are working our asses off to make the fucking world go around."

"I don't really know what to say to that."

This client, Ben continues, whose name is Giles—Ben isn't supposed to reveal this information, but as his conversations with Sammy continue, his discretion tends to wane—is fixated on a particular protestor, this guy in one of those crocheted rainbow Bob Marley hats who's always dancing around the borders of the park, dancing while the rest of the world is trying to get to work, while the rest of the world is *late for work*, because of his stupid fucking dancing. "I will bash his skull in," says the Terminator. "I will play patty-cake upon his bones."

"Jesus," Sammy says.

Ben says that in order to deal with Giles, and many more like him, he has had to extend his hours. He is seeing patients until nine each night. "I'm absolutely exhausted," he says, "from writing prescriptions. I've worked my fingers to the very bone." He's being theatrical as usual, overstating everything. Ben is someone whose personality has been shaped almost exclusively by an accident of fate: that he bears a shocking, almost unbelievable likeness to Orson Welles. He has the same dark hair and eyes, the same square jaw, the same hairline, the same broad build. When he was a teenager, and this likeness first announced itself, Ben began to talk in a Wellesian manner, narrating relatively mundane events as if they were scenes from a Shakespearean tragedy, speaking in sentences festooned with metaphor and dependent clauses. The trick was a hit with his friends and teachers, and soon enough what had begun as a joke had taken over, had become his public persona. In recent years, to complete the effect, Ben had gained a good deal of weight and grown a full beard, cultivating his likeness to Welles to the point that people sometimes called after him in the street: *Rosebud!*

"I can't go on like this," he says now. "It's inhumane, the conditions I'm enduring."

"Oh, please," Sammy says. She is one of the few people who takes a pin to the Welles balloon. Though she seems to like Ben's Orson well enough—Orson is fun, after all, and charming—she often checks him, cuts the scene, tells him to try it again, but with less feeling.

"But it's *exhausting*," Ben insists, pushing it a bit further. "By the time I said goodbye to the week's last patient I could hardly drag my hand across a prescription pad. My hand has stiffened into a claw. I can barely lift this piece of shrimp to my lips." He pops a pink crescent into his mouth, crushes it with his teeth.

"Is there really no one?" Sammy asks. "Not one of your patients who finds this protest sort of interesting? Sort of a dialogue between opposite sides of a culture? Is there anyone experiencing even a flinch, just a pang of, I don't know, self-doubt, or reflection?"

"You must be joking," he says.

"Well, I mean, that's sort of how we're talking about it on campus. You know, in our little professors' lounge."

"Oh, the lounge," he says. "The seat of power itself."

They are switching over to her now, Sammy realizes. It's time for her to start weaving a web, pulling together the loose strands of her daily life in such a way that they hold together, make some kind of sense. And funny! She should try to make it funny. The trick is to take something that's sort of pathetic, and then twist it so it plays for laughs. "We're discussing Occupy," Sammy says, "in several different ways, sometimes in terms of its literary antecedents. Hugo has come up quite a bit, and Shakespeare, and of course Dostoevsky. And we're also talking about its aesthetics." It embarrasses her to confess this. "This week we were talking about the situation of the camp as a painting, you know, the composition of it, how in all the pictures in *The Times*, there's this play of light and shadow. The architecture of Wall Street itself, its massive buildings, the orderly grid of them, versus the melee of the tents in the park, the sort of chiaroscuro of it all, the light hitting the buildings and reflecting off them, against the dark camp, there's been some mention of Caravaggio." She cringes.

"I don't know how you sit through this bullshit," Ben says.

"I don't either," she says, though she herself was the one who had contributed the bit about Caravaggio.

"You're really on the cutting edge," he says. One of his little jokes, the joke being that out in the Midwest, what Sammy is on the edge of is oblivion.

Her life, Sammy has to admit, must seem small to Ben. *Is* small, in fact. She teaches English literature at a state university, in a City of No Importance, as she calls it. Her department shares a building with philosophy and history and foreign languages and classics, and in the afternoons their faculty gather in the basement lounge, forming what they fancy to be an Algonquin Round Table, though admittedly falling short of the original group in wit and youth and especially influence—no one is taking notes, no one wants to hear what they have to say.

Except Ben. For reasons Sammy has never quite understood, Ben loves hearing about the professors' lounge, the people who gather there and the opinions they formulate. Contemplating the lounge and its inhabitants is an experience, she imagines, somewhat akin to visiting a zoo, to gazing upon a group of strange creatures, ill-suited to their climate, their rarity and isolation and captivity rendering them incapable of breeding, of surviving in the real world. Ben once asked Sammy to text him pictures of the lounge and its inhabitants, so she furtively took shots with her phone. The pictures had come out looking especially bleak. In the fluorescent light of the lounge her colleagues' skin appeared sallow and speckled. Relaxed in their chairs, their bodies seemed boneless, their limbs sort of adrift, undulating, like creatures in an aquarium. Ben texted back that if he had to spend more than five minutes in that room, he'd kill himself.

Don't insult us, she returned. If you cut us, do we not bleed?

I can't help you, he wrote, until you're ready to help yourself.

We're fine here. We're okay, you're okay.

You're not okay, he wrote. Trust me.

Often in these little exchanges, Sammy took up the defense

of her colleagues, but in reality, she had to admit, maybe they weren't quite okay. Most of her colleagues were males, in their sixties and seventies, who wore moth-eaten cardigan sweaters with suede elbow patches and leather-covered buttons. Their eyebrows were wild and they had tufts of white hair extending from their inner ears and nostrils. They stank of pipe tobacco and blew their noses loudly into handkerchiefs and often coughed great globs of phlegm into them, as well, which they inspected and frowned at before folding them up and returning them to their pockets. Each day they gathered at the table and took out their lunches—sad affairs crumpled in paper sacks—and then, while eating, opened their newspapers and read out headlines from *Le Monde* and *The Times* to each other. They griped about the state of the world, discussing the news and then spinning it, taking the clay of experience and then throwing it on a wheel. They ran it between their hands, shaped it, spun it, thinned it out until it collapsed in a heap. The feeling in the lounge was that cultural and political events themselves were of no real importance—rather, their value had to do with the stories one could make with them. There was no event on earth, not even the falling of the Twin Towers, that in the halls of academia hadn't been spun into some kind of narrative, some kind of metaphor, which had the effect of undermining what had actually happened, the moment itself lost to the theory of the moment. At heart, Sammy believed, this was an insult to life itself, though the professors argued otherwise: it was the putting of life itself in context, the organization and categorization of events, that really mattered. Or at least ultimately, that was all they had.

"Everyone here sympathizes with the protestors," she says now. "Of course. Everyone identifies with them. But still I kind of wonder what life would really be like if they were in charge. If they had their day."

"It would be anarchy," Ben says.

"That's just it."

As these things go, Sammy continues, if lines are being drawn, obviously she's on the side of the protestors. "I mean, it's in our *blood*," she says. "We were just the same." She refers to their time on the campaign, the air of revolution about them. That year, the Democrats' rallying cry had been the same as the protestors'. They wanted corruption to be brought to trial, wanted to take all the money being spent on weaponry and redistribute it to education, wanted businesses and banks to be regulated, wanted to shove the face of the Republican Party in a pool of its own spilled oil and blood, all the usual bullshit. And even now, Sammy says, her favorite students are the same, the angry ones and the romantics, those fueled by ideas of the way things should be, politically or philosophically or both. She has one or two of them in class every year, kids carrying around volumes of Marx or Keats or Whitman, their hearts stuffed with speeches and verse. These kids always look like they just, as some kind of initiation rite, rolled themselves through the mud of Woodstock: their hair is unwashed and standing on end, their faces pitted with acne, their teeth crooked and coffee-stained, their clothes gray and limp, their fingertips callused from playing guitar. Each of these students thinks himself unique and, she allows, it would be wrong to say otherwise, though by now, with years of teaching behind her, these kids have begun to blur, to form a type. She explains to Ben that she tends to think of these kids as all having a single name, Fergus, which was the name of the first student of this sort she could remember having, a kid who lived for a while in a tent on the center of campus. He was protesting homelessness, though for some reason she failed to understand this and thought he was actually homeless, thought he lived in the tent as a matter of necessity. But in any event, when the tent was eventually removed by campus police, and Sammy asked him where he was living now, half the class laughed. Apparently it was well known that Fergus was a member of one of the richest families in the city. All kinds of buildings and public squares were named after them. Fergus was only here, at their crappy satellite state campus, because he had been kicked out of Harvard, then Northwestern, then the flagship state campus; his presence now in her classroom was just some kind of socialist exercise, he was *walking amongst the people*, as it were, and had disguised himself so well that his professor had mistaken him for a person actually living in a tent and was asking now where he lived, how she could help. *Where does Fergus live?* a classmate joked. *Oh, just the east wing of the museum.*

"So I have to admit," Sammy continues, "they drive me crazy, too. Fergus and his brethren are always missing class, then showing up to office hours to explain where they were, some protest or rally or musical benefit, which they recount in excruciating detail, and then they want even *more* of my time, want me to go over with them, personally, what they missed in class, they want their own private lecture delivered right there on the spot. And in addition to missing class," she says, "Fergus, and every other Fergus like him, is always turning in his assignments late, not because he isn't doing the work but because he falls down into the ambiguities of Wallace Stevens and falls so deep he can't get out, he can't function; on the day a paper is due he'll miss class, then show up at her office clutching the pages of his tear-stained draft, his notes scribbled frantically in the margins, the backs of the pages marked up with arrows and charts indicating the flow and structure of his ideas, whole passages crossed out with violent slashes of ink." Sammy imitates Fergus now, pitching her voice into a falsetto: *The indifference of the universe as envisioned by Stevens, that art and meaning and God are just, just a fiction, well, I don't know if I can handle it, I mean, it makes me want to fall down and die.* Here Fergus collapses in tears, she explains, a scene which, over the years, from one Fergus to the next, has less and less effect on her. She has begun to keep a box of tissues at the edge of her desk so she can hand them out, not as a means of saying: *You poor thing, allow me to support you in your moment of insight and vulnerability,* but rather as a means of saying: *Wipe your fucking tears, you are weeping at the wrong feet, though I was once a refuge for broken hearts and lost souls, I am almost forty now, and tired, and have a child of my own at home, and there is nothing left.*

"Wallace Stevens," she is always telling Fergus, "spent all day at a desk working for an insurance company. He got up every morning and put on his suit. He walked to work and did his work. He produced. Try to remember that." Here she ends things by offering the tissue.

"It's all in the motion with which you pluck the tissue from its box," she tells Ben now. "Quick, with a flick of the wrist, a whoosh that says: *Good day.* This is how to handle a Fergus. Really," she says, "your clients should just march down to Zuccotti Park with a box of tissues and give it a try."

"So I guess it could be said," she continues, "that I am, in my own small way, turning into a Wall Street type. I have been swept up by the tide that overtakes us all, insofar as I have my own office, insofar as I have a steady income and a place to live."

Ben cuts in here to remind her that her salary would make one of his patients, if he happened to hear this figure while taking a sip of scotch, laugh so violently that he would spit out that mouthful of scotch, and just that small amount of scotch lost to the air, *aerosolized,* he says, would be worth more than Sammy made in a day. "I have clients who pay someone twice your annual salary to *walk their dogs,*" he says. "In fact, I don't know why you don't move up here. There are people making ninety thousand a year in downtown Manhattan walking the overly-large hounds of

Wall Street executives, who are fond of bull mastiffs." Something to do with the market, he says. These Wall Street types aren't entirely without a sense of symbolism, of humor.

"That's why no one has a pet bear," she says.

"Exactly."

Everyone in the entire city of New York, come to think of it, Ben tells her, is making more than Sammy does. Of everyone he knows, including his doorman, who is nearly eighty and morbidly obese, who has lost the use of his left arm and is blind in one eye due to a recent stroke, he can't name another person worse off than Sammy, even the homeless guy on his block, even *this* guy is making more than she is. Whenever Ben sees him, he's drinking a venti cappuccino from Starbucks. "Which," he says to her, "you probably couldn't afford."

"Please," she says, "I get it."

Ben and Sammy have been mock-fighting for twenty years, carrying out a little class war, Ben making fun of Sammy because she has never had any money and never figured out how to get it, and Sammy reminding Ben that he's sort of an asshole, a rich kid who never did anything to deserve his wealth, the kind of person who would have been beheaded in the French Revolution.

But it's still true, Sammy says now, she's more Wall Street than Occupy, insofar as she has a kid to take care of, rent to pay. She needs systems to be in place, roads and bridges and schools, a vaccinated peer group for her kid; she needs the economy to not collapse; she needs her university to not put everyone on furlough, as it has threatened to do every semester since 2008, and she needs tenure; she needs the grid to remain intact to heat her house; she needs the internet, she needs police to patrol the streets to keep her city's violence in check, she needs murderers and sexual predators locked away in prison; she needs the garbage trucks to run; she needs hot running water; she needs groceries abundant on store shelves, and though she doesn't like to really think about it, she needs the bounty provided by genetically modified agriculture, to keep things affordable, she needs industrial farming; generally she is a vegetarian, but occasionally she needs a hamburger; generally she's a pacifist but she supposes, if it protects her and her loved ones from harm, she needs the occasional highly-specific bomb dropped on a highly-specific target; at heart she's an animal, she admits, a little cluster of needs, needs, needs. "I need all of these things," she says, "because I have another animal depending on me, because I'm a single mother with no family in town, I don't even have any friends to call on in times of need, I don't have a network of people with whom to *barter* should my income fail or fluctuate. The Occupy way of doing things, of upturning the system and living communally, just doesn't work for me, not because I'm opposed to it but because nobody likes me. Which I understand," she says, "I don't particularly like being around myself. So in a way," she concludes, "even though I'm an English professor at a third-rate school making forty-three thousand dollars a year, which is a joke to you and your clients, even so I can still relate to the establishment, to the suits. I can at least acknowledge that the quality of my life, such as it is, depends on the system they keep in place."

She is finally done. She has said her piece and is, after talking so long, a little embarrassed. This is usually how conversations go between Sammy and Ben. Ben calls and starts talking about his life and work, and Sammy listens more or less quietly, until something Ben says unlocks something in her and out pours a flood of social theory she didn't even know she'd been harboring. Essentially, the trouble is this: Ben is Sammy's only friend, the only person she can really talk to. When he calls Sammy it is a matter of critical importance to her, a lifeline, but their talks, she suspects, are not nearly so important to him. Ben has a great number of friends, many of them famous—there's a Kennedy in his address book, a Roosevelt, a handful of Guggenheims—and so the whole time she's talking she's vaguely aware that she is wasting his time and also pretty sure that he's put the phone on speaker and is pursuing other interests, flipping through magazines and scrolling through channels, surfing the internet.

"God, I'm sorry," she says now. "I shouldn't have talked so much. I'll shut up." She is always doing this, breaking the basic etiquette of the telephone. Everyone knows the whole point of a phone is, well, bullshitting is the point. Light banter. Shooting the breeze. She keeps misusing the medium, trying to score a symphony when all anyone wants to hear is a pop song.

"It's really no problem," Ben tells her. "I was making myself a drink. I didn't hear a word you just said."

He starts in on something else—the latest gala he attended, all the inane conversations he endured about Telluride. "And Beyoncé," he says. "For some reason there's a preponderance of rich, anorexic white ladies in love with Beyoncé. They're obsessed with the exact nature of her besequinned butt, the mechanics of its movement. I find this phenomenon fascinating."

"You're not alone," Sammy says. "Somewhere at this very moment a graduate student is hunched in a library carrel working out this same idea. Multiple graduate students, actually, fighting one another for supremacy."

Ben takes up this baton and runs with it, starts suggesting medical diagnoses regarding our cultural obsession with Beyoncé: Beyoncéitis. Beyoncéphalitis. He rattles off a list of symptoms, but Sammy doesn't really hear them. Her attention has been pulled away by a kind of sixth-sense—she can tell that her daughter has abandoned the television and approached the kitchen. Ava is probably bored, and hungry. Sammy looks behind her, off into the living room, where Ava had been sitting cross-legged in front of the TV, watching *Tom & Jerry*, and confirms that Ava has indeed left her spot. But where is she?

Sammy turns back to the stove. Gives the pot of not-yet-boiling water a threatening look. "And another thing," Ben is saying. "All these galas have to have a signature cocktail now. Everyone is desperate to create something different. You wouldn't believe what they were serving. Some ghastly blend of tequila and coffee liqueur."

"Yeesh," Sammy says. But she is wholly distracted now, wondering about Ava. She steps out of the kitchen and finds that Ava is crouched just on the other side of the kitchen wall. She is on her hands and knees, looking up at Sammy pleadingly, her eyes wide and dark. She shakes her whole body like a wet dog, and her dark curls go flying. Sammy reaches down to scratch them. "Good girl," she whispers, trying to sound cheerful, though her heart is heavy.

Ava has been doing this a lot lately—crawling along the perimeters of the house, sniffing, panting, pretending to be a dog she calls Alfred. Some sort of compulsion has taken over. Earlier that week, Ava's teacher had sent a note home from school, saying that she was crawling around the playground. "Though it is not unusual for children to still play pretend at this age," the teacher wrote, "I thought I would let you know, because she has stopped playing with other children, and this might be a sign of some sort of trouble." The letter had gone on to suggest Sammy and Ava meet with the school counselor. Sammy had written back saying she would handle it herself, and brokered an arrangement with Ava. She could be Alfred at home as much as she wanted. But not at school. This was the best Sammy could do, at the moment—keep the strangeness of her household within its walls.

Ava rises up on her knees, folds her hands down like paws, makes a whimpering noise.

"Are you hungry?" Sammy asks.

And Ava nods her head, pants.

"I gotta go," Sammy tells Ben. She retreats back into the kitchen. "Someone's on the other line. I think it might be my dignity calling."

"Finally," Ben says. "Send my regards."

After they hang up, Ben sits in bed for a few minutes, staring out the window. He can see the lights of Central Park, its winding paths. He knows he is one of the relatively few people on earth with such a lofty view, and lounges in the feeling of it. Whenever he hangs up with Sammy he feels the pleasure of his own life more acutely. It's like the feeling he always had back in med school, and then residency. When, after a long shift, he walked out of the hospital, and across the street, and then stopped for a moment to regard the hospital from a distance, its many floors and many, many dark windows. Behind each window a patient was in bed, probably suffering, but not him. He was still young, and healthy. He was rich. And he was free.

1992

Sammy is exhausted from talking with the Tsongas boys. She is not used to talking, in general, and these boys in particular are difficult, talking so fast, and alluding to so many obscure people and things, she can hardly keep up. She had been thrilled, briefly, to be able to return some of the comments lobbed at her—by some fantastic stroke of luck, she happened to be studying Keats in school, and had read *The Sound and the Fury* the year before—but she has been wobbling the whole time, balanced on a blade.

The tall boy—Rosenberg, they called him—is examining the pictures on the wall, just like Clinton did. Sammy wonders if she should try to talk to him again, but isn't sure what to say. Maybe she should ask him about the campaign? The book he's writing? Keats? She scrambles after the right words. Falters.

But just then the boy steps in. "Why don't you come out with us?" he asks. "See what campaigns are made of. Give us a bit of the local gossip. You're closing anyway, right?"

She feels herself blushing. Tries to act casual. "I guess," she says, looks at the clock. Still thirty minutes before closing, but who cares, she thinks. She calls her father, makes up some story about a group project at school, classmates picking her up from work. Then she starts closing the shop in a flurry. Covering things with cellophane. Wiping down surfaces. She sees the near-empty jar of mayonnaise, which she should hand wash and put in recycling, but tosses it in the garbage instead. Then she starts throwing all kinds of things away that don't really belong in the garbage. Plastic ware that should be washed to reuse. A dish cloth. *Fuck it*, she keeps thinking, borrowing one of Kurtz's favorite phrases. She is going to do something for once, to go find out what campaigns are made of, what life is made of. *Fuck it*.

It turns out Kurtz's car is an old VW, yellow and pocked with rust. Its most salient feature, which Sammy has noticed from afar, is a honking alarm that goes off whenever one of its doors is opened. Kurtz opens the door and the honking starts. The tall boy leans down and pulls a lever that folds the front seat forward, motions to Sammy to get in with a sweeping gesture, as if he has opened the door to a vault of treasures. Then he climbs in back with her, Kurtz and the foreigner take their seats up front, and they are off. The horn honks for a full minute, during which Kurtz yells back at Sammy to explain that the alarm is haywire—*fucked*, is the word he uses—that it costs more to fix than he can afford, so they just live with it, this blaring spectacle that announces their coming and going dozens of times a day. "Rosenberg doesn't drive," yells Kurtz, "or else we'd be riding in style, we'd be in a fucking Jaguar if he bothered to get a license, or a Benz, or whatever the fuck it is you rich people are into these days."

And that seems to be it, what politics is made of—one insult after another. The boys drive around the city cursing and deriding one another. Occasionally, when they see a Clinton sign on a lawn, Kurtz stops the car and the foreigner jumps out, sounding the alarm, and steals the sign, struggles back into the car with it. Then, when they've collected a few signs, they pull into a fast food parking lot and toss them in a dumpster. They do this again and again, driving in a zigzagging, random pattern. At a certain point, it occurs to Sammy that these boys aren't running the Tsongas campaign, not at all, that they are low-level functionaries at best, possibly not even official volunteers.

The car alarm keeps sounding and Sammy squirms with anxiety. She is trapped in a car with a group of bandits who announce their every crime and then leave a trail of honking prints in their wake. "Aren't you afraid of getting caught?" she ventures, leaning into the front seat and yelling over the horn.

"This is important work," yells Kurtz. "People see a Clinton sign and they think, *Hey, maybe this fucking, this fucking Appalachian Godzilla is okay, I keep seeing signs all over the place so he must be okay.* Politics isn't just local it's like, super local. It's like in a ten-foot radius of every voter."

About an hour into this caper, they stop for Slurpees at an ampm in Sammy's neighborhood. In fact, her house backs to the gas station lot and she can see—through the slats of the long, leaning fence that serves as a border wall between her neighborhood and this stretch of commerce, this half-mile expanse of gas stations and dry cleaners and credit unions and muffler garages—the yellow light of her father's bedroom window. He must be waiting up for her. Here she is out with three boys, vandalizing property, and he is home waiting with the light on. Suddenly she can't stay another minute.

"I'm going to walk home," she tells the tall boy, shouting over the alarm. "I live close by. And I have school in the morning."

"Let Kurtz drop you," he says.

"It's really, it's fine. I'm just right there." She gestures toward her house.

"Don't be ridiculous. We're gentlemen, underneath it all. We're not animals, we're not going to abandon you in a parking lot."

"Really," she says. Not wanting the boy to see where she lives.

"Suit yourself," says the boy, giving her a critical look. A few steps away, she turns and gives him a wave, then practically runs away. Maybe she'll never see these boys again.

But when she reaches the edge of the parking lot, Sammy hears the boy calling after her. "Hey!" he shouts. She stops and turns. "My name is Ben," he says. For a second she is frozen, her brain racing, making calculations. Maybe he wants to be friends, she thinks. Otherwise, why would he tell her his name?

The next night the boys come in to Bobbi's again, and this time they draw Sammy even further into their arguments, ask her to sit at the table to again provide the local point of view on various topics: acid rain, affirmative action, tax cuts versus tax credits, the NRA, the ERA. "I don't know," she keeps saying. "I don't think people here really care about that. Jobs," she says. "I think people just care about how much money they make." She closes the shop early and goes riding around the city again, seeing it from the eyes of strangers, through the eyes of a campaign looking to interpret and manipulate the locals. *We need these votes*, is the thinking, *we need to guess what these people want and play to it.* Or maybe: *We need to change what these people want, we need to tell them what to want.*

Then the next night the same thing, and the night after that, and on and on through the next two weeks. Ben and Sammy are always in the back together, Ben telling her about every bit of gossip he picked up in the campaign office, mostly having to do with Clinton. Periodically they pull into a parking lot and get out of the car and stick a bunch of fliers under windshield wipers, but mostly their work is the desperate sort, Kurtz pulling up to houses and Boris jumping out to pluck signs from lawns, then Kurtz speeding away with the horn honking.

Through this stretch of days, Sammy is distracted at school, often daydreaming about the previous evening, going over the transcripts—everything Kurtz and Boris and Ben said to each other and to her, everything she said in return, or wishes she'd said. She is so preoccupied, it becomes obvious even to her father.

Every day after school they go through the same routine: they come home and walk their dog to the am/pm behind the house, where they stop for a snack. Though Sammy and her father don't tend to talk much on these walks, still her father notices. "You're off somewhere again," he says one afternoon. The next day, he starts reciting Robert Frost's "Stopping by Woods on a Snowy Evening"—a little game of theirs. "Whose woods these are I think I know," he says. And then it's her turn to say the next line. Back and forth like that—he's taught her dozens of poems this way. But she doesn't really hear him, or hears him but forgets the game. "His house is in the village though," he continues. Then waits again. Then he says: "Jesus Christ."

This, she hears. "Sorry," she says. "The woods are dark and deep, or whatever."

"Or whatever," her father says, "being one of Frost's signature phrases."

A beat skips where they both try out lines in their heads.

"Something there is that doesn't love a wall," Sammy says, "that wants it down or whatever."

"I'll follow you and bring you back by force," her father says, quoting one of Frost's lesser-known poems, "Home Burial," his favorite. "I *will*. Or whatever."

They arrive at the ampm and Sammy's father hands her the leash. She always waits outside with the dog, Lou Grant. Technically he is Lou Grant the Second, the second basset hound they have had in nine years. Rescuing hounds from shelters is her father's weakness, his only sentimental flourish, something he started the year after Sammy's mother died. They have no idea how old this particular Lou Grant is, though he appears to be near the end: he is slow and stiff in his movements, so overweight that his stomach drags on the ground as they walk. By the time they stop for a snack, he is panting.

One of Sammy's habits is to talk to Lou Grant while her father is inside, picking out the day's delicacy—maybe a stick of beef jerky, or a can of roasted peanuts, or a Snicker's bar—as well as his daily six-pack of beer. Her routine is to pretend the dog is haranguing her, asking a series of increasingly incriminating questions, like a *60 Minutes* reporter.

"I don't know," she says to Lou Grant. "I wasn't there."

The dog looks up at her, the flesh under his eyes sagging, little crescents of tortured pink.

"You've got it wrong," she says. "I'm not saying it was necessarily my colleague. I'm just saying if I were you, I'd be asking him questions instead of me."

They regard one another.

"Okay, fine, it was me. I had my reasons. What do you want me to do, kill myself?"

Then Sammy hears a horn honking and sees, from the corner of her eye, the bright yellow Beetle pulled up at a gas pump. She sees that Ben is striding toward her, and panic sets in—some part of her calculating instantly that Ben will stop to talk with her, which means he will meet her father as he emerges from the store. She turns her back, pulls the dog away from the entrance. Her plan is to duck around the corner of the building before Ben sees her, but Lou Grant won't budge. She gives him a little tug, then a yank, but he still doesn't move. "I swear to God," she says.

Then Ben is standing right next to her. "Is this your dog?" he asks.

She looks down at Lou Grant. "No," she says. Meaning it. Wanting to disavow Lou Grant, to renounce everyone and everything with which she is currently affiliated. But it comes off like a joke—of course it's her dog—and they both laugh.

"You're just standing in front of the ampm with a random basset hound," he says.

"Yes," she says. "I am."

He smiles. Or rather, turns up one corner of his mouth, an expression she finds so winning in its coolness, so suitable for so many occasions, she has practiced it in the mirror at home.

"I think I know what's going on," Ben says. He pulls a pack of clove cigarettes from the inside pocket of his jacket, taps one out, sets it in his mouth, fishes for his lighter. It's not in the first pocket he searches, nor the second, so he keeps rifling through his coat and pants. "Goddamn Kurtz. Always stealing my lighter." He lets the cigarette rest on his lip.

Then it is just as Sammy imagined: her father comes through the door, and stops next to Ben, and their meeting is inevitable. At first, Ben is so consumed with the search for his lighter, and the narrative he is producing, that he doesn't quite realize what's happening.

"You're just, like, standing here with this dog to create the illusion of casual innocence, when in reality you're, you're..." Sammy watches as a notion registers on Ben's face—that the man stopped beside him wants something, has something to do with them. In another second, he makes the connection. This man is the person Sammy is waiting for, the reason she's standing outside with the dog. This is her father. Sammy watches as Ben takes in her father: a tall, bearded man in blue coveralls, a man carrying a six-pack of canned Schlitz, a stern man, a man not particularly happy to find his daughter talking with a boy.

Ben has stopped mid-sentence. His gaze goes from Sammy to her father and back. This would be a good place for her to step in and introduce her father, Sammy realizes. Or for her father to introduce himself. But neither of them is very social, so they both just stare at Ben, waiting for him to finish his sentence.

"In reality you're a trained killer," he says.

Another awkward beat passes, and then Sammy and her father, through some sort of silent agreement, like the instinct that governs the movement of flocks of birds in flight, shift away. "See you," Sammy tells Ben. She tugs at Lou Grant, who follows her this time. She gives a quick glance over her shoulder, waves. Ben raises his hand. His brow is creased, as if he's puzzled.

Then Sammy remembers: she had told Ben her father was a teacher. It hadn't been a lie, entirely—he *was* a teacher, at one point. But of course he was a janitor now. It's all probably obvious to Ben, she thinks, not only that she lied, but the reasons for it, some feeble effort to impress him, to cover up something she was ashamed of.

When Ben comes into Bobbi's later that night, there is no mention of this little scene—everything is back to normal. Sammy makes the boys' sandwiches as usual, sits with them as they talk strategy, closes early and rides around with them. But at the end of the night, instead of having Kurtz drop Sammy at the ampm, Ben leans forward and gives Kurtz a series of directions—turn right, turn left, right again—directly to her house. The car stops in front of the house and everyone stares at it, this sagging little cottage, the one she so desperately wanted Bill Clinton to see, so he would understand something about her, that she came from the same circumstances, had the same ambition to rise up from them. But what she wants now is the opposite: not to be seen or understood at all, to remain anonymous, a mystery.

"How did you get my address?" she asks Ben. There are dozens of Brownes in Manchester—the phone book wouldn't be help much.

"The campaign pays for all kinds of information," he says. "You'd be surprised how much you can learn about a person."

"Oh," she says. She wonders what this means. What else does he know?

"Well, thanks," she says.

Boris opens the door, and folds his seat forward, and Sammy climbs out of the car. When she crosses the street and turns to wave, she sees that Ben is staring at the house with rapt attention. She watches his face, wonders what he sees there. It is as if the house is telling him something about her. Perhaps, in light of the house, he understands her character—how her love of beauty has been formed in direct proportion to its absence here in Manchester. For her part, she thinks she sees quite clearly now her place in things, in Ben's life and in his book. She understands that she is only a minor character, a specimen of humanity, a diversion. The kind of character who appears in chapter three, then catches tuberculosis and dies in chapter four.

Kurtz drives away, and Sammy turns and walks to the door, her head hanging. There is a heaviness in her chest. There is nothing to be embarrassed about, she reminds herself. She didn't do anything wrong. This just happens to be her house, her life. So what is this feeling?

On the morning of the primary, Sammy tells her father she is sick, then walks to meet the Tsongas boys outside a polling station—an old, gothic-looking church. It is bitterly cold and most of the incoming voters are eager to get past them, into the warmth of the church. Most are scowling and tired of people telling them who to vote for. They just want it to be over. The aggressive advertising, the fighting, the pleading. They want it to be over, but Sammy wants it to go on forever.

She loves watching Kurtz operate, how he approaches voters and walks alongside them, rattling off the reasons to vote for Tsongas: his proven track record of reaching compromise, his sensible energy plan, his impressive polling data against Bush. And she loves the desperate little pleas Kurtz makes when voters push past him: *It's the right thing to do, Ma'am!*

Meanwhile, Sammy notes, Boris is useless, or worse—he seems to be actively driving voters away. "You will vote for Senator Tsongas," he says, his accent somehow worse than ever, bordering on villainous, yet too lame to pose any real threat, like The Count from *Sesame Street*. She wonders what Boris is really doing here, what his story is, what he hopes to gain, what he is trying to make himself into. But the thought passes.

Because really, her focus is Ben. For their part, Sammy and Ben are the backup singers, handing out fliers and buttons to the voters Kurtz and Boris miss while they pursue others. Through much of the morning, Ben and Sammy play a game where they watch a voter pass, then imagine his name and occupation, his innermost secrets and desires. "Bruce Biggerstaff," says Ben, after a giant of a man in coveralls is safely out of earshot. "Muffler mechanic. Never married. Goes by 'Bucho.' Secretly wants to be the lead singer of a Def Leppard tribute band."

"Marlene Fitzpatrick," Sammy says, of a diminutive woman dressed in a tweed suit, a duffel coat, rain boots. "Secretary at a Catholic school. Two kids, both grown, never call. Husband dead of a heart attack. Spends her free time reading *National Geographic*, updating and maintaining her deceased husband's stamp collection. Innermost desire is...." She falters. "Well, I guess her innermost desire is to be the head secretary at the Vatican."

They go on and on like this, Ben imagining lives that are mock-heroic, his characters outsized—the humor coming from the absurdity of their exploits, the magnitude of their failures. Meanwhile, Sammy's characters are quiet, meek, the humor coming from the smallness of their pleasures and desires, one man, for instance, wanting nothing more than to hear his own voice on the radio.

Just before noon, Kurtz takes a call on his briefcase phone and then announces it's time to move. "Points west," he shouts.

"Now, now, now." Clapping his hands together as if moving a platoon through hostile territory, as if there weren't a second to lose.

Ben looks at Sammy, shrugs. "Points west, I suppose," he says. There isn't any time for pleasantries. Ben touches two fingers to his eyebrow, then pushes them toward Sammy in a salute.

"Wait!" she says. Actually reaching out for him. "Um, I mean, good luck. I'll be rooting for you."

Ben seems to sense what she wanted to say—that she wants to keep in touch. "Don't worry," he says. "I'll call you."

"Do you want my number?" she asks. She is delaying him with this petty business, she knows—Kurtz is already in the car—but she can't help herself.

"I already have it," he says. "Maybe we'll see you down in Virginia. Good luck, kid."

Sammy stands and watches him climb into the car, watches Kurtz drive away, and even when it is out of sight, she listens to the diesel engine rattling, the car alarm sounding its final flourish.

Kid, she thinks. *I suppose I'm a kid.*

That night it is just Sammy and her father sitting in front of the television. They watch the returns come in announcing Tsongas as the winner, but Clinton hogs up all the coverage. He comes so close to winning, even amidst all that scandal, that he brands himself The Comeback Kid. In the following weeks Sammy watches the coverage of the campaign, always hoping for a glimpse of Ben or Kurtz or Boris, though soon enough no one is covering Tsongas anymore—Clinton is the presumptive nominee. He is always pictured making his way through a crowd, people putting their hands on his shoulders and arms, leaving their prints on him. He keeps winning primaries in exactly the way Sammy had tried to describe to Kurtz—a phenomenon she now hears people talking about on television. Bill Clinton is out there, reporters keep noting, walking the streets, introducing himself to everyone he passes by—not by obligation, as is the case with other candidates, but by some kind of bizarre compulsion, some kind of genuine need. In particular, reporters note, he seeks out workers moving about the periphery of his campaign, the flight attendants and chauffeurs, the secretaries, the wait staff, the people washing dishes in the back room, the skinny kids hauling bags of garbage out to the dumpsters behind fast food establishments, the cashiers and gas station attendants and traffic cops and road construction crews. He wants to meet all of them and shake their hands, he wants to tell them his heart is with them. Anyone wearing a uniform. Anyone with callused hands. Anyone stiff with arthritis. Anyone who has worn through the soles of his shoes. Anyone who goes home at the end of the day and soaks his feet in Epsom salts. Anyone with a herniated disc, with carpal tunnel syndrome, with black lung, anyone who stinks of propane, of garbage, of deli meat. He wants them to know he is going to help. With education, with loans, with job training, with higher wages, with tax cuts, with healthcare. If they give him the chance, he will take them up, make them his cause. They have only to meet him, and they will see. They will believe. He is out there at all hours, pounding the pavement, pressing flesh. He won't stop until he has appealed to everyone, personally taken their hands in his. He is on the lookout for the undecided, the apathetic, the lost. And they are out there, as always, hoping to be noticed, hoping someone will come along and claim them, like the crappy luggage circling on a rack at the airport—these people, Sammy's people, they are just there for the taking.

One afternoon not long after the primary, when the excitement of the campaign is gone and Manchester has returned to its grim, cold self, Sammy checks the mail while her father is leashing up Lou Grant for their afternoon walk. She finds an envelope from Virginia—just a regular, letter-sized envelope, a rejection, she assumes—and stuffs it in the pocket of her coat, not wanting to open it in front of her father. Wanting, instead, to watch her dreams die in the privacy of her bedroom. On the walk, Lou Grant looks particularly mournful and lame, the freezing drizzle coating his fur in tiny pellets. When they stop at the ampm Sammy waits outside, staring down at the dog, who stares back at her, his face collapsed into long jowls, his ears drooping, and she tries to adjust to the idea of staying in New Hampshire, attending the state school. After graduation, probably coming back to Manchester to teach English in the same school she attends now, she and her father riding to work together in the morning, walking Lou Grant, or some future Lou Grant, in the afternoons, the world having passed her by....

"I don't know," she says to Lou Grant. "I wasn't there."

And then, after a beat, "You can't prove anything."

Back in her bedroom, she opens the letter and finds it is from the financial aid office—a scholarship offer that has somehow arrived before her acceptance. The letter is from a man named James W. Ramsey, who is pleased, he says, to offer her not only a full tuition waiver, but funding for room, board, and book expenses as well. He has also included, he writes, a stamped envelope for her reply, so that her acceptance will come at no personal cost to her.

The phrase that runs through Sammy's mind is: *How poor do they think we are?*

She has won this scholarship, she knows, based on the essay she submitted—a portrait of her father as a middle-aged man. The essay began with an image of him mopping the floor of her high school cafeteria. Then she explained how her father had once been an English teacher there instead. How he'd gone to school on the GI Bill, gotten his bachelor's and master's, completed his teacher training, started teaching and even started working on a doctorate. But then Sammy's mother had died, and something had changed with her father—he was unable to be around people, unable to talk aloud to a group, and so now here he was, she wrote, circling that mop, with verses of Shakespeare running through his head: *Our doubts are traitors, and make us lose the good we oft might win, by fearing to attempt.*

What had gone wrong, she asked in the essay. She went on to tell all of her father's secrets, the things he never talked about, and advised her never to talk about. She talked about his poor Irish upbringing, his drunk father, his time in Vietnam—the damage it had done to him, the anxiety he suffered, his desperate need for solitude. She talked about his occasional attempts to recover, to believe again, to join himself with a group. The time he tried to return to school, the time he'd spent working for Gary Hart, the hope he'd felt for the 1986 Red Sox team, all of which had ended in heartbreaking disaster. She talked about this belief resurfacing now, in her. The belief that she might go to school and redeem things, make good on his dreams.

At the end Sammy had placed herself in the essay, a kid sitting in the cafeteria watching her father work. She talked about the hunch that had developed in her father's spine, how so many years bent over a mop had bowed him, given him the posture of a supplicant. She made reference to Quasimodo. She said how the curve of her father's spine looked to her like a question mark, and the question was: Is this really my father's life? And from there, more questions: *Will it ever get better? What can be done? Is this my life, too? Will it be the same?* She talked about standing over her own mop in Bobbi's Hollywood Café, wondering what would happen next. *It's up to you*, the essay was saying. *If you want to leave a kid standing over a mop, well, so be it.*

Now Sammy feels bad about what she wrote. The essay was overdone, and touched with cruelty. Her father was a quiet man who valued his privacy, and she'd taken his story and profited from it. It takes her a week to show her father the letter, so egregious in its generosity that she fears it will betray her, that her father will sense what she'd done. But he just takes the letter and unfolds it, and a smile forms at the corner of his mouth. "You did it," he says. They hug, and she starts crying, which she tries never to do in front of him. But she can't help it. "You did it, Pal," he says.

The spring and summer pass slowly. Sammy wades through the final days of school, then the summer at Bobbi's, where no one interesting comes in, just the women tired from shopping next door, at the plus-sized fashion outlet. They come in with their bags and lift their faces to the menu. They order the chicken salad. While Sammy makes their sandwiches, they talk to each other about their purchases. "You did well," one says to the other. "You'll be able to wear that suit anywhere."

"I just hope it's okay for a wedding," the other says. "I wanted a dress, but the suit hides more."

As Sammy rings up their orders she stares at their feet, which are swollen and stuffed into leather sandals. Their pedicures are chipped.

Then the women sit at the little round tables and eat their sandwiches. The girl stares at them and thinks about spending the rest of her life in Manchester, of getting married and having kids and buying a plus-sized suit for an upcoming wedding. A scrambling feeling comes over her. She feels like something will go wrong, some sword will come down and cut off her route to a better life. If she doesn't leave town immediately, it seems, she will be stuck there forever. She can't stop thinking about it.

On Sammy's last day of work, Bobbi Woolworth brings in a bag of samples from the makeup counters she frequents. She makes Sammy sit at one of the tables while she transforms the blank canvas of her face. While Bobbi works she gives Sammy a lecture about starting over and the importance of never revealing where you came from, who you once were. "That's what Marilyn did," Bobbi says. "She left that little town and that shy girl behind." Bobbi puts up Sammy's hair in a series of pins and clips. She paints Sammy's mouth red and draws a mole above it with liquid liner. "It's important to start over with a new look," Bobbi says. "If you keep up this routine you'll find a rich husband and one day you'll be living in your mansion." She holds up a mirror and shows Sammy her garish face. "One day you'll be living in your mansion," Bobbi says, "and it will be like none of this ever happened."

So much of Bobbi's life, Sammy thinks, has been an effort to pretend certain things hadn't happened, that times had changed, that she had grown older. And all those girls who had gone through the sandwich shop before Sammy, who had worked for a year, then left and never returned—there was a bit of sadness there, too.

"I'll write you," she tells Bobbi. She is suddenly on the verge of tears. "You can come visit me in the mansion."

Bobbi hugs her tight. Sammy is awash in a cloud of Chanel and can hardly breathe. "Don't you ever look back," Bobbi says. "You just walk out that door and keep on walking."

1992

Ben calls his mother every Sunday night, or else she worries, and takes it out on him the next time he does call. "I was *worried*," she says, in her glorious New York accent—something he never thought he'd miss, but is now happy to hear. "You said you were going to call, but you didn't call."

So he calls her from the road—a payphone at a truck stop. He has closed the folding door of the phone booth, but he can still barely hear over the diesel engines, the rushing traffic.

"Benny!" his mother says. "You called!"

"Of course, Ma," he says.

"I was telling your father earlier, I hope he calls, I hope he calls so we can see how he's *doing*."

"Not great," he says. The campaign is winding down as they lose ground to Clinton. The polls aren't looking good. There is talk, on the level just over their heads, amongst the paid volunteers, that Tsongas will pull out by the end of the week.

"Where are you?" she says.

"Somewhere in Illinois. I think."

"Chicago?"

"Not even close."

"Oh," she says. Pauses. "Well, I can't think of a single thing to say."

"There's nothing," he says. "Nothing here at all."

"Well," she says. "I mean, we're watching the news. I know it's not looking so good for you."

"Any day now."

"Come home. Just come home. You've done enough."

"I guess." He sighs. "I just wanted, I just wanted to take it all the way. This isn't how I wanted the book to end, you know?"

"Well," she says. "You can always, I guess you can always make up a different ending."

He can picture her perfectly. She is standing in the bathroom, inspecting herself in front of the mirror. The phone is on speaker, so she can make adjustments to herself. She is plucking at her bangs—she has worn her hair in a bob his entire life—lifting up strands and letting them fall. Or she is applying red lipstick, which she does all the time, even at night, when there's no one to impress. Or she is trying on various necklaces—she is fond of necklaces with large, dangling pendants. Possibly she is poking at the flesh of her upper arm, watching it swing back and forth. She always stands in front of the mirror when she's on the phone, a ritual he has never quite understood, something he has filed under the category of: Women.

"I just wanted it to be true," he says.

"Oh," she says, sighs. "You're so young."

He asks what's going on at home, and she tells him about an exhibit she saw at The Met. Some contemporary artist he's never heard of, a painter obsessed with garbage. It was interesting, she tells him, though not in the way that will last. "You'd hate it," she adds. She knows his taste—knows it because she formed it with her own hands. Practically every Sunday of his life, she took him to a museum. Even when he was a toddler, and had to be carried through the rooms, she took him. This is worth looking at, she told him. Or: This is worthless. His love of Titian, Renoir, Dubuffet, Basquiat, Keiffer. His total aversion to Stella, Koons—she had shaped it all.

"How's Dad?" he asks.

"Nothing new," she says. Her standard answer. Ben's

father is the most stoic and unchangeable man he has ever known, or ever hopes to know.

"It's a Carson night," his mother says. "You're missing out." She refers to *The Tonight Show*, which they always watched together when Ben lived at home. *The Tonight Show* was past his bedtime, but he suffered the same ailment his mother did—he couldn't fall asleep before midnight. His mother had understood him, indulged him. Almost every weeknight from the ages of ten to eighteen, he had sat next to her on the couch watching Carson, leaning against her. She pulled him close, her arm around his neck, her hand occasionally running through his hair.

Now Johnny Carson is easing into retirement. Half the shows, lately, are hosted by Jay Leno, who his mother hates. Whereas Carson is cool, sly, a bit cagey, Leno is a lumbering buffoon. A tactless man launching simple jokes in a high-pitched voice, leaning forward, desperate for approval. "Why those *idiots* at NBC think, for a *single second*, that fans of Carson will join a church led by that, that *giant moron*, is, well it's just *unfathomable*." She is truly distressed, he can tell. "What are we going to *do* at night?"

"Letterman?" he suggests.

"I tried him," she says. "He leaves me cold."

"Dick Cavett?" he tries again.

"Dick Cavett is insecure," his mother observes. "He uses his intellect as a shield, in my opinion."

"I'm not going to argue with that."

"He's not even on the networks anymore. Just imagine how smart he is now."

They are quiet for a minute, during which Ben considers how long he's been gone, how long his mother has lacked a companion in the evenings. First he was off to college, then Europe, now this business with the campaign.

And then, because they are still so close, because they so

often are thinking along the same lines, she says, "Just come *home*, Benny. I miss you. Come watch Carson with me. Come home."

"Okay, Ma," he says. "Okay."

He gets back into the car. *For one of the last times*, he thinks to himself. He is relieved, in a way. Tired of this life. The thought of going home settles on him. He thinks of the king bed in his room, how dark and warm it always is, how the velvet curtains block out all the light. He thinks, too, of his own private bathroom, just steps from the bed. And the food—he's missed his mother's cooking, the dozens of restaurants within walking distance. Most of all he's missed the city itself, the feeling of stepping out in the late morning onto the bustling streets, the crowded sidewalks, the lanes of traffic, the honking horns.

Okay, he thinks. *I'm going home*. He's not happy about the way the book is ending. Maybe Kurtz will have to kill himself? Or fall into drug use, crime, bribery, eventually jail? Maybe Boris will be revealed as a KGB agent? But even without an ending, at least he's going back to New York.

Not an hour later Kurtz answers a call on his briefcase phone, then hands the receiver to Boris. Boris is reserved for once, professional. "Yes, Ma'am," he says. "Absolutely. Anything you need. We'll do anything at all." Then he slams the phone back in its case. "Yes!" he cries. "Yes!" He grabs Kurtz by the shoulders, shakes him, even though Kurtz is trying to drive. The car weaves in and out of its lane. "We did it!" Boris screams. And then Kurtz screams, "Fuck, yes!" He pounds on the steering wheel. Leans on the horn. Lets out a barbaric yawp.

In the following moments Ben learns that what they have done—what Boris has done, actually—is get them jobs on the Clinton campaign. Paid jobs. Kurtz is, at this very moment, trying to figure out which exit to take. They are turning around. Heading for Florida.

So Ben yanks himself out of his dreams of home. He's come this far. He can't leave now.

He calls his mother again the following night and explains the situation. That they are working for Clinton now. Part of a winning team that really will make its way to the White House. "I can't really explain it," he says, "but I feel like I have to see this through."

"Of course you do," she says. "Of *course* you do."

"The only trouble is school. I already deferred a year. I can't again."

"I know," she says. "I'll fix things with your father."

"He's going to lose his mind."

"Leave him to me," she says. "I can handle him." Then adds, "Don't talk to him for a couple of weeks. I'll work him over. Just let me know where to send you money."

"Thanks, Ma," he says.

And just like that, he's bought himself another year. He feels guilty about disappointing his parents, asking for more money. The feeling he materializes as a lead cube, the size of a microwave. This feeling is easy to visualize because it is so familiar. He feels bad about money, quite often actually. All his life he has had access to so much, and has never really had to do anything for it. The only thing that has ever been asked of him is that he become a productive member of society. There has never been any question, really, about what he would do—he would follow his mother's profession, because he was *interested in people*, as she phrased it, in the same way she was. But now he is making her wait. He is making his father explain, when his colleagues ask about his son, that he is still *taking time off*. Dabbling in politics.

The feeling is too heavy. So Ben does what he always does when he wants to get rid of it. He makes a plan. He'll reapply to med school in the fall. Maybe try NYU instead, go back to the city. Live at home, consult his mother about study questions. Not because he needs her help, but because it will make her happy. There, he thinks. That's settled, that's what I'll do. And he puts down the cube.

2011

Sammy is on the floor of her daughter's room, a stuffed dog in each hand—two terriers, Irish and Scottish. The dogs are named Lenny and Squiggy, and she is pretending to make them hide from Ava's dogs, two German Shepherds out for blood. These days, Sammy spends more hours of her life playing with these dogs than she spends doing anything else other than sleeping. They have been playing *Dogs!*—Sammy and her daughter call it this, *Dogs!*—for weeks now, a single, perpetual game of *Dogs!*, with the same feuds playing out nightly, certain groups of dogs against others. Ava has dozens of dogs, living in piles along the borders and in the shadows of her room, little shantytowns divided into groups, terrier and toy, working and sporting, nonsporting, herding, hound. The game is essentially this: that Sammy's dogs are walking about the room, minding their own business, until Ava's dogs come on the scene, at which point Sammy's dogs hide, but are discovered, followed by a gradual buildup of threats and evasions that always end with one of the dogs sinking his teeth into another's neck, the injured party bleeding out and then being thrown in a mass grave. It's a classic game. Cops and Robbers. Jets and Sharks.

They are playing with dogs lately as a means of not pretending to be dogs, themselves. A little adjustment Sammy has made, something she considers an improvement. A point in the win column, such as it is.

This particular game has been going on for a while, Sammy's

dogs running and hiding, Ava's dogs giving chase, and now finally the time comes: Ava's dogs, Ludwig and Friedrich, pounce on Lenny and Squiggy, and there's a frenzied battle, growling and yelping, and then, suddenly, silence: Lenny and Squiggy are dead.

Lately, to entertain herself, or perhaps to forge some kind of connection between her life and the larger world, the real world, as she thinks of it, Sammy has been taking pictures of the *Dogs!* carnage, after the fashion of the photos she has been seeing for years on the front page of *The Times*. She has come to think of herself as something of a war photographer. The feud she is most fond of documenting is something she calls The War on Terriers. Sometimes she texts these photos—groups of dogs lined up on their backs, covered by a blanket, only their tails sticking out—to Ben, along with little headlines: FIVE DEAD IN SURPRISE THANKSGIVING ATTACK, or, PEACE TALKS TURN DEADLY. Ben seems to understand that she is not, in fact, sending him these pictures for their own sake but instead attempting to communicate something desperate and hopeless, something along the lines of: *Look at my tiny little life. Look how ridiculous.*

Now she arranges Lenny and Squiggy in hopeless, defeated postures, then takes out her phone and snaps a picture, sends it to Ben. Ambushed, she writes.

CNN is running a crawler right now, he returns. They're not identifying the names of the dead until the families are informed.

It's nice of you to play along, she writes.

Of course. These are very serious matters.

This isn't exactly how I imagined my life would turn out, she writes.

He replies by confirming the smallness and absurdity of Sammy's circumstances, which is exactly what she wants. You could have been somebody, he writes. You could have been a contender.

Her thumbs hover over the screen. She is considering telling Ben about her plan to redeem herself, bring herself back into contention: that a handful of good jobs have just posted in her field, and she is putting together some applications. There's a position in Jersey, one in Connecticut, two in New York. A year from today, she could be texting him from the same time zone, somewhere closer to him, closer to her father. She is excited to tell Ben, but something stops her. She puts down the phone, wonders what it is. *Bad luck*, she decides. *Bad luck to tell him too soon.*

Though underneath this, lurking, is another notion, one she's harbored for years: It just might be that living so far apart has been the very thing keeping her and Ben together all this time. A strange notion, but a persistent one.

There is only one way to find out, and she's not particularly sure she wants to know the answer.

In any case, she puts down the phone.

1992

Finally, the day comes when it is time for Sammy to leave home. Over breakfast she and her father regard a map spread across the kitchen table. The map is so old it is faded and torn along the creases, and so the route her father has marked traverses, in places, uncharted and missing lands. Instead of taking I-95 he has traced a path down 81 through the countryside of Massachusetts, New York, and Pennsylvania. He is avoiding the highway, he says, because there is some question as to the roadworthiness of their Buick, which is twenty years old—there is some question about its ability to maintain high speeds for hours on end. Sammy's father has packed the trunk with several gallons of water and pints of oil and coolant, a spare tire and jack. He has also packed and settled behind his seat a cooler full of Schlitz cans and candy bars and beef jerky. They are ready for anything.

They leave after breakfast and wind through the countryside, passing farms dotted with sheep and cattle. The engine keeps getting hot and they pull over to let it cool. During these interludes Sammy's father stands leaning against the car, smoking a cigarette, his legs crossed at the ankles, and in this pose he looks to her like an advertisement for cigarettes—a man on a lonely country road stopping to take a moment to himself, to think his thoughts. What he is thinking is a mystery to Sammy and always has been. Whether he is sorry to see her go, or glad to be free, is impossible to say. She can't tell whether he is proud to be taking her to school, or disappointed. She is going off to do what he himself had done, what he loved, so there is a chance he is pleased. But then again, she thinks, he has turned away from it all and perhaps doesn't care to be reminded. Once her father had explained to Sammy his decision to leave his teaching post in terms of the higher dignity of manual labor, of quietly doing something that needed to be done. There was just as much honor, he'd said, in mopping a floor than in teaching a class. And it suited him better. The pace. The quiet.

Then again it would be hard, Sammy often thought, to clean toilets in a local high school all those years and to remember all the while that one's work was an act of dignity. Of course her father must have struggled. He always carried around volumes of poetry on his custodial cart, issues of *Dissent*—he couldn't quite disappear entirely into his new identity. What he enjoyed most about his job, it seemed to Sammy, was the half-hour or so after school when he stood in the hall talking to a French teacher named Mr. LaCroix, an old-timer who wore the same cardigan sweater every day, and whose addiction to cigarettes was so profound he often lit up in class, took a single drag, then stabbed his cigarette out on the blackboard. They stood in the hall and talked philosophy and politics and poetry, and complained about pop culture. What Sammy knew of her father she knew from listening to these conversations, in which her father's ideas and opinions came flooding out. When her father found someone interesting to talk to, someone who had read the right novels and philosophical tracts, he grew animated, you might even say chatty, which revealed something, Sammy thought—that he wasn't quite satisfied with the quiet life of repetitive labor he had chosen, that something was stifled in him, that he wanted something more.

But in the end she can't confirm any of these theories, because her father never speaks of them. Most of their lives have unfolded in companionable silence. The longest conversation they have on the drive to Virginia is in response to a billboard they see in Pennsylvania, advertising a restaurant that serves homemade scrapple. They don't quite know what scrapple is and can only imagine it has to do with undesirable portions of animals. Every mile or two they offer a new suggestion: the lips of goats, the ears of cows, the tails of pigs.

Not long after they cross into Maryland Sammy's father stops at a roadside diner of the sort pictured on postcards, with chrome accents and a bright neon sign. They seat themselves in a booth and a waitress wearing a mustard-yellow polyester uniform and white nurse's shoes comes to take their order. They order burgers and Cokes and fries, and then wait. From the speakers overhead comes a kind of music Sammy has only heard before on *The Muppet Show*: classic country. Willie Nelson and John Denver and Dolly Parton. Watching *The Muppets*, Sammy had thought the whole thing was maybe a joke, a genre of absurd excess—the godawful banjo, the twanging, the absolutely unbelievable breasts—but here it seems to be offered in earnest. In the context of the diner—its patrons, men in dark, stiff jeans and flannel shirts, hunched over their plates—it occurs to her this music might be serious. That the longing and heartbreak it expresses are true cries for help. *Everybody's lonesome for somebody else*, Hank Williams sings. *Nobody's lonesome for me.*

It is getting dark outside, the time of day that puts Sammy and her father in a thoughtful mood. They look past their reflections and out at the road, the passing traffic. They have spent so many hours quietly staring out of windows that Sammy is surprised when her father clears his throat and speaks. "We should probably have a talk," he says. He is turned away from her to such an extent that she considers it might be possible he is talking to the man behind him, in the next booth.

Then it occurs to Sammy that her father is trying to fulfill his parental duty regarding sex education. "It's okay," she says. "I don't need, I don't need a talk. I already talked to, I already talked to Bobbi." This isn't quite true, but is close enough. Bobbi had made certain recommendations to Sammy about sex appeal. "What I like to do," she said, "is give myself a squirt of perfume right down my pants. You never know when someone might be down there."

"It's not that," he says. "It's about." His eyes dart. "It's about something I guess you might call the family gift."

"Oh," she says.

"I don't think it's something you need to worry about. But you should know there's a certain." He falters again. "There's a certain predilection," he says. "A certain problem managing, I guess you'd call it excess."

"Oh."

"You know your mother," he says. "It's true it was an accident but it's also true that. It's also true she was drunk."

"I know," she says.

"I just mean. Once you start it's hard to stop. And you're getting this, you're getting this from both sides, you might say."

"I know." Sammy is fiddling with the salt and pepper shakers, rotating them in her palm.

"Just try to steer clear. You're going to be down there with lots of opportunities to, well, lots of ways to go wrong."

"I *know*," she says. "I *get it*."

"Okay. Okay. I just felt like I had to tell you."

Then the waitress brings their Cokes and they tap their wrapped straws on the table, unsheathe them, plunk them into their drinks, suck, swallow, exhale loudly through their mouths. The Cokes cheer them and they start talking again. "Ahh," the father says. "This is good."

"We should drink more Coke."

"We should keep this in the fridge at all times."

"I don't know why we don't have this, like, every day."

"It might be the best drink in the world."

"You don't really need anything else, ever. It's like, completely satisfying."

"It quenches."

"It's sweet, but there's also this sharpness to it."

"That's the thing. If it were just sweet, it wouldn't work so well."

They drink until they are out of Coke and stare at the bottom of their red plastic glasses with despair. When the waitress brings their food they ask for more. In the minutes between her leaving the table and her return with more Coke they are despondent. But when she arrives with two fresh cups they perk up again. She gives them two new straws, and they push off their wrappers and plunk them in. There is no limit to anything, it seems. Everything is new and when it isn't anymore it will be replenished.

They have a third Coke before they leave and are sort of flying on their way back to the car. But in thirty minutes or so they crash, melancholy overtakes them. Sammy slumps her head against the window. It is dark now. She closes her eyes. Her breathing slows. Some moments later she hears her father fumbling in the back seat, hears the lid of the cooler swing open, then the crack of an aluminum can opening, the first slurp of beer.

In no time, it seems, her father nudges her and she sees they are winding through the streets of campus. All along the sidewalks young people are walking together in groups, many of them shouting and laughing. Behind them, across expanses of lawn, stand red brick buildings with beautiful white columns, lit by floodlights, brilliant. As they wind through campus Sammy begins to sense that the Buick is disturbing the peace, polluting the environment. More times than can be attributed to chance, kids turn their heads and stare at it, their heads pivoting toward the awful noise of its engine, like the low grumbling of a three-headed beast napping at the gates of hell. The car is so out of context here they might as well be traveling by horse and buggy. For a period of time they are stopped at a red light behind a blonde girl in a convertible two-seater Mazda Miata, which seems to be the polar opposite, automotively speaking, to the Buick. The blonde in the car actually turns around to see what is behind her. They present her blank faces. She smiles weakly and turns back around.

"I wonder what would happen to that girl in an accident."

"She would be crushed like a bug," Sammy says.

Though they say no more on the subject, Sammy is sure they are both picturing it, the death and dismemberment of this blonde, the crushing of her little red car. Generally she and her father believe themselves to be good people but displays of wealth make them petty, vengeful.

She starts turning the campus map this way and that, trying to figure out the relationship between where they are and where they need to be. The Buick crawls along, and the father keeps asking her whether to turn or go straight. "Uh, straight," she says. When they finally arrive at the right street, it is more or less by chance. The street winds up a hill, behind a row of dorms, and comes to an end at a roundabout. They stare up at the buildings, sensible brick structures with wide rectangular windows. Every window is lit. They can see a few people moving about, and all of them look like the girl in the red Miata. "Do you want to come up and see my room?" Sammy asks.

"I don't think I can leave the car here," her father says.

"Right," she says. "Are you staying the night? Should we meet for breakfast?"

"I think I'll just keep driving. Head back. I'm not tired. All that Coke."

"Okay," she says.

She pulls her bag out of the back seat and gets out of the car. Her father waves and puts the car in drive. He starts off, punches the horn twice with his fist. She stands on the sidewalk and watches the Buick's taillights and then, after the car has turned onto the main road and she can no longer see it, listens to its engine rumbling, listens until it fades away. A panic settles on her. She has the feeling that she is facing one direction, her father and the life she has always known, but when she turns around and walks up to the dorm, a new life will begin, and she doesn't want to live it. Suddenly, terribly, it occurs to her that she doesn't belong here. The only thing she can think to do in a place like this is mop the floor.

She stands for several minutes with her bag slung over her shoulder, pillow tucked beneath her arm, trying to talk herself into doing what needs to be done. Then she remembers the five-dollar bill that Bill Clinton had given her, remembers it is still folded up in the pocket of her jeans. She'd left it there all these months, because she had wanted always to be carrying it. Every few days she would take it out and unfold it and think of those few moments she spent with Clinton, and wonder if the bill would be worth something someday, wonder if Clinton would win the election and she would have some connection, however small, to a president. The bill has gone through the wash so many times there is no trace of him left, but still she takes it out once more and unfolds it, regards Lincoln's face, and feels a chill. Maybe, she thinks, this little scene is just the beginning of what will turn out to be an extraordinary story. A girl looking at the face of a president, given to her by a future president—each having come from nothing but having persevered and transformed. She feels again the way she did the night she met Clinton—that perhaps she is a character in a book, perhaps something interesting will happen, perhaps she will win in the end. The only reason things feel so bad now, she tells herself, is because this is how stories always start: a character newly orphaned, lost to uncertainty and despair. But things will get better, she thinks, because they have to, because that's how these stories go.

1992

One truth Ben would like to make clear in his book: Campaign offices are all alike in that they are shitty, but each is shitty in its own way.

This particular one (Tucson? Phoenix? Flagstaff? They have been driving around for days and Ben doesn't even know where they are...) is shitty in the sense that it is in the middle of a strip mall, in a space that was most recently a plus-sized clothing outlet. Lucky Lady, it was called—the name is still painted in giant red letters along one wall. The space has been emptied out and repurposed. There are desks here and there, and up front, two couches. But there are still remnants of the outlet. Three stalls of changing rooms in the back. And shoved in the far back corner, an empty clothing turnstile, with a lone blue dress suspended from a plastic hanger, the tag still on it: $28.99.

He and Kurtz and Boris are sitting up front with a few other staffers, bullshitting. Kurtz is always cornering the policy makers and speech writers, launching phrases at them, trying to impress them, wanting some kind of foothold to the upper reaches of the campaign. Because they are still doing the grunt work. No longer pulling up signs from lawns, but not much higher. "The future," Kurtz is saying, waving his hands, "what we need to do is get people excited about the fucking future." The volume lowers in the room suddenly, though Kurtz doesn't notice—he just keeps trying out phrases. "Building a bridge," he's yelling, excitedly. "Building a bridge to the next century."

Ben turns his head and sees a small cluster of people in suits at the back of the room—the high-level staffers—and rising above them, a head taller, the silver hair of the candidate himself. Clinton is standing in front of the food table, surveying it, looking at the open boxes of pizza and donuts. His staffers are chattering, all talking at once. Clinton is nodding, smiling a bit. He picks up a donut, takes a bite, chews absentmindedly. "I like that," Ben hears him say. He is much quieter than everyone around him, but Ben manages to tune everyone else out, tap into Clinton's frequency. "That's good," he says. "I like that." He finishes the donut on the second bite, just folds it into his mouth. Chews, listens some more. Sucks the tip of his thumb. "Work it up," he says. He picks up a slice of pizza—it's been sitting out all day, but no matter—and starts wandering toward the back. Disappears.

That's it. The first time Ben actually sees Clinton. He remembers what that girl said back in Manchester: *a bit of a star quality*. It's true, he realizes. He didn't believe it then, but now he sees it's true.

Clinton is gone now, but Ben is still frozen, staring at the food table. He starts to think, really and truly, that Clinton will win. That by some crazy chance, Kurtz has actually found his way onto the staff of the candidate who will win the presidency. Ben scribbles down a few details. Lucky Lady. The blue dress hanging in the corner. The donuts, the bit of frosting on the candidate's thumb. This is the stuff that will make up his novel. He is stunned, a bit giddy. Charged again. Like's he's stuck a knife in an electrical outlet.

Then someone comes through the back door—a blond woman in a blue pants suit who cuts a quick line through the room, all the way out the front door. "That's not what was supposed to happen," she says over her shoulder, to a staffer following behind her. Her voice is low but somehow sharp. "Call him and reschedule." Then she's through the door, gone. Hillary Clinton.

2011

They play a game sometimes, by text, a series of volleys that lasts all day long. Ben will send something to Sammy in the morning, some type of low-level complaint, and they'll go back and forth throughout the day, jockeying for position, each trying to have it worse than the other.

My back hurts, he writes one morning.

And she replies: My kid woke up crying three times, and in the brief stretches when she was asleep, she was kicking me in the spine.

An hour later he sends: I think maybe I can't get away with wearing pink dress shirts anymore. My complexion has changed. There's no longer any contrast between me and the shirt. I look like a giant hot dog.

That's a sad story, she writes.

It IS sad. It was a three-hundred-dollar shirt.

A while later she sends: I can't exactly say that I find meaning in my work. I just tried to teach "The Metamorphosis" to a bunch of kids whose response was along the lines of: "This dude's family needs a giant can of Raid!" Jesus.

At least you can say you're an educator, he writes. I'm passing out tissues to people who are upset with their kitchen remodelers.

Later she writes: I can't stop sneezing.

I think I need reading glasses, he replies.

My car is leaking antifreeze.

I got stopped in the hall by Mrs. Henderson, the compulsive chatter. Her cat has diabetes now. Kill me.

It's snowing here. Again. I'm going to have to wake up fifteen minutes early tomorrow to dig the car out.

I'm out of Scotch.

My bras have lost all their elastic.

My last blood pressure reading was 160 over 110.

Jesus, she writes. Fine. You win.

Ben is, more often than not, the person who initiates these little dialogues. Perhaps because he spends his days listening to other people's complaints, and wants a forum of his own. Or perhaps because he is simply bored, caught up in the work week and wanting some relief from it.

Over the years, these texts have become their own genre, governed by a particular code, one of Ben's design. It is very important, he feels, to preserve and uphold the traditions of the genre, traditions mainly having to do with tone. A certain offhandedness is key. No matter how long Ben contemplates a text, it must present itself as having been tossed off, typed while he is in the middle of something else, something much more important. Too, in his case, the texts must be touched with irony. Every time he registers a complaint about his lavish circumstances, he is in fact performing a little flogging ritual, acknowledging his privilege, the shamefulness of having been given so much. For Sammy, the tone is different, more frantic than ironic, sometimes bordering on slapstick, because in her case, the complaints are real, rooted in the constraints of her circumstances, the meagerness of her income and the constant unrelenting hassle of being a parent. But still it is important, for the sake of the ritual, to keep things light, to make herself the butt of the joke, as in: *Look what I went and did now.* Sometimes she forgets this, and Ben has to reel her in.

For instance, on this particular day, not long after Sammy declares Ben the winner—his blood pressure being, after all, practically lethal—she comes back with: Wait, maybe you don't win. My kid doesn't have any friends.

What is he supposed to do with that? Before he can think of anything, she sends another: And my mother never loved me.

Jesus.

He shoots back the only thing he can think of: My mother loved me too much. I'll never experience that level of devotion again and will spend my life looking for it.

She doesn't respond right away. He spends a moment wondering which is worse, to have been given too much, or to have been starved your whole life, starved of something you always wanted. When he was younger, he would have said the answer was easy, but now he isn't sure. It's a trick question.

The whole thing is dragging him down. Two middle-aged people complaining of never having been loved, of having been loved too much. Does she have to ruin everything?

But then, she redeems herself. "Well, I'm allergic to shellfish," she writes. She probably had this waiting, Ben thinks, a little dagger concealed in her cloak. She probably dragged him down into the muck just so she could stab him. He feels a little surge of admiration. Texts her right back, tells her she's won the day.

1993

After Sammy is off to school she doesn't hear much word from home, and so on that cold January afternoon, when a girl she doesn't know knocks on her door and tells her there's a phone call, some guy on the line on the lobby phone waiting to speak to her, the first thing that comes to mind is her father, that something has gone wrong. As she walks barefoot down three flights of stairs the idea coalesces, becomes so certain and so clear she can see it, a desperate tableau: her father at home, lifeless in his recliner, mouth open, the TV running, Lou Grant barking plaintively, so much so that the neighbor lady, Mrs. Fitzgerald, out walking her own dog at six a.m., hears him scratching at the door, his whining and barking so out of character that she calls the police, who come upon the scene some minutes later and find her father blue and bloated in his chair, like something washed ashore by the tide. They find his beer cans littered on the floor, crushed in the middle, etc. She can see the police scribbling on their notepads, Mrs. Fitzgerald in her puffy coat and boots, wringing her hands, telling her story: *I heard the dog. The dog was making an awful racket.* The police noting: *Found by neighbor. Drunk, no evidence of foul play.* She sees a fire truck pulling up to the house, then an ambulance, she sees her father laid out on a stretcher, covered with a sheet, carried outside, she sees the neighbor kids, too young for school, watching from the windows of their living room, their fat faces pressed to the glass...

In the dorm lobby, kids are sitting around on couches and in giant lounge chairs. The TV is running, some rap video with people on a yacht, wearing white, sipping glasses of champagne. Two kids are rolling across the carpet, wrestling, taunting each other—*Eat my balls,* one says—and she stops to watch for a moment. Everything is brilliant, and shimmering at the edges, underscored with a driving beat. *This is the scene,* she thinks, *the absurd scene in which I find out my father is dead.*

The moment passes and she regards the receiver, dangling on its cord. She picks it up and holds it to her ear. "Hello?" she says. She doesn't even know who to expect on the other end. Maybe it's the police or hospital. Or Monsieur LaCroix.

"Get your ass ready," says a voice. She recognizes it but can't place it. "We're fucking coming for you." And then she gets it: Kurtz.

"Oh," she says. "Hi."

"Benny says we owe you for all those sandwiches. So we're picking you up. We're already in the fucking car."

"Oh," she says. "Uh, okay."

"Put on your fanciest shit," he says. "Black tie. All out."

"Uh," she says.

"This is the social event of the decade. You can't possibly overdress is what I'm saying."

"I don't understand what you're taking about," Sammy says. This is a new technique of hers, something she learned from a professor—it is the professor's chosen response to the nonsensical theories and rantings of the student body: *I don't understand...* This line is, Sammy has noticed, remarkably effective. Making the professor seem earnest and the student obtuse.

"The inauguration of our new president?" says Kurtz. "Fucking *hello?*"

"Oh," she says. "Really?"

"What the fuck is going on down there?" says Kurtz. "Doesn't anyone watch the news?"

She looks at the television. The rap video has ended and there's another rap video playing. Instead of a yacht there's a rooftop. People are still in white, drinking champagne. Maybe it's the same video, after all. "Not really," she says.

"To be clear, I'm inviting you to the inaugural ball. You're an eighteen-year old kid from Manchester, New Hampshire with a chance to go to a presidential fucking ball. Inside access. Backstage, staff-only type shit."

"Oh," she says. "Wait, you guys are working for Clinton?"

"Obviously. When Tsongas tanked we jumped on the wagon. No loyalty in politics. So get your fucking shoes on."

"Jeez. I don't know." She is suddenly burdened with the problems of Cinderella. "I don't have a dress. Or shoes. Or any money." Worse, she doesn't know anyone—there is no one she can ask for help.

"Jesus Christ," Kurtz says. "Borrow something. There's a million rich kids down there, just walk up to the first girl you see and tell her you need a ball gown. See what happens. Don't you get how anything works?"

"No," she says. "I think that's been, you know, established."

"Well, I'm not your fucking nanny. Figure it out."

"Okay. I'm at this dorm called Baltz."

"I know that. I'm the one who called you, Dummy."

"How did you?" she asks.

"Sandwich shop," he says.

"Oh." She imagines Bobbi talking to Kurtz, thrilled that a boy is looking for her, giving him all the information he wants and then some.

"You're not that hard to find," says Kurtz. "You're not exactly a mystery. Not that anyone's really looking." And he hangs up.

The two wrestling kids have stopped fighting each other and are lying with their arms and legs intertwined, watching another video. Rap is the only word Sammy knows for it—but she's not quite sure it's the right word. Since the moment she arrived on campus she has been suffering from a crippling uncertainty about what things are called, an inability to bring the right words to mind, even when she does know them. In her first days of school, she'd frozen up whenever someone tried to talk to her—she could barely return a greeting. She suspects this problem has to do with the fact that every girl on her hall is blonde and blue-eyed and petite, with delicate, doll-like features, and every single one dresses in a uniform manner, in pearls and heels and flowered dresses, as if they had come to some kind of agreement before arriving on campus. By contrast Sammy is walking around in jeans and t-shirts and sneakers. She is dark-haired and absurdly tall, with an angular face similar to the ones in a Picasso painting she once saw reproduced on the side of a bus. She didn't know then how famous *Demoiselles D'Avignon* was, didn't realize it was a portrait of five whores. She had only recognized the disturbingly sharp cheekbones of the women, and their noses, which looked as if they had been forced askew with the heel of someone's palm. She just saw the painting and thought: *There I am naked on the side of that bus.*

In any event the difference between Sammy and everyone else at her school is so profound and embarrassing that she has found herself incapable of navigating even the simplest social exchanges. Her problem has been compounded by the fact that, by some administrative mistake, she has been given a handicapped single-occupancy room at the end of her hall. The room has its own large bathroom, with rails along the walls and an elevated toilet. The private room is the envy of all the girls on the hall, though in its way it is a curse—Sammy doesn't have a roommate, doesn't have anyone who is more or less forced to be her friend. So she's just been wandering around by herself. A few weeks into the year she began to sense that, due to her general awkwardness and the handicapped room, people had come to believe she was deaf—an assumption she didn't bother to correct. Now the idea has taken hold, and so whenever people speak to her—rarely—they speak with exaggerated tones and gestures. She just nods and mumbles in reply. *Okay,* she tells herself. *This feels right. I have a communication problem. I'm handicapped. I'm deaf.*

Now she is a deaf person charged with communicating with people, asking them for help. She walks up to her floor and just sort of stands in the open doorway of a room in which several girls are gathered, watching MTV. The same video is on from downstairs, or maybe it's a different one. "Um," she says. "Hi." She waves, to make herself clear.

"Hi," one girl says.

"What's up?" says another. Their voices are ear splitting.

Sammy spills out her problem. Without quite realizing what she's doing, she speaks more slowly and deliberately than normal, as if repeating phrases uttered by an instructor in a foreign language class. "So I guess what I'm wondering is," she concludes, "if anyone has a dress I can borrow? And maybe some shoes?"

For a moment they all stare at her. She flushes—a sweat breaks out across her whole body. She writhes in the feeling she has just told a preposterous lie. But then one of the girls switches the TV to coverage of the inauguration, which shows Bill and Hillary Clinton walking down Pennsylvania Avenue, waving to the crowds that line the streets, and this seems to verify everything Sammy has just said. A girl from Louisiana named Lara Gardner, the hall's leader, jumps up. "Oh my God this is so exciting!" she says. "Oh my God! Everybody up! Go get your formal wear!" She claps loudly, and all the other girls—five or six of them—scatter to their rooms. Sammy watches as Lara goes through her closet, angrily pushing hangers back and forth on the rail. Though Lara is cheerful and accommodating in all that she says and does, there is something fearsome about her. She has the haircut of a politician's wife—a short, severe bob—and Sammy can't figure out why someone so young would do something like that to her hair. It's like she's presenting a future version of herself to the boys here who might be interested in running for office, who are looking for sensible helpmates. Along with the severity of the bob, Lara has an underbite that gives her a determined and somewhat defiant look. And her eyes, which are pale blue, have an iciness that is off-putting, sort of terrifying. A shiver had gone through Sammy when Lara approached and introduced herself on the first day, held out her hand, spoke her name with startling volume. Sammy had floundered, but Lara carried on as if she hadn't. Lara's manners were impeccable, Sammy had to admit.

One by one the other girls come back into Lara's room, carrying ball gowns of various lengths, in various colors. The inauguration coverage is still on TV and the other girls keep looking at the screen, then looking back at Sammy. It seems to be passing through their minds that Sammy might have hidden depths, important connections. "I thought you were deaf," one of the girls says.

"Partially," she says. "Totally in one ear and like fifty percent in the other." The bullshit is just flying. "I almost drowned, is what happened. I went through the ice. Technically I was dead for a few minutes but you know how, you know how the cold saves you. The only thing that really happened was I lost my hearing. But I get by, I read lips."

A tremendous amount of good will goes around. "Oh my God," the girls say. "That's so sad."

"I'm just happy to be alive," she says.

The coverage finally breaks to commercial and suddenly

everyone is up and moving around, coming in and out of the room with various items. A project is made of Sammy's grooming that has the feel of a cross-cultural exchange. She is reminded of a documentary she saw the previous semester in an anthropology class, where a man in explorer khakis had demonstrated his clothing to a tribesman in Papua New Guinea. The explorer took off his vest and handed it to the native, who put his arms through the holes with what looked like a great deal of trepidation. Once he was fitted into the vest he looked down at it and laughed, as if the idea of wearing such a thing were absurd. The whole class had laughed in response, though Sammy's feeling had been different: Why bother these people? Why outfit them in our own fashion? Why humiliate them, film them? Why not just let them be?

Someone appears in front of Sammy and presses against her a white sequined dress that is supposed to fall to the knee but which, on her, hardly covers her butt. It is a ludicrous garment, something Goldie Hawn would have worn on *Laugh In*, but all of the girls approve. "Perfect," they say. There is a sudden tugging at Sammy's sweatshirt and then it is up over her head. She stands awkwardly with her arms crossed over her chest. "Arms up," someone says, and she obeys, like a child. They fit the dress over her head, fit her arms through the holes. The dress falls over her, heavy as chain mail. "Turn around," says one of the girls. And she does. There is a tugging at the dress's zipper. "Turn around again," she hears, and so she turns. Every time she moves the dress makes a stiff crackling sound.

"You're totally pulling this off," one girl says.

Then there is a bit of a fracas over shoes. Sammy's feet are too big for every pair of heels presented to her, and Lara has to walk down to the next floor, then the next, to find someone with bigger feet. Eventually she comes back with a pair of gold lamé shoes only a size too small, and a satiny gold cape and matching purse. "It's freezing," she says, draping the cape over Sammy's shoulders, "but you can't wear a winter coat. You have to just deal with the cold."

Sammy thinks she is done, but there is still more to do—hair and makeup and nails. The girls keep holding products in front of her and she makes a face, sort of rippling her mouth with uncertainty, like Charlie Brown. "Just try it," the girls say. "Just let us."

"Okay," she says. She sits still as they run brushes and sponges and tubes across her face. Her hair is put in rollers and sprayed with aerosol. Her fingernails and toenails are painted. As a final adjustment, Lara takes away her glasses. "You can't wear glasses with a formal dress," she says. "It's forbidden. It's out of the question."

"I can't really see," she says, "like, anything."

"Can you see me?" Lara says. She steps back an arm's length, then two. Her figure becomes a blur.

"I can tell there's a person there," Sammy says. "But that's about it."

"That's all you need," says Lara. "All you really need to do is not bump into anyone."

"She can't be blind *and* deaf," says one of the girls. "You can't keep her glasses."

"But she looks so much better without them," says Lara.

"True," says the girl.

"This is the *inaugural ball*," Lara says.

"Maybe you could give them back to her for, like, emergencies," says the other girl. "She can keep them in her purse."

"No," says Lara. "She'd just wear them all night."

Lara stands with her hands on her hips and stares at Sammy for a long moment. Her expression is inscrutable. She starts picking up segments of Sammy's hair and squeezing them. "I have to go to class," she informs the room. "Don't let her mess up her makeup. Or her hair or nails."

"We won't," the girls say.

"This took a lot of work," Lara says. "But we did a good job. Let's try not to ruin it."

After Lara is gone the other girls go back to watching MTV and don't notice, or don't care, when Sammy leaves the room. She shuts herself away in her single occupancy and settles herself on her unmade bed. She arranges herself with care, arms crossed over her chest like a corpse. The night's activities rise before her with the sublimity of a mountain range: all the talking, the bustling around in a gigantic ballroom, the anxiety of performance and the scrutiny of said performance. She starts to panic. So she does what she always does when faced with this kind of trouble. She worries about it until she falls asleep.

When a knock comes at the door, sharp and loud, it takes Sammy a moment to remember what is going on. She sits up and rubs her eyes. Her dress rustles, moves stiffly against her. There's another knock, more of a pounding made with a fist, and she scrambles up, opens the door.

And then they meet again.

Ben is standing in the hall. Tall and handsome, in a tuxedo with the tie untied, the collar open, the black coat. *I didn't think I'd ever see you again*, is what goes through Sammy's mind, but she doesn't say it.

Ben runs his eyes over her. "You clean up," he says.

"None of this is mine," she says. "Obviously."

"Let's go." He puts his arm behind her, leads her toward the stairs. All the way through the dorm he has an air about him of a person practicing patience and magnanimity, a high-rolling lawyer escorting a client out of jail. As if it belittles him to be in that space, amongst those teenagers dressed in their slippers and pajamas. Sammy is keenly aware of this and also aware that she is a glittering spectacle, wearing a sequined cocktail dress in full daylight. Everyone turns to watch her, something she cannot stand, something she feels working against her physically. But soon enough they are out the door, and she sees Kurtz's car idling—rattling, really—in the circle drive where she was first left off by her father. Ben opens the door for her and the alarm goes off, like always. Sammy and Ben climb in back and then they are off, honking down the drive and then through campus, people in their coats and hats turning to look at them, Sammy looking back with a bit of a smirk, because finally she is doing something, she is doing something and other people are the ones watching.

Once the horn stops, and they are past campus and on the road, Kurtz turns his attention to Sammy, looking at her in the rearview. "So what's your deal?" he says.

"I don't really have a deal," she says, "I don't think. I'm just, I'm just sitting here."

"I mean, how's school? What classes are you taking? Who are you fucking? Have you stopped wearing a bra and shaving your legs? Have you gained fifteen pounds? Are you a lesbian now? What's your story?"

"This semester," she tells him, "I'm taking Shakespeare, and contemporary American lit. And a class on the philosophical movement of Pragmatism as it applies to literature. And poetry, modern poetry."

"What the fuck are you gonna do with all that literature?"

"I don't know. I haven't really thought about it."

"You need to diversify your portfolio," he says. "If you want an internship, or a job, you need to take some different classes."

"I know," she says. Her advisor had told her the same thing, and only reluctantly signed off on her schedule.

"What about econ?" he says. "What about poli-sci?"

She just gives him a blank look.

"History?" he says.

"I have some sort of block with history. I can never remember anyone's name, or the dates of anything. I have a very loose grasp on what's happened in the world, up to now."

"Jesus," he says.

There is a heavy silence.

Then Kurtz says, "You shouldn't admit things like that. You should keep quiet about it and then when you get home, like, the next chance you get, what you do is, you read a history book. Get down the basics at least."

"I tried that already," Sammy says. "Last year." Which was true. When she first met these boys, when they started coming around the shop arguing history and policy, making constant reference to various wars and dynasties and heads of state, debating the merits of the governments of Pinochet and Castro and Perón, Sammy had felt like she was drowning, awash in a language she couldn't understand. Suddenly it seemed like everyone in the world had this shared knowledge, that she was far behind where she ought to be, that she didn't have what was needed to survive and maybe never would. So she had started reading, taking out an armload of books from her school library, but then she'd found her brain couldn't hold that kind of information. She could recite the details of what any given maid or factory urchin or bartender was wearing in a Dickens novel, but couldn't date the conquests of Attila the Hun within five hundred years, couldn't even remember the basic century in which Napoleon asserted his influence across the whole of Europe. Was it Europe?

"It just baffles me," Kurtz says, "what you poets think is going to happen when you graduate. Like someone's going to be waiting for you with a car, like a stretch limousine, after you walk across the stage and get your diploma. Like, 'Hi, I'm your limo driver. I'm here to take you to your castle, where you'll be studying, you'll be pouring over…'" He was cracking himself up, he could hardly even get the words out. "'*Villanelles*! And, like, the occasional *pantoum*.'"

"I'm kind of impressed with how much you know about poetry, actually," Sammy says.

"I know enough," he says, "to know it's not going anywhere. It's like, a dead language."

"I can't help it," she says. "My parents, my dad sort of read a lot of poetry there for a while. He even named me after a poet. It's like, the family business or something."

"Most people," Kurtz says, "name their kids after presidents and kings."

She considers this. Maybe everything that is wrong with her has to do with her name.

"I bet you have some hippie parents," Kurtz says.

"Why would you think that?" she says.

"It's like a gift I have. I can talk to someone for two minutes and turn around and tell you everything about them, down to what brand of socks they're wearing."

"Okay."

"Let me do you," he says. "Let me tell you about yourself."

"Okay."

"I bet your dad burned his draft card and your mom was, like, playing the guitar and singing Joan Baez songs all the time, and your dad was playing the bongos, I bet they were wearing ponchos and smoking dope and you all just, I bet you all slept in the same bed and wore shoes made out of rope." He is tapping his fingers frantically on the steering wheel. "And composted your leftovers and filled up the toilet with piss before you flushed it and never had chocolate in your whole life, because you were always eating carob, and your mom took in like a bunch of cats and started a greyhound rehabilitation shelter and then started sponsoring kids in Africa." He laughs. "Oh, man."

"You're way off," Sammy says.

"Okay fine," says Kurtz. "Fine, it was either that or fucking, your dad's a fucking Vietnam vet who went to school on the GI bill and fell in love with poetry because it expressed the inexpressible suffering raging in his head and he met, while he was in school he met your mom in an English class and they had all these fucking romantic ideals, they hated Nixon and wanted peace on earth and all that shit, but then they had a kid and they got sucked into paying the mortgage and most of their life turned into drudgery and disappointment, though they still had their old ideals hovering over them, meanwhile the very kid that pushed them to the brink of suicide is named after the poet they love, they have to look at her and say that name a hundred times a day and each time it tears a little piece of their soul away, and they've still got a picture hanging in the living room of the Kennedys playing football, or the one of Jack and Bobby sitting together in silhouette with their heads tilted together, when they were on the campaign trail, just to remind themselves of who they used to be."

Sammy feels herself blushing. In fact, her father once had a poster of Bobby Kennedy pinned up in the basement, over the washing machine. Bobby had his hands on his hips and wore a look of determination, staring off at some distant horizon. It was like he could see things as they should be, could see the path toward them, knew the exact length and direction of the road forward, what it would cost to get there and what rewards would be reaped along the way. The poster had warped with humidity and one corner had fallen down, had hung like that, dog-eared, for a year or two, then one day had collapsed entirely behind the washer. It was still there.

She spends a long moment trying to put into words the feeling that comes over her when she thinks about this poster, when she thinks about the fact that all of her father's heroes—the Kennedys, Martin Luther King, Abraham Lincoln—were shot, gunned down in their prime. *Fallen heroes*, she thinks, is the phrase a poet would use. The image of the poster behind the washing machine would go nicely. Or maybe not. Maybe that's piling on, maybe it's cheap. What's the phrase, then? How should it go?

When she comes back to it, Kurtz has moved on, fighting with Boris again about something. But a feeling lingers, of having been scanned and processed. Of having been understood, though not in a sympathetic way. Acknowledged and dismissed, is the feeling.

1993

Ben and Kurtz are sitting in a diner, a little place in D.C. around the corner from the apartment they've been sharing with a handful of other staffers. Clinton has won the election and they have been working on the transition—just the inaugural committee, grunt work again, but it's kept Kurtz in play for something better. Today is the morning of the inauguration, and Kurtz is running out of time. If he doesn't find a position today—if someone doesn't call him back, toss him a bone—it's all over.

Kurtz has his briefcase phone on the table between them. Even though it's six o'clock in the morning, he's already making calls, working his way down a list. "I'm looking for something more central to the administration," he's saying now, using his most professional, reserved tone. "West Wing if possible." There's a pause, during which Kurtz drums his fingers manically on the table. "Yes sir," he says. "I appreciate that, sir. I'll look forward to hearing from you."

With an uncommon gentleness, he places the receiver in its holder.

"Motherfucker," he says, quietly. He covers his face in his hands, and it almost looks as if he's praying. "None of my connections are working," he moans. His face is still shrouded beneath his hands. "None of my connections with the goddamn *Kennedys* are worth shit with these fucking, these Appalachian *hill people*. Fucking Bigfoot and his completely unintelligible Cajun sidekick."

"Arkansas isn't part of Appalachia, technically," Ben says.

"Whatever," says Kurtz. "South of the Mason-Dixon, it's all the same shit to me."

They are silent for a moment. Ben has never seen Kurtz like this before. He remembers the little paper cutout of the White House Kurtz used to keep tacked up in their room. Something has gone wrong—he has neglected a stone on the path and he has lost his way.

"Don't worry," Ben offers. "You'll find something. You'll find a way in."

"I think I'm going to cry," Kurtz says.

Ben goes back to his notebook. This is his last day in Washington, and he is scrambling to get down the final details for his book. For the last twenty minutes he has been trying to pin down a metaphor. He wants to contain everything he has to say about politics in his description of Kurtz's car. A machine of German ancestry, sputtering with every shift of its gears, the wind coming through the doors and even up through the floorboards. There's 183,000 miles on it, but it's still going. It's a workhorse. Or rather, an insect madly going about its business. A cockroach that could survive the atomic bomb. What Ben has to say about politics, the American dream, is that it is a taped-together import. At its helm, he has placed an Ahab-mad captain. A man chasing something he will never quite catch. The system is both falling apart and yet robust, is what he wants to say. It is a machine that pursues in vain, but never stops its pursuit. The most important point he wants to make is: this machine called politics—only the crazy people think they can run it.

Kurtz will never win—that's what he hopes to suggest with this rattling car. Because even if Kurtz does win, he will still lose in the end. Winning, in this case, is just part of a cycle—a story meant to convince the American people they live in a democracy, a place where dreams come true. Even if you grew up barefoot in a shack, which was Lincoln's story, and Clinton's too, practically. Every once in a while, the system has to let someone like that through, to renew the belief of the proletariat. But what the people don't understand is that they are being tricked—the reigns they have been handed are attached to a horse, yes, but it is the wrong horse. Just a ceremonial horse. The real horses, the ones that matter, well, they are running free. Offshore somewhere. Out of reach. Beneath the radar.

Somehow Ben has gone from cars to horses and then possibly airplanes and submarines—things undetected by radar. The metaphor has scuttled away from him. He can't seem to pin it down.

Ben looks up for the waitress—he finished his coffee a while ago and has been waiting for a refill. But the waitress here is no good. In fact, he's decided, there isn't a decent waitress outside of Manhattan. This past year, in all the towns he's passed through, he hasn't found another place that functions like New York, where unspoken but immutable laws govern the behavior of the population. Observing these laws has always come naturally to him, he realizes now, only now that he has toured these lawless places. The thing about New York, what makes it work, is that it is an agreement. Between waiters and cabdrivers and doormen and mailmen, between the police and firemen and EMTs, the transit and construction workers, the businessmen, the prostitutes, the museum guards, between the deli and bodega workers, the newspapermen and newscasters, the students and artists, the couriers, the editors and publishers, the entire population of Wall Street, even the kids, the very smallest New Yorkers. Everyone agrees on the rules. Move fast, take what you need, keep your head down. Do what you're supposed to do. Keep moving. Everyone knows when it's okay to cross against the light and when it isn't.

When to hustle through and when to wait your turn. When to bribe and when to complain. When to make a scene and when to move along. In New York, it's only the tourists who don't know how these things work, but in the rest of the country, no one seems to have come to an agreement on how to do anything. It's making him crazy.

This waitress, for instance, doesn't understand the tenets of her profession. She is standing behind the counter, with her butt sort of propped up on it, her back to him. She is flipping through a magazine. *Cosmopolitan*, probably. He stares at her for a long moment. She flips the pages of the magazine quickly, angrily. Like she is trying to find out the answer to the problem of her existence, and they are hiding it from her.

Finally, he can't stand it anymore. "Can I get some more coffee?" he calls out. She lingers over the magazine for a few seconds, then sets it down, goes over to the coffee pot, lifts it lazily, comes over to his table. "Sorry," she says. Gives a little laugh. "I was absorbed in some important reading." She is trying to get on his good side, and might have, though something about the way she looks annoys him. She isn't unattractive—she has dark hair and light blue eyes, a good combination—but neither is she quite beautiful. Something about her jaw is off—it is too wide, and juts out, giving her face a vapid, defiant expression. She looks like a seventh grader who's just been asked a question about Charles DeGaulle. Colleen is her name, or so it says on her nametag.

"Thanks," he says. A bit too snidely. Colleen goes back behind the counter. Rests her butt on it again. The counter, where people eat.

Colleen, he writes in his notebook. Diner. Butt on counter.

Then Ben remembers the girl who made them sandwiches in Manchester. She was just a kid, gangly and awkward, but there was something graceful there, too—she was a good waitress. All of her movements were as swift and unobtrusive as possible. And she was a reader, a real reader—always reading Dickens behind the counter. He had liked her.

"What was the name of that place back in Manchester?" he asks Kurtz. "Remember that girl, Sammy, that waitress?"

"Bobbi's Hollywood Café," Kurtz says. Of course he remembers. It has often occurred to Ben that Kurtz is touched with some form of autism—his memory for names and dates and figures is astonishing.

"Wasn't she supposed to be going down to college?"

"Virginia," Kurtz spits out. "Majoring in English." He is dialing his phone but can still answer questions about a girl he met briefly the year before. He will do well in politics, Ben thinks.

"I wonder if she got in," he says.

"Call her up and find out." Kurtz hangs up the receiver and spins the case around to Ben.

"Never mind," Ben says. "It was just a passing thought."

"You know what your problem is? You keep acting like everything in life is some ineffable fucking mystery. When really all you have to do is make a couple of phone calls."

"It's too early," Ben says. "Plus she's off at school somewhere. I don't know how we'd find her."

"Observe," says Kurtz. He opens the case and picks up the phone, which makes a high-pitched squealing sound. Kurtz will probably die of a brain tumor, Ben thinks, from that fucking phone.

Kurtz calls Manchester's information. Then Bobbi's Hollywood Café. No one answers there, so he hangs up.

"I guess it's an ineffable fucking mystery," says Ben.

"No, it isn't," says Kurtz. "I'll prove it. This is my mission. My mission is to show you how shit gets done. Consider it my parting gift."

It occurs to Ben that all this time, Kurtz has been under the impression he's been propping Ben up, carrying him along, showing him the ropes. A burst of laughter escapes him—a short bark.

"You'll see," Kurtz says. "Just wait."

They carry on with their morning, and Ben forgets about calling Sammy. But later, while standing in the crowd waiting for the swearing in ceremony, Kurtz takes out his phone and calls Bobbi's again. This time he gets Bobbi herself on the phone. He scribbles down a name on his palm. Then he calls information in Charlottesville, then the help desk at the University. All the while he narrates to Ben what he is doing, in a condescending tone, to demonstrate how it is that an ordinary person accomplishes a simple task. Then he dials the payphone on the first floor of Sammy's dorm, and gets into some protracted conversation, trying to describe her. Larkin, he calls her—that's her real name, Ben remembers. "Tall," Kurtz says. "Frizzy brown hair. Kind of mopey." There's a long wait. And then finally, he's gotten ahold of her, and is asking her if she wants to come up to the ball. What are you *doing*? Ben mimes. He makes a slashing motion with his hand. But Kurtz ignores him, turns away.

"I've been meaning to check out Charlottesville," Kurtz tells Ben, when his call is finished. "I'm thinking maybe law school. Let's be honest," he says, nodding to the crowd of well-wishers lined along Pennsylvania Avenue. "This administration isn't exactly fucking working out for me."

Now Sammy is here with Ben in the back seat, and they are headed to the ball. The whole time Kurtz is talking to her, trying to ask her about UVA, she keeps fidgeting, pulling her dress down. There are moments when she seems self-conscious, exquisitely aware she is on stage—she tries to sit up straight, and hold her hands in her lap in a delicate clasp. Then she forgets herself, slouches, stares off out the window, leaves her mouth slightly open. Then she remembers herself again, corrects her posture. This whole endeavor is hard for her, Ben can tell. Probably her first invitation to a formal event. He should help her, ease her mind. But then again, watching this sort of thing—the awkward fumbling of a person helplessly out of her element—fills him with tenderness. It's a rare feeling, one he enjoys.

Sammy turns to him suddenly. Excited, it seems, because she has thought of something to say. "How's your book coming?" she asks.

The perfect question. Ben pulls his notebook out of his coat pocket, leans toward Sammy. He opens the book and shows it to her. He is embarrassed, slightly, by his handwriting, which is so tiny and cramped and slanted it seems to implicate him—it makes him look crazy. He does this, he thinks, so that others can't decipher his writing, his thoughts.

"I couldn't have asked," he nods toward Kurtz, "for a better subject. He thinks I'm writing a book about the campaign, about the candidates. But I'm really writing a book about him."

Sammy makes a surprised face.

Then Ben begins to read from the opening pages of his journal. "Central to understanding Kurtz's character," he says, "are his humble beginnings, as the son of a housekeeper. But not just any housekeeper—his mother worked as a housekeeper at the Kennedy compound in Hyannisport, the beach house where the first American family played football and went sailing."

"Really?" she says, and Ben nods. But then he realizes: All those years in Cambridge, he never once met Kurtz's mother. Even though Hyannisport was hardly an hour away, Kurtz never once invited Ben home. Ben had always assumed Kurtz was embarrassed, didn't want anyone to see where he'd grown up. But now Ben wonders if it might have been something else, if Kurtz was hiding something.

"To hear Kurtz tell it," Ben reads on, "he had practically grown up in the compound, playing in closets and cupboards with the Kennedys' discarded toys while his mother vacuumed and polished silver and rubbed wax onto floors and banisters. Lo even before he was born, he claimed, he knew the Kennedys, he was there walking about that magnificent house even in utero. So complete was his identification with the family that they had practically made a mascot of him. His head had been tousled by many generations of Kennedy men, their hands callused from sailing. In fact, it was the Kennedys who had gotten him into Harvard. With a single phone call they had secured his education and place in the world. Or at least this is the story he was always telling once he got to campus. You couldn't be around Kurtz for more than five minutes without him mentioning the Kennedys."

"That's true," Sammy nods. "Now that you mention it."

"Kurtz had been studying politics since birth," Ben reads, "in much the same way that other boys studied baseball. He knew the name and capital and leader of every developed nation, its gross domestic product, its closest allies and worst enemies, statistics regarding its military and arsenals, imports and exports. He was familiar with the economies of every European nation, knew the level of debt they carried, their trade partners and policies. He knew the names of dozens of revolutionaries rotting in dozens of prisons. Domestically, he was schooled in the basic history of every presidency. He knew the names of every current cabinet member and secretary, of every senator and a good percentage of Congressmen. He was familiar with the demographics of key electoral states, the current poll numbers, district by district, of the candidates running for congress. In this one area, his performance rivaled that of an autistic savant."

"Also true," she says.

"What was most interesting about Kurtz," Ben continues, "was the fact that he was obsessed with a profession in which he would never personally succeed. Kurtz himself would never be a candidate, this much was clear, because there was something wrong with him, a disorder or imbalance which seemed to share certain qualities with Tourette's syndrome, and certain qualities with Dustin Hoffman's character from *Rain Man*. Kurtz's head was so full of information that it was bursting, and the pressure of all this knowledge seemed to override his very body, causing it to tick and jerk, often making his speech pressured, tremulous. This is why he used the word *fuck* compulsively, for the release it gave him. He simply could not steady himself, could not practice moderation or diplomacy, could not manage a basic conversation, the easy back and forth between the partners in a dialogue. When confronted by an opposing point of view, or one that he found ill-informed, Kurtz would fly into rants, forming elaborate counter-arguments, quoting long lists of statistics, making his case like a geometric proof. He could defeat any opponent by burying him in facts. But he couldn't do it without violating the dignity of public office, or the general social contract held between people of good faith."

"I feel sort of embarrassed," Sammy says. "I mean, it's like, we're looking at him naked."

"That's what I'm going for," he says.

"Well, please don't ever write about me. I mean, yeesh."

"Kurtz's ambition, then," Ben continues, "was to be chief of staff to a powerful man, to find the right person and attach himself to him, to make himself indispensable, anticipate his candidate's every need and tend to it, anticipate every disaster and avert it, to research and craft the policies the candidates would espouse, to do the silent, dirty work the candidate himself couldn't do, to make the calls and threats, to make the kills and clean up after the bodies and dump them in the rivers, to walk behind the candidate with a mop, to stand between the candidate and every bullet. He knew this about himself. Behind every great candidate, he often said, is a Kurtz. It was the Kurtzes of the world—the unseen and unsung Kurtzes—that made it go around."

Sammy is staring off now, looking troubled. Maybe guilty. He is having an effect on her. Which is good. It's just what he wanted.

He reads on. "Kurtz could be associated with, and in fact was inseparable from, certain objects about his person. He carried around at all times a cellular phone, an early-model machine encased in a padded leather bag, and was so attached to it he often used it as a pillow. Attendant to the case, and even more important to Kurtz, was his address book, which he carried in his pocket and was always pulling out and flipping through, muttering to himself, as if praying some kind of rosary: Robert, Jr., Ted, John, Jr., Caroline, Radziwill, Schlesinger, Shriver. This was his religion, his altar, these were his saints."

Ben stops for a moment, regards Sammy, raises an eyebrow. "What do you think?" he says.

"I think you kind of nailed it," she says. "I mean, absolutely. I just feel kind of sorry for him. Like, he's so exposed."

"It's not so bad," he says. "He loves attention, it doesn't matter what kind. Plus I'm just running him down so he can become the hero later."

"Oh," she says, frowns. "I suppose that's the way it works."

"Then there was Boris," Ben continues, "a tag-along volunteer, a minor villain. Boris was thin and pale, with a narrow face that came to a point at his spear-like chin. He had a long nose and unsettling black eyes. His hair was black and he wore it long, parted on the side. His eyebrows and sideburns were untamed, and he wore a long, drooping mustache. Overall, he gave the impression of someone who had been pulled out of the last century. His clothes appeared to have been made by hand. He wore the same thing every day—a pair of brown suede pants and matching jacket, and a blue t-shirt with uneven gray stitches at the neck and hem. His t-shirt was so worn that there were holes all around the neck, through which his chest hair, which covered him like a pelt, poked through. His shoes were made of a heavily cracked orange leather, with an inch-high wooden heel, and came to a curved point at the tip. His only accouterment was a silver cigarette case, which he kept in the inside pocket of his jacket. He was always pulling out his case and rolling his own cigarettes, which he didn't smoke so much as gesture with, pointing them at people as he spoke."

"Aren't you worried they'll hear you?" Sammy says.

Ben scoffs. They both regard Kurtz and Boris in the front seat. For the moment they have stopped fighting and are singing along with the radio—AC/DC's "Back in Black." They are both playing air guitar, pitching their heads forward and jerking them back.

"Never mind," she says.

Ben continues. "Why he was involved in our politics, no one really knew. Perhaps, having survived the Soviet regime, he found democracy to be a church in which he must participate. Or perhaps he was a spy. Sent here by the Kremlin to make connections. His mysterious appearance at the Manchester headquarters of the campaign, the way he'd found Kurtz, attaché of the Kennedy family, and attached himself to him, had *all* the markings of an infiltration. In any case, he couldn't be trusted."

"*Really?*" Sammy interrupts. "Or is this just to make the novel more exciting."

"Seriously," Ben says, "I wouldn't doubt it."

Sammy looks at Boris with what appears to be new interest. She sits up straight now, takes hold of her knees and squeezes them. She seems to like the idea of riding in a Volkswagen Beetle with a Russian spy. He has made her life more interesting.

"Of course, the best character is Ben," he tells her. "But he needs no introduction. All you need to know about him is, well, he's basically an old-time movie star. Basically Orson Welles."

"That's not necessarily a good thing," Sammy says. "I mean, young Welles or old?"

"Young," Ben says. "Young and handsome. And so fucking talented no one can believe it."

"But the thing is," she says, "you can see the old version of Welles embedded in the young version. You look at him when he's young and handsome but something's off, you know, you can tell he's just going to blow up. It was all there all along."

"But imagine," he says, "if he controlled himself. If he possessed even a modicum of discipline. If he had the resources, the guidance. If he didn't have to worry about funding. Imagine what he would have done."

"I don't know," she says. "I don't think it works that way. Like, you can't separate the crazed ambition from the lack of control, you know? Like, in order to have a grand vision, you sort of have to be a maniac."

"That's a fallacy," Ben says. "A classic romantic view of the artist. Any real artist, anyone who endures, always has discipline." He is arguing this, but doesn't really know if he believes it. In fact, he has taken Sammy's view on this topic more often than not. He doesn't know why, around this particular girl, he tries so hard to sell himself as an authority, a statesman. He feels the need to uphold certain ideals. Practices. Codes of conduct.

"Maybe you're right," she says, seeming to concede the point, and he is satisfied for a moment. Then she circles back. "But I sort of doubt it."

2011

Sometimes, it must be confessed, Ben and Sammy call each other to talk about poetry. Ben sees a poem in *The New Yorker* and, overcome in a brief moment of weakness, calls Sammy to read it to her. Or Sammy is preparing to teach and digs up her old volumes—*Leaves of Grass, Life Studies*—and calls Ben just to tell him about a line, a line that made her feel alive again, if only briefly.

Sometimes they text. Bitter little stanzas, desperate ones. "Life, friends, is boring," Sammy sends to Ben. "We must not say so. Ever to confess you're bored means you have no inner resources." And then, right on its heels, another text: "Now I must confess I have no inner resources, because I am heavy bored."

Occasionally someone hits the wrong button, or auto-correct does horrible things, so that *I Wandered Lonely as a Cloud* comes out as *I Wandered Lonely as a Clown*, and another time *We must love each other or die* goes forward as *We must love each other or dine*. When they see these errors, all the pain and longing with which the lines had been typed goes flying off, and they can only laugh. They laugh and never manage to read the lines again with the same solemnity.

Now and then Ben will send Sammy a stanza from Larkin, the dour poet after whom she was named. However much she would like to be associated with love, with a poet like Keats, who saw beauty everywhere, even in death—instead from Ben she gets this:

They fuck you up, your Mum and Dad
They do not mean to but they do.
They fill you with the faults they had
And add some extra, just for you.

He sends these lines to her semi-frequently, two or three times a year, a bit of cruelty, she thinks. To him it is only a joke but to her, someone who indeed has been fucked up in what she often considers a genetic way, fucked right down to her DNA—it is not quite funny. And after she has a daughter, a daughter she worries she is fucking up not only in genetic terms but also, she often feels, in environmental ones, well, it's a bit of a cruel joke. Sometimes, complaining about his patients and how much they blame their parents for their suffering, Ben goes even further, and sends:

Man hands on misery to man.
It deepens like a coastal shelf.
Get out as early as you can,
And don't have any kids yourself.

He writes it but he doesn't really know what it means, Sammy thinks. He doesn't have a child of his own, and likely never will. All of this is just a bit of posturing, just a bit of cool cynicism. Possibly it's a defense against something he might, in certain moods, want for himself—a kneejerk reaction against certain longings. But in any event, it isn't funny when you have a child of your own. That's one of the things standing between the two of them, the one thing about her, Sammy thinks, Ben can never understand.

They talk about poetry most in the fall, Ben has noticed. Probably something to do with the leaves changing, the cold setting in. This year, the mood between them is especially wistful—it is as if they have, without quite realizing what was happening, crossed a threshold. Suddenly they are middle-aged. Much about their lives has become inscrutable, inexpressible. And so, poetry.

One October afternoon, that Updike poem appears again. Ben had first come across it in *The New Yorker* back in the nineties, and had called Sammy and read it to her, then clipped it from the magazine and tucked it away in a book. Then, twenty years later, in a moment of distraction, he pulls the book off the shelf and the poem comes fluttering out. He calls Sammy right away to read it to her again.

The poem is about an older man recalling a lost lover. A man whose body is falling apart, whose eyebrows have grown wild and whose underwear has begun to smell rank. *Aches and pains!* cries the speaker.

> *...The other day*
> *My neck was so stiff I couldn't turn my head*
> *To parallel-park: another man*
> *Would have trusted his mirrors, but not I;*
> *I had the illusion something might interpose*
> *Between reality and its reflection, as happened with us.*

Though Ben had been young when he first read it, he had known that someday the poem would ring true, someday he would relate. And indeed something has shifted with him in recent months—he is starting to feel old. His back hurts almost constantly. When he wakes in the morning his joints are stiff and his breath foul—in a different way than it had been when he was young: there was something necrotic to it now. What is going wrong with his body is starting to change his thinking, too. He no longer talks boundlessly of the future. These days, when talking to Sammy, more often than not he speaks of the past.

"Something might interpose between reality and its reflection," Ben repeats to Sammy, when he calls her to read the poem that second time, "as happened with us." Sammy doesn't answer for a stretch, maybe ten seconds.

"I remember that one," she finally says. He can tell from her voice that she is choked with something. Nostalgia, maybe. Wistfulness. "I remember when we first read it, thinking it was good, knowing it was good, but not being able to feel it, you know, in my body. But now it stings. The poem stings."

"That's exactly the word," he says. This is one of the reasons he values her. She can always find the right word for something.

Then, abruptly, she says, "I have to go. Ava's going to be the last kid standing in the parking lot again."

"Leave her there," he says. "Insecurity breeds resilience."

But she says she has to go, hangs up, dashes off to her daughter.

It is always like this between them, Ben thinks. They keep coming close to something, right up to the edge of it, but at the last minute one of them always swerves, retreating to the obligations of daily life, or the comfort of humor and sarcasm. Then the other sulks for a bit, wounded. They keep circling, approaching each other and then turning away, random in their comings and goings, impossible to predict, like the pattern of bees in flight.

1993

Sammy tries not to get too excited when they cross the bridge over into the city. She wants to crane her head, look around for monuments, but doesn't want to with Ben watching. Around him, it is important not to do that kind of thing.

She is disappointed by how quickly they come upon the convention center—it is just about the first thing they drive past. People are everywhere in the streets, huddled in groups, rushing toward the ball. Kurtz seems to be playing some sort of video game whose object is to come as close to pedestrians as possible without actually hitting them. His car lurches towards clusters of people in black tie, then halts, lurches and halts. "Take your time," he keeps saying, waiting for people to cross. "I have all fucking day."

What Sammy sees of the city she sees because they have trouble parking. The streets are clogged with limousines, and many are blocked off by police and security cars. Kurtz steers the car outward in concentric squares, leaning forward over the steering wheel, craning his head left and right. They pass several parking lots and garages, all of them full. "What the *fuck*," he says.

They keep drifting, past apartment buildings and churches and parks. They make so many turns Sammy loses any relationship to the convention center.

Finally they find a spot on the street and Kurtz maneuvers into it. They get out of the car and start walking. It is bitterly cold and Sammy is wearing almost nothing, so Ben drapes his coat around her shoulders. The coat is filled with the warmth of his body, and his scent—a cologne she doesn't recognize, though it smells like a pine tree and a campfire, like the great outdoors, the kind of New England she never lived in.

Just ahead, Sammy sees a man in a heavy garment pushing a shopping cart toward her. The cart is piled high with the man's possessions. One of its wheels is off kilter and runs amok, it squeaks and drags. The noise of the city disappears and all she can hear is the sound of the cart approaching. The man slowly comes into focus. He is hunched, hooded, his face lost to shadow. As they pass each other the man looks up at Sammy and they regard each other for a moment. Her dress catches every bit of light from the streetlamp, reflects it, while the man is in shadow, so dull and dark and loose he bleeds into the night itself, and Sammy feels, for the first time, the sensation of being better off than another person. A squirming feeling comes over her. Some kind of desperate urge to explain. *This isn't me*, she thinks to say. *I'm not really here.*

In the lobby of the convention center ticket takers are standing in front of banks of escalators, taking tickets from people and ripping them in half. Sammy waits in line with Kurtz and Boris and Ben. When Kurtz reaches the ticket taker he works through some sort of preordained, complicated handshake. "My man," Kurtz says. There are no tickets in this world, per se. There is only Kurtz.

They ride up the escalator and emerge into a huge room—a warehouse, really—with hundreds of people standing around in clusters. There are places where lines have formed to buy drinks and food, and tall tables are set up with people standing around them, holding plastic cups and containers in their hands, shoveling food into their mouths with plastic forks. At the far end of the room is a stage with a band. A handful of people are dancing in front of the stage. From the way they are moving—stiffly, carefully—they appear to be not quite drunk enough, struggling against the confinements of their formal clothes and their dignity.

At first they are clustered in a group, walking along the perimeter of the room. Kurtz is in the lead as always, and seems to be looking for someone or something in particular—he has some kind of goal in mind. But whatever he is looking for, he can't seem to find. They circle and circle. As Sammy passes groups of people, she listens to the conversations they are having. A sort of groupspeak has come over the room. "He's on his way," someone shouts. "First he's doing the New York ball and all that shit, and then he's headed over here, where his real friends are." Then she moves ten feet and hears basically the same thing. "He's getting New York and MTV and everything else out of the way first. This is going to be his last stop. He's saving Arkansas for last, because these are the people who elected him. All the people here are the people who got him elected." People are moving their arms constantly, talking constantly. "He's saving the Arkansas ball for last," one woman screams, "because we're his people, we're his fucking *family*!" She stabs herself in the chest with a manicured nail.

Eventually Kurtz seems to find what he was looking for— two men, stout and red faced, who are standing with drinks in their hands talking about college football. He walks right up to them. The men look like they had once been football players themselves, though now their bodies are long since ruined by red meat and alcohol. They have potbellies and bulbous noses, and their hair has all but disappeared, but for a rim above the ears. Great veins stand out on their skulls, throbbing. Sammy is amazed when Kurtz just walks up and inserts himself into their conversation. "No one was going to beat Alabama this year," he says. The men regard him for a moment, warily. "It just was never going to happen," he adds.

"Maybe," says the silver-haired man. "But you don't need to go rubbing people's faces in it."

"I'm not, sir," Kurtz says. "They're not my team, personally. I'm more of a Harvard fan."

"Harvard?" says the man. Instead of a bow tie he is wearing a turquoise bolo. It is the kind of move, Sammy calculates, only the very rich or very poor can afford to make. "Fuck Harvard," he says. "Harvard is nothing but a bunch of pantywaists." He opens his mouth and let out a long, hoarse laugh. The entire top row of his teeth is capped, perfectly white.

"Pantywaists!" says his friend. He stamps his foot. Sammy notices both men are wearing cowboy boots with their tuxedos. "I'd like to see one of your Crimson little bitches, I'd like to see one of them take a run at my Razorbacks," he says. "You ever get a pig stuck up your ass?" The men throw their heads back and laugh.

Kurtz laughs too, introduces himself, then Sammy. And it is only at this point she realizes that Boris and Ben are gone—they have drifted off on their own. She looks around in a panic. It seems to her she should be able to spot Ben—he is so tall—but the room is full of tall men, all of them in black tuxedos.

The man in the bolo tie says his name is Tex, and his friend is Jed.

"Shit, you're tall," Tex says to Sammy.

"And skinny," says Jed.

"Like a goddamn giraffe!" Tex says.

"Where's my rifle?" says Jed. They laugh.

Thereafter Sammy stands quietly as Tex and Jed and Kurtz talk about football, throwing out not the names of teams but their mascots, none of which mean anything to her. A cartoonish battle rages in her head, with gators pitted against tigers, elephants fighting off wildcats, bulldogs chasing down roosters. From there the conversation turns to increasingly obscure clubs and groups, from the Boy Scouts of America to Greek fraternities and then to the best hotels in Venice. Sammy stands and struggles to do something with her face that resembles interest and recognition.

At one point Tex says he has to take a piss and disappears, and Kurtz talks with Jed for a while about the surprising roominess and comfort of Ford trucks with extended cabs. Then Tex reappears with an entire bottle of Wild Turkey and a handful of plastic cups. He passes the cups around and fills them. Sammy takes a sip and the bourbon slides down her throat. She manages not to choke but it is a profound inner battle. Everything around her, all the people and noise, disappears and it is just her and this feeling, this surging heat. As soon as she recovers she takes another sip and the whole process starts again. She drinks until she is flushed. A line goes through her head, one she's heard on countless soap operas and television dramas: *I've never felt this way before.* Usually this is whispered between lovers but here it is between her and bourbon.

Tex refills their cups and Sammy drinks hers down, remembering the words of her father: *You might say a certain proclivity.* It occurs to her she has discovered a hidden talent. Something she is good at. *Intermediate Bourbon,* she thinks. When she finishes her second cup Tex raises his eyebrows, winks at Kurtz, refills her cup. "Looks like you got yourself a keeper, there."

Then they are exchanging cards—Kurtz actually has cards, which surprises Sammy—and hatching plans for Kurtz to come on down to Houston for a visit. They'll drive up to Lake Pontchartrain, God's Country, where Tex has a cabin and a boat. After that, says Tex, they're going to shoot some deer. Tex knows a local farmer who lets him hunt his land, for a price. "Ain't no seasons," he says, "when you know the right people." He says this with the full confidence of a man whose candidate has just taken the White House. His candidate and way of life have won the day, and there are no rules. None that apply to him.

Then Tex and Jed say they need to go find their wives. They clap Kurtz on the back and wish him luck. "You're not so bad for a pantywaist," Tex says.

"I appreciate that sir," says Kurtz.

"That was someone important," he says, after they wander off.

"Really?" Sammy says.

"He sort of runs an oil company," says Kurtz. He has pulled from his jacket pocket a little black book and is transcribing, with a tiny pen, Jed's phone number.

"Oh," she says.

"You have to know who's important in a room," says Kurtz. "You know how you can tell?"

She just gives him a look, like: Please.

"The shoes," he says.

"Okay."

"Those were thousand-dollar boots. You know what they were made out of?"

"Leather."

"No shit. But what kind."

"I don't know," she says. "Panda."

"Don't be cute," Kurtz says. "This is the shit that matters, that gets you places. You can't just keep acting like everything's a joke or like it doesn't matter. It fucking matters, believe me. I'm trying to help you."

"I don't think I can be helped," she says.

He rolls his eyes.

They stand still for a while.

"They're ostrich," he says. "You can tell just by looking, the sheen."

170

They wander around some more. The crowd has thickened even further and the music is louder. New musicians keep joining the stage, though the musicians already occupying the stage don't leave—they just make room. A sort of Sgt. Pepper's situation is forming. Sammy recognizes the faces and voices of some singers from her father's era, singers who made their names in the sixties and then lost themselves to drugs, then staged comebacks in the eighties. The songs from their comeback tours had played on the radio all throughout her childhood, and they are all mixed up in her mind. She is always confusing members of The Eagles and The Doobie Brothers and Fleetwood Mac and Creedence Clearwater Revival, confusing Bruce Hornsby and Dan Fogelberg and Glenn Frey. Their songs are all about loss, about broken marriages and bodies, about paths grown over with weeds and brambles, about untaken roads, about trying to get back something precious that has been lost or ruined or discarded. They are singing with a desperate earnestness, looking at one another plaintively.

Sammy and Kurtz wander away from the stage. She is looking everywhere for Ben, but can't spot him. Meanwhile Kurtz is casting his eyes over everyone he sees, looking at their shoes, their tuxedos, their watches, the jewelry bedazzling the necks and ears of the women. He gravitates toward a middle-aged couple, a sandy-haired man and a blond woman whose dress is reminiscent of aluminum foil. The couple is standing listlessly, disappointment radiating from them, not only in the event but with each other— they seem like people who ran out of things to talk about many years ago. Kurtz just walks right up to them and starts talking, asking the husband where he's from, how he knows Clinton, what he does for a living. The husband is jovial, delighted to have a young person take an interest in him, whereas the wife remains mostly expressionless, staring off, except when she is asked a question or when her husband makes reference to her, at which point she smiles automatically, as if a switch has been flipped.

The man tells Kurtz that he is the president of a branch of banks spreading across northeast Arkansas. "Customer service," he shouts to Kurtz, "is what we're known for. It's what keeps people coming back. What we do is, if there's a kid in line with a mom, we still give out lollipops. We're the last bank to keep doing that. And the moms love it. Twenty-three branches with folks lining up for high interest mortgages, it all comes down to a couple hundred bags of lollipops!"

"That's brilliant," says Kurtz. "I'm going to keep that in mind."

Suddenly it occurs to Sammy that the couple they are talking to look like Pat Sajak and Vanna White. The resemblance is so strong she can't believe it didn't hit her sooner. Then it occurs to her that maybe they are Pat Sajak and Vanna White, working undercover, like maybe at some point in the evening they'll be brought on stage to conduct a round of Wheel with audience volunteers. She is overcome with excitement. Kurtz and the man are still talking, but she interrupts them. "You look like Pat Sajak!" she says. "From *Wheel of Fortune*. Did anyone ever tell you you look like Pat Sajak?" The man is staring at her blankly. "And you," she says, turns to his wife. "Oh my God, you look *exactly* like Vanna White!"

The wife is thrilled. "I've heard that before," she says. "People are always saying that."

"I mean, *wow*," says Sammy. "I have this overwhelming urge to buy a vowel."

The wife laughs again. "I've heard that before, too."

"When?" says the husband.

"Lots of times," says the wife. "When I'm out in public, people come up to me."

"I feel like I'm meeting America's favorite couple," Sammy says.

"Except they're not a couple in real life," says the wife.

"They're not?" Sammy asks. "I thought they were married."

"Pat only *wishes*!" says the wife. She gives her husband a lighthearted slap on the shoulder.

"I guess you're right," says Sammy. "I guess a man like Pat would be lucky to land a woman like Vanna."

"That's what I keep *telling* him!" says the wife. The wife is really excited now, like this is the best conversation she's ever been a part of.

There is nowhere left to go with this topic, but Sammy keeps going. "What you should do is," she says, "you should put a wheel right in your living room, and you should have a stage and letters, and you should do puzzles with the kids at night, if you have kids."

"We do!" says the wife. "Three boys."

"Perfect," Sammy says. She carries on about bribes and prizes for the kids, a wheel with colorful slices having to do with rewards based on their performance at school and behavior at home. Her plans are elaborate. She has a grand vision. But then something happens. As she is describing this vision she begins to notice that almost every couple in the room looks exactly like Pat Sajak and Vanna White. They are everywhere, in duplicate and triplicate, paired off in innumerable clones. She trails off mid-sentence.

Then the bank president is excusing himself, saying he sees someone he needs to say hello to, he is pulling his wife by the elbow. Kurtz doesn't even have time to offer his card. He turns and fixes a hateful look on Sammy. "What's *wrong* with you?" he says.

"I don't know," she says. "I think maybe I'm drunk."

"You think?" he says. He looks her up and down, like he's never seen anything so bizarre, like he can't believe she exists.

"Jesus," he says. "You're a fucking mess."

"I'm sorry."

"You really blew it," he says. "One of the things I'm considering, one of the careers I'm thinking about, if politics doesn't work out, is finance. That guy could have been a good contact."

"I kind of doubt it," Sammy says. "He was so, he was so short."

"You know how I could tell that guy was important?" Kurtz says.

"I guess I don't care," she says.

"You will someday," he says. "And you won't know what to do. You'll fall for some cheap imitation. Some small time luxury, like a Rolex. People think a Rolex is a sign of wealth but really it's a sign of aspiring wealth. Anyone can buy a Rolex."

Sammy is looking up at the ceiling at this point, as if appealing to the heavens. How much longer is this going to go on? When can I get out of here?

"But this guy was wearing a Breuget," Kurtz says. "It means he travels. It means he's got, like, fifty grand to throw down on a timepiece."

"I thought," she says, "we just elected someone who was, you know, a champion of the little man, someone who walked amongst the people. I thought tonight was supposed to be a celebration of the return of power to the middle class, like, the microphone was being handed off to the working man so that he could take the stage and air his grievances."

Kurtz smiles fully for perhaps the first time all evening. "That's cute," he says. "That's adorable."

They wander around, bickering constantly. Sammy says something and Kurtz tells her what a stupid

174

observation it is. Three out of four times she agrees. But the fourth time she mounts a counter-offensive. "How come every stupid thing that comes out of your mouth," she says, "is valid? Why are you always right and I'm always wrong?"

"Because what I say meets with agreement," he says. "Most of the population sees things the way I see them."

"But that doesn't mean what you say is necessarily true," she says. "You're just rattling off opinions the same as I am."

"But my opinions reflect and correspond to reality as it's known by the people I'm speaking to," he says. "Which is more important."

"Agreement is more important than truth?" she says. "Really? Is this really the like, philosophical stance you're taking here?"

"All I know is I'm not the one going around telling people they look like Pat Sajak," says Kurtz. "When they don't. Not at all."

Normally this little spat would have silenced Sammy for the rest of the evening, but the Wild Turkey seems to have transformed her. She finds it important to communicate to Kurtz everything she is thinking, everything that is passing through her mind. "I have standards too, you know," she says, "but they don't have to do with money, they have to do with dignity, and refinement, and comportment, and like, matters of the soul." She explains that she is looking around with the same critical eye he is, and is also disappointed for the most part, though not because of something so ridiculous as a Rolex. We have elected a new president, she says. And if you believe the rhetoric, this will be the leader who lifts our people from despair and carries us into a bright, gleaming new century. This will be someone who restores our dignity. But to celebrate all of this we have tiny meatballs on toothpicks, we have small portions of wine in plastic cups, we have aging musicians wearing garish amounts of makeup, musicians hopping foolishly around on stage, musicians who in a few hours will be back in their hotel rooms rubbing Bengay into their joints to recover from the antics they'd performed. As for the audience, we're all standing around having the same stupid conversations we always have, talking about taxes and property and sports, stuffing our fat faces and talking with our mouths full. So, what I want to know, she says, is this: Where's the dignity? Where's the largesse? Where's the magnanimity? All around us is baseness, crude avarice, cheap plastic, people shouting and dancing badly and laughing like hyenas. Where is the crystal? Where are the linens? Doesn't anyone at least speak French?

"In churches all across the world," she adds, "sacred cloths are spread over altars, golden goblets are filled with wine and lifted heavenward and, like, held in beams of light that slant through stained glass windows, there are careful and meaningful rituals observed—you can say what you want about the Catholics but at least there's solemnity involved, at least there's beauty, there's a sort of hushed silence, there are pristine white robes and red shoes and golden, pointy hats, they know how to usher in their leaders is what I'm saying, with the smoke and the balcony and the pomp, and don't we need some of that here, now, at the dawn of a new era in our nation's history? If not now," she says, "when? If not us, who?"

"The *Pope*?" says Kurtz. His face is a mask of angry frustration. "You want the inauguration of our new president to be like the electing of the fucking *Pope*? You want the celebration of a democratic election to resemble the inner workings of the Vatican, all that shrouded bullshit, that smoke and mirrors hysteria?"

"Maybe not," Sammy says, deflated. "Maybe not exactly like that."

"What did you expect?" says Kurtz. "This is life. This is pretty much as good as it gets. It's not like there's some secret back room behind here with better people in it. I got news for you. This is the back room. You're in it. Maybe you should just be happy to be here. Maybe you're lucky someone drove four hours to pick your ass up and drive you here."

"Oh, God," Sammy says, suddenly mortified. "I'm sorry." Suddenly she remembers she is a kid from Manchester, New Hampshire, the daughter of a janitor, and here she is complaining about the inaugural ball. All of the conviction goes out of her in a rush, like the air going out of a balloon. She covers her face with her hands.

Then all of a sudden there is an eruption of screams and applause. Everyone is jumping up and down. The president has taken the stage, along with Hillary and Chelsea. They stand waving. The president is magnificent, a giant, even bigger and brighter than Sammy remembers. He is a head taller than everyone else, his skin pink and gleaming, his hair flecked with sparkling gray. The room is in a frenzy, everyone reaching their arms out. It seems like the laws of physics have been suspended, like everyone has joined together, like people are made of plasma more so than flesh, like they are swirling together, the boundaries between them fluid.

Sammy thinks how the previous semester, in an art history lecture, she saw a picture of Christ entering Brussels on a donkey. The scene was painted in tortured Expressionist colors, dark reds and greens and browns and blacks, and Christ, barely noticeable in the crowd, was surrounded by throngs of people. The people were all wearing these grotesque masks, and looked like devils, with horns and sharp teeth. Sammy hadn't been sure what to make of the painting when she'd seen it—why Christ was surrounded by maniacs and demons—but now she feels she is beginning to understand. The crowd around her isn't made up of people anymore, but animals and spirits. There is some kind of electricity in the air, also a sense of terror. People's mouths are open and their eyes are gleaming, they look capable of anything, good or ill. It is dark on the floor but the lights on the stage are reflected in the eyes of the audience. All the brightness and energy coming off people's faces suggest that the world isn't going to be the same. It is going to change in a big way. Maybe for good. By the time I get out of college, Sammy thinks, there might be no poverty or war or illness or suffering. On top of which, artists will make the same living as doctors. We will be a great society.

When she turns to say something to Kurtz—something stupid, like: *Wow!*—she realizes that he too is gone. She turns in circles, scanning the heads around her, but no Kurtz. Probably he has tried to advance toward the president, drawn to his power. On stage, the president is dancing with his wife. Sammy wonders what it would be like to have so many people staring at you. The whole thing makes her queasy but she just stands there and takes it in. Her logic is to stay in the same place. Kurtz will come back for her, she thinks. Or someone will.

There is more music, more dancing. The failed middle-aged white musicians are joined by a group of exuberant black soul singers. The music is upbeat now, celebratory. An old black man playing an electric guitar hops across the stage on one leg, and Sammy recognizes him as Chuck Berry. She tries to calculate his age. Sixty? Seventy? At one point the president plays the saxophone to wild applause. The President of the United States, Sammy thinks, is playing the saxophone. We are living in a new kind of world. The music goes on and on, becomes repetitive, then shapeless. It is as if the people on stage are trying to find new limits. The song they are playing teeters perpetually on the verge of collapse but somehow keeps going. The crowd is held in thrall, wondering how long it can go on, wondering how it will end.

Finally, the music comes to an abrupt halt, and the president sweeps his wife and daughter next to him and they all stand waving to the crowd, taking in the applause, again for a much longer time than the girl thinks anyone could possibly stand, and then they disappear off stage. The musicians keep playing but it isn't the same. People start milling around, heading for the edges of the room. Everything changes back to the way it was before. The lighting is unflattering, the air is thick with sweat and cologne and alcohol. Already a staleness is coming over everything. How quickly all that promise has turned to disappointment.

Sammy starts wandering around. She is looking for Ben or Kurtz or Boris—it doesn't matter, she just wants to get out of there, to go home, to go to bed. She wanders around, coming close enough to each cluster of tuxedoes to distinguish faces, then turns sharply away. There is still some excitement in the air, though it is being produced only by drunk people, people who haven't yet realized the party is over.

Then she sees Ben. He is leaning against a wall, his shoulder pressed against it, his back turned. His head is inclined downward. She thinks he is alone and downcast, and rushes toward him. But when she gets closer she sees he is in fact leaning in close to talk to someone—a young woman, short and slight, her blond hair slicked back, her mouth painted red. She is leaning into Ben, swirling her drink around, staring into it, meditatively. They are standing so close. Whatever they are talking about seems to be a secret, something intimate.

Sammy flushes—she feels startled, embarrassed, like a kid walking in on her parents. She darts away, hides herself behind a cluster of men in tuxedos. Then files onto an escalator and rides down to the lobby. Downstairs there is a bank of pay phones filled with drunk men in tuxedos, shouting. "Kenny Loggins," one man is saying. "And Bruce Hornsby. And Chuck Berry!" Suddenly she wants to talk to someone, tell someone where she is, before it's over and doesn't matter anymore. She waits for a phone and then dials the operator, asks to place a collect call to her father. When she'd left home he had told her to call collect any time she wanted, even just to say hello. He'd said he would be waiting to hear from her. Now the idea that he has been waiting to hear from her—the idea that he is still in the house, still in that chair in front of the television, and she hasn't called all this time—comes down on her like a hammer.

The phone rings and she is filled with a nervous, sick feeling. "Hello?" says her father. She can tell he is drunk, can hear the television in the background. She waits while the operator asks him to accept the charges.

"Go ahead," says the operator, and clicks off.

"Hi, Dad," Sammy says. "Guess where I am?"

"Jail!" he says. Like he's been waiting to use that one.

"Nope," she says. "Guess again."

"I don't know," he says. "Tuscaloosa."

"Dad. I'm at the inaugural ball."

"Jeez, Lark. That's great. That's great." He is trying to wake himself up, trying to be sober. "I've got it going here on the TV," he says. "The news. They've got reporters out in the streets there. They're freezing their asses off, it looks like. Hold on, let me see what they're saying." He fumbles. She hears the volume go up. Her father tells her that multiple television cameras are pointed at the building from which she is calling. This is a first, he says. No one in their family has ever been somewhere that was being covered live on television. No one has ever been warm, inside, with reporters freezing their asses off outside, no one in their family had ever so much as...

"It's actually not that big a deal," she says.

"Are you kidding? Not a big deal? You're talking to, you're talking to a kid from Hubbardston, here."

"I saw Chuck Berry."

"No kidding!"

"He was doing his thing, you know, with one leg."

"He's still doing that," he says. "Huh."

"And Kenny Loggins."

"No kidding!"

"And Michael McDonald. And I saw Kenny G for a second, I think."

"Wow."

Sammy and her father are acting like these people are really important, like being in a room with them is some kind of life-altering event, when in truth these musicians are just people who have recorded a few songs, and smiled and posed for cameras, but are otherwise just slobs like everyone else, or so it is starting to seem to Sammy. Now that she is standing on the inside, in the warmth of it all, it doesn't seem all that special.

"You're talking to a guy," her father says. "I never even set one foot..."

"In an Italian restaurant," she says, "until your thirties. And when you did you ordered a hamburger."

"That's right. That's goddamned right." This is one of her father's ongoing narratives, the story of his childhood. How sheltered he was growing up, how Irish, how poor. How little he knew of the world. How the first time he went to an Italian restaurant he ordered a hamburger off the kids menu, not knowing what lasagna was, ravioli.

"You thought pizza was an exotic food," she says.

"And I didn't have a cup of coffee until the Army."

Sammy can't think of anything to say. She had been dying to tell him where she was, but now it doesn't seem worth mentioning, in fact it is an embarrassment. "I don't want to run up your bill," she says.

"My kid," he says. "My kid's at the inaugural ball."

"I saw the president."

"My kid saw the president."

Sammy knows well the phases of drunkenness her father cycles through. The initial burst of loquaciousness and good will, where he tells jokes and talks about his childhood, about movies and books he likes, where he's excited and wants to impart the life's wisdom he's accrued. Then something shifts and he turns forlorn, rueful, and also sort of embarrassed—suddenly he wishes he hadn't gone on so long, revealed so much. Now, Sammy realizes, she is doing the exact same thing. She was excited to call him but now regret has her by the collar.

"There are lots of people waiting for the phone," she says. "I don't want to tie up the line."

"Okay," he says. "You get back out there and have fun. Get up there on stage with Chuck Berry and, you know, show him a thing or two."

"I will," she says.

As Sammy walks away from the phone a strange spinning sensation comes over her. She steps onto an escalator and leans heavily on the railing. As she rises she has the feeling something is pushing her to the side. She watches a series of steps flatten and disappear. The task of negotiating herself off the escalator looms with a terrible sense of difficulty and likely humiliating failure. When the time comes she summons her inner resources and steps off, rights herself. She sees a sign for a restroom and walks toward it with careful steps.

The ladies' lounge has multiple rooms. First a wide room lined with mirrors, with gold satin couches, then a room with sinks and counters, and then, in the furthest room, a series of toilet stalls whose doors stretch all the way down to the floor. Sammy enters a stall and sits on the toilet for a long time, thinking about her current problem, the fact that she is shut away in a toilet stall at the inaugural ball, somehow having a bad time when she is supposed to be having a good time. Something is wrong with her, and it occurs to her that if she can figure out what it is, she might be able to fix herself. She sits and thinks: Why can't I talk to anyone? Why can't I just have a normal conversation? Why do I get so flustered, so nervous? Why do I keep thinking of myself as the wronged party in every social encounter, when in fact I'm the one causing all the problems? Why do I feel so sorry for myself? Why do I believe that fate has treated me so unfairly? Why am I convinced that I am good and deserving but tragically overlooked, while everyone else around me is small and petty and compromised, but still somehow successful? Why do I think I'm special? Why do I think I'm the only one in the room who sees what is really going on, what really matters, what matters to the soul, while everyone else is distracted by bullshit? And if I am really the only person in the room who sees what's really going on, why don't I ever do anything about it? Why don't I try to make things better? What's my goal? What's my ambition? Am I really going to sit around for the rest of my life, criticizing people and reading books? Is this possible and if so, is it okay to spend one's life this way?

On top of these problems—a running list she cycles through on a daily basis—now she has a new one: the family gift. All her life Sammy has stood proudly apart from it, imagining herself as a noble figure, a young person of uncommon strength and conviction, like Joan of Arc. Her plan has always been to stand armored, protecting herself and her children and all future generations of Brownes from this gift, a heavy sword raised against it. Her plan was to stab and kill the gift, skin it, and fold up its pelt and put it away in a locked chest, like a trousseau. Now and then she would kneel with her children before the chest and unlock the gift and take it out and unfold it and hold it before them. *Behold the gift*, she would tell them, *which I have killed and skinned and locked away in order to keep you safe. Behold its terrors, its destruction.* The children would stare wide-eyed. In their awe they would reach out to touch it, to stroke its fur, but she would yank it away. *You must be careful never to touch it*, she would say. Then she would fold the gift and put it back and make a display of locking the cabinet, hanging the key over her neck. *I carry this for you*, she would tell them.

Thank you, mother, they would say. *For slaying the gift, for locking it away, for enduring the heaviness of the key that hangs from your neck, always.*

But now she is drunk, in a bathroom in a strange dress, two hours away from school, with no money, confused and adrift from the people who brought her here, who seem to have abandoned her. She is lost to the gift and will never be right again. A little sob escapes her mouth.

Sammy holds her head in her hands. She is breathing through her mouth, heavily, as if she's just run a race. She can feel herself tipping to the side. It suddenly doesn't seem like such a bad idea to curl up on the floor. No one will know, no one will mind. She stares down at the tiny white tiles, little rectangles arranged at odd angles, abutting and adjoining one another in a complex, inscrutable pattern. The tiles swirl around each other in a kind of dance.

Two women come into the lounge, talking to each other. They have thick accents, slow southern drawls. "God what a man," one says. She has a hoarse voice, crackling with phlegm. "That was a real man out there in that room."

"That's a *beautiful* man," says her friend, whose voice is small and high.

"He's absolutely not human," says the first.

"I agree," her friend says. "He's superhuman. He's a superman."

"I'm too tired to fix my makeup," says the hoarse woman. "I'm too old. I don't matter. Nobody cares what you look like at my age," she says.

"Just do your lipstick," says the other. "A good lipstick fixes everything."

"You mean it distracts from everything."

"However you want to put it."

They are silent for a bit.

"That man," says the first, "I knew it from the first time I saw him way back when at the state fair. I saw him shaking hands with people and I said, 'That man's going to be president.'"

"It's been a long time since we've had a president like that. A president who has something in his *person*, if you know what I mean, something of a natural leader in his *person*."

"They tried to screw him out of it."

"But we didn't let them."

There is a brief silence. Then the hoarse woman speaks out sharply.

"What do you think of our new president?" she asks. Sammy thinks for a moment that she has been spotted somehow, tucked away in her stall, spotted and called to question. But then a third voice speaks.

"I can't say," says the voice. "I can't say as I know too much about him."

"He was just in the next room," says the hoarse woman. "Five minutes ago you were standing just feet away from the most powerful man in the world, and you didn't even know it."

A beat skips wherein the third woman seems to conclude that she is supposed to act impressed, grateful. "It kind of gives you chills," she says flatly.

"That's right," says the hoarse woman. "That's goddamned right."

Suddenly Sammy wants to join the conversation. She feels a desperate need to be a part of this, perhaps tell her story about making Clinton a sandwich. She stands up and comes out of the stall and walks carefully into the room with the sinks and mirrors. There are two sets of sinks along opposing walls. She stands at the sink opposite the women, washing her hands, and steals glances at them. They are quite old, in long, sequined dresses, one gold and one black. The woman in gold wears a white satin turban with a large pink jewel at its center. The woman in black has a puffy nimbus of peach hair and a fox stole draped around her shoulders. They are fixing their makeup, leaning toward their reflections. Suddenly Sammy realizes a third woman is standing just beside these two, a large black woman in a navy blue dress with a white collar. She seems to be keeping guard of a small basket of perfumes and lotions. Somehow Sammy hadn't noticed her when she'd come in.

She turns her attention to her own reflection. All the makeup Lara had put on has slid off and collected under her eyes, giving her the look of a football player. She wets her fingers and runs under her eyes and rubs. The makeup smears and gives her a ghoulish quality. She wets her fingers again and goes back at it, but the makeup only turns into a sort of black paste. Now she looks like a domestic violence victim in a bad TV movie.

"Oh my Lord, you look fabulous," says the woman in black, the hoarse one. "Your dress doesn't fit and your hair's a mess, but God you look fabulous. You're so young," she says. She says to her friend, "Look how young this girl is."

"Look at that neck," says the other.

They cross over and stand beside Sammy, one on each side.

"Promise me something," says the woman in black. "Enjoy your youth."

"Okay," Sammy says.

"I want you to promise. I want you to swear on your mother." The woman is squeezing Sammy's arm, now. She looks in the mirror back to the attendant, who gives her a look that amounts to: Don't ask me.

"Okay," she says.

"Repeat after me," the woman says. "I swear on my mother's life to enjoy my youth. I promise not to waste any opportunity that comes my way."

"And I promise to sleep," says her friend, "with lots of men before settling down and getting married." She giggles like a girl.

"And not to have kids," says the woman in black. "Dear God, not to have kids until at least thirty-five."

The woman in the turban is playing with Sammy's hair now, twirling little sections of it around her finger. "Don't give up your job," she says, "when you get married."

"Don't ever give up your options," says the other. "Because then if you want to leave, you can't."

"All the power is on their side," says the turban. "All their friends are lawyers and judges, so if you want to leave, you have nowhere to go. It's like living under a dictatorship."

"Keep your friends," says the woman in black. "No matter how much you rise in stature when you get married, keep your old friends. Have them over. Even if they're the type not allowed at the club, keep them around you."

"You're going to need them," says the turban. "They're the only people who can help you, at a certain point."

"They're the only people you can call in the middle of the night," says the woman in black, "and say: *I'm in trouble. I need you to come here with some plastic wrap and a shovel.* They're the only people you can call when the shit really hits the fan, pardon my French."

"And you never know," says the turban, "some of them might become powerful."

"Swear," they say.

"I swear," Sammy says.

"Who are you with tonight?" says the turban. "Someone with potential? Someone in government?"

"No," she says. "Just a campaign worker."

"Oh God," says the fox stole. "Ditch him. Don't waste your time." Sammy can't stop staring at the fox stole. It seems to be making some kind of statement. The woman who wears it is no longer young nor beautiful, but, the stole suggests, she can still command the fate of an animal, a life can still be taken for her comfort, embellishment. The fox is orange and narrow and it appears to have secured itself around her neck by biting its own tail. Its head rests on her shoulder, its little legs dangle. Its eyes are yellow glass, and seem to be staring right at Sammy. They have an imploring expression. Who knows how many years this fox has been hanging around this woman's neck—it is probably desperate, Sammy thinks. It must have heard all of her stories a thousand times, it must be tired of the sound of her voice. If it could come back to life and bite her through the jugular, it would.

Sammy reaches out to stroke the tail of the fox, which is fat and striped, and the woman flinches. "I'm sorry," Sammy says. "I was just admiring your fox."

"I want you to go out there," says the turban, "and find somebody to sleep with."

"Someone with money," says the fox stole.

"Someone with power," says the turban. "A candidate, not a campaign worker."

"Go sleep with the president!" says the fox stole. They both cackle.

"You might as well," says the turban, "start at the top."

For a moment, they all regard themselves in the mirror. Sammy is standing between them, and it seems to her that she might be, in some way, in some parallel universe, the child of these women, an heir to their twin fortunes. Here beside her, finally, are two women who know how things work. Perhaps they will adopt her, will take her home and tell her their secrets, they will take her back to Arkansas and make something of her. She sees herself, like Elly Higginbottom, under the direction of various tutors, taking elocution lessons and etiquette classes, walking with a stack of books balanced on her head, learning tennis, ballroom dancing. She imagines a gray-haired, hunchbacked tailor bent before her, measuring the length of her leg, making plans for a series of dresses and suits. She sees a butler unfolding a cloth napkin and spreading it in her lap. Then she is riding a horse across a green pasture, jumping a fence. Then she is on a veranda reclined on a chaise longue, between these two women, a Tom Collins in her hand....

The fox stole breaks the spell by slapping Sammy on the butt. "Well, God love you, you young thing," she says, and turns on her heel.

"Have fun!" says the turban. She wiggles her fingers in the air. Then they are both gone.

Sammy stands facing the mirror for a long time, feeling deflated. She starts to cry.

Eventually the attendant approaches with her basket and asks if she needs anything.

"I'm sorry," Sammy says. "I don't have any money."

"It's complimentary," the attendant says. She sets her basket down, unscrews a tiny bottle and holds it out. Sammy is supposed to take it from her, but she cups her hands like she had always done for communion, back when her mother used to take her to church. The attendant squeezes a dollop of pink lotion into each palm and the girl rubs her hands together, then over each other, fast, like a squirrel turning a nut.

189

"What's the problem?" says the attendant. Sammy is really blubbering, now.

"I don't know," she chokes.

"Everything's gonna get better," the woman says. The girl sniffles, nods. "Everyone's been saying, with the new president, everything's about to get better."

They look at each other for a moment. The attendant is short and squat and has her hair pulled back in a tight bun. Her expression is solemn. A bright red vein has burst in one of her eyeballs, running from the inside corner to the pupil in a red squiggle that looks like the fanciful signature of an artist at the edge of a painting. Sammy cries even more. The attendant holds out a tissue.

"I'm sorry," Sammy says. She takes the tissue and presses it against her face. "I'm so sorry."

1993

The president has left and the ball is winding down. Ben circles through the rooms, looking for the white sequins of Sammy's dress. He had caught glimpses of her all night, wandering around with Kurtz, her dress flashing. She'd looked nervous, turning her head this way and that, in search of something, probably him. Several times he had thought to approach her, to rescue her from Kurtz, but then again, he was curious to see how she would hold up. And too, if he left her alone, maybe she'd meet someone, find herself swept up in a new crowd. It would be good for someone her age to make some connections.

At this point, though, he hasn't seen her for an hour or so, and he's starting to worry. Plus, he's frustrated—he hates staying past the height of a party. It's time to go.

He spots Kurtz and Boris. Asks if they've seen her.

"She probably met someone," Kurtz says. "Let's just go, man. She'll catch a ride with someone else."

"Maybe she met someone," Boris says, "who works at a Subway, and they hit it off, and the next thing you know they will be having little sandwich babies."

"Jesus," Ben says.

"We're going out for a cigarette," says Kurtz. "Don't take too long."

"I'll be right out," Ben says. He rides up the escalator again—most people are on the way down, now—and right at the top, he practically collides with Sammy. "There you are," he says. "I've been looking all over."

"I thought I lost you!" she says. She bursts into tears. "I thought you took off with, I don't know, I was just, I was just wandering around and I don't have any money or even a coat, just this stupid..." She holds up the gold wrap, now hopelessly crumpled, like a used tissue.

"Relax," he says. "Everything's fine. Let's go." He is surprised at her distress. Then again, he thinks, he did consider leaving her. Just for a second.

Ben puts his arm around her and guides her onto the escalator. They ride down to the lobby, then make their way out the door. He spots Kurtz and Boris standing in a huddle smoking, their bowties untied. Neither of their tuxedoes fit—they are much too big. They have the look of cater-waiters on break behind a restaurant.

"Look who I found," Ben says.

"Let's go," said Kurtz. "We've been waiting forever."

They start making their way to the Beetle. Kurtz and Boris walk ahead, bickering, pointing their cigarettes at each other. It is a long walk, and Sammy leans against Ben. They are both sleepy, walking slowly. The streets are still busy but the festiveness and excitement are gone, the cars moving languorously. The expressions on the faces of the limo drivers are weary.

In the car, Ben explains to Sammy that an arrangement has been worked out in advance, involving the whole group driving her back to Charlottesville so that Kurtz can ambush one of his idols, a political scientist who teaches classes on campaign strategy. This professor is some sort of celebrity, in Kurtz's world. "We're gonna go check this shit out," Kurtz says now, speeding down 95. "I hear there's this diner he likes, this breakfast place, it's like 24 hours, and supposedly what he does is, he goes in really early every morning so he's like the only one there."

"And he can eat in peace?" Ben says. "Without anyone bothering him?"

"Exactly," says Kurtz. "And read the newspapers. Except what we're going to do is, we're going to find him and bother him."

"I know that place." Sammy explains that there is only one place in town that stays open all night, where drunk kids flock to eat at three in the morning, when the other bars close—they will just beat the rush. The diner's signature menu item, she says, is a cheeseburger with a fried egg on top.

"We're just gonna sit our asses down," says Kurtz, "and wait. We're just gonna order up four of those burgers and sit there and eat until he comes in. Then we'll eat again, we'll just order whatever he orders and strike up a conversation about how we happen to love the same food. Boom. We're best friends."

Sammy leans against Ben in the back seat. Up front, Kurtz and Boris start arguing about someone named Ted. Ted is, according to Kurtz, a mouthbreather who can't take two steps without stepping in a pile of shit. "So his parents knew Carter," says Kurtz. "Big fucking deal. My mother is practically a Kennedy. Ted doesn't know shit. Can't tell what Clinton plans to do with the economy, doesn't know shit about energy, doesn't know shit about trade, doesn't know shit about Russia or Israel of Afghanistan or Cuba." He is driving erratically, seeming to accelerate and decelerate and change lanes as a means of emphasizing whatever he is saying at the moment. "Dude doesn't even read the newspaper. He's the one who gets us jobs?"

Boris shrugs. It is the shrug of a communist who is used to oppressive and unfair systems of governance. "He's on staff. He's our best connection. We must deal with him."

"This is bullshit!" Kurtz yells, and pounds the wheel. "Commerce is a second-tier gig. It's not a first-class operation, not at all."

A sour mood settles over Ben, and he tries to figure out where it's coming from. Maybe it's just that he's reached the end, the end of his year on the road with Kurtz. Or maybe it's the view from this new vantage point, in the back seat, watching Kurtz and Boris up front, plotting their future—maybe it's the feeling of having been replaced. And worse, by such a cheap knockoff, something slapped together in a Russian warehouse.

Ben pulls a flask from his pocket and draws from it, offers it to Sammy. She takes a drink, then passes it back to him, and they continue like that back and forth. "Kurtz just got an offer to work for Ron Brown," he explains to Sammy. "And even though this morning he would have killed for it, would have taken anything, now that he has it, he's trying to get something in the White House instead. He's very impressed with himself. He values his contribution to the party at a higher level, apparently, than the party values it. But Ron Brown isn't a bad place to start, if politics is your thing."

Sammy nods like she understands, like she knows who Ron Brown is, but Ben can tell she is just going along.

"Chair of the DNC?" he says. "Future head of Commerce?"

"Oh," Sammy says. "Right."

"Kurtz is going to be doing advance."

She nods again, though in a way that conveys her total ignorance of advance work.

"That's when you go somewhere before the guy you work for gets there, and make sure everything is set up."

"Oh," she says.

"You know, set up security. Make sure there's a functioning microphone at the podium. Check the entrances and exits, set up the transportation, the hotel, make sure there's a little glass of water, all that."

"That doesn't sound so good."

"You live on the road," he says. "But you feel important, apparently."

"Are you going along?"

Ben shakes his head. "Absolutely not. This is my last night. Tomorrow I'm going home to write the book."

"How long will it take?" she asks. The very question that has been plaguing him. He is due to start medical school in the summer, and has just a few months. This doesn't seem like long enough to write a book, but then again there was Rimbaud, who worked in fevered brilliance. And Van Gogh, who painted dozens of masterpieces in the months before his death. It will come upon him, Ben thinks. He is smart, and young. Why not?

Suddenly Kurtz turns his attention to Sammy. "Hey, Sammy Browne," Kurtz says. He fishes out his address book from his jacket pocket. There is a tiny pencil slotted into the spine of the address book and he takes it out with his teeth. "What's your phone number?"

"I don't have a phone," she says.

"No shit," he says. "I mean, in Manchester."

"Oh," she says. "Why?"

"Because this is how the world works. I put everyone I meet in my book, and they put me in theirs. People do this because you never know who you're going to need to call in the future. I can't think of a single reason I'd ever need to call you, but these things can't be predicted. Maybe twenty years from now I'll see you on *Meet the Press* and I'll be like, 'Goddamn, when I met her she was just this gangly sandwich kid who couldn't tell her head from her ass but now look at her,' and I'll want to call you and reconnect. I'll be staring at that screen like, 'Holy shit, I can't fucking believe this.' And what will I do? I'll pull out this book and *bam*, Sammy Browne. I'll call the number. Who knows what will happen. Maybe it will be disconnected. Maybe it will belong to a Chinese restaurant. We don't know. But we can make efforts."

"I'm not going to be on *Meet the Press*," she says.

"You don't know that." His eyes are shifting from the rearview to the road.

"I do. I believe there are some things that can be ruled out."

"I can rule out that I'm not going to fuck a sheep later," he says. "I think we can put that squarely outside the realm of possibility."

"I wouldn't say that," says Ben.

"Fuck you," says Kurtz.

Then Kurtz explains to Sammy, "Your being on *Meet the Press* in twenty years is still within the realm of possible experiences. Maybe next semester you'll take a political science course and something will spark in your brain, you'll figure out how the world works and want to be a part of it. These things happen."

"I think it's more likely," Sammy says, "that if you ever call me, you'll be looking for Ben."

"Why would I lose touch with Ben?"

"Because people drift apart."

"Not me," says Kurtz. "I keep my connections. Anyone valuable, I keep up with them. Take Ben. Ben is valuable, Ben is worth a fucking fortune. I've got six possible phone numbers for Ben in this book. Because connections are the one true capital we have in life. I have the updated number of the Kennedy compound in here and why? Because I keep up with the housekeeping and landscaping staff. I send Christmas cards. I call on holidays and birthdays. Is this number useful to me at the moment? If I called it right now what would it do for me?"

"Nothing," Sammy says.

"Wrong," says Ben. "If he called it he would know that an action he took produced a tone in a house far away, that something he had done with his own hands had taken an effect, however small, in an historically important environment, an environment in which some remnants of the Kennedy brothers, the sounds they made, were still resonating in the house, however slightly, and now into this same air will come the shrill ringing of a phone, which he produced." That's good, he thinks. He'll have to use that in the book.

"That's exactly right," says Kurtz. "Who else in this car has that power, that opportunity?"

"Who else would want it?" Sammy says.

"You know, your little girlfriend seems nice," Kurtz says to Ben. "She seems quiet at first, and pleasant, but at her core she's kind of a bitch."

"I know," Ben says. "That's why I plucked her out of obscurity."

"Flags have already been speared in this moon," Sammy says. "You're not the first person to disembark from a shuttle and walk on the face of this particular topic. This isn't, like, news to me." Ben is impressed with her, for the first time all night. She is keeping up.

"I'm just verifying, then," says Kurtz. "I've surveyed the area and made my assessment. I'm adding to the chorus."

An hour later, they are pulling up in front of the famed all-night diner. Even at three in the morning, two black men in blue coveralls are seated at the counter, either coming off shift or about to go on shift somewhere. They are hunched over their plates, in their posture more a sense of fatigue and routine than of existential despair—this isn't a Hopper painting. A tall, skinny cook is leaning against the counter, smoking a cigarette, dressed all in white, a paper hat in the shape of an ocean liner perched on his head. Ben reaches for his notebook—a compulsion, by now—but then decides against it. Decides to just observe, and remember.

Kurtz pulls open the car door and the horn starts again. He folds the front seat forward and Sammy climbs out, a bit wobbly. Then Ben. They file into the diner, where Kurtz greets the cook and the two workers like he's known them for years.

"What's happening, my friends?" he says, spreading his arms wide. "How's everybody doing on this fine evening?" The men regard Kurtz warily, but he doesn't seem to notice—he just takes off his tuxedo jacket and settles it on a stool at the middle of the counter, then sits on it. Boris sits next to Kurtz on one side, Ben on the other, and Sammy sits next to Ben. This places her closest to the black men, who are staring at the group with what looks like disbelief. Ben watches as she gives them a sort of apologetic nod. Like: *I'm sorry we're here.*

Kurtz orders burgers for everyone, and the cook ducks below the counter to retrieve burgers and eggs from the refrigerator. He slaps four patties on the grill and cracks four eggs next to them, then stands over the grill while everything hisses. The cook keeps a cigarette in his mouth while he works, its ashes accumulating slowly, dangling over the meat and eggs. Ben watches the ashes, transfixed, first as they glow orange and then turn gray. They sort of bob as the cook talks, trembling. They seem to be defying the laws of physics. At what must be the last possible second before they collapse takes the cigarette from his mouth and flicks the ashes in a mug, and the whole process starts again.

Kurtz has started talking to the two men at the end of the counter. "We come here tonight," he says, extending an arm toward them, as if he's Winston Churchill delivering a speech to his public, "as representatives of the new administration, because we want to get a feel for where the country's at, where real people are at, at the start of this new presidency. Because this is going to be an administration that keeps in touch with regular people. If you don't mind my asking a few personal questions," he says, "I'd like to know more about your lives, like how much is the mortgage, what does food cost you, how much would you say you have to spare, if anything, at the end of the week?" He says all this in a single breath, his voice escalating like a preacher's. The men stare at him for a moment, and Ben wonders if some violence will break out. But then one of the men answers. "I don't really know," he says. "I turn things over to my wife. I just give her the check and she takes if from there. I just take whatever she gives me for walking around money. Ten dollars here and there, what have you." According to the patch on his coveralls, his name is Leroy.

"What about kids," Kurtz asks. "How many people are you trying to support."

"Three kids," says Leroy. "But they're grown now."

"What's your salary?" says Kurtz. "When's the last time you got a raise?"

The man keeps answering Kurtz's questions, though for what reason, Ben can't imagine. Maybe they're just being polite, maybe they are letting Kurtz go on out of largesse. But there is something else—the feeling in the air of people answering questions at customs. It is obvious Leroy doesn't want to talk to Kurtz, but understands some system is in place, compelling him. An uneasy feeling settles over Ben, but Kurtz just keeps going. "Do you have a credit card?" he asks the men.

"No, sir," says Leroy.

"Do you keep your money in a bank or at home?" says Kurtz.

Leroy shoots his friend a glance. It is the wounded expression of a man who has been mistaken for a fool. "My wife takes the checks to a bank," he says. "If that's what you're asking. Not keeping anything under the mattress if that's what you're saying."

The cook sets Kurtz's plate in front of him and Kurtz takes up the burger and shoves it in his mouth. A bright line of yolk runs down his chin. "This is fucking delicious," he says.

"Glad you approve," says the cook.

"Do you have a car?" Kurtz asks the men, right back at it, his mouth full.

"Mercury," says Leroy.

"I like a Mercury," Boris muses. "I'd drive a Mercury over a Cadillac any day."

"How much is it to fill the tank?" says Kurtz.

"Twenty," says Leroy. "Thereabouts."

"And what about a pack of cigarettes?"

"One eighty-nine," says Leroy.

"Have you ever used a personal computer?" asks Kurtz.

"What for?" says the other man. The patch on his coveralls says *Edward*.

"You know, keeping documents and correspondence."

"No, sir," says Leroy. An incredulous expression takes over his face, like he can't believe Kurtz exists, like he couldn't believe the world is in the hands of someone with that kind of face and haircut.

Sammy seems to be in a state of quiet agony, hunched in on herself, taking very small bites of her food. She is in that stage of drunkenness, Ben can tell, where it takes concentration to perform even the most ordinary maneuvers. A shred of lettuce, dotted with mayonnaise, drops from her burger and lands on the sequins of her dress. He reaches out and pinches it, smears it on his napkin, without her noticing.

"What do you think of all these statues everywhere?" Kurtz continues. "All these confederate soldiers enshrined all over the place?"

"Don't really care," says Leroy. "Never thought about it until this minute." He starts laughing. "Is this what you white people sit up in Washington talking about?" His friend starts laughing too. At least maybe this is funny, thinks Ben, an amusing break in their routine. Maybe they'll go home later and tell their wives about the ridiculous policy makers they met.

"Is your boss white?" Kurtz says to the cook.

"Owner's white," he says. "Don't see much of him. I'm the boss here, basically."

"Does he treat you fair?" says Kurtz.

"Can't complain," says the cook.

"What do you do, if you don't mind my asking?" Kurtz says to the men.

"Maintenance," Leroy says.

"My mother does maintenance," Kurtz says. "Well, housekeeping."

"So does her father," Ben says.

Sammy nods vigorously. She seems eager to have it known she isn't a rich kid.

"My whole family are union, plumbers and pipefitters," says Boris. "My mother, my brothers and sisters, my cousins and uncles and aunts." He goes on talking about his father and the work he does as an industrial plumber. As a boy, Boris says, he apprenticed himself to his father for years. He knows it well, hard work. He was born into it, it runs through his veins.

They are saying these things, it occurs to Ben, to let the cook and Leroy and Edward know that they are all friends, all cut from the same cloth—basically they are trying to do what Clinton did. But they aren't doing a good job. One of the problems here, which is perfectly obvious to everyone except Kurtz, is that they are in formal wear and these men are in coveralls, that they are white and the men are black, and even though their parents have the same kinds of jobs as Leroy and Edward, and even though there is no cash value whatsoever between them—except for Ben, of course—even accounting for all of this kinship, these similarities, at the end of the day they are still four drunk white kids who have just stumbled out of the inaugural ball. They all have college degrees, or will someday, and there is little chance any of them will ever be working second shift maintenance at the age of fifty.

Suddenly, with a hard smack, Sammy places her forehead down on the counter. Almost as if she's passed out.

"Uh-oh," says the cook. "Better get your friend taken care of."

"I'm fine," she mutters.

"We don't like drunk kids passing out in here," says the cook. "We're not that kind of establishment."

"She's cool," says Kurtz. "Sammy, tell him you're cool."

"I'm cool," she says, though she doesn't lift her head up. "I'm just tired of this conversation, is all."

Edward and Leroy and the cook burst out laughing. Ben is happy again. If nothing else, she is adding a bit of fun to the night.

"What do you want to talk about?" says Kurtz. "What does the youth of America want to talk about instead? MTV? Frat parties? Spring break? Who's sucking whose dick in, like, whatever dorm you live in? Which of the RAs is hot?"

"I don't really care," she says. "I just don't want to hear any more about, like, the government or whatever. I don't think anyone here wants to talk about the federal government."

"Oh really?" says Kurtz. "You presume to know what people are interested in talking about? Really?"

"Well I don't really want to talk about the government," says Leroy, "for one."

"Me neither," says Edward.

"Okay, fine," says Kurtz. "Fine. What should we talk about?" He balls up a napkin and sort of throws it on his plate. "The floor is open. Don't let me crowd it. Don't let me ruin your good time by talking about something, you know, actually relevant."

204

Nobody says anything for a while. Then the cook comes forward. "What we were talking about when you came in," he says, "if I recall correctly, was Leroy's people. We were asking after his mother in the nursing home."

"Oh," says Kurtz. "Oh, sorry." He rubs his eyes with his fists. "I'm sorry, man."

"That's alright," says Leroy.

"Alzheimer's," says the cook. "About the worst thing that can happen to a family."

They all hang their heads over their plates for a moment. Then Kurtz, quiet for as long as he can stand, says: "What's your healthcare situation? Medicaid? How's it working for you? Is it easy to navigate? How much time would you say you spend per week on paperwork?"

"What he's interested in," says Ben, solicitously, "is what government can do to make people's lives better."

"Leave us alone," says Leroy. Edward cracks a smile.

"What does that mean, to your mind?" Kurtz says. "For government to leave you alone, what would that look like, how would that be different from now?"

"Social security," says Leroy, "is always sending letters to my mother. Making her prove she still old or something. Always some new kind of form to fill out."

"Okay," say Kurtz. "What else?"

"I don't need warnings printed on my cigarettes, for another thing," says Leroy. "I'm not a child."

"Okay," said Kurtz. "Good. What else."

"I don't like having to register my car every year and go through all that rigmarole."

Kurtz nods. "What else?"

"Don't know," says Leroy. "I'd have to think."

"What about taxes?" says Boris.

"I pay them," says Leroy. "But I don't favor them. Don't favor having to file them and don't favor having money held back all year just to get it back."

"What about things like roads and schools and police and all those services, are you happy with things in your neighborhood?"

Leroy shrugs.

Suddenly Sammy cuts in. "I have a question," she says. "Please excuse me, I'm just trying to understand how politics works." She turns to Edward and Leroy and addresses them, as a means of apology. "I'm just a visitor here," she says. "I'm not part of the campaign or anything. I'm a newcomer, I don't really know what's going on, I don't know anything about politics at all, this isn't even my dress."

They nod.

"I guess the thing I don't understand with politics," she continues, swiveling to Kurtz, "is, like, whether or not there comes a time to actually, like, do something. Like, there's all this talking all the time, and arguing, and all these questions and all this strategy, and there's the polls and statistics and media and everything, but I don't get how, or when, or even if things actually ever, you know, *happen*?"

Everyone laughs again, in a way that seems to implicate Kurtz, that seems injurious to him. "You're one to talk," he says. "The sum total of what you've accomplished in life is, like, you figured out how to make a fucking sandwich."

But people are still laughing.

"I'm not trying to be funny!" she cries. "I'm honestly curious about how all this talk, how it eventually turns into anything, how it turns into laws or policies or actual physical structures, with people in them, like, living in a different way than they live now. Like, how all this talk about urban strife is going to actually someday transform into a building with people in it, and kids, you know, playing on a playground or something. Because I sort of think, well, I hate to say it but I sort of suspect, well, I think maybe nothing ever changes."

Ben is laughing, has lost his composure, a bit. He's laughing because Sammy has just put into words, in her bumbling fashion, the central question of a longstanding feud he's had with Kurtz. The feud is over whether there is any point getting worked up about social policy, whether things can actually be built and changed, whether it is worth caring or believing or trying. Or whether politics is an endeavor that only distracts the romantic, to the great amusement of the rich, who continue to run things as they like.

"Fuck all of you," Kurtz says. He gets up to use the bathroom and Boris follows. While they are gone Ben reaches furtively into Kurtz's tuxedo pocket and pulls out his address book, slips it into his own pocket. Sammy watches with amazement, slaps his arm. "No way!" she hisses. "Put it back!" But Ben won't look at her, only stares ahead, smiling.

When Kurtz returns, he shifts gears, asking the men which sports teams they root for, what they like to do on weekends, but the spirit has gone out of the room, the mood has changed—it's no longer an adventure. The men stand up to leave, unfold their wallets, deposit bills on the counter. "Goodnight," Leroy says, and looks them over, gives them a two-fingered salute. "Good luck to you." Kurtz jumps up and shakes their hands, offers them his card. "In case you ever need anything from the federal government," he says. "That's my cell number. I hope you'll call me." The men regard the cards, smile, tuck them in their pockets. "Thanks," they say. Amused. They turn and walk out the door, and the bell clangs merrily.

Not a minute later, while Kurtz is shaking the cook down for more information, Sammy tugs at Ben's sleeve. "Thanks for taking me out," she tells him. "I'm just gonna walk back to the dorm. I'm so tired."

And so Ben turns to Kurtz and tells him, "I'm walking Sammy home. I might be a minute."

"It's okay," Sammy says. "I'm fine. It's not far."

"Don't be ridiculous," he tells her. He is not only obligated to walk her home—he lives by a certain code of conduct—but happy to do it. He is tired, and drunk, and stuffed—he could use a walk, maybe a quick nap.

"Don't leave without me," he tells Kurtz. He hands over forty bucks. Because he pays for everything, always.

"You're missing out, man," Kurtz says. "This is going to be legend."

"I have no doubt," Ben says. Striking, he thinks, a note of sincerity, or something close to it.

Outside, they are only a few steps down the sidewalk when Sammy sees two white cards on the ground, and bends down to retrieve them. "Oh," she says. Tenderly. The cards are soggy, and one of them is splattered with mud. "Poor Kurtz."

"Don't feel too bad," Ben tells her. "He knows most people don't keep his cards. He just gives out as many as possible. The shotgun theory of public relations, he calls it. A thousand little pellets, spread all over."

Sammy lets the cards drop, and they flutter back to the ground. "What I don't get," she says, "is how is he still so *awake*."

"Cocaine," Ben explains. "Why do you think he's always disappearing into bathrooms?"

"I don't know. Like, I guess I thought he was using the bathroom?"

"You're adorable," he says.

They walk back to Sammy's dorm, the whole time only encountering one other person, a boy in just khakis and a t-shirt trudging in the opposite direction, a boy so drunk Ben can smell it. They reach the dorm and climb its stairs to her room, which is small and dark and in a state of considerable disarray, with piles of books and clothes all over the floor. Sammy rushes to her bed and plucks up a small teddy bear, shoves it back underneath a pillow.

Then they fall into bed together, pull the blankets over themselves. At first they have their backs to each other but there isn't enough room this way, so Ben rolls over and drapes an arm across her. The sequins of her dress rustle. "Jesus," he says. "Take your dress off. It's like sleeping with a fucking lizard."

She does what he says, first tugging awkwardly at the zipper in the back, squirming out of it inelegantly, then pulling off her hosiery. Now she is just in her underwear. She rolls over to face him, buries her face in his chest, wraps her arm around him, pulls herself closer. He considers kissing her, but something stops him—her body is so slender and childlike. He takes her jaw in his hand and feels two things simultaneously—the urge to protect her, for she is so fragile, and yet also the urge to crush her. He feels that just by squeezing his hand, he could break her jaw. He has never experienced such a strange combination of feelings. He flushes, buries his face in her neck and kisses it, sort of with a smack, the way you'd kiss a baby. "Get some sleep," he says.

In just a minute she is asleep, curled into him with the trust and abandon of a child. Her mouth open. She isn't snoring, exactly, but breathing heavily through her mouth. He made the right choice, he thinks—for it is clear to him now how young she is. Really, she is just a kid.

2011

Sometimes late at night, Ben calls Sammy and asks if she's awake, and even though she isn't—she has fallen asleep in her clothes again, grading papers—she claims to be. "Of course," she says, her voice groggy. "I mean, you're interrupting some gripping reading material here. But for you, anything." These nights, they are usually both too tired to make conversation, so they just turn their TVs to the same station and watch the news together, occasionally venturing a comment or question, but mostly just sitting in companionable silence, watching the footage of the train wreck that is the world.

One night, they are watching CNN together when the news breaks to footage of the president walking down a hallway, head down, a group of men hurrying behind, and that's when Sammy sees him, his unmistakable slouch, his furrowed brow, his unkempt hair. Kurtz. Walking behind the president.

"Holy shit," she says. "It's Kurtz!"

"Yup," says Ben. Casual, unimpressed. As always.

"That was Kurtz!" she says. "He's like, a foot away from Obama!"

"Of course," says Ben. "He's special advisor on the Middle East now. He just replaced the previous guy because the previous guy, well, he killed himself."

"Oh, wow. That's like, that's serious. Boy. I didn't realize Kurtz was so high up in the administration."

"Well, you know what he's like," says Ben. Meaning, she imagines, how much information Kurtz has in his head. He probably knows the names of every major player in every relevant country, plus the names of their wives and children, every sordid detail of their various human rights situations, the leaders of their militias and the rogue groups poised to overthrow them, the names of every dissident and terrorist rotting in every prison in the region and the names of *their* wives and children. Yes, Sammy concludes. Someone like Kurtz would be valuable. Invaluable.

"How is he? Do you still talk to him?"

"Not as often," says Ben. "He's pretty busy these days."

"Right. I guess he would be."

Kurtz is off screen now. But Sammy is still in awe, still fixated on him. Someone she knows is walking a foot behind the president. She is silent for a while, thinking back to that time, the brief stretch of days when she knew Kurtz. She wasn't sure, back then, what would become of him—whether he would claw his way into the White House, or wind up in a locked ward. "Wow," she says again.

They watch a bit longer. The program breaks to a pharmaceutical ad—yet another drug pitched to senior citizens, showing them the kind of life they could have if they only took the time to visit their doctors and ask for a prescription. An older man and woman, dressed in white linen, are walking along a beach, holding hands. The wind is tossing their hair about. The woman points to something out over the water and the husband nods, smiles—they both stare up in delight, as if regarding the majesty of God's face. But then the camera pans back and Sammy sees they are looking at a prop plane, trailing behind it the name of the drug. Yet another pill designed for erectile dysfunction. Sammy flushes. Even though she is older now, and should have outgrown such things, she is still so often overtaken with embarrassment. In this case, she is remembering what happened between her and Ben all those years ago, the last time they tried to have sex, and it is still so painful to her that she turns red. She scrambles to change the subject. "How's your mother?" she asks.

"Okay," Ben says. "Her boyfriend died but she got a new one. I think she met him at the old boyfriend's *funeral*. Some guy named Sherman. *Shermy*, she calls him."

"Ugh," Sammy says. "That's just. I kind of can't. I can't quite imagine her down there. She was such a New Yorker. It doesn't compute. And with *boyfriends*."

"I don't really want to know the details."

"No, no."

"But she keeps making all these allusions. She keeps calling him her lover. Sherman is such an attentive *lover*, such a robust *lover*, that sort of thing."

"Stop!" she says.

"They take long walks on the beach holding hands."

"I have a cramp in my brain." Somehow they are right back where they started—the older couple on the beach. She can't get away from it. "I just can't imagine any of this."

"She keeps trying to get me to visit. You, too—she says to bring you."

This, too, is awkward. Ben's mother was always trying to bring them together. But it hadn't worked out, it just hadn't worked, and now the whole topic of Ben's mother is sort of veiled in disappointment, at least for Sammy. She tries to get away from it.

"I just can't see us down there," she says. They have always been city people, fighting to cross the street, standing in line in stifling, pungent delis. "Like, what would we do? All that fresh air and sunshine. All that happiness and relaxation."

"Well, *somebody* has to do it."

"Just not us."

"Would it kill us?" he asks.

They both think for a minute. Then laugh. "I think it might," she says.

And he agrees. It would probably kill them.

1993

When Sammy and Ben wake a few hours later, the sun is up, and she feels suddenly exposed. She searches for her regular clothes on the floor, jeans and a t-shirt and sweater, sneakers, a giant winter coat, and throws them on quickly. Then she and Ben walk across campus toward the diner, squinting in the bright morning light. They hardly say a word to each other. At one point Ben comments on Thomas Jefferson's architecture—all the brick buildings with white columns, one after another after another. "This place has a serious case of the Harvards," he says, and throws his cigarette on the ground.

Inside the diner it is the same scene all over again, Kurtz and Boris sitting on stools, inclined toward the cook—the first cook has gone off shift and has been replaced with a new one, all the better for Kurtz, who is battering him with the same old questions. Ben sits next to Kurtz, but Sammy just stands in the doorway and watches. As Ben settles on the stool next to Kurtz he turns to Sammy with a questioning look, wondering why she isn't joining, but she just waves and smiles a little. He waits a beat, then seems to understand. He touches his fingers to his mouth, then pushes them toward her, a kiss of sorts. She catches it, then turns and walks out.

This is how she is. Again, she turns the question in her mind: What it is, exactly, that's wrong with me? Being around people—normal people, as she thinks of them—is thrilling to her, until suddenly it isn't and she scrambles off, puts herself into exile. It's something to do with growing up in her father's house, she thinks. She is so used to quiet that she doesn't really know how to be around people.

The whole walk home she worries she's fucked everything up. Ben had driven all the way down here to get her, brought her up to the inaugural ball—and for what? She got drunk and then cried and then fell asleep and then ran off.

Sammy hears a bell toll on the half hour and realizes she is missing her Shakespeare class. Realizes she has forgotten, for twenty-four hours, who she is and what she is supposed to be doing. She rushes toward Cabell Hall. Inside, the foyer resonates with the sound of Martin Luther King's "I Have a Dream" speech—being played for a large class in the auditorium. She slinks through the foyer, feeling as if she is interrupting, as if she has walked into a temple with her shoes on. When she pulls open the door to her classroom, King's voice floods in with her. The Shakespeare professor, who is ranting about Iago, stops and glares at her. "Glad you could join us," he says, probably an insult, though she can't read his expression because she doesn't have her glasses. She slumps into a seat in the back, flushing with shame— she is not only late but doesn't have her books. She tries to look interested, engaged, tries to look like someone who is prepared for class, but then some time later wakes up with her face on her desk.

Back at the dorm, Sammy goes to return the dress and wrap and heels and rhinestones to Lara Gardner, who is excited and wants to hear every detail about the ball.

"It was fine," she says. "Like a high school dance, but for older people." She is doing the thing with her voice again, speaking a bit too slowly, as if communicating is a struggle.

"Did you meet the president?" Lara asks.

"I did," she says. Not at the ball, technically—she is referring to the night in the sandwich shop—but who cares.

"Oh my God," Lara says. "Oh my God. Did you get a picture? Did you get his autograph?"

"I don't really," she says, "I don't really put much stock in these things. I care more about, about how average people are doing. How a president can help working families, and kids, and things like that."

"Oh my God," Lara says. She looks at Sammy with an amazed expression. What Lara thinks she is looking at is a brand of quiet dignity she will hold as an ideal and strive for the rest of her life. *I once knew this deaf girl*, she would tell people, *who had struggled her whole life, not only was she deaf but she was also poor, and yet somehow she had a grace to her, I mean true class, the kind you can't really fake or even learn.* Though what Sammy is really practicing is an absurd pettiness. She wants Lara to feel bad for her relative wealth and privilege. She is enjoying Lara's sympathy, her admiration. She basks in it. Since the previous afternoon in Lara's room, preparing for the ball, when she first pretended to be deaf, when she was first surrounded by so much good will and pity, she'd felt better than she'd felt all year, maybe ever in her life.

"You're a truly exceptional person," Lara says.

"Not at all," she says.

Lara pulls Sammy's glasses off her nightstand and hands them to her. She puts them on, and the world comes into sharp focus. It is too much. She takes them off and doesn't wear them again for a long time.

After Sammy finishes freshman year and leaves the dorm, she will only talk to Lara Gardner once more. One day the following year, as she is sitting alone in the cafeteria—she is always alone, that year, reading—Lara approaches her table. She comes right up and puts a hand on Sammy's shoulder. "I just want you to know," she says, very loudly, "I wish we were friends."

"Oh," Sammy says. "Well, okay."

221

"I try to surround myself with good people. It's important to me to, you know, be around people who inspire me. I hope we can see more of each other. I hope we can be friends."

"Sure," Sammy says. "I'll see you around." She goes back to her book. That year she is toying with the idea of becoming a philosopher, and making her way through Nietzsche's oeuvre. As far as she can tell philosophy involves long stretches of solitude, and eventual derangement brought on by loneliness and poverty. But out of this derangement sometimes come great ideas, and this seems like the only prospect for Sammy, the only occupation for which she might be suited, the only thing for which she might be said to be in training. All of the awkwardness and yearning to fit in she'd felt in her first year at school has fermented, and turned into something else, a simmering hatred for the life and people around her. Lara is the last person she wants to talk to, but Lara will not leave. She wants something more, something Sammy isn't giving her. "It was really nice to see you," she says, and Sammy waves, like: Thanks, but please go away so I can contemplate the death of God.

Sammy watches as Lara walks off, and considers what must be happening in her mind: Lara has reached the outer limits of the people she knows—she can already see where they are going to end up, and it isn't far enough. And so she is trying to find new people. Maybe she thinks Sammy is some kind of dark horse, that she will become someone worth knowing. If it was possible for Bill Clinton, a kid from nowhere, and nothing, to become president, then it might also be possible, by some sort of inverse property, that the kids Lara knows, all those rich kids, aren't going to amount to anything. Maybe the world has changed in such a way that, in order to rise through its ranks, a person has to have suffered first, to have prevailed in a long struggle. Sammy concludes that the way things are going in the world has thrown Lara Gardner into some kind of spiritual crisis. The President of the United States is a former pot smoker and draft dodger. Kurt Cobain is slouching around in his pajamas and cardigan, and kids have made him their hero, pinned up posters of him on their doors. The most popular song of the year is Beck's "Loser," anthem of the downtrodden, ballad of the unskilled and apathetic and unrepentant. Its lyrics are hard to decipher but there is something about a trailer park and something about Cheez Wiz, something about suicide, and then that refrain—*I'm a loser baby, so why don't you kill me*. People are singing it all the time. Why would people sing something like that, Lara must be wondering. She is trying to understand.

Then Sammy won't see Lara again or even think about her for twenty years, until one morning as she is getting her daughter ready for school, and the TV is running in the background, and she's sort of half listening to a story about a short-term loan company that has preyed on and defrauded millions of its customers. "We provide a much-needed service," says the voice, the company's CEO, "to the working poor, providing funds to populations no one else would even consider helping. This lawsuit is a politically motivated *sham* that will end up hurting the poor while helping politicians who only care about their public image." Sammy looks up at the screen recognizes instantly the short, orderly bob and icy blue eyes of Lara Gardner. "We *will* prevail in this lawsuit," Lara says, smiling. "And America will thank us."

A few days after the ball, someone comes knocking on Sammy's door again, saying she has a phone call in the lobby. The whole scene repeats itself from the inaugural morning, with all kinds of imagined tragedies presenting themselves as she descends the stairs. When she reaches the lobby the scene is the same as before, a group of kids watching MTV. "Hello?" she says, convinced this time maybe someone really is dead.

"You need a phone," says Ben.

"Oh," she says. "Hi."

"I can't get you on this line," he says. "Half the time no one answers."

"Right," she says. "Sorry."

"And then the other half, except for this once, people answer but they have no idea who you are. I'm running out of ways to describe you. No one there is familiar with the comedic awkwardness of Carol Burnett."

"You have to ask for the deaf girl," she confesses. "People think I'm deaf."

"You're kidding me."

"I'm not. I don't know how it happened."

"That's fucked up."

Sammy is nervous and can't think of anything to say.

"You there?" Ben asks.

"Sorry," she says. "I didn't hear you. I'm like eighty-percent deaf."

"Jesus Christ," he says. Laughs.

Then Ben tells Sammy a story about the ride home, how halfway between Charlottesville and D.C., Boris was driving while Kurtz was trying to get some sleep in the passenger seat, and just as Kurtz was drifting off he reached into his pocket, sort of the way a kid reaches for a security blanket, and found his address book missing and had gone berserk, insisting Boris turn the car around, which of course Boris refused to do, and they'd fought about it, screaming profanities, and Kurtz kept jerking at the wheel and covering Boris's face with his hands until Boris grabbed Kurtz's briefcase phone, somehow steering with his knees and simultaneously rolling down his window, and he held the briefcase out the window, telling Kurtz he was going to drop the fucking phone right on the fucking road if Kurtz didn't fucking let it go, and somehow in all the commotion the alarm started again, and Ben sat and watched from the back seat laughing, thinking how this was the end of the line for him, the perfect way to end his novel, two psychopaths ready to rule the world, fighting one another for supremacy.

"So that's it," says Ben. "That's how the book ends. The fate of Kurtz's briefcase phone hanging in the balance. All I have to do now," he says, "is write it." He says he has a writing schedule, eight hours a day. He'll be done in six weeks.

Then med school will start, and he'll be busy again. But, he says, he wants to keep in touch. "You should visit some weekend," he says. "Come up to the city sometime. I'll show you around."

"Okay," she says. "Sure."

"We'll talk soon," he says. "Let's just agree to call each other. I left you my card."

"Right." She remembers finding the card on top of her dresser, with the number of Ben's pager service embossed in black.

"You're not going to call, are you?"

"I'll call," she says. But he is right—Sammy is thinking even then how she won't, how she will most likely lose the card, either by accidentally throwing it away or sticking it in a book for safekeeping, but then losing track of it. She is the opposite of Kurtz, she thinks, destined to lose the one number she wants to keep track of.

"It's really not a big deal, Sam," he says. "I don't want to marry you. I just want to keep in touch, know what you're doing. Help you out if you need it. It's what people do."

"Right," she says. "Okay. I know. Thanks." But what she's thinking is: Is this really what people do? She doesn't know how any of this works.

A week later a package arrives for her and she tears it

open recklessly, right in the mail room—it is the first package she has ever received. Inside the package is a telephone and three hundred dollars in cash. There is a note. *Hook this up*, it says. *Page me with your new number*. Also inside is Kurtz's address book. *For safekeeping*, Ben has written. *Be sure to call the Kennedy compound now and then, just for kicks*. One night, quite late, after Sammy finishes a paper on Robert Lowell and is feeling wistful about old New England money, she calls the Kennedy house and lets it ring. She imagines a black rotary ringing on a small antique table in a dark hallway, a shrill noise going through the place, the place where Bobby and Jack and Teddy had grown up and returned, as powerful men, for vacations with their own families. It is still winter, and there is probably no one there—she imagines the couches covered with sheets, the shades drawn, mice scurrying in the walls. She imagines the halls echoing with the ringing of the phone, and beneath that, so faint it is almost indiscernible, what Ben had described in Kurtz's car—the still-resonating echoes of the Kennedy boys as children, their footfall as they came running in from their sailing adventures and football games. She imagines their voices—that accent she knows so well—calling to each other, yelling at each other. She imagines the voices of their mother and their maids, calling them down to dinner, telling them to wash their hands and their faces, to change their clothes, to make themselves ready for what the world expected of them. A chill goes through her.

Ben calls every week, always at strange hours, two or three in the morning, and he is almost always drunk—she can tell because when he is drunk, he talks so freely. Sammy lies in bed, barely awake, and listens to him talk about what Kurtz and Boris are doing. Kurtz is working advance for Ron Brown, and Boris, through mysterious connections of his parents, has secured a spot in the White House. Ben has recently done some digging and discovered that Boris is actually massively wealthy, despite the front he put on, the stories of his harsh Communist upbringing, all that bullshit about his blue-collar family. His membership in the Democratic party, Ben says—his credentials as someone who identifies with suffering—are forged. "Which I knew all along," he says. There are so many things about being rich, Sammy thinks, that only the rich know about and recognize. While it is possible for poor people—for her and Kurtz—to overlook them, Ben no doubt recognized at once who and what Boris was. There is a bitterness when Ben mentions Kurtz, how he and Boris are living together, how he never calls anymore. Ben is about to start medical school, and will soon be surrounded with new people, new interests, but for the moment he is wounded, lonely. It occurs to Sammy that Ben might only be calling her because he tried Kurtz first, and couldn't get ahold of him.

Sammy keeps that phone for years—all through college and graduate school and into her thirties, until the world gives up on landlines—and all that time Ben is practically the only person who calls her. Over time they speak less and less of Kurtz and Boris—of the people and circumstances that drew them together. As Sammy progresses through college she becomes the person Ben calls when important things happen in the world. She picks up the phone and he says: *Can you believe it?*, referring to some event of global or national significance—Blackhawks down in Mogadishu, Waco, Oklahoma City, Vince Foster's suicide, the peace accord between Rabin and Arafat, tsunamis in Japan, the passing of NAFTA, Rabin's assassination, the reemergence of Tsongas's cancer and his subsequent death.

In the early years, Sammy never knows what Ben is talking about. She doesn't have a television or a radio in her room and doesn't read the newspaper—her head is always buried in a novel or philosophical tract—and when Ben calls she either hasn't heard the news or, if she has heard, it has barely penetrated her consciousness. *I can't believe it,* she says, automatically, though most of the time she doesn't know what it was she is professing not to believe. Ben sees through her, chastises her for not living in the world or caring about it. *I do!* she says. *The world is, like, really important to me. I just happened to miss the paper this morning.* Then she goes off to class and criticizes her peers—silently, smugly—for not knowing what has happened in the world, for sitting and talking about the parties they attended. *People are dying,* she thinks. *But go ahead and talk about how drunk you were Saturday.*

Of course, they talk about Clinton. Probably more than anyone or anything else. They love watching him fall into and wriggle out of various scandals—love both the flaws that get him into trouble, and the skill he deploys to get out. Since that night in the sandwich shop Sammy has felt a strange connection to him, and she is always remarking on it to Ben. There are a number of instances in which Clinton seems to betray the very people who elected him, turns his back on the characters whose poverty and desperation he claimed to share, to understand, to remember. Whenever she sees him taking questions—on the giant screens in the student union, or the bar televisions in the restaurant where she waits tables—she stops and stares, recognizing a guilty look in his eye, and she feels a kinship with him. She takes up his side in debates, the kind people are always having in classrooms those days. "It's about integrity," another student says. "It's about loyalty. It's about character." And she says, "It's about the job." She thinks of Clinton as someone who is just trying to get things done while people take shots at him, grab at his ankles, bitch and moan about everything he does—all because he came from nothing, because he didn't strike them as presidential. Give him a break, she thinks. Maybe he lied a little, maybe he cheated. Maybe he didn't make good on all his promises. Maybe he threw a few of his friends under a few oncoming busses. So what?

In her own version of this narrative, Sammy cannot shake the feeling that she has betrayed her father. The longer she stays in school, the more esoteric her studies—the farther she falls down the rabbit hole of literary theory, poetry, philosophy—the stranger she becomes, until she is at last a stranger to herself and the life she came from. Over the years she finds it more and more difficult to return home. Eventually she visits only once a year, just a few days at Christmas, and she spends the whole time in a desperate, clawing mood. The air that fills the house is stifling, heavy with accumulated failure. It is as if the house has died and a blanket has been draped over it. Every surface has gone soft, slicked over with the grease risen from the stove, and with the steam from the radiators, then layered over with dust.

Every year, on her way out of town, Sammy passes the former Bobbi's Hollywood Café. Not quite a year after Sammy graduated college, Bobbi Woolworth had killed herself. She had crawled into bed, naked, and taken a bottle of sleeping pills. Supposedly she had left a note saying it was too hard to keep up anymore, that she wanted to be released from the effort life required her to make; the little shop with her name on it had failed, she wrote, failed to satisfy her need to see her name in lights. Sammy passes Bobbi's and wonders if this is the nature of things: Ruin. Or if it is just the nature of things for some people, some places.

All these years later, she still thinks about that night at Bobbi's, with Bill Clinton and the chicken salad, all the time. She has made a little diorama—a miniature sandwich shop, its tables and its deli case, with miniature figures interacting—and set it on the mantelpiece of her mind, enshrined it. How often she stands before it and stares, considers the angles. She calculates the probability of Clinton walking through the door. Of all the sandwich shops in all the world.

She sometimes thinks, too, that the clanging of that little bell announced not only the moment of Clinton's arrival onto her personal stage, but also the world's, because by all accounts he won that election by walking through every single door of every single shop in every single city, and so that little bell clanging was the opening note of the song that had been playing ever since. Initially that sound was what people wanted to hear, it was what the country loved about him—he was a real person who walked the same streets regular people did. But in that bell, too, was the call to arms for the other side, the machine that would drown it out—the grinding of the wheels of the printing presses, the newspapers and gossip magazines that would generate the investigation of Whitewater, of Paula Jones, of Monica Lewinsky, that would crank out the Starr report, that would impeach the president. And you could take it even further, Sammy often thought, if you wanted to. It might be said that the only reason we later elected Bush was to undo our electing Clinton, to restore what was presented as dignity to the office, to undo whatever sins we perceived the Clintons to have committed. And from that colossal fuck-up, you might also say, came everything after, all the calamity and atrocity of war. In a sense, you could say that what started with a bell, musically, escalated and evolved, was laid over with the churning of the presses, then crescendoed into bombs and machine gun fire and the slamming shut of the cells of Guantanamo, the desperate gasps of the water-boarded, the clicking shutters of the cameras at Abu Ghraib, the veterans home from war putting bullets through their skulls, the mad buzzing of fleets of drones, a total calamity.

Yes, Sammy often thinks, you could say that if you wanted to. If you were the kind of person who thought about these things, thought about them perhaps too much. If you were the kind of person who looked at the world and wondered what had happened to it. If you believed in cause and effect—believed things could be considered, decoded, explained.

"This isn't a novel," Ben reminds Sammy, whenever she tries to string these narratives together. "Things aren't going to necessarily work out in the end. The good guys might not win, the bad guys might get away with it. Whatever dramatic irony you're seeing is purely coincidental. There's no author here."

"I know," she tells him. "You're right." But she keeps spinning tales, weaving webs. Believing there is some design to it all—something to be deciphered and understood. She persists in believing there is a solution to be found, a true path. She can't help it. She's read too many books.

1993

Ben and his two partners are standing around their station in the anatomy lab. The room is more hostile than Ben anticipated, the air bitterly cold, the lighting harsh. And the smell, the choking smell of formaldehyde and phenol, is so potent Ben struggles to breathe. He closes his eyes. Counts to ten. This is what he does when he thinks he is about to puke.

"Remember," their professor says. The professor is making his way around the room, weaving through the tables. Probably enjoying himself. Because everyone in the room—these rich kids, these future doctors—is afraid. "Your first order of business is to name your cadaver. This is the first step in developing the respectful and sacred relationship with the human being who donated his body for your edification."

Ben opens his eyes, regards the table in front of him, the cadaver zipped in a black bag. Students at other stations have already revealed their bodies. At one station, even, they have begun turning the body prone, to start their dissection. But Ben is just standing there. He is still queasy.

Ben has been paired with two lab partners, Annie and Annie Two. They are both blond and small, the kind of girls who wear full makeup to class, who go clacking around in high heels. "Oh my God," Annie says. "I don't think I can handle this."

"Oh my God, me neither," says Annie Two.

No help there. They are both looking at Ben.

"Can you, like, do everything?" Annie says, clasping her hands together under her chin, using the voice of a child. "Please, oh pretty please?"

"Please, please, please," says Annie Two, jumping up and down a little. "We'll be your best friends."

He gives them a cutting look. "Can you at least think of a name?" he asks.

"We need to see him first," says Annie.

"We can't very well name him without looking at him," says Annie Two.

Ben has no idea what he is about to find—the students have been given nothing more than the age, race, and sex of their cadaver. In this case, they have before them a fifty-seven-year-old African American male. What he was like in life, why he donated his body to science—or if he didn't expressly donate it, how it wound up in an anatomy lab—none of this is known.

Ben unzips the bag, pulls away the sides, then pulls back a sheet to reveal the head. He is shocked by the man's skin, which is not brown but gray and chalky-looking. Ben pulls the sheet down further, past the man's shoulders, which are thin and bony, delicate. Then further, to reveal his torso. A tattoo arches across the man's heart, a single word in a delicate, looping script: *Mother*. This man before him, he was a man who loved his mother.

"Benjy," says Annie. When no one responds, she follows up with: "No, that's not quite right. Maybe, maybe Buddy?"

"No," says Annie Two. "He's too old to be a Buddy."

"True," says Annie.

They think for a moment.

"Hermy!" says Annie.

"He totally looks like a Hermy," says Annie Two.

"Hermy it is," says Ben, snidely. He surges with hatred for the Annies. He hates them so much he considers dropping out of medical school right then and there, just to punish them.

He closes his eyes again, collects himself.

Then he opens his eyes, and then there is nothing left between him and the job that needs doing.

When the lab is over, and Ben is undressing in the locker room, he peels off his gloves directly into a trash can, as he's been instructed to do, but somehow, something wet leaps up and splashes his cheek. "Fuck," he says.

This, Ben thinks on the walk home, this awful ritual of dissecting a body, is why no one really talks much about medical school. Both of his parents went, and hardly ever spoke of it. They just sent him along, let him find out for himself.

Well, now he knows.

It takes them all semester to dissect the body. Lab is once a week, on Friday afternoons, and Ben finds himself, as each week progresses, growing heavy with dread. *I didn't know it would be like this*, is the phrase that keeps going through his mind. Sometimes he goes further, asks himself: *Well, what did you expect?* And answers: *I don't know. I have no idea, actually. But not this.* Nothing about the body is quite what he expected. There are so many surprises. The aorta, for instance, is stronger than he thought, tougher, like a garden hose. And the brain is so delicate. The brain is the body's most important structure and yet it has the fewest defenses. You can slice right through it. Untold millions of lives have been destroyed by relatively minor injuries to the brain. Something goes wrong even with the lining, which is somehow tough and flimsy at the same time, and forget it. Lights out. End of story.

Ben leaves the lab every Friday and heads straight home to shower. He walks, for the fresh air, hoping to dilute the smell of the lab. But in little gusts, the smell rises up and envelops him—it is like he is being haunted. Often he considers Herman, as he calls him, for he refuses to call him Hermy: Who he was, what his life was like, and the unlikely fact that their lives have converged in this exceedingly strange manner. He knows nothing of Herman's life, beyond what can be discerned from his body. The joints in his hands, which are deformed from arthritis, perhaps brought on by repetitive labor. And the tattoo, of course. The tattoo gets him every time.

Even after a shower, Ben can still smell Herman. Faintly. Ben thinks, in some way, it will follow him the rest of his life. He feels his life has changed in a way he can hardly explain, only that there is everything before Herman, and everything after. The point is, knowing all this about the body—its frailty, its inevitable decline, what it looks like in death, how *utterly devoid of life it is*—puts a barrier between you and other people. Because you understand this frailty now so intimately, and other people don't. That's what doctors never tell you about medical school. That's why they don't tell you. You think you're signing up to help people, but in the end, a screen comes down between you.

Ben needs to talk all of this through. He can't talk to his father, who would only tell him to tough it out, deal with it. Plus, since retiring, his father is down in Florida most of the time. And Ben can't tell his mother, quite—they simply like to enjoy themselves together, eating dinner, sharing a bottle of wine, watching TV. Neither one of them wants to ruin that by talking about medicine. He could talk with his fellow med students, but they all seem too young to him. And overly confident in their views—they are simultaneously ignorant and yet sure of themselves. Whenever he hears them talking, it is never about anything meaningful. He once had to endure a thirty-minute conversation between Annie and Annie Two about a Coach handbag. He tries Kurtz, but Kurtz is always running around, in a different city every time he calls, it seems. "What's cracking?" Kurtz says, when he answers the phone these days. And Ben isn't quite in the mood. Kurtz hits a different note with him, now.

What Ben needs is someone who will listen to him talk about his week, and then offer him a bit of encouragement, or some pleasant distraction. So he calls Sammy. She's always there, always interested in what he has to say. Impressed with his observations. Duly horrified and amazed, as the case dictates. "Hermy?" she'd said, when he told her about his lab mates and their cadaver. "*Hermy?!*"

And then, she always has some little surprise in store, some pleasant distraction. "I set aside this poem," she tells him, "because it reminded me of you." She reads out these lines as if they are all that matters in the world, as if they matter at all. *They say the more sin hath increast in the world*, she reads to him one night, *the more grace has been caused to abound*. He listens to her read it, and feels happy, in a way—perhaps the way parents feel when they watch their children discover something, the first time they notice a rainbow, or score a goal, or taste a plum. None of it matters, really, but it's a pleasure to watch someone think it does. That's what Sammy is like, always trembling with the excitement of some discovery. He loves this about her.

And Sammy is in love with him, he can tell. She can never quite hide how happy she is when he calls. Mostly, he thinks, it's harmless—it's good for a girl her age to have someone to love, someone safe. But he is careful to keep things under control. Now and then, he says something a bit cold, asks her if she's found a boyfriend, or mentions the name of a girl he works with, even though he doesn't really date these days. What he does most often, to keep a bit of distance between them, is add a little flourish, a touch of Casablanca charm, to the end of their calls. "Goodnight, kid," he always says. He doesn't want her getting carried away.

2011

One morning Ben arrives at the office to find that his first patient has cancelled. Instead of catching up on paperwork, or any number of other things he should be doing, he props his feet on his desk and opens up the newspaper. He still enjoys reading an actual paper, taking cover behind it, disappearing for a while.

He flips, flips. Reads a few sentences of each article. Runs his eyes across the advertisements. Takes a stab at the crossword. Then, in Science, he comes across a neuroscience piece about aging and the perception of time, and he reads it straight through. The younger brain, the article explains, during its teens and twenties, records everything it experiences in a kind of high definition. Which is why we remember exactly what we were wearing, and exactly what we said, during so many key scenes from our younger years. And why time, in one's teens and twenties, seems so expansive. Why life can seem like such a long sentence, practically endless.

Then our brains change, he reads. Somewhere in our twenties, we stop recording in such high definition. Sometimes we barely record at all. Maybe because we've seen it all before. There is so little that is new, so little that surprises us, compels us to remember. So we're more forgetful, less intense. This isn't all bad, the article notes—it's not entirely about loss. We become better able to put events in perspective. We understand that dramatic events, both good and ill, pass and diminish. We achieve equilibrium. We make peace.

Then we forget everything, and we die.

Ben feels as if he has come across the explanation for a phenomenon he has been troubled by of late: Nothing he does or says or witnesses, now that he is past forty, seems to make any impression on him. He meets perfectly charming people all the time—smart people, funny people, extraordinarily good-looking people—but even before the initial introductions are finished, their names have floated away. He has categorized everyone, and dismissed them, because he knows already what becomes of each type: the ambitious people will fly too high and then crash to the ground, the beautiful people will fall into the water gazing at their own reflections. What this article has brought to light is that the friendships of Ben's youth were forged in a blazing fire, full of mystery and possibility, the kind of fire that consumed him, and this is why they have endured. Whereas now, there is nothing to excite him, compel him—only weak sparks. You can't go home again, is the message.

He is so taken with this article that he clips it from the paper, tucks it away.

Later that morning, he finds the article online and emails it to Sammy. That evening, she writes him back: Oh my God. That article was horrifying. Basically we're just skimming across the surface for the rest of our lives. It's all just sand through the hourglass. Nothing is ever, like, going to matter to us again. I guess we're stuck with each other.

And he writes her back: What article?

1993-98

In the early years of their friendship, Sammy visits Ben on spring and winter breaks, and he serves as her tour guide, taking her all over New York, to all the tourist traps he hasn't visited since childhood. They have lunch at the Russian Tea Room, go ice skating at Rockefeller Center, watch The Rockettes. They wind through the Guggenheim, stand in front of the terrifying T. rex at the Natural History museum, behold the Vermeers at the Frick. He takes her to her first musical, *Phantom of the Opera*, and her first Broadway play, *The Producers*. All of this with a slightly bored affect, as if indulging a child. Which she is, basically. Sammy is still in so many ways a child. She has never seen anything and has never been anywhere. The sum total of what she knows about the world is now to Ben's credit.

Sammy's favorite thing to do in the city is walk. They leave Ben's apartment and he tells her to pick a direction, any direction, and then they let themselves be swept up in the crowds of people moving down the sidewalk. They wander for a few blocks, stick their heads inside a shop or a garden, a church, a fire station. They take so many turns, right and left and right again, left and right and left, that she loses all sense of direction. But Ben is never lost. They'll be in the thick of it, surrounded by tall buildings, and all of a sudden he will point, and here comes a park, or a plaza, some wonder arising from seemingly out of nowhere. Once, winding through streets, they suddenly come upon the Empire State Building, and Sammy throws her head back so she can see it. Her mouth is wide open. "Please," says Ben. "You're going to get us mugged."

Sammy is used to Ben doing everything in terms of navigating the city. But one night they are standing on a street corner and he instructs her to reach up. "Like you're picking a hanger off the rail in your closet." She does what he says. "Now raise up your index finger," he says, and she does. "And kind of wave it a bit." She does, not quite sure she is doing it right, but within a few seconds a cab drifts toward them and stops in front of them, and Ben opens its door for her. "Congratulations," he says, "you hailed your first cab."

One year, early on, they attend the Macy's Thanksgiving Day parade, and stand shoulder to shoulder—it is so cold that year—watching Snoopy and Woodstock fly overhead, and Sammy has, for the first time, the experience of finally seeing something in person she had only seen before on television. A peculiar feeling comes over her—that she is at last, after all these years, a real person. She and Ben stand with their arms around each other, their heads flung back. Her chest feels like it might split open. She thinks of that James Wright line—*if I stepped out of my body I would break into blossom.* James Wright had recorded this feeling after an experience with the natural world, when a pony approached him and nuzzled his palm, and Sammy is feeling it now, standing with Ben, watching a giant Snoopy balloon fly overhead. But whatever, she thinks. Whatever.

By far the most startling thing about New York is the experience of being part of a family. Ben lives with his mother, and so when Sammy visits him she becomes, temporarily at least, part of the Rosenberg clan. Ben's mother looks almost exactly like him—or rather, Sammy supposes, he looks nearly exactly like her. But because she knew Ben first, or perhaps because the features Ben and his mother share are more befitting of a man, Sammy thinks of Ben's mother as an altered version of him, basically Orson Welles with different accessories, Orson Welles in long, flowing black robes and pearl chokers. Orson Welles with a red mouth, with a shiny black bob.

The first time they meet, when Ben presents Sammy to his mother at a restaurant, she stands and takes Sammy's face in her hands, kisses her from cheek to cheek, once, twice, three times. "Mwah, mwah, mwah," she says. "I'm always so happy to meet one of Benny's friends."

"Benny!" Sammy thinks. "Benny!"

All through dinner that night, and many thereafter, Ben's mother has a way of including Sammy in circles and conversations she in fact knows nothing about. "You know how Uncle Leo is," she says, rolling her eyes at Sammy in an expression of collusion, though Sammy in fact has no idea how Uncle Leo is, in which particular way he is unbearable. But she just goes along. Yes. Uncle Leo is being Uncle Leo again.

Ben's parents are, by the time Sammy enters the picture, living apart, his father having more or less permanently retired to their place in Florida. Though separated, the mother and father talk on the phone every day, sometimes three or four times in a single evening. The mother puts the phone on speaker, ups the volume so the whole apartment resonates with their conversations, which are shockingly loud and acrimonious. Never before in her life has Sammy heard people speak to one another in this way. "I *told* you," says the mother. "That's what I've been *telling* you. You don't *listen!*"

"I swear to God," says the father. "I swear to God." The father's voice is hoarse, crackled, perhaps damaged from yelling his way through their entire marriage.

In the early years of her life with the Rosenbergs, Sammy assumes Ben's parents are on the verge of a divorce. But then no, she finally realizes, this is just their marriage. Just marriage in general. She doesn't know anything about it because she's never really seen it.

She's never really seen it, a family. The first night she stays at the apartment, Ben's mother makes up the spare room, a small office with an iron daybed. She makes up the bed with flower-patterned sheets and a matching bedspread, leaves a glass of water by the bedside. When Sammy says she's tired and going to bed, Ben's mother makes a big deal of showing her to her room and turning down the bedspread, fluffing the pillows. "Here," she says. "Here. Try it. Lie down. See how nice?" She pulls the covers over Sammy, tucks them under her chin. "See how comfortable?" Sammy's eyes well with tears. Because it is indeed comfortable. And because she can't remember the last time she was fussed over. Ben's mother kisses her on the forehead, turns out the light. Sammy can't ever remember being tucked in but something in her body seems to recall the sensation. Her own mother must have done it, all those years ago.

Sammy comes to love Ben's mother. Loves sitting at the kitchen island watching her cook. She is always up to her elbows in something, sticking her hands up carcasses—partridges? Cornish hens?—stuffing their body cavities, tying their little legs together with string. Or she's making a roast of some kind, rubbing spices into a cut of meat. One time, her hands slick with fat, Ben's mother touches Sammy's neck, puts her hands around it in a strangling gesture. "That neck," she says. "I'd kill for that neck." Whereupon Sammy notices that Ben's mother doesn't really have a neck—she is so short and squat that her head just sort of rests on her shoulders.

Ben's mother is always pressing bills into his hand, money with which to entertain Sammy. "Here," she says, "take this, have a nice time, treat yourselves." The mother lords over and underwrites all those years they spend together, all through college and grad school, and then even more school, straight through their twenties. They never quite escape his mother, never stop being her children.

When they are alone, out of the apartment, Sammy teases Ben. "Benny!" she calls him. Pinches his cheek. He brushes her hand away, a bit riled—he is probably always being teased about his mother's love for him. "I didn't know," she says once, "all this time I didn't know you were a *Mama's* boy!"

"Don't," he says, cutting her off. She has angered him. Truly angered him for the first time.

"Sorry," she says. And then a bit later, "I'm just jealous." Which is true. All she ever wanted in life was a mother like this. If given the chance, she would fall down at his mother's feet in a pile of tears and beg to be loved. She would marry Ben immediately if he ever asked, if only to have a mother like his.

It is Ben's mother, finally, who asks Ben the question Sammy has been wondering about since the night of the inaugural ball. "What *is* it with you two?" she asks him one night, as they are finishing dinner—Chinese takeout in front of the television. The spring break of her senior year of college, just before graduation. "Are you together, or what?"

"Jesus, Ma," Ben says.

"Can't I ask a question?" she says. "It seems like a perfectly reasonable question." And though this is exactly what Sammy has been thinking for years, she is embarrassed to hear it spoken out loud. She sinks down into the couch.

"Oy," Ben says, in a tone he uses only with his mother—a particularly aggrieved Yiddish. It's part of a little play they are always putting on—her nagging, his protests.

"All I'm saying," she says, "is that two young people who get along, and who look good together, what's the *issue*?"

Ben gets up from the couch, walks off toward the kitchen. They can hear him dumping the rest of his food in the trashcan. "I told you," he calls from the kitchen, "I'm never getting married."

"Don't you dare say that," his mother calls back.

A bit later, Ben and Sammy leave for a movie—it is a warm night and they are walking to the theater. "Sorry about my mother," Ben says. "All her friends have grandchildren. She's obsessed."

"Oh," Sammy says. "It's no problem. I get it. Mothers are like, I guess they're like that."

A beat later she ventures: "So you never want to get married? Like, ever? Or were you just trying to drive her crazy?"

"I don't know," he says. "I kind of doubt it. Let's just say it's getting harder to imagine."

"Oh," she says. "Well, I get that." Often it has occurred to Sammy that she is deformed in some way, some way that makes her incompatible with others.

"Despite certain appearances, I'm just a very private person," Ben says.

And even though Sammy understands, is in fact the same, she feels deflated. Ashamed somehow. Why? she wonders. What is this?

She tries to recover. "I'm from a long line of like, pathologically guarded people." She tells him about one of her father's favorite quotes, which he'd written out on an index card and stuck to the refrigerator with a magnet. She could still call it to mind, in her father's cramped handwriting. "I hold this to be the highest task of a bond between two people," she says. "That each should stand guard over the solitude of the other."

"Rilke," Ben says. Warming. He loves nothing more than identifying the source of a quote.

"Was that Rilke?" she says. "All this time I thought it was Jerry Lewis."

He laughs, turns to her. She has won him back. So often it is like this for her. A tense game, the spaces in their conversations like held breath. She watches her favor, her fate, all her little wagers dance along the roulette wheel, bouncing and spinning. This time landing safe.

They go out to a movie. Tom Hanks plays an astronaut whose safe return to earth is imperiled. "*Excellent*," Ben says, as they leave the theater. "Tom Hanks is really an *excellent* actor."

And Sammy laughs. "Okay!" she says. "I surrender! He's *excellent*!"

They are having a good time again. Careless, happy, the little episode from before well behind them now. The night is warm and they enjoy walking. Sammy doesn't know quite where they are—she never really does—and is surprised when Ben takes her hand and pulls her toward a doorway, the entrance to a hotel. The Carlyle, it says on the awning, black with gold script, beautiful.

A doorman holds the door for them and they walk through the lobby, black and white, elegant. A concierge nods to Ben, as if familiar with him. He pulls her along—he knows just where he is going—to a bar, smallish, dimly lit, with a high-backed maroon booth running along the perimeter of the room. Above the booth, the walls are painted amber, and covered in childish sketches. The drawings seem familiar, somehow. Sammy regards a gathering of animals, all wearing suits, sitting around a table, having an outdoor luncheon. "This is *adorable*," she says. Ben points, directs her attention to another drawing—twelve school girls in blue dresses, marching in two lines before a nun. Sammy remembers the image, from the Madeleine books she had read as a child.

"He painted the whole room," Ben tells her. "In exchange, they let him live in the hotel while he worked."

They sit and have a drink, and Ben tells her more about The Carlyle, its history, the celebrities who have been known to stay there. "You never know who you'll see," he says. "Jackie O. used to eat lunch here once a week."

"Like, right here in this bar?"

"Sometimes," he says.

Sammy is struck by the notion she might be sitting in the very same spot as Jacqueline Kennedy. A dizzy feeling comes over her. So much of the world has always been obscured to her, and whenever she is let in on one of its secrets, she feels dizzy—a feeling she has only ever felt with Ben.

They finish their drinks, and Ben excuses himself for a moment. When he returns, he pulls Sammy by the hand. Unusual, this gesture, this force, but she follows along. In the lobby, he surprises her by stopping at the elevator. Presses the button. The elevator arrives and the door swings open, and they step inside. She has no idea what is happening. Maybe he's just taking her to a high floor, to show her the view. Maybe there's some kind of restaurant up there, or pool. Or maybe not.

They float up, and the door opens, and he leads her down the hallway to a room. And she finds herself wondering again: What is this?

The room is dark, lit only by a shaft of light coming through the imperfectly drawn curtains. She can see the outline of a bed, a desk, a chair. He pulls her into the room, pulls her close. He holds her head in his hand—one hand cradles the back of her head, the other takes up her jaw. He kisses her. She falls into him. Then he is pulling up on her shirt, and they are each taking off each other's clothes in a frenzy. Shoes and socks, shirt and jeans. He slides off her underwear, then his.

The sex isn't, she supposes, even while it is still happening, anything terribly special. He stares at her while he moves, keeps her jaw clasped in his hand, and she holds his gaze, and briefly there is something between them, a direct line, and then it breaks, and he closes his eyes, his head falls onto her shoulder, he collapses onto her, and that's it. It is nothing much different from the scenes she's seen played out in countless movies. But it is special to her, her first time.

They are both embarrassed after. She pulls the blankets over her, and he smokes a cigarette with a casual flair that seems studied. They don't speak. After a while he gets up and gets dressed, and she does the same, and they leave the hotel and walk back to his apartment, where they part ways—his bedroom is off past the living room, hers is in the other direction, and that is all there is to it, their first time together.

After that, they don't mention it. And when she visits again, the first two nights are the usual routine, staying in the apartment. But the third, the night before she leaves, they go to The Carlyle again. They are better this time, slower, shifting through different positions, but after, they are embarrassed again in a way she can't describe—maybe because they've known each other for so long. They walk back to the apartment in silence. Holding hands for a bit. But then, one of them or the other, it is too subtle to really discern, lets go, and they are just friends, walking side by side, Ben and Sammy, same as it ever was.

They do this again and again. All through her master's degree. A little routine, a cycle of anguish and thrill. What does it mean? Sammy wonders. She wants nothing more than to know what it means. For the fog surrounding this question to lift. But she never asks, sensing that if she did, it would ruin things between them—that the only reason Ben keeps her around is precisely because she doesn't ask this type of question.

Then, finally, things come into focus.

It is March, the final weekend of Sammy's spring break, and she takes the train up to New York, just for an overnight. Ben meets her at Grand Central and tells her, first thing, he is taking her somewhere. They catch a cab and Ben tells the driver to take them to the World Trade Center. Though she has seen them from afar, Sammy has never been to the towers, and when she emerges from the cab she is shocked—somehow it is still possible to be shocked in this city—by their size. She is awestruck, though not quite in a delighted way. A bit of terror runs through her.

"This is the best view in the city," Ben tells her, putting his hand on her back, shepherding her along in that gentle way of his, which she can never resist.

In the elevator, they are pushed to the back, crowded by a group of young tourists—high school kids, all wearing the same letter jackets. The backs of the jackets are embroidered with their school mascot, a swirling tornado. The Topeka Twisters, they're called. The kids are all inordinately large, Sammy thinks—broad-shouldered, big-boned—and they are unbelievably loud, without a trace of self-awareness. They don't seem to realize, or care, that there are other people in the world. "Dude," one kid says to another. "Dude, when we get to the top, all I'm saying is you better watch your back." The kid pushes his friend, and the friend stumbles forward, into an older woman. Sammy wants desperately out of the elevator but it is taking a long time—they are riding to the observation deck. The Top of the World, Ben calls it.

"This might not be the best time to tell you this," Sammy says, "but I'm like, terrified of heights."

"Really?" he says. "I don't think I knew that. You never mentioned it."

"It's like, a textbook phobia situation. I might not be able to walk around out there."

"Just give it a try," he says. "It's an experience you won't forget. It's unlike anything else in the world."

"The thing is, I think I might throw up."

"You won't."

"But, my dignity." She is always worried about her dignity. She would never recover from something like throwing up in public.

"Just think of this like aversion therapy. It will be good for you."

The doors open, and they are carried along by the Twisters out onto the foyer and then, through its doors to the terrace. It is a sunny day, the sky a brilliant blue, streaked with only a few wisps of clouds. The wind is strong. Sammy's hair goes flying all over, and she struggles to contain it—concerned with her dignity again, which is always coming unleashed, skittering away. She gathers it all up into a fist and then twists it into a knot.

Ben puts his hand on her back again, and they inch around the terrace, regard the river, the bridges stretching across it. From this height, all the other buildings in the city, even the tall ones, look like buildings children have constructed with Legos. Ben nudges Sammy along, and they weave through small groups of tourists, clusters of people speaking French, Russian, Mandarin. "This might be the very pinnacle of humanity," Ben says. "One of the greatest testaments of man's achievement here on Earth." His voice is resonant, the way he makes it when he's feeling something, when he's in love with the world.

"I'm having more of an Icarus feeling about humanity," Sammy says. She is taking the smallest steps. Practically shuffling.

"What are you afraid of?" he asks.

"Falling," she says.

They are both giving each other the same look of utter incomprehension: What are you, crazy?

"This is as great as any temple," he says. "Any cathedral."

"I'm not saying it isn't." She is creeping along, clinging to his arm. "I'm just saying, it takes a fair amount of hubris to build a temple."

By now they have walked right up to the edge, which is too much for Sammy—she can't look, closes her eyes. "Don't look down," he tells her. "Look up."

She tilts her head back, looks up, and has the impression that she is not looking up at the sky, but is in fact in the sky. "That doesn't really help," she says. She presses her face against his coat, and he puts his hand against the back of her head. He seems to be amused by her fear.

He starts telling her, in soothing tones, about the history of the World Trade Center. Its architectural features. The express and local elevators. The built-in sway. How Le Corbusier was hated, then loved, the city working against him and the towers, then the flipping—once they were finished, the city had come to see itself as defined by them. He mentions, too, the extraordinary caper of Philippe Petit, the French acrobat who walked a high wire between the towers in 1977. Has she heard of it?

"No one would do that," she says. Right into his coat.

"A wire between the buildings," he says. "Thirteen hundred feet off the ground. He walked back and forth for over an hour."

"Now I feel even worse. Just thinking about it."

"You should feel better. He survived on a tiny wire. But you, look at all this room you have. You could do a cartwheel."

She laughs a little.

Then Ben's tone changes. "I used to come here with my dad," he says, softly. "Once a year." Ben hardly ever mentions his

258

father. It occurs to Sammy that Ben is taking her to a place that is special to him, a place that means something—he is letting her in on a part of his history, his family. She is the only one who really knows him, she thinks.

Just then a configuration of the Topeka Twisters stumbles past them—one boy hoisted atop another's shoulders. "I'm king of the fucking world!" shouts the lofted boy. And Sammy catches, briefly, the same expansive feeling—like she has been lifted off the plains of her former life and is soaring. She leans against Ben and looks out again at the city below. She has the feeling that whatever ruin men are making of their lives down there is immaterial, will never touch them.

Later, at the Carlyle Bar, Sammy drinks a bit more than usual and becomes loquacious. She talks excitedly about the trouble she's having finishing her thesis. How, a few nights ago, in a manic state, she had thrown her thesis in the trash and started over—she had been seized, she said, with some *Totally New Fucking Approach to Robert Lowell*. Here she holds her hands in a frame, as if setting her words against a lighted movie sign. Now playing: Delusional Master's Student Has Never-Before-Conceived Idea.

But then, she admits, the next morning, she couldn't even decipher her own notes, and what had hours before presented itself as a towering new insight into *Life Studies* seemed like a house of cards. "And that's not even the worst part," she continues. "Two of my committee members, like, *hate* each other, and they're having a protracted argument *via my thesis*. One will ask me to make changes and then the other, in response to those changes, makes me do something else, and none of the changes are for the sake of the study, they're just, they're just middle fingers going back and forth."

"What's their argument?" Ben asks. He is scanning the bar,

not really seeming to pay attention. But Sammy has known him long enough, by now, to know that this is when he's really paying attention. Or at least she thinks.

"Well," she says. "My advisor is the usual tweed jacket kind of guy, he smokes a pipe, that sort of thing, and the other committee member is a feminist with pink hair and a motorcycle jacket."

"I see," he says.

"And you know, so of course she has a problem with Robert Lowell."

"Because…."

"Because." She pauses. "Because he drove his wives completely batshit."

"I didn't know that."

"Jean Stafford," she says. "Elizabeth Hardwick."

"Never heard of them." He shrugs, swirls his drink, seems a little embarrassed.

"They were, they were brilliant. Better writers than him, maybe. But he, he…" she trails off. "He crushed them."

"And the feminist has a problem with this."

"For some reason," Sammy says. "But that's not my biggest problem. My *biggest* problem is that I don't have any idea." She is really drunk, she realizes. Swirling. "When I finish this fucking thesis, I don't have any fucking idea what I'm going to *do*!"

And so it is finally out there, the thing that has been bothering her. Not just the end of her studies and the void it represents, The fact that she is about to be free—completely, utterly, terribly free for the taking. Yet with no takers.

"What does a person typically do with a master's in poetry?" Ben asks.

"That," she says, pointing at him. "That right there is the problem."

Then Ben says, offhandedly, "Why don't you come up here for a while? Stay with me, figure something out. There's got to be a few of you sad poet types working in publishing. Or teaching at expensive private high schools." He says this with the force of a new idea, one that has just occurred to him, though Sammy has spent many hours imagining this very thing. Hoping it would one day occur to him.

She tries to play it cool. Furrows her brow. "Well, maybe." But just seconds later she is on a rant, imagining their life together in New York. "I can't really afford rent for the first bit," she says, "but I could pay you in other ways. I could make your lunch in the mornings. You're always complaining about the cafeteria food. And I could..." She can't think what else—the Rosenbergs already have everything they could ever need or want. "I could walk your nonexistent dog. That Irish Terrier you never wanted. I could take him to the vet. Groom him. Take him to the park. Ride him around the city in your nonexistent car, so he can stick his head out the window. He loves that."

She carries on, imagining the possibilities, but soon notices an odd expression on Ben's face—a weak smile, something she doesn't quite know how to read. He catches the waiter's eye and signals for the check, and she falls silent. She often feels this way with Ben, like she's gone too far, taken off running in the wrong direction. He'll be warm, and then suddenly curt, and she halts like a dog yanked back on a leash. She watches Ben pull bills from his wallet and count them out—twenty, forty, fifty dollars—and toss them on the table with a nonchalance she still can't fathom, no matter how much time they have spent together. And so added to the feeling of being a dog on the leash, she feels like a poor dog on a leash.

They are quiet as they make their way up in the elevator. In the darkness of the room, Sammy feels as if some sort of test is underway; whatever happens here will determine the future, it seems.

Normally she waits for Ben to start things, to kiss her, unbutton her cardigan and push it off her shoulders, but here she doesn't wait—she finds him and clings to his waist, pulls him to her. They move toward the bed. He sits, and she climbs on top of him. Kisses him. But then he pulls away.

"I'm sorry," he says. "I had too much to drink."

She kisses him again, not quite getting what he means. They have always been drunk together. It has never mattered before.

He takes her by the arms, pushes her away. "I'm sorry," he says.

"Oh," she says. Finally getting it.

Then he does the thing he always does—he holds her face in his hands. It is a tender gesture, though there's something about it that makes her feel young, and foolish—it is the sort of thing she's seen parents do to their children: *Yes, we'll get a dragon for your birthday, of course.* Her eye twitches, very slightly, and she worries she has given herself away, that the effort it took to keep her disappointment from registering on her face was visible to him.

"Tell me more about your thesis," he says. "Your totally fucking brilliant interpretation of whoever." He lies back, fishes a cigarette from his pocket, lights it. He always smokes in hotel rooms—a quality that Sammy has sometimes found thrilling, sometimes arrogant. He has no regard whatsoever for other people, she thinks now.

She is so desperate to fill the air, she chatters on as if nothing were wrong. "Well, there's this one poem, where Lowell walks out on his back steps at night, and sees a skunk rooting through the garbage, sticking its snout in a container of sour cream. And that's basically, you know, the secret to all of his poetry, the key to unlocking all of its meaning, maybe all the meaning of all the poems ever written, or at least it seemed that way for a few minutes."

"Everyone knows that already," Ben says. "That's the first thing they teach you at Harvard."

"The skunk *won't scare,* is the line, and when you pair it with an earlier line in the poem, *nobody's here,* you start to see the poet as a something nonhuman, something wild," she says. She is waving her hands, working off nervous energy. "The poet is on level with the skunk. And the skunk is, you know, kind of a rodent, nobody likes a skunk, but then again it's a mother skunk with her kittens, which is tender, there's creation afoot, but then again it's eating sour cream out of the garbage, which is gross. There's a mix of good and bad connotations, is the point," she says, "There's some likeness being made between the poet and the skunk. Some form of recognition. And the message is: you can feast on ruin. You can survive on it, if you're an animal. I don't know. It all made sense for a minute. I don't remember."

"I think maybe it's a good thing your program's over," he says, clicking a button on the remote, bringing the television to life. "You've driven yourself completely fucking crazy."

"I know," she says. She covers her face with her hands. "Robert Lowell has that effect on people."

"You'll be okay," Ben says, in a detached way—a way that makes clear he will have nothing to do with it. "You'll land on your feet."

She has no idea what happened. Only that, an hour ago they were planning to live together. And now they aren't. The room is spinning and she is lost in it. What happened, what happened, what happened.

The next morning, they make no mention of the night before. They get through breakfast, sitting side by side reading the paper together, letting the crossword fill their time. What is the capital of Djibouti? they wonder. And laugh. How should we know? What do they want from us? We can't know *everything*. But just beneath the surface, the mood is strained. Sammy leaves for the train station an hour before she needs to.

Then she has five hours to stare out a window, and piece together all the dots, every encounter she has ever had with Ben, until it forms a clear picture. It is as if she is a child at work on one of those books of puzzles people give to kids on long road trips. She is trying to figure out what just happened—the particular laws of physics governing the bewildering catch-and-release maneuver they just performed. She was too much, she thinks, too excited about moving up to New York. Probably he had only been kidding when he mentioned it, or said it before he really thought it through. Then she'd taken up the idea and run with it, ruined it, like a fool.

But then again, she thinks, her shame turning to indignance, he was the one who brought it up.

You were the one who called me, she thinks. All these years, you called me. You sent me the fucking *phone*.

2000

Ben is standing in a treatment room at the hospital, observing an ECT session. He and another intern, plus several med students, are clustered behind their attending, who stands beside a patient—a middle-aged woman made anonymous by her hospital gown, the green paper cap covering her hair. As an instructive measure, the attending ties a tourniquet just below the patient's left elbow, so that the sedative they are about to deliver, which will relax the rest of the body, won't reach the patient's forearm. After the patient is sedated, and the current is delivered to her temples, and while the rest of her body displays no sign of disruption, the attending indicates the muscles in the patient's left forearm, twitching and grabbing—evidence of what is happening in the brain.

"Why does this work?" one of the med students asks. Her name is Jenny. She is short and stout and inelegant, with orange hair cut like a man's, freckles all over. She is overbearing. Always asking questions. Always pushing it. Ben hates her.

"Electric stimulation to the brain," the attending says, robotically, "is known to alleviate the symptoms of depression." He speaks as if to a child. Everyone knows this.

"But why? Why does it work?" Jenny asks. "What are the mechanisms?"

"Well," the attending falters. "That we don't really know."

"Then aren't we, like, playing with fire?" This is exactly

what Ben has been wondering for several years, he hates to admit.

"We're doing what we know works," the attending says. "For some people, it's the only thing that works."

"But we don't know why."

"Correct."

Then the attending gives another current. Ben watches the muscles in the arm work again, the only evidence of what is going on beneath the otherwise placid surface of the patient's body. Somehow, this is helping.

After the session, Ben can't stop thinking about it—the patient's arm, how it twitched. He wonders what, if anything, might be going on beneath the surface of his consciousness. What currents might be vibrating, unbeknownst to him. Because the last several years, he has felt less and less. By now, in fact, feels almost nothing. Medicine has done something to him. Hollowed him out.

He knows enough to know this is temporary—just a mood that has consumed him, perhaps one of the side effects of being a resident. But even with this knowledge—that however convincing and permanent moods may feel, they always shift—he wonders if he will ever change. Worries that he is becoming, essentially, his father. That he will feel this way, cold and calloused, for the rest of his life.

Until, suddenly, he doesn't.

One September evening, his shift just ended, Ben is walking down the long hall toward the exit—the exit that leads, on this particular day, to an entire weekend off. He is nearly there, hungry for it, gleeful, when something stops him—he decides to turn into the art therapy room end of the hall. He stops because there's a piano at the back of the room, an old upright no one ever plays, and he suddenly has the urge to play it. The room is dark, and he makes his way gingerly, past eight long tables set up for creative work time in the morning, covered in brown butcher paper. There is a long row of metal lockers along the wall to his left, filled with art supplies. And along the opposite wall, a large aquarium, bubbling, lit with purple and green lights. A few orange fish drift back and forth, their fins and tails trailing, undulating. They never really sleep, either, Ben thinks. Even when he sleeps these days, he isn't really sleeping.

He sits down at the piano, an old Baldwin, and lifts its cover. Hits the C chord. It's out of tune but he carries on. Tinkers for a bit. He still knows a whole cache of songs he had learned to play as a child. His mother had insisted on lessons, and for a while playing the piano was one of the things he wanted to do when he grew up. He remembers his parents taking him to Café Carlyle to hear the great blind master, George Shearing. Ben had watched him, inscrutable behind his dark sunglasses, his head inclined now up at the ceiling, then off across the room. He didn't need to see the keyboard—the songs were just in him. He was *one with the piano*, as Ben's piano teacher used to say, though in Ben's case she used the phrase to indicate something he couldn't quite achieve: *You are not one with the piano*. Eventually his teacher, Mrs. Greene, had told him he didn't quite have the talent, or the temperament, for serious study—she was breaking up with him, didn't even want to take his money anymore. "But at least now," she told him, "you've learned enough, you will be able to appreciate a well-played piano."

He makes his way through the opening bars of "Guilty." *If it's a crime then I'm guilty, guilty of loving you.* Then he just lets his fingers wander the keys, a way of emptying his mind. This, too, is something his mother had instilled in him. The best way to think was not to think at all, she always said, but to occupy the body with some sort of manual activity. Then the thinking you need to do could go on in the subconscious, unbeknownst to you.

Ben is sometimes able to pull this off, sometimes not. At

the moment he is failing, thinking of the patients he saw earlier in the day—how hopeless they were. All the work he did here, all the progress he made with patients, was temporary. The patients stabilized to the point they could be released, then went out in the world until they were dragged back in. On and on, over and over. That's what's been bothering Ben the most lately—that nothing he does here really helps, not in an enduring way. He might as well go into private practice with his mother. Listen to the neurotics fuss about the nature of their souls. He is disappointed with himself for losing hope, giving up on the hospital. He wishes he were different. Made of tougher stuff. But he isn't. He just can't help it.

Suddenly one of the nurses comes barging through the doors. Her name is Meg and there is something of Mia Farrow about her, which is to say she looks like an elf, short and slight, with blonde hair cut close to her scalp, but for a few wisps that frame her face. Her eyes are large and dark, her nose upturned, her mouth full and pink. In her green scrubs, she really does look like a woodland creature. A creature of delight and magic.

Except she isn't. In her case, it is as if being so small and fair has fueled something in her—she is the loudest, meanest nurse on the ward, the most brash and confrontational person Ben has ever worked with. Ballbuster, people say. Stay away from her. She'll bust your balls.

He's stayed away from her so far—he has been on this rotation three weeks—but now here she is, leaning into the room. "We can hear you all the way down the hall," she says. Her voice is sharp. Almost braying.

He does a thing he does sometimes, cocks his head, gives a bit of a smirk. "Is that so?" he says. He is used to flirting with nurses. Has made a game of it.

"It *is* so." She is not amused.

270

"That's a bit of a quandary," he says.

"It won't be," she says, "if you shut the fuck up." Then she disappears. The door slaps closed behind her.

He is stunned. Kind of impressed. He can't think of another person who has spoken to him this way, who was so immune to his charms. Just Kurtz. But there was something wrong with Kurtz, so he didn't really count.

Ben doesn't know how to respond. But he feels he can't let her go unanswered. He breaks into a loud *Rhapsody In Blue*, but just for a minute. Then he shuts the fuck up. Walks home.

Thereafter, the mood at work changes for him. He is aware of Meg in a way he wasn't before. It is easy to hear her—her voice cuts through whatever room she's in and even down the hall—and he finds himself listening to her, tucking away bits of information. "We're going up to Westchester," he hears her saying. "Pick some fucking apples or something." He notices she is married, though judging from the size of her ring, not to anyone very impressive.

She says nothing to him for several days, and he thinks perhaps the moment they had in the art room is gone, it was nothing. But the following week, toward the end of his shift, he hears piano music coming from the art room. One of Chopin's nocturnes. He walks down the hall and pushes open the heavy wooden door and sees it's her playing. Of course. She is a much better than he is. Bent over the keys, lost in it. One with the piano, as it were.

"I won't be challenging you to a duel anytime soon," he says, when she finishes. "I don't really have the chops to keep up with you."

"Well," she says. "I didn't want to say anything."

That's it. She gets up and walks out. Right past him.

After that, he thinks about her all the time. Does all the

things people do on the internet. He finds her address, but almost nothing else about her. Just her name listed as a participant in a few marathons. A testimonial to a personal trainer on the website of an athletic club in Brooklyn. *Things weren't quite coming back together after the birth of my son*, she had written. *But Andre whipped me back in to shape in no time.*

One night, about a week after he finds her playing Chopin, he is walking home from his shift, just off hospital property, and suddenly she is right next to him—he looks down and sees her bright purple clogs keeping pace beside him. "Hey," she says.

"Long day," he says. The most inane thing.

"I'm ready for a beer."

"I'm buying," he says. It's a bit of a gamble, but it turns out she's game.

"Great. That's what I wanted you to say."

They turn into a small Indian place and settle into a booth and Meg orders right away, as soon as the waiter comes over. Two beers, garlic naan. Tandoori chicken. She starts talking like they've known each other for years. She doesn't do it like other people— doesn't take time to ask him questions, or orient him to the basic landscape of her life. She just launches in. "My parents refuse to eat Indian food," she says. "I keep trying to take them every time they visit, but it's like they don't want to eat in the city, they're afraid of catching something. That's why I had to get out of Westchester. I mean, the whole culture there is being afraid of the city. It's fucking ridiculous."

There's a manic energy to her dialogue, but he rolls with it. She tells him about growing up in the suburbs—her father a school teacher, her mother a nurse. She tells him about the punk band she started in college and the years she spent after graduation, touring, playing in dives all across the country. "Even like fucking

Oklahoma," she says. She talks about giving up the band after three years and coming home, moving back in with her parents, enrolling in nursing school. The defeat it represented to her initially. But then its surprising rewards. She tells him about the worst cases she's seen on the ward in the three years she's been there. She tells him she's applying to medical school, because she can't stand taking orders from doctors. "I'm smarter than any of you anyway," she tells him. She wants to be a psychiatrist, too, thinks she will make a good one. "I love telling people what to do."

"The first thing you ever said to me," he recalls, "was to shut the fuck up."

"Well," she says. "You have to admit, that's pretty good advice."

Halfway through dinner—there is still food on their plates, food on the serving dish between them—she checks her watch and stands to leave. "Gotta go," she says. "My son is waiting for me." She smacks Ben on the shoulder on her way out, two quick taps, the way you'd congratulate a kid for making a basket. Then she leaves him to finish his meal, pay the bill. Leaves him to wonder.

This goes on for a few weeks. A meal here and there—Indian again, Italian, Ethiopian—Meg talking the whole time. Each time, just when Ben is getting comfortable, Meg suddenly stands to leave—her son, her son. Then one night, Ben tries his trick at the Carlyle—the bar and its charming murals—and she stays. She is right there with him. There is no mention of the son or husband. He doesn't even have to suggest going upstairs, because she does. Or nearly so. "I've always wanted to stay here," she says, "see what the rooms are like." And in no time they are in the elevator together, and she is leaning against him.

Ben is surprised how easy it is. He had expected to be nervous, troubled by the complications of sleeping with a nurse, not to mention another man's wife. But Meg is relaxed about everything. With other girls, in bed, Ben is used to a certain degree of playacting—the lusty stares, the deep breathing—or in Sammy's case, a shyness, the way she blushed, looked away from him, closed her eyes. But Meg is relaxed, business-like. It's as if she's had a hundred prior affairs. She climbs on top of Ben and places one hand on his chest. Marks him.

After sex, their heads together, Meg shows Ben pictures of her son—a little gallery bound in her wallet. At first the son, Wells, is a baby, all swaddled up. Then he is sitting up, wearing a red onesie and posed next to a stack of Christmas presents, his hands brought together in a delighted clasp. He is cute, in the way all kids are cute. Big brown eyes, light hair. Then Meg flips to another picture of the son. Here, he is suspended in a carrier, worn by the never-mentioned husband, who, like Meg, also looks small and elf-like, delicate. His hair is pale brown and curly, thin, receding at the temples. He is wearing one of those bright ponchos with an Aztec pattern. He looks like the kind of guy you meet in college in an anthropology class. Then marry in an outdoor wedding at the foot of a mountain. Then divorce.

"That's Milo," she says. "He was the drummer in my band. Now he mainly just takes care of Wells. Plays the occasional wedding with his jazz trio. Just riding the cymbals," she says, and mocks him for a few beats. Ben doesn't know what happened between them, but to go from punk to jazz is a downgrade in Meg's book, this much is clear.

The husband looks surprised in the photo, caught off guard, his head turned toward the camera because his name was called. At your service, is the expression. Ben feels a pang of something for the husband—pity, maybe regret. But he pushes it away.

Then for a few months it's as if he's under a spell. He thinks only of Meg and the moments they have or might steal together. Nothing else matters to him. Not the undecided presidential election, the battle between George Bush and Al Gore that is consuming the whole country, that has pushed Kurtz to the verge of a cerebral hemorrhage. By year's end, Ben is sick with desire. Ready to make any promise, break any law that will bring them together.

He spends New Year's Eve as usual—going out to a movie with his mother, then bringing home Chinese food and eating it in front of the television, *Dick Clark's New Year's Rocking Eve*. It's just the two of them—his father is in bed early, as always—and Ben makes his way through the evening, making small talk, commenting on the movie, the food, the terrible musical acts on TV and the insanity of the crowd gathered outside in the cold. But the whole time he is thinking of Meg, waiting to hear from her. He is suffering, for the first time in his life, from the sentimentality depicted in movies—that clichéd desire to be with the person you love at the start of the new year. "What's going *on* with you?" his mother asks him, twice. "Nothing," he tells her.

When his phone finally rings, he jumps up and pulls it out of his pocket with an uncommon urgency. His brain is racing, thinking already of the excuses he'll make to his mother. He'll grab his coat and be out the door in under a minute...

But when he flips open his phone and the screen lights up, everything that was soaring in him crashes. It's only Sammy.

2011

Sunday mornings, Ben calls Sammy and they read *The Times* together. They sit down at their respective tables, drinking their respective cups of coffee, and flip through the pages. When they were younger, they went after the headlines, wanting to know everything there was to know about the world, but now they dispense with the news in the time it takes to turn the page. "Dreadful," Sammy says this particular morning. And Ben says, "Wanton destruction, plague, blah, blah, blah."

They keep scanning. Science, books, film. But nothing really catches their attention. They even flip past the crossword, which they used to do all the time. There is no longer much fun in knowing these things: who starred in which movie, when a certain country annexed part of another. What used to make them feel cultured now just makes them feel old.

Finally, Ben finds something that interests him, in Vows & Engagements—an article about a couple whose relationship started as an affair, two parents who met at their kids' kindergarten holiday party. "Jesus," he says. "Scandal at the kindergarten holiday party. *The Times* is really down in the gutter, here." He is so entranced, he starts quoting directly from the article: "'I was instantly smitten,' the groom was quoted as saying. 'I was so upset,' said the bride. 'I was like: Why did life flaunt him around on a platter when I can't have him?'"

"*Why did life flaunt him around on a platter?*" Sammy says. "Barf."

"The worst," Ben says, "Though I suppose it's nice to see this sort of thing come out of the shadows. I mean, it's all around us."

"I don't know, though," Sammy says. "Maybe there's a reason to sweep these things under the rug. I feel bad for the exes. They wake up on a Sunday morning and try to read the paper, and then, blam. There's the affair, the most painful experience of their lives, right in the world's storefront window, laid bare for everyone to see."

They keep reading. The article goes so far as to include the details of the bride and groom's first tearful confessions of affection, their first illicit meeting in a hotel. But the worst part, the most painful part, Sammy thinks, is the accompanying photo, showing the couple at their reception. The bride is sitting in the groom's lap, and he has his hand on her ass. Their children stand around them looking variously nervous, sad, angry, bored. Whatever mania or desperation has taken hold of their parents, whatever mess they have made of their lives, whatever disavowals and commitments their parents have made, these children want nothing to do with it.

"I have to say though," Ben concludes, sounding truly impressed for once. "I think this one is going to last."

Sammy laughs along, though something is off. Reading these announcements isn't as much fun as it used to be. They are too old for Vows & Engagements, too old to be mocking the people who choose to announce their happiness, or delusions, to the world. The math has changed: There is something wrong with *them*, now, for never having married. She tries to express this sentiment. "I wish them the best. Who are we to judge?" After all, she is a single mother whose last date—with a real estate agent/amateur bodybuilder who referred to eating dinner as *powering down some fuel*—was so bad it had turned her off dating altogether. "It's not like either one of us has exactly figured it all out," she ventures.

"Well," he says. "Maybe the answer is right under our noses. Maybe we should get married." He muses for a moment, in a theatrical voice that makes it known he is only kidding, about how their story would play out in print. "The first time they met," he says, "she made him a sandwich. A sandwich so good he decided to marry her."

"Roast beef," she continues. "With provolone and mayo."

"And a giant pickle on the side. A pickle for the ages." His voice has a wistful quality now. He'd been joking at first but the joke has swerved, gotten away from him. Maybe his life, Sammy thinks—all that money and status, all his friends and connections, that beautiful apartment overlooking the park—maybe it isn't quite enough. Maybe he's a bit lonely, too.

She flips the page and is mesmerized by an advertisement for a satchel, offered by world-renowned makers and purveyors of fine leather goods. The bag is so beautiful it seems to sweep away within itself, in an instant, all of the atrocities and horrors on the newspaper's first pages, just swallow them up in its depths. She directs Ben to it. "When you turn the page and see these bags," Sammy muses, "all is forgotten, all is forgiven. You imagine that your life, should you own such a bag, would be magically transformed. That a person carrying such a bag could not possibly fail in any social or professional setting. In my case, I could carry that bag around campus and no one would question me again. Students would pay attention in lecture. Colleagues would assume I had something worthwhile going on in my head."

"Agreed," says Ben.

"What is it?" she asks. "Why is this bag so powerful?"

"There's something hypnotic about the dimpled surface of the leather," he says. "It's as if the cow has been killed in a state of excitement, and the goosebumps on its flesh are somehow preserved through the skinning and tanning—the bag seems to contain all the struggle and glory a dying soul undergoes. It's almost still alive." He draws on his cigarette. "It's as if instead of having a child on one's arm, one has a bag. They are both tender and succulent packages of flesh."

"You're onto something," she says. "Although there's a crucial difference. One draws from you, the other returns to you. Whereas the child draws on your resources, and confuses you, and drags you down in the world, the bag does the opposite. It's better than a child."

"It's the opposite of having a child, then. Whatever is encompassed in that bag," Ben says, "the portions of your life you're carrying around, seem to be of a higher quality, in better order."

Sammy loves when Ben plays along with her. His usual response to her posturing is to endure it, rolling his eyes or scoffing, and he only very occasionally contributes. But this particular day, with these particular bags, he is all in. Right there with her.

"And anyone can carry one," she adds. "Even the old, even the ugly. It's not like skinny jeans, which don't work for most people. Bags don't discriminate. Bags are for everyone."

"I happen to look great," says Ben, "in skinny jeans."

"You do," she agrees. "You certainly do."

After they hang up, Sammy considers their story, as viewed through the lens of *The Times*. How typical it was. They started out on the front page, wanting to know everything, to inspect everything, to approve or disapprove. They sought to take in the world together, figure it out, pin it down, refine and settle their opinions. Decide what mattered, what didn't. What to value, what to dismiss, what to praise and what to mock. Then for a while they diverged, Sammy taking a morbid interest in the war, and Ben falling prey to distractions. Each tried to tempt the other. Look over here, over here, over here. They went back and forth, indulging and begrudging one another, until finally they grew weary, and did the only thing left to do: they set it all aside, the politics and crime, business and arts, sports, weather, science, travel—the great American novel they'd been reading their whole lives. They turned that page and decided to do what middle-aged Americans do next, and do best: they washed their hands of it, stared at the pretty things, those small luxuries manufactured in far-away lands. They drank from the cup of forgetting. They went shopping.

2001

Sammy is walking between rows of desks in a third-grade classroom at St. Mary's Elementary, where she is employed as a substitute teacher. "A *sub*!" the kids cry out, in every classroom she appears. "We have a sub!" There is always excitement in their voices, intrigue. They are going to get away with something, or even better, they are going to get away with doing nothing. The underlying implication of the word *sub*, in this case, is a bit of subterfuge. That's the word they're really looking for.

Today she has been instructed to keep the children busy with worksheets, which are fresh off a mimeograph machine. The ink is purple and smudged, the pages damp. Though it is March, the school is still using Christmas-themed crosswords and word-searches—page after page decorated with candy canes and stockings, gingerbread houses, Santa and his reindeer. The kids are bent at their desks. Some of them are like little cartoons of concentration, working their pencils, their tongues sticking out of the corners of their mouths. Others are slumped, staring out the window at the falling snow, which is coming down fast. Sammy thinks of correcting them, reminding them of their work. But then again it doesn't really matter. Not much point finding the word YULETIDE in the middle of March.

One girl, her blonde hair pulled back in a tight ponytail, which is tied with a green velvet bow, shoots her hand into the air. "Mrs. Browne," she says. "I can't find Santa."

"Keep looking," Sammy says. She is pacing slowly, her hands clasped behind her back. She is hoping to project wisdom, authority.

"I've been looking," the girl says. "It's not there."

"I'm sure it is," Sammy says, though she is inclined to believe this particular girl, an unusually serious student. She is always raising her hand with the answer to Sammy's questions, bringing her classmates into line when they're out of order. She is the type of girl who has written her name, J. Corning, in dark black marker, in large block letters, on all of her possessions—her notebooks and pencil cases, her back pack, the tag of her jacket. "It isn't there," she says again, plaintively.

Sammy comes and stands behind her. Peers down at the worksheet. The word search consists of a block with a list of words beside it—elf, snow, sleigh, claus—all of which J. Corning has dutifully circled and checked off her list. But not Santa. Sammy finds the problem quickly enough. An error at the printer's. Instead of Santa, it says Fanta.

"There *is* no Santa," J. Corning says. Distraught now.

"There's no Santa!" cries one of the boys at the back of the room. "There's no Santa!"

The class erupts into giggles and chattering. "Hey, Fanta," Sammy hears. "I wanna ride in your fleigh."

J. Corning's fists are balled up, pressed against the desk, little pistons about to fire. This is unacceptable to her. Something is wrong in the world, and it must be fixed. But how?

"These things sometimes happen," Sammy says. "People make mistakes." J. Corning's face fall into confusion, then disappointment. Then anger.

"They shouldn't make mistakes," J. Corning says, "*on a children's worksheet.* It's not fair."

Something petty rises up in Sammy—a feeling that first announced itself when she was a child, then grew and grew. "When

I was your age my mother died," she thinks of telling J. Corning. "If you want to talk about not fair." But there's no point doing this, Sammy has learned. In fact it is important for people like J. Corning to grow up as they do. A certain percentage of the population needs to proceed unhindered, free of skepticism and self-doubt, they need to *never have suffered*, is the way Sammy thinks of it, so they can maintain the gall they need to become surgeons, or business owners, or politicians. Otherwise no one would do these things.

The bell rings and everyone pushes their chairs from their desks, scrambles, scatters. J. Corning walks solemnly to the row of coats on the wall and plucks her duffel coat off its hook. She puts on her hat, mittens. All of this carefully. Then she fits her arms through the straps of her backpack and hoists it onto her shoulders. "Now my whole weekend is ruined," she says. She turns and trudges away.

Sammy straightens the teacher's desk, turns out the lights, walks home. Snow is still falling, though lighter now. The streets are so quiet she can actually hear the snowflakes landing on her shoulders, the hood of her coat. All the way home Sammy wonders if something will be waiting for her in the mail—an acceptance from one of the many doctoral programs she's applied to. Going back to school is, after two years away, the only thing Sammy can think of doing next. She remembers, with a little flush of embarrassment, the way Kurtz had mocked her during their ride up to the inaugural ball, way back during her freshman year. Did she think someone was going to pick her up in a limo when she graduated, and install her in a castle, and provide her a stipend to read and write? Is that what she thought was going to happen?

Well, of course she didn't think that.

Except maybe a little. She has to admit, in terms of doctoral programs, she's basically looking for a stipend to study poetry. Maybe not in a castle, but a small room in a turret would do.

She arrives at her apartment building and pulls open the lid to the mailbox, but there's nothing in it, nothing but a catalog for children's clothing, addressed to the previous tenant. She hears a loud yowling and looks up to see the stray calico she has been trying to court. There is a patch of scruffy woods behind Sammy's apartment building and the cat seems to live there. She comes out whenever she sees someone coming or going from the building. Sammy has named her, something about her face suggesting a Karen. "Just a sec," she tells Karen. Holds up a finger. She lets herself into her apartment and rummages through the refrigerator for a piece of cheese. But when she comes back outside, Karen is gone.

Cats. She doesn't understand cats.

So she goes inside and settles in for the weekend. Puts on her pajamas. Opens a bottle of wine and pours a glass. A familiar feeling comes over her—that this life she's living, this life of subterfuge, is okay, that it will do, so long as it's temporary.

She sits on the couch—abandoned by the previous tenant, presumably because it is so ugly, upholstered in brown and yellow plaid—and flips through the catalog of children's clothing. Cute, all of it, overalls and booties and little hats. Cute but useless. The idea of having a child is so foreign to her, so absurd, the items in the catalog look like props from a science fiction movie. Then the phone rings and she races to it. It's Ben, just as she hoped. "Hey," she says. "I was just thinking about you, I mean, I wanted to tell you something funny."

"I have something to tell you, too," he says. Something in his voice is off. Someone died, is Sammy's first thought.

"Okay," she says. There's an awkward beat of silence. "What is it?"

"Well," he says. "It's good news, at least I think."

"Oh, good," she said. "Because you sounded a little, you sounded kind of weird."

"Oh," he says. "Well." He clears his throat. "It's just that. Well, I'm getting married."

The rest of the conversation sort of goes by in a blur. She says things like: "That's great! Wow! Who is she? When did this happen?" Her questions tumble forth, all except the one she really wants to ask, which is: "Are you fucking *kidding* me?"

Then, mercifully, Ben does what he's been doing a lot these past few months, which is to say he is busy, is being paged, has to go. *Of course*, she says.

She hangs up, and plunks down on the couch, stunned, in a sort of trance. She goes over everything Ben told her. The girl's name is Meg, a nurse on the psych ward with a three-year old kid. They've only known each other six months or so. No particular date set, but he'll let Sammy know, he wants her to be there, it wouldn't be the same without her.

She goes over it again and again, until the last of the light goes out of the sky, and then she is sitting in the dark.

She hears Karen crying, and comes back into the world. Sammy can see her through the window, sitting in a little circle of light created by the streetlamp. Her calls are loud and desperate, but her bearing is still somehow regal.

Sammy gets up and goes to the refrigerator, finds the cheese again, puts it on a little plate, goes outside and kneels down, sets the plate on the ground in front of her front door. Karen does nothing but stare. Sammy pushes her door open wide, and extends her arms toward the apartment, like a game-show model showing a prize to a contestant, as if to say, *all this could be yours*. "Want to come in?" she asks Karen. Karen blinks. Blinks again. "Come on in," Sammy says. "I can't stand here all day."

Then Karen springs up and turns away, trots off into the woods.

And so, Sammy thinks, our heroine has been rejected by a stray cat.

"Fine!" she calls after Karen. "See if I care." She goes back inside the apartment, slams the door. She is filled with bright rage. It's not Ben, she tells herself. Ben she can handle. It's just this cat, this fucking cat. The disappointment she feels about the cat—really, she reminds herself, this is about the cat—has brought to light how long, without even quite realizing it, she has harbored the belief that she and the cat would end up together, in the end.

"Now my whole weekend is ruined," she says, to no one at all. "It's not fair."

2001

Looking back, Ben would have to say it started with the apartment.

The problem was that Ben and Meg didn't see much of each other. They both worked long hours. And then after work, she took a train to Brooklyn, went back to her family. There was only this small pocket of time between work and the train she could work with—she could say she got caught up in something, that one of the other nurses was late and she had to cover. They'd rush to a hotel and then, as soon as they were done, Meg would run off. Ben would stay in bed for a while, order room service, watch television. He spent many of those hours in bed thinking about their problem, how to solve it. Meg had never once mentioned leaving her husband, but he was preoccupied with the idea. The possibility of having her to himself.

Now he remembers it exactly—the moment they first spoke of living together. It was a Friday in late January, and they'd rushed to a hotel after work. After, lying in bed, their heads together on the same pillow, he'd used their hands to approximate the circles of a Venn diagram, representing their commitments and their obligations at work, her obligations to her family. He'd grabbed her hand, placed it on top of his, to indicate their work schedules, then grabbed her other hand and placed it off to the side, to indicate her family.

"If you were single it would be so easy," he'd said.

Removing her other hand. "We'd have all this time." There was a considerable amount of overlap between their work schedules, but the time beyond that, which he indicated by tracing a circle around their hands, they could spend together.

"Well, I'm not," she said. Placing her hand back. Overlapping all the time they might have together. He felt a little stab of something.

"But even if I were," she said, "we'd hardly see each other." The circle she drew to indicate the boundary around their work schedules was considerably narrower than the one he had drawn. It was more accurate, he had to admit—work really did take up most of their lives. "And you have your family, too. And friends and whatever else."

"At least we could fall asleep together," he said. "If we lived together."

"True," she said. "But you live with your parents."

This was something that embarrassed him. But right on the heels of this shame he reminded himself: If she saw his parents' apartment, she'd understand. A person didn't just walk away from a place like that, a building like that.

"If you had your own place it might be different," she said. "I could see maybe staying over."

This was the opening he'd been looking for. "What would you tell your husband?"

"I need some space," she'd said. Coolly. "I'd just tell him I need some space for a while."

Then she'd gotten up, gotten dressed. Left him alone.

Thereafter, the pattern with Meg was: She'd mention something, something Ben didn't quite want to do. And then she'd leave. And a kind of desperation would come over him. Whatever it was she mentioned, he'd do. He was bewitched.

In this case, what he did was buy an apartment in his parents' building. A starter place, one of the few in the building that hadn't been remodeled, made into a little palace of luxury. It was a two bedroom on a low floor, with views of the courtyard instead of the park. It had been untouched since the sixties. The floors were old and scratched and the walls, yellowed with cigarette smoke, were a sour white. The lighting was bad. The bathrooms were ghastly—one of them tiled in pink, the other in mint green. And the kitchen—the kitchen was a nightmare. It was smaller than his bedroom closet at his parents' place, and fitted with cheap white appliances: a refrigerator that rattled constantly, a stove with coiled burners that glowed orange. But nothing was quite so bad as the smell. The place was musty, and underneath that, in little pockets as you made your way through the rooms, pungent. Cats had lived there.

Ben's heart sank a little, the first time he walked through it with Meg. He was preoccupied with comparisons to his parents' place, every surface of which was heirloom-quality. The kitchen and bathrooms were tiled in marble. The walls refinished with Venetian plaster, the moldings custom made from oak. Everything was heavy, solid. Mined from some exotic location and shipped across the ocean. He could hardly believe the two apartments were in the same building.

He kept apologizing all the way through the new place, depressed by its ugliness, when, coming up behind Meg as she turned into the bathroom, he caught her face in the mirror. She didn't have many tells—of all the people he knew, she was the hardest to read—but for a second her saw that eyes were wide. Rapturous. Ben had to remind himself that real estate in Manhattan, virtually any real estate—well, there were people who would kill for it.

"It's not much," he said. "But the building is good. The building is what really matters. Everything else can be fixed."

"I love it," she said. "I don't care what it looks like." She'd turned and kissed him. Started undressing him right there in the bathroom.

But then, as it turned out, she did care what it looked like—she wanted to bring in contractors, she told him, not even a week after he'd shown her the place. "We can't move in yet," she said. "The contractors will need this place to themselves for a few months." She'd gone into a frenzy, gotten bids for everything. He started to feel queasy whenever he talked to her—like he was being dragged into something he wanted no part of, something beneath his dignity. "Hey," she said, whenever he tried to avoid picking out paint, or tile, or carpet, or drapes. "I need you to focus. We're going to have to look at this the rest of our lives."

And that's when he realized—it wasn't just that he had bought an apartment. He was asking her to live with him. Which, because she was married already, meant he was asking her to marry him. That was the opening bid, with her.

Soon enough she spelled it all out for him. She had been accepted to med school and was going to be quitting her job. Her situation was delicate. She needed something she could depend on. "I can't just move in with you for the hell of it," she said. "If I'm going to leave my family, I need some assurances." So that weekend they'd gone to Cartier to pick out a ring. She was still wearing her old set and had to take it off in order to try on her new prospects. That's when Ben realized how complicated everything had gotten. How messy. What he'd gotten himself into.

Then it was time to introduce Meg to his mother. He set up a lunch on a Sunday, walked with his mother to their favorite bistro. Meg was more than an hour late—they had two Bloody Mary's before she even arrived. When she finally did, sweeping through the door in a gust of frigid air, she didn't apologize—just sat down at the table and started complaining about her commute. "My God," she said. "It was a fucking nightmare getting here." She didn't even take off her coat, which was dotted with snowflakes. Ben watched as his mother eyed Meg in quick, cutting glances. "Wells absolutely wasn't having it," she said. "I was almost out the door but he started crying." She rolled her eyes. "So you know, I had to coddle him for a while." She looked at Ben's mother. "You know how it is." She reached up and tousled her hair to shake off the snowflakes. She was still wearing her old wedding set—the new ring was on a chain around her neck.

Ben's mother was unusually quiet, which was a trick of hers—she was letting Meg talk herself into extinction. When the waiter came, Meg ordered first, a mimosa and a Denver omelet. She slapped her menu closed and shoved it at the waiter without even looking at him. Ben's mother ordered next. "If you please," she said at the end, closing her menu and offering it to the waiter, gracefully, as if a gift.

Ben tried to make the kind of small talk that would flatter Meg—he told his mother about Meg's acceptance to med school, her skill on the floor. The way everyone respected her. The good humor she displayed with patients. But Meg kept missing his lobs, sometimes ignoring his cues altogether. "What is this place? she said, turning her head this way and that, regarding the tables, covered in white table cloths and set with patterned china, the heavy chandeliers, the oak paneled walls, the taxidermy animal heads affixed to the walls. The restaurant was doing its best to suggest a country club from a bygone era. But even though it was old fashioned, admittedly a bit pretentious, Ben and his mother had always loved it. "It's like Teddy Roosevelt puked everywhere."

Their food arrived, and his mother took over. "Congratulations," she said. "I heard you'll be moving. Won't have to take the train to work. You can just walk."

"That's true," Meg said. She was buttering a piece of toast in quick, angry strokes, the knife scraping, crumbs flying.

"And then medical school. That's wonderful."

"Well, it's complicated," Meg said. "My son is three. It's not going to be easy."

"Yes," his mother said. "I understand. I remember."

This might have worked, might have bonded them together, but Meg didn't want to be understood. "But I don't have," she said, "I don't have the same footing you did." Meg didn't want an heiress to claim she knew what it was like to work and have a child. Because even though Ben's mother had worked hard, through med school and residency, still, she didn't know. She had all that money to fall back on. She didn't know.

After Meg finished eating, but before Ben or his mother did, she excused herself from the table to go outside for a cigarette. She stood on the sidewalk, directly in front of their table, in full view, tilting her head down as she drew on her cigarette, then lifting it up, stretching her neck taut, blowing smoke straight up in the air. A man in an army jacket stopped and asked her for a cigarette and she gave him one, lit it for him. They stood together for a moment, chatting back and forth.

Ben and his mother were both mesmerized, staring. "What is it?" she asked Ben. What is it you see in her, she meant. He had never introduced a girl to his mother before, except Sammy, and Sammy didn't really count.

"I don't know," he said.

"May I suggest," his mother started.

"No, you may not."

"That she's not unlike your father."

"Don't start."

"So fickle with his love it sent you chasing."

"Please."

"And so compact. Flinty."

"Stop," he says. "Or I'm leaving."

They sit in silence for a bit.

"Well, she's pretty," said his mother. "I'll give you that."

Ben had a weakness for beauty, his mother always said. Whenever they walked through a museum together, they quibbled about it. "That's nice, but it's simple," she'd tell him, of a painting he admired, a Botticelli or a Titian. "Look here," she'd say. Pointing to a Schiele, or a Kiefer, or a Dubuffet. "This is where things get interesting." But he couldn't help it. He wanted beauty. He liked standing before it.

They continued to regard Meg, who had managed to enthrall the man in the army jacket. He was gesturing wildly, telling some kind of story. Then Meg threw her head back, broke out in a laugh. It was so loud they could hear it through the window.

Well, what is it, he often wondered after that, what is it? Meg was unlike any of the girls he had dated, all of whom, in one way or another, were bound to certain conventions, conventions having to do with etiquette, rank, reverence. She wasn't unlike Kurtz, he thought again. Why was he so drawn to them? What did they give him? He didn't know.

He didn't know, but he moved along, because he was compelled. He couldn't explain it any other way—just that he was *compelled*.

Then the contractors finished their work and they were free to move in. That first weekend, Meg brought her son to stay. It was the first time Ben had met Wells. Meg came through the door carrying him on her hip and Ben was struck by how alike they were. The boy's face was round, like Meg's, and he had her big brown eyes and wispy blond hair. Some part of him hadn't seen

Meg as a mother yet, he realized. Nor the boy as a person, a real boy.

"Can you say hi to Mr. Ben?" Meg said. And the boy turned his head away, buried his face in his mother's neck.

"I'm Ben," he said, trying to undo the strangeness of Mr. Ben. As if he were a neighbor, or the mailman.

He was able to win the boy over by showing him around the apartment, the room they'd decorated for him—a bed made up with dinosaur sheets, a big stuffed dinosaur resting on top, a small bookcase filled with colorful picture books. A reading lamp in the shape of a rocket. And then dinner had gone well enough—Ben had cooked spaghetti, the boy's favorite. Then they'd all sat on the floor of the living room, because Meg hadn't decided on furniture yet, and watched *Looney Tunes*. Things were still tentative—several times Ben caught Wells eyeing him warily—but they were going well, Ben thought. A few times, when Daffy Duck tripped and fell down a flight of stairs, or the coyote fell off a cliff the boy had lost himself to laughter. A good start.

Then it was time for bed, and Meg carried Wells into his room. Ben stood just outside the room and watched Meg getting him ready. She knelt on the floor, peeled off his clothes, put on a diaper, pajamas, all of this quickly, efficiently. The boy was only three and still clumsy in his movements, working his feet tentatively into the legs and arms of his pajamas. His head got stuck in the neck hole of the pajama shirt, and Meg helped him with a gentleness Ben had never seen from her before. They had done this together so many times that they anticipated each other's movements, worked together wordlessly. It struck Ben that he had never done anything like that, had never cared for anyone in this way, and he was moved by all of it. It was a currency he wanted to acquire.

Meg put Wells in bed, kissed him, turned out the light,

closed the door, and they settled back in the living room. Then Wells started crying. *Mommy, Mommy.* Ben watched Meg to see what she would do. And what she did was nothing.

Wells kept crying. Ben was irritated at first, and on top of that, suffered a bit of anxiety about the neighbors—no one wanted to listen to this. "Does he just?" he asked. Not quite knowing what the possibilities were. Calm himself down? Pass out?

"Eventually he'll give up," she said.

They were trying to watch the news, to stay informed about the world they lived in, but Ben couldn't concentrate for the noise, the unrest in his own household.

"Should we help him out?" he asked.

"I'm done for the day," she said. "I'm off duty. My light is off."

Her expression was so stern she looked different to him. The fineness of her features appeared suddenly too sharp.

The crying went on and on. It became plaintive, then truly distressed. "Mommy," Wells kept calling. "Mommy."

"Go to sleep," she yelled once.

"I want you," he gasped.

"I'm not coming. Go to sleep."

At some point it occurred to Ben to ask: "Why doesn't he come out?"

"I trained that out of him a long time ago," she said. "He wouldn't dare."

Eventually Wells started kicking his feet against the wall—the whole apartment shook.

"It's his first night here," Ben said. He stood up. "I don't want it to be, like, traumatic."

"What are you," she asked, smiling at him coyly, "a psychiatrist?"

He went toward the room.

"This just means," she said, "when he wakes up again in an hour, you're dealing with him."

Ben let himself in the room, knelt down next to the bed. "Hey, Buddy," he said. The boy turned himself over and crawled off the mattress, settled himself in Ben's lap. His arms were around Ben's neck, clung tight. By this time Wells was hyperventilating, shuddering as he inhaled.

It took him several minutes to stop gasping.

"I want Mommy," he said, when he was able to speak.

"I know," Ben said.

He could smell that Wells's diaper was wet, could feel its bulk in his lap.

"How about we fix your diaper?" Ben said. "And read a story."

The boy nodded.

"Hey, Meg?" he called.

"What?" she yelled back.

"His diaper is wet."

"Okay," she said. "Change it then."

He paused a moment. "I don't know how," he confessed.

"Are you fucking kidding me? I can't marry someone who doesn't know how to change a diaper."

So Ben did his best with the diaper, which wasn't as complicated as he thought it would be. Wells was resigned now, standing with his arms limp at his sides. He didn't move his body to help Ben, didn't know how this particular dance went. Ben got him changed and then laid him back in bed. He was practically asleep already, so tired from crying, but he placed a hand on Ben's shoulder. Stay. Ben knelt by the bed and waited for the boy's breathing to slow. He tried to get up once and Wells stirred, opened his eyes, so Ben squatted back down next to the bed and waited. Finally something shifted, and the boy started breathing through his mouth, with abandon, was how it looked to Ben, breathing with abandon. He took the boy's hand off his shoulder and rested it gently on the bed. He stood up, stretched. He felt scorched. Exhausted. He wondered how long this phase would last.

He went back out to the living room and sat next to Meg. "You're a pussy," she said. Not even looking at him.

Something turned in Ben. What initially struck him about Meg as a refreshing disregard for ceremony, as boldness, he now saw as crass, even cruel. The feeling gathered for a few days. He carried on as usual, went to work, picked up takeout on the way home, listened to her chatter over dinner—she talked almost exclusively of her coworkers, how stupid they were. Then one night, quite suddenly, as she was talking with her mouth full and sawing at a strip steak, slicing through the meat and then, for no good reason, scraping at the plate, he realized something: He hated her.

It was a mess after that.

Somehow he thought Meg wouldn't take it so hard, when he told her at dinner a few nights later, using the plainest and most clichéd language he could think of: *It's not you. You're perfectly wonderful. It's just something with me. Something I don't even really understand.* He'd looked past her as he said these things, staring out toward the living room in a way that he hoped would seem sorrowful, pathetic even. It was a pageant, but the whole thing had been a pageant, he believed—she didn't really love him, wasn't even capable of love.

But instead of taking it easy, she'd flown into a rage. Screamed so loud the neighbors could hear. *I left my husband for you. I broke up my family.* She took the chain from her neck and threw it at him, so hard the ring hit the floor and bounced.

"You can keep the ring," he said. Holding up his hands, surrendering. "It's worth a lot. You can sell it."

She stopped. Stood with her hands on her hips, her head down. Then she told him, without looking up: "I don't want the ring. I want the apartment."

In the following days they came to an agreement—she could live in the apartment through med school. This meant they'd be living in the same building for four years.

Then, it wasn't long before Meg's husband moved in. Ben should have been able to predict this, but he was somehow surprised by it. Coming back home from getting bagels one Sunday morning, Ben caught sight of the husband and Wells. The husband was playing with Wells in the courtyard, kicking a ball back and forth. The husband didn't see Ben watching, so he lingered for a moment. The husband looked out of place, nervous. He was still wearing that stupid poncho. Wells kicked the ball and it rolled toward one of the large planters—there were beautiful potted plants all around the courtyard—and the husband panicked after it. He was a man who was afraid of breaking something. A man who didn't want to get into trouble. It must be strange for him to be living here, Ben thought. Where people broke things all the time, and left their mess for the staff to clean.

He wondered what Meg told her husband. She probably never really left him, he realized—just said she needed space for a while, needed to think about things. The husband probably didn't even know Ben existed. Meg probably explained the apartment away, some bullshit about a doctor she used to work for. Someone who got married and was willing to rent out his old place for next to nothing.

A few weeks after that, in the mailroom, there was a run in between Meg and Ben's mother. His mother turned around and there was Meg, holding Wells. "Hi, there!" she said, as though they were old friends. "Wellsy, can you say hi to Mrs. Rosenberg? Can you say thank you?"

Ben's mother related this little scene to him in a high, mocking voice. Which wasn't that far off from Meg's actual voice. "Can you say thank you, Wellsy?" his mother said again.

"Well," Ben said. "She was just being nice."

"She was taunting me. She knows, ultimately, it's my money she's living on."

Ben scowled. The parameters of this whole mess kept getting wider.

"He's a cute kid," said his mother. "That was the one thing I was looking forward to."

A gloomy mood came over Ben, contemplating the next four years, the awkward encounters that might come upon him at any moment. Always the threat of running into Meg. He felt bad for his mother. And, strangely, he felt bad for the building, which he had always treasured. It was as if he had gone on some strange vacation, and returned with a parasite—something that would draw on his refuge, put it through a season of suffering. Everything was sour. He had failed, and now they were going to have to steep in it for a while.

"That woman," said his mother. "She played you like a fiddle."

"It was my fault," he said. "I made promises. I left her. It wasn't her fault."

Though from then on, he wondered—wondered if he was played. Often he considered the absolutely maddening ending of Henry James's *Portrait of a Lady*, where Isabel Archer, that bright young debutante, has given herself away to a man who was only after her money—money he needed to support his daughter and lover. Ben had always hated that book, hated to see a character duped like that. Made such a fool of. The ending of that novel gave him the worst feeling he had ever felt, reading a book. He couldn't stand it.

No, he told himself. It was me. I left her.

But the whole thing made him wince, like the memory of a bad illness.

He cheered himself up by thinking about selling the place in five years. He'd probably make a good profit, far beyond what he'd spent on renovations. In this city, real estate went nowhere but up.

II.

Boy meets girl, is how this particular story goes. And then there's not so much of a chase as some other type of game, one with long stretches of back and forth, maybe tennis, the ball crossing the net from boy to girl to boy to girl. On and on, until they are lulled into a rhythm.

Then, quite suddenly, the boy lets a ball go by. He sets his racquet down and walks away.

Well, the girl thinks, what was that? What the fuck have we been doing all this time? She throws her racquet down, stamps her foot, a little John McEnroe. She wanders off the court, looking around for some type of line judge to appeal to, someone to yell at: *You can't be serious, man. You cannot be serious. How can you possibly call that out?*

Then the boy returns. Picks up his racquet. Twirls it in one hand. Starts calling the girl, bouncing the ball at the serving line. Tossing it up in the air and letting it drop. *Like I'm ever,* the girl thinks. But then, telling herself she is bored, that the boy is at least a good partner to practice with, practice for whatever will be coming next, the real match, whatever and whenever and whoever that might be, she comes to the line.

Quiet please, says the judge. And the boy says *Fifteen love.*

2001

One bright morning at the start of her first semester at her new school, Sammy is walking to French class, making her way through the student union, head down as always, weaving through clusters of people—undergrads, she thinks of them now that she is pursuing a doctorate—and something, some difference in the light, or concentration of darkness, or maybe it is the silence, that sudden pocket of silence, makes her look up. There in the union, people are standing shoulder to shoulder, frozen stiff, their faces lifted to the twin televisions mounted on the wall. Normally these televisions run a loop of messages from the University, messages about upcoming events and elections, but now Sammy sees on screen the New York skyline. She sees that one of the twin towers has a gaping hole in it, a smoking black hole. Something has crashed into that sleeve of brightness and now it is on fire.

Sammy stands in that group of strangers—silent, all of them—until the second plane hits and the group breaks into gasping, then moaning, then chatter. *Fucking terrorists*, she hears. *This is fucking war*. She stands there for an eternity. Long enough to see, time and again, the faces of newcomers as they pass by. Innocent at first. Then vaguely aware of something wrong. Then curious. Then solemn. She watches and watches. Is part of a cluster, then a group, then a crowd, then a swarm. Until the first tower falls. Then the second. Watches all the faces passing by as they fall from not knowing into knowing.

Eventually, when there is nothing more to see—or rather, when the war she will be seeing for the rest of her life has completed its overture, its leading actors falling to their knees in a terrible curtsey—she walks home. She is living then in a studio apartment that is so cheaply built she can hear every footfall of the neighbor with whom she shares a wall, every sigh and sniffle. Her neighbor is Sameer Srinivasan, a Ph.D. student in film studies who had knocked on her door one day in June, shortly after she moved in, to explain the noises coming from his television. "I am completing a dissertation on 1970's gay pornography," he said, in a thick accent. "So I am sorry for anything you might hear of a disturbing nature." He was holding a ceramic cooking dish and pushed it toward her slightly. "Paneer," he said. "With my apologies."

Soon after she and Sameer had fallen into the habit of cooking for one another, and sharing meals at Sameer's, sitting on the floor in front of his television. Sammy had never seen pornography before in her life and flushed with embarrassment as they watched what Sameer called "the classics": *Blow Job, My Hustler, Flesh*. Though by the time they got to *Boys in Sand* and *Nights in Black Leather* it had all become strangely routine to her—she had come to understand the conventions of the genre and could watch it like anything else, with a critical eye, an ability to stand outside it and consider its narrative construction and arc. Much of what she saw became routine, boring even. Here comes the part, she started saying. Where this guy notices that guy. And then that guy sucks the other guy's dick.

But this September night they sit on the floor watching ABC's coverage of their national tragedy. They say almost nothing to each other. Just sit there. Occasionally getting up to use the bathroom, refill their glasses of water. At one point, Sameer tells her he is supposed to leave for his shift at 7-11, where he works the register, but he already understands the new rules of the game in this country. "You think I'm going to report to that fishbowl," he says, "and make myself a target for a bunch of rednecks riding around looking for some Arab to shoot? Fat fucking chance."

Sammy's mind hasn't yet crossed this threshold nor even approached it. But of course, she realizes. Of course it will be harder now to have brown skin in this country. Oh, shit, she thinks. Seeing both ways now. Not only the horror that just unfolded but all the horror to come.

Finally, after waiting all day, Sammy hears her phone ringing on the other side of the wall. Gotta go, she tells Sameer, for she knows it is Ben. Ben calling, finally. She scrambles out the door, then into her apartment, panics after the phone. "Ben?" she says, desperately, holding the receiver tight against her cheek, as if it will bring him closer. A few seconds pass where she thinks there is no one on the other end of the line—where she thinks she has just missed him, that the silence she hears is the silence before the call disconnects. But then he speaks. "Hey, Sam," he says. His voice heavy, flat.

"Oh, my God," she says.

"My God," he says.

"This is just…"

"I know."

"I'm so sorry." She doesn't quite know what she means. Just that he is from New York. And likely knows someone lost. Several people, maybe.

"I know," he says.

Then she hears a high-pitched, rhythmic sound, like a machine spinning to a stop—Ben is crying. Sammy is too stunned to say anything. They just stay on the phone, Ben gasping a few times, collecting himself. Sammy making the occasional involuntary noise.

"Are you still watching?" he finally asks.

"ABC," she says.

"Switch to CNN."

"I can't. I don't have cable."

"Okay, fine." He switches his channel and then Sammy, who has the volume of her television turned all the way down, can hear the voice of Peter Jennings coming through the phone, a beat removed from his corresponding image on screen. Peter Jennings' head is tilted thoughtfully, wearily. He has not taken a break all day. There have been no commercials. Only the anchor at his desk. For a man in the midst of an unprecedented crisis, a crisis unfolding just outside his door, he is oddly composed. It is as if he has been waiting all his life for this moment. He says he is still trying to make sense of it all, in real time, but in a way it seems he already has. He narrates this new tour of hell with a smooth, calming voice. We are all moving to a fiery pit underground and he is our butler, showing us our new quarters. Here is the room of darkness, here is the room of suffering, here is the staircase leading down to even greater depths of sorrow and shame, here are the prisons, the caves, the bunkers, here is the room where the bombs are made, here is the room where the coffins are made, here is the room where the coffins are stored, mind the flames that spring up from the ground, here is the river of death and forgetting, here are the tiny wooden boats that will bear you along.

At one point Peter Jennings explains that the current violence in Kabul (Where is Kabul? Sammy wonders, for the last time; this is the last time she will not know where Kabul is…) is merely an intra-Afghan affair, a burst of sectarian violence with which the United States has nothing to do.

Now and then the camera breaks away from the news desk and runs the same looping footage of the planes hitting the towers. Then the towers collapsing and the enormous clouds of black blossoming outwards. Then the smoking piles of rubble. Then the smoldering Pentagon. Then the burnt field in Pennsylvania where the fourth plane crashed. Then there is Diane Sawyer reporting from the street. And back to the news desk. On and on in a continuous loop.

An hour passes, two. Several times they reach a point where Sammy thinks to get off the phone—where she normally would have gotten off the phone—but this is different. This is ongoing. She cannot imagine, were she to put down the phone, what she would do next.

"What do we do now?" she asks Ben at one point. "Like, get up in the morning and go to work?"

"I don't know," he says. He has only just started at his mother's practice, doing the most basic work, med checks, chart reviews, and he doesn't really know what to expect. He had spent the day at the office, talking with the other partners in the practice, trying to come up with some sort of plan. It was all still unfolding but they could see what was coming next: In the following days people would be anguished, desperate. Clinics and ERs would be overflowing—they were all going to have to dig in. "I have no fucking idea."

They stay on the phone until two in the morning. At which point Ben acknowledges he should get some sleep. There is work ahead of him.

"Yes, get some sleep," she says.

"You too." Though neither of them do.

The next morning, not knowing what else to do, Sammy walks to her French class again. The Gideons are out on the street corners in their suits, distributing their little green Bibles, and she takes one, palms it, stuffs it in the pocket of her coat. Just on the edge of campus she passes a café that had opened two weeks before, a little place serving falafels and hummus. The proprietor, a new businessman who had saved for years to start his restaurant, according to an article she had read in the student paper, had named the café after himself, and so the name of the café, which had been written in gold across the storefront window, was Osama's. But now the window is gone, someone having thrown a brick through it, and so instead of reading the name Osama she reads, spray painted on the brick above the window: *Die Motherfucker.*

For the next several weeks Sammy's routine goes on like this. School, then dinner with Sameer, during which they watch the news, their new porn. But Ben's calls are always interrupting their evenings together. Whenever they are getting comfortable, Ben calls and she races over to her place and they talk while watching the news together, sometimes for hours. Whatever trouble had passed between them earlier that year, that whole business with Meg, has disappeared—they are once again each other's confidantes, outlets, lifelines. Ben reports that indeed the clinics are overwhelmed with patients. Trauma, anxiety, depression, suicidal ideations. On top of the usual amount of trauma and anxiety and depression and suicidal ideation. It's an all-hands-on-deck situation. He is tired. And angry. And overwhelmed. And sad.

He is also, he says, a person with a fortune at his disposal who doesn't need this shit. "I'm thinking," he says. "I'm thinking, fuck it."

"You can't quit," she says. "You worked so hard to get where you are. You're just starting out."

"That's the point of saying fuck it. It only counts *because* I worked so hard."

But in the end, it isn't Ben who says fuck it. One October afternoon, Sammy comes home to find an old box sitting in front of her door, a note taped to it. The note is from Sameer, who explains that he has gone to live with his brother in Canada. "Fuck this shit," he has written, in a beautiful, looping script at odds with its sentiment. "It's only a matter of time before some frat boy blows my head off." In the box he has enclosed his VHS player, and a small trove of gay pornography. *For your viewing pleasure*, says the card. Sammy will never watch these movies again, she knows, but also can't throw them away, can't throw away the memory of Sameer, who had been her only companion in this strange Midwestern town. She carries the box inside, dumps it on the floor of the coat closet. Now she is a person with a secret box of pornography. *It's not what it looks like*, she imagines herself saying. Though to whom, well, that she doesn't know.

2002

It isn't long before, at least in midtown, most traces of 9/11 have disappeared. There are more American flags than usual, displayed in storefronts. And for a time, people are wearing little flag pins on their lapels. Sometimes Ben passes a storefront and sees a grainy, photocopied picture taped up, facing out into the street, usually from a wedding or high school yearbook; the bereaved have hung these photographs of their beloveds. But on the whole, the city is back to itself relatively quickly. "Go shopping," the new president has instructed. And so people do. They get back to it.

Ben is, for all outward appearances, back to normal, too. He gets up every morning and goes to work. People are anguished about the attacks, of course, but by the end of their sessions they are back to talking about petty grievances. Promotions they failed to land at work. Things they hate about their husbands. "I know I shouldn't be complaining," they sometimes say. But it doesn't stop them.

Still, something has changed in Ben. Though he is getting up and going to work, seeing friends on the weekends, his mood has taken a turn toward the somber. Even a year later, on a cool fall day, the clouds stretched thin across the sky, windblown, he looks at them and considers they are stretching across the flight path of the planes—the clouds look to him like a scar. He can't look at the skyline without noting where the towers should be.

Ben is, he supposes, depressed. In a state of chronic

disappointment. He has not dated since Meg, and is still unsure about the choices he's made, whether he really wants to take over his mother's practice. Worst of all is this new knowledge, that the world he thought he was living in—that glorious, shimmering world, where anything was possible and there was nothing to fear—had been, his whole life long, a fiction. He should probably talk to someone, find a way to dig himself out, but he doesn't want to. Eight years of training have made him skeptical of his own profession.

What he manages to get away with—because he doesn't have time for appointments, or because he already spends so much time in this sort of dialogue and is tired of it, or because he already knows exactly what another therapist would say, or perhaps because he doesn't really respect many of his peers—is a therapy of his own devising.

He has four strategies. First is something he calls the walking cure, a half hour or so at lunchtime where he wanders the city. On weekdays, he simply walks the streets, taking turn after turn, trying to lose himself for a bit. Weekends, when he has more time to spare, he walks through the museums, or through Central Park, past the zoo and then the carousel. Sometimes he strolls through Barney's, or a bookstore, running his fingers across various items, though rarely buying anything.

At the end of his walks, Ben stops to register his impressions in a small notebook. He still retains the old habit he started years ago on the campaign, though his aspirations have narrowed—what he hopes to produce now are short poems tossed off in the moment, little impressions of New York life, like Frank O'Hara had done with *Lunch Poems*. O'Hara knew there was enough to observe on an hour's walk in New York to justify a poem, though in 1959, Ben thinks, it was even better—the world was more interesting. There was that poem about Kruschev arriving at Penn Station on his state visit. Or the one about Miles Davis beaten by a cop outside Birdland. And then of course "The Day Lady Died", his poem about walking past a newspaper box and seeing Billie Holliday's picture on the front page of *The Post*. Ben had memorized the last line of that poem, where O' Hara succumbs to a memory of leaning on the door of a bathroom in 5 Spot, listening to Holliday sing, mesmerized: *Everyone and I stopped breathing.* He wants to write a poem like that. Something beautiful, arresting. He would be happy with a single line, actually. Something that cuts to the quick. Something that matters.

Another thing Ben does, to help himself through, is drink. He starts drinking the moment he comes home from work, and keeps drinking for the rest of the night. He is familiar with addiction, is aware of what's happening, the dependency he is forming. But it doesn't stop him. His mother drinks, too. Often when they watch TV together at night, they are both quietly drunk. It is their favorite time of the day.

What walking doesn't solve, what drinking doesn't dull, Ben works out in his brief nightly meditations, wherein he imagines he is a guest on *The Tonight Show* with Johnny Carson. He sits down and tells Johnny what has been going on in his life, and Johnny listens, nods. Sometimes asks a question. Occasionally offers a bit of advice. He is surprisingly empathetic, this imagined Johnny Carson, who is always wearing the same thing—a plaid blazer with brown and blue stripes.

One particular night, they have been visiting for longer than usual, and have gotten past the standard opening bit of chatter. They have gotten down to it. They have gotten onto the topic of Ben's fourth, and most secret form of therapy. The one he never talks about. The one he can barely admit he engages in, even to himself.

"I don't know," Ben says to Johnny. "Define prostitute." He

is propped up in bed, swirling a drink. Still in his work clothes.

"Oh, we're defining prostitute, now?" Johnny says. He shoots the audience a confused look. "I mean, I think it's a fairly well-defined concept. And a simple one, not to mention."

"It's a legitimate question," Ben says. He picks up his tie—a pink one he bought at Barney's last week. Or salmon, might be more accurate—they always call it salmon, with men's clothing. He runs his hand down the tie. It is patterned with diagonal stripes of varying width and sheen. He loves this tie. He has had to force himself to wear other ties all week and now, Friday, he has indulged himself.

"Well," says Johnny, "how would *you* define it?"

"I suppose," says Ben, "from my point of view, I suppose a prostitute is someone who has sex with another person for money."

"I think you nailed it," says Carson. The audience laughs. "Was that so hard?"

"It's just, sometimes these things can fall into a gray area."

"In what way?" Carson says. "If you don't mind my asking, in what way is there a gray area about sleeping with someone, and then handing them a little pile of cash?"

"Well, sometimes it's a check," Ben says. The audience laughs. He likes to give himself a few good lines.

"Do they take American Express?" Carson says. The audience goes in bigger for that one—they like Johnny better, of course.

"I guess the gray area, the confusing thing is, it's not always spelled out."

"So you can understand the language, but you can't read or write it."

"Yes. Correct."

"It's all some sort of code."

"You see what I mean."

"I think I'm getting there. But give me an example."

"Well, let's say this certain girl makes your coffee every morning."

"Okay."

"And she's very friendly, and so you chat for a bit. Find out that she's in school. Or was in school but had to drop out to take care of her mother. But she's saving up, hoping to go back. She wants to major in marketing."

"Sounds fascinating."

"Then let's say she's gone for a week or two, and when she comes back, she tells you she had all this trouble with the landlord. The landlord said his son was moving back home after failing to make it in LA as an actor, and so the girl and her mother are suddenly being evicted from their apartment. So the girl had to take time off work to find a new place, one that has wheelchair access for her mother or whatever. But they're having a hard time, and don't have the deposit back yet from the landlord, so can't get together the deposit for a new place, et cetera."

"We're going to have to break for commercial," Johnny says, "if you don't get to the point."

"Okay, fine. They're having trouble, so you give her your card and say you might know a lawyer who can help. And she calls and leaves a message. You meet up for coffee and you end up giving her a thousand bucks so she can move, and she's sort of gushing. Later that week, she asks if she can buy you a drink. Then, that's pretty much it. You have a drink, preferably in a hotel bar. Head upstairs."

"Okay," Johnny says. Sort of snidely.

"Don't act like you don't know. These girls are young, they'd do anything for money—you know what it's like."

"I don't have the slightest idea what you're talking about."

The audience laughs.

"There's nothing wrong with it."

"Well, I guess I just have one question then," Johnny says, "If you're not ashamed, why are you talking to me about it? Why not talk it through with your mother?"

He looks at the audience. Makes a face. "That's an excellent idea,' he says. "I think I'll go wake my mother up right now and tell her all about it."

He gets a laugh.

"Fair enough," Johnny says. Frowns. He is a serious person, actually. Not too many people appreciate that about him. "But you take my point."

"I take your point," he concedes.

Perhaps there is a bit of shame, he admits. No doubt having to do with Meg, the disaster of Meg. He is still frayed from all of that, singed—he can't do that again. And even if he wanted to, so much of his emotional life is taken up by others—he doesn't have the patience, the compassion, left over for another person. Now sex is something partitioned off from the rest of his life, something along the lines of an extracurricular activity, like racquetball. Something he does once or twice a week. It is as easy as he described to Johnny, or sometimes even easier—he has only to stop in at a certain bar after work.

"But isn't it better when you actually care about someone?" Johnny asks. "What about Sammy? It seems like there might have been something there."

"There was," he says. "But I sort of dropped it. Broke it. However you want to put it." He still doesn't know quite what went wrong there. Only that, when it came down to it, he knew she loved him. And that, given his own limits—and without wanting to, yet also not being able to help it—he would crush her. "Anyway she's still a kid."

Johnny nods, knowingly. "I had her on the show once," he

says. "She tripped on her way out. Ed caught her by the elbow but she was about to go face down on the stage."

"That's unfortunate," Ben says. He can picture it.

"She wasn't much of a hit with the crowd. All she wanted to talk about was Emily Dickinson. We had to cut the whole thing."

"I get it," he says. "She's an acquired taste."

"Speaking of," Johnny says. "That's your fourth scotch. And you're not exactly pouring with restraint."

"I'll just finish it quick."

"Or maybe just leave it."

"It's expensive."

"You can afford to let it go to waste. That's one of the benefits of being rich."

"You're right. I should probably go to bed."

"Don't forget to set your alarm."

2002-2007

Sometimes it seems to Sammy that, even though it didn't touch her directly, 9/11 is nevertheless altering the course of her life. She is a person who, just on the verge of adulthood, saw the adult world, the world she was preparing to inhabit, go up in flames, right in front of her eyes. It was like she was a runner poised for the fourth leg of a relay, but just as the baton was about to be passed to her, it was dropped. And not just on the ground— more like dropped into the abyss.

Just act like there's a baton, is what she's decided, just start running, and so she does, mostly, though there is no real feeling in it, and often she simply stops, just stops running and stands there aimlessly while others keep running past her, because it seems so foolish, so foolish and embarrassing to be running along, as if it mattered, as if the race hadn't already ended a long time ago. All her ideas of responsible adulthood, everything she's ever been taught or experienced, it all goes out the window. The basic feeling is: Why bother? Who knows what the world will look like in five years? We could all be dead. The feeling is: There are no rules anymore.

A dark nihilism takes hold of Sammy, and the particular form it takes is that she starts fucking just about everyone she meets. All kinds of different boys. A sad boy who plays the guitar, who sits under a tree on campus singing Dylan songs through his nose. A fellow English graduate student, who wears tweed blazers and tortoise shell glasses, who likes to quote Samuel Johnson. A tattooed boy whose slender body is covered in an arsenal of weaponry, axes and blades and guns and even a cannon. A pudgy slacker boy who wears the same thing every day, rust-colored corduroys and a black Neil Young t-shirt, who rolls a joint before he even gets out of bed in the morning. More boys. Boys she meets in bars, in the coffee shop where she works, in the library, in the park. All through college, and through her master's degree, there was only Ben. Ben and her ridiculous, deluded love for him. But here in this small Midwestern town, love has fled, and it is as if, instead, she is trying to win some kind of contest.

The boys she sleeps with fall into two camps. Half of them are clingy. Asking her to stay the night. Calling or stopping by the coffee shop. The other half worry that Sammy is trying to ensnare them. "I gotta go," they say, pulling on their clothes. "I'll call you, okay?" These boys are poised for some kind of argument. Then surprised to find Sammy doesn't care, doesn't care one bit. Which turns them into the first kind of boy. Calling. Stopping by the coffee shop. But she just slips away. Runs through their fingers. She doesn't know what she's doing, or why, only that she has lost hold of the feeling that someone is watching, that it matters what she does or fails to do. She keeps telling herself she'll stop. But it goes on and on. Six months, nine months, a year.

She is using condoms, mostly, and taking the pill, mostly, except for the nights she forgets and falls asleep in her clothes. But still. Not far into the second year of her program, Sammy realizes she is pregnant.

She needs to do something and tries to figure out what that might be. She's in Missouri, so there aren't many options. She thinks and thinks about it. She can't make up her mind. Weeks go by. She keeps thinking maybe the problem will solve itself. Maybe she'll have a miscarriage. Maybe if she ignores it, it will just go away. This is how she usually handles things, and so far she has gotten by just fine.

More time goes by. One day she finally calls a doctor, schedules an appointment. It's another two weeks before she can get on the schedule, and by that time, it's too late. She's just going to have to have the baby.

When she finally tells Ben about this, it is in a halting, circuitous manner, involving noncommittal pronouns and passive verbs. "And so in this way," she says, when she at last gets to the point, "it was discovered that there's going to be a baby."

"Get an abortion," he says.

"It's too late," she tells him. "I sort of didn't realize what was happening for a while."

"How could you not realize you were pregnant?"

"I don't know. I guess I don't really keep very good track of things."

"Are you fucking kidding me?"

He seems angry with her. Like she's failed him, ruined something between them. Questions keep occurring to him, and he launches them at her. Who's the father? Are you going to drop out of school? What are you going to do for money? How can you not know who the father is? How many men are we talking about?

"I'm not really sure about that either," she says.

There is a long pause. Then Ben says, "Well, can't you line them all up for a DNA test?"

"I don't really want to. I don't want anyone else involved."

"You're going to need money. I don't think you're considering how expensive this is going to be."

"I've got it covered. I think."

"How much is your stipend?"

"Thirteen thousand," she says.

"Are you fucking kidding me?"

"Well, thirteen-five. And it's, you know, it's cheaper to live out here."

"Jesus, Sams," he says. "You're like twenty-grand under the *poverty* level. You're not even going to be able to afford *diapers*."

Sammy starts crying, but doesn't want him to know. She puts the phone down on the couch beside her, presses her face in her hands. "How could you *do* this?" comes Ben's voice. But it is small and distant, and the least of her problems now.

Then, in spring, the little girl, Ava, is born. Only five pounds and impossibly tiny. Her hair is thick and dark, almost black, and it is wild—there are little whorls all over her head, a cluster of small hurricanes. Her upper arms and shoulders are covered with a downy fur, the softest thing Sammy has ever felt. When the little girl opens her eyes, Sammy sees that they are a light, sparkling blue. Ava looks nothing like Sammy. Nothing like anyone Sammy knows, or ever has known.

One curious feature of Ava's birth is that it coincides with the US invasion of Iraq, March 2003. Sammy goes into labor that morning, and by the evening, when she calls Ben to tell him she had the baby, he asks if she's seen the news. "No," she says. "Turn it on," he says. She finds the remote control, which is also the nurse's station call button, attached to the hospital bed with a fat beige cord. She presses a green button and the wall-mounted screen comes to life.

A nighttime cityscape, a nocturne. Then the bright trail of rockets across a dark sky. In flashes, Sammy makes out the Baghdad skyline, blasts in the background. A mosque. A few palm trees. It looks like a nice city. A nice city being bombed. The baby is asleep in an isolette next to Sammy's hospital bed, and she makes a little squeak. Sammy turns to regard her. She is wearing a long sleeve white top with mittens attached to the cuffs, folded over her tiny hands. Just that and a diaper. She is covered in a fleece blanket, white with teddy bears printed all over it, bears with yellow and blue and pink ribbons around their necks. Sammy looks back and forth between the baby, so tiny, fast asleep, and this new war. Back and forth. Back and forth.

"I'm not trying to rain on your parade," he says. "Just thought you'd want to know."

"Well, I do suppose there are other things going on in the world." She acknowledges this, but still she feels, for the first time, a wall come down between herself and Ben. He's still living in that old world, she thinks. The world before the baby. He doesn't understand what's happened.

In the nights following, when Sammy is back at home in her apartment, she is terrified of being alone with the baby so keeps the television on twenty-four hours a day. She watches footage of the war, and more footage. The war is more or less being broadcast live. A camera has been set up along the bank of a river, which is lit up with streetlights and their reflection in the water. And beyond the river, a row of tall buildings. And beyond those, bright explosions, blast after blast, occasional bursts of rapid fire. She imagines people cowering inside the buildings, wondering what will happen, how close the fighting will come and when it will end. A beautiful city, she keeps thinking. Most of the action sounds remote, but once she is startled by a fireball, which appears just in front of the camera, and which calls to mind the burst of flames in which the wicked Witch of the West appears in *The Wizard of Oz*. Sammy has been able to compare war, up until this point, only to fiction. But a new feeling comes over her, too, no longer fiction but a desperate, visceral feeling that somewhere in that fiery city there is a mother with a newborn at her bedside—many, many mothers, in fact—who have just brought life into this world. She sees everything now as having to do with the baby. It is a twist in the narrative she didn't see coming. The war, which had sent her into a dervish of nihilism, of *fuck it*, wound up producing the behavior which produced the one thing she now cares about—the thing which pulls her out of it, brings her back into the world again.

Sammy's father flies in from Manchester to visit and he holds the baby for hours and hours, holds her tiny head in the palm of his hand. He cries noiselessly. Cries and then collects himself. Cries again.

He has brought the Burger King crowns he and Sammy used to always wear, a tradition begun on her fifth birthday, when she asked to be taken to Burger King. Her father had kept the crowns ever since. They always wore them around the house on Sammy's birthday, or when she visited home. Now there is a little girl whose birth must be celebrated. So they sit around Sammy's studio apartment in their crowns, the television running. Her father fashions a little crown for the baby out of paper. For the three days he visits, the baby is never put down. Someone is holding her at all times. The baby sleeps on top of Sammy, and her grandfather, her eyes shut tight, her little fists clenched, her crown askew.

Over the next three years, through graduate school, until Sammy gets her first job, she survives because her father sends her money. He has saved quite a bit, living so modestly, and he is happy to do it, he says, because Sammy and the baby are his only family, the heirs to his fortune as it were. All he asks is that he be allowed to visit, and that they visit him when they can. Sammy accepts all of this, but she feels bad. She feels bad. She feels bad all the time.

Sammy's entire life revolves around the baby and during these years, it must be said, she and Ben grow apart. Ben is busy with his practice, taking over more and more of his mother's patients as she semi-retires, spending long weekends down in

Florida. Ben is busy, busy building his life. Going out to dinners and concerts and gallery openings and charity galas. Busy taking up the mantle, becoming the person he was born to be. And the person he was born to be has nothing to do with babies in cities of no importance.

Sammy's life, meanwhile, has shrunk down to the square footage of her studio apartment. In the early days, the kind of attention the baby requires involves feeding and holding and changing, and these things alone take up more or less Sammy's entire life. Later there is a long stretch where the baby must be prevented from killing herself, from climbing tall objects and then falling off, from choking, falling down sets of stairs, running into the street. Between these pockets of anxiety there is boredom, heavy boredom. There is crying and there are crying cessation efforts; there is mess-making and cleaning up, scooping crumbs out of the bucket of the car seat, scrubbing dried pea mash from every crevice of the high chair; folding and unfolding strollers, buckling and unbuckling buckles; there is a running soundtrack of electronic toy noises and manic, sing-songy children's music; there are trips to Target for diapers and wipes, baby food and baby clothes.

Once the outright survival stage passes there comes language acquisition, single words at first, and then a bead-strung, relentless inquisition regarding those single words, not just what they are but why the exist, what they do: *What is this, What is that, Why is this, Why is that, Look, look, look!* Then, finally, comes a bit of abstract thinking, an understanding of how things relate to one another. One day Ava points to a cloud and says it looks like a Hot Pocket, and lo and behold, Sammy sees overhead a cloud that does, in fact, look exactly like a Hot Pocket. Sammy is proud her little girl has developed this affinity for metaphor and yet ashamed of what she has compared the heavens to. I cannot tell this story, she thinks, it is so cute, and yet I cannot tell it due to the shame of feeding my daughter this frozen processed food, microwaved until it is molten in the center, until the filling bursts from the pocket itself.

Ben doesn't want to hear about any of this, anyway. When Sammy calls him, and talks about what's going on with the baby, she can recognize the sounds of impatience coming from his end of the phone. The TV running rapidly through channels, the flick of a cigarette lighter. And when Ben calls her to talk, wanting to work out some theory or encounter, she often has to hang up because Ava is crying, or in the bathtub endangering herself, or wandering off in some way that requires the use of both of Sammy's hands. Sometimes Sammy tries to get away with putting Ben on speaker, but he hates being on speaker and figures it out almost instantly. As soon as he hears his own voice resonating through Sammy's apartment he says: "Am I on speaker? Did you put me on fucking speaker again?"

"I'm sorry," she says, "I'm sorry, I'm sorry, I'm just, it's impossible to talk while holding the phone anymore, Ava is, like, nonstop, she's like a little traveling disaster...."

"You did this to yourself," he tells her. "This is what you wanted." And he hangs up.

This stings a bit. Why does he treat her this way? Why must he punish her? If she had any dignity, she often thinks, she would stop answering his calls. But she can't hold onto these grudges for long. These days, she can't hold onto anything.

If Ben happens to call when Ava is asleep, Sammy can't really talk then, either, because she needs the time to grade papers or finish her dissertation. Basically she is trying to cram all of her doctoral and teaching work into the twenty-minute windows while Ava is occupied during the day, and then into late-night sessions, when Ava is finally asleep, by which time Sammy's brain is limp, lagging. Perhaps for this reason she shifts the focus of her dissertation away from the sprawling, manic work of Walt Whitman—which he never stopped revising, which he was adding to and adding to and adding to right up to the moment of his death—to the exquisitely controlled miniatures of Emily Dickinson. Each poem a little piece of origami. Phrases compressed and folded into sharp edges and angles. Sammy works in vicious, concentrated bursts. Attacking a single poem under a bright light. Then another. She unfolds each poem and lays out all of its meanings. Then folds it back up again. She makes seven different groupings of poems, a chapter for each. Her work is highly organized and striated. Compartmentalized. Her brain only works for about fifteen minutes at a time; this is the best she can do.

So in effect, Sammy is now a girl whose life is unfolding in isolation in a tiny room, writing about another girl whose life unfolded in isolation, in a tiny room. And this isn't very interesting to Ben because, Sammy has to admit, why should it be? Ben has written her off, she can tell. She imagines if he ever mentioned her to other people, which he probably wouldn't, he'd say something like: "One of my friends had a kid and it's all she talks about. It's fucking unbearable." She supposes it is. She is. Unbearable.

They talk less and less. Ava turns one, two, then three, and by this time Ben and Sammy are only talking maybe twice a month. They keep saying they will see each other soon, but Ben never wants to set foot in the Midwest, and Sammy can't leave Ava. A stalemate.

Then Ben's father dies and, even though they weren't close—in fact, Ben and his father had hardly spoken after Ben left for college—he is devastated. Instead of the relief he thought he would feel on his father's death—the lightness, the freedom from his father's judgment and cruelty—Ben feels sick all the time, tight in the chest. He is always on the verge of tears. And more than anything else, he has a manic urge to talk.

So he calls Sammy in the early hours almost every morning, four or five o'clock, wanting to talk through his memories. Sammy watches the sun rise as she listens to Ben, watches her room light up, watches the outline of her sleeping daughter emerge next to her in the darkness, then develop slowly, until her daughter materializes fully—her mouth open, an expression of complete tranquility on her face, her favorite stuffed dog snuggled underneath her chin, gripped tight. Over the course of several weeks, Ben goes through his whole childhood—the dark shadow his father's presence had cast over almost every aspect of his life. Ben describes his father as a man of almost pathologically regular habits. Every morning he had woken early and performed a series of calisthenics—a routine that never changed: jumping jacks, push-ups, squats, lunges, sit ups, three rounds each—and then went for a run. Then he showered and went to his office, or the hospital—he had clinic days and surgery days. He worked until eight each night, was home by eight-thirty. He ate his dinner, read the newspaper. Took a walk. Returned home for a drink and a cigarette. Then he went to sleep. Ben and his mother barely saw him during the week. And when they did, he was in the midst of his routine, not to be interrupted.

On weekend mornings, he did the whole routine with the calisthenics and running, then checked in on patients at the hospital. On the way home he stopped for bagels. Often he was able to eat his bagel and read the newspaper before his wife and son emerged from their bedrooms. "I got bagels," he told them, a bit of disdain in his tone. Somehow he managed to emphasize, in just three words, that he had gotten up long before they did—he had already gone out and worked a bit, and seen the world, and brought a bit of it home, for their enjoyment. The rest of Saturday, and all of Sunday, was a bit of a dance. Ben and his mother would have plans in place: Hebrew school, in Ben's early years, then outings to museums and movies, or trips into Connecticut to see his mother's cousins, piano lessons and recitals, soccer games, and, when Ben was in high school, rehearsals for the plays and musicals he acted in. They would always invite the father, and he would either attend, his frustration visible the whole time—he would pace with his hands in his pockets on the sidelines of games, or behind the last row of seats during productions—or he would stay home. In which case Ben and his mother were relieved, free to enjoy themselves, though they paid for it inevitably—the father was sulky when they got home, as if he had been kept away, asking bitterly whether they'd had fun, whether anything exciting had happened without him.

His father, Ben says, was especially unkind to his mother, mocking the comforts she afforded herself, the money she spent. Often she would spend an entire Sunday morning preparing a meal—fixing a roast and various sides, a pie for dessert—and he would stand watching her, eating a peanut butter sandwich, saying he had all he needed right in his hand, for forty-seven cents; then he wouldn't touch dinner. But by far the greatest insult was that he was skeptical of the mother's profession. He never wanted to talk about feelings, or hear about anyone else's. How Ben's parents had married—how they had ever managed to get through a date—he could never understand.

Perhaps it was because his father was so handsome, Ben muses. He was small but muscular, powerful. His face was beautifully sculpted, with high cheekbones and a strong jaw, a strong nose at a slight angle. His eyes were a deep bluish-green, his skin a rich olive color, his hair silver and wavy, parted on the side. Dashing, was the word people used to describe him. He carried within him, within his *person*, a mysterious power. "It's hard to explain," Ben tells Sammy. Again and again. He keeps working out the same theories. "She must have just been....in love with him."

"What a disappointment," Ben keeps saying. Meaning himself. Or his father. Or what they amounted to, together. Sammy doesn't quite know. Doesn't know and doesn't ask. That's always been the trick with Ben. To keep quiet, to wait and see. She just listens as he cycles through these stories, then repeats them. He has lost control of himself for the first time, has become the person talking, raging, churning—the person on the couch. "Yes," Sammy offers, every so often. Or, "Of course." Ben always talks for just under an hour, as if governed by the same contract he has with his patients. He rambles on, relaxed, rueful, pausing often, sighing. Then, always abruptly, he collects himself. "I'll let you go," he says. Clears his throat. "Sorry to call so early." Each time he hangs up it seems to be with finality. Like he's done with the whole thing. But he keeps calling. For weeks and weeks.

At the end of that semester, Sammy decides to visit Ben, who seems to need her. She flies home to Manchester with Ava, then leaves Ava with her grandfather, takes the train to the city. It is the first time Sammy has ever left the baby, as she still calls her, and she is nervous the whole train ride, sick with worry, hatching a plan to turn right around as soon as she gets to the city. When she arrives at Grand Central she rushes up to the lobby, to the bank of pay phones, and dials her father, expecting to tell him she is on the way back. "How is she?" she says, when her father picks up. She is clutching the phone, which is grimy and keeps slipping, so she clutches it harder, presses it right to her cheek, though it smells of gasoline. "She's *fine*," her father says. "Sleeping like a baby."

"Really?" she says. Frowns. She was expecting some kind of extended tantrum. But Sammy's father informs her that Ava has been happy all evening, and has given him a new nickname, Grampuddy. "She just came out with it," he says.

So she goes out into the city, to Ben's apartment. The bubble she has been living in for four years finally bursts and she can breathe in the outside air. When she arrives at his door, and knocks, she is suddenly anxious. Panicked. Ben opens with a flourish and looks her over. "You look exactly the same," he says, sounding surprised. "You haven't changed at all." He is moved, it seems. Happy she has come.

For Ben's part, he has gained a good deal of weight, and grown out his beard. But to Sammy, he is the same, exactly the same. His confidence. The air about him. "You haven't changed either," she says.

And so they are back. They are back and it's like they were never apart.

2007

It's the cat lady again. The woman who is grieving the death of her cat, Ramone. Has been grieving the death of her cat, Ramone, for months.

"I named him after The Ramones," she tells Ben. "I don't know if I mentioned that last time."

She had.

"Because he was so sleepy," Ben says. Hoping to stop her from telling the story again, but she starts telling it anyway.

"I wanna be sedated," she sings. "It was just so funny, how he was sleeping, like, dead asleep while all his brothers and sisters were jumping all over the place. They always say, when you're picking from a litter, to choose the friendliest one. But he was just so peaceful looking. So sweet. I knew the instant I saw him."

"This is just, part of life," he offers. "When you love something, you're bound to lose it eventually. That's what makes love so hard to let into your life, for many people. You should be glad that you did." Now that song is stuck in his head. *I can't control my fingers, I can't control my brain.*

"I know," she says. "I know you're right. I just can't stop being sad."

This woman is prematurely old. She is just over forty, but has given up any care for her appearance—has cut all of her hair off, wears no makeup, goes around in sweatsuits. Last year her father died and left her money—millions—but she's not yet figured out what to do with it. She just sits around her apartment with her cats.

Hurry, hurry, hurry, before I go insane.

"I keep trying to enjoy what I still have," she says.

"That's a good exercise," he tells her. "You should even write those things down. The things you still have that make you happy."

"At least," she says, starting to cry again. "At least I still have Reggie!" Her other cat. She bursts into fresh sobbing.

They decide to tweak her meds, more of this, less of that, and then the hour is up, thank God. He stands and walks to the door, opens it. The cat lady hugs him on the way out—she's a hugger, and he has sort of given in to it, extending one arm so she can close in on him, then tapping her lightly on the back, twice.

It's the lunch hour, and Ben takes his usual walk. He spends a few minutes wondering, as he does more and more lately, whether this is what he should be doing with his life. In med school and residency, psychiatry had seemed so vital to him, so urgent. He can think of dozens of cases that took hold of him—the patients so desperate in their suffering he could feel it in his own body. One woman in particular comes to mind, a schizophrenic who came in for a med check. He'd read her file and knew what questions to ask—whether she was taking her meds, whether she'd been seeing the demon again. Traygor, she called him. A red, horned devil with yellow eyes who reared up in her mind and threatened her. Just the mention of the demon had set the woman trembling. She was in her thirties, but perhaps because of her hair, which was cut in a short bob, or perhaps because the features of her face were so small and delicate, she looked like a child. "No," she'd whispered. Her voice quivering. She'd curled in on herself, as if afraid of being struck. Her suffering was palpable.

Now he is tweaking meds for cat ladies.

He is winding through the park, past the zoo and carousel, all those kids circling around, bobbing up and down, their parents standing along the circumference, waving. The parents seem deranged, their faces contorted into manic expressions. Maybe they really are that happy, Ben thinks, but probably not—probably they are making the faces they think they are supposed to make, or are compelled, biologically, to make, to demonstrate to their offspring the depths of their love.

Just past the carousel, Ben watches a balloon vendor, leaning to present a balloon to a small child. The vendor has made a loop with the string and is fitting it around the child's wrist. The child—a young boy with dark curly hair, wearing a striped shirt, khaki shorts, loafers, sort of pudgy, close to what Ben had looked like as a kid—watches solemnly, as if being offered communion. Ben feels a tenderness, and considers how we only feel affection toward children who are our own, or who remind us of ourselves. He keeps walking. Not ten seconds later the balloon whisks past him. He turns and sees the child is stopped in his tracks, watching the balloon ascend, the look on his face one of total surprise. The sadness of having lost his balloon has not yet set in. For the moment he is suspended in the shock, amazed that something could fly away so quickly.

Later that night, Ben is in the kitchen, listening to the radio while he prepares his dinner. His doctor has recommended he stop eating out so much, try cooking for himself. So he is attempting a lentil soup, unenthusiastically peeling a carrot.

The news drones on, something about a coup in an African nation. *Soldiers raided the village*, Ben hears. *Beaten and killed... set fire to the villagers.* And he wonders what he just heard— whether fire was set to villagers themselves, actual people, or whether the announcer was using the plural possessive, perhaps the *villagers' homes* was what he said. He doesn't quite know, and realizes he doesn't care. It is all too much. He snaps the dial to the left, turns it off.

He goes back to his cookbook. His mother's cookbook, is how he thinks of it. How he still thinks of everything in this apartment. His mother's stockpot, his mother's knife set, wooden spoon. She has been gone for six months, and he still isn't used to it. Still doesn't know quite what happened. She had gone down to Miami Beach to meet with a realtor, sell the condo. The condo she had always hated. It had been his father's, mostly—he was the one who loved the sun, loved to escape to the beach in winter. Then he'd died, and Ben's mother was relieved, excited even, to rid herself of the property. She had expected to stay in Miami only a few days. But a week went by, then two. Then she'd come back home, but only for two months. To give her notice at the practice, tie up loose ends. "The sun," she kept saying. "I need to feel the sun on my face."

The phone rings—Sammy, a welcome distraction—and he picks up. She is in a state. "Oh my *God*," she says. "I had the worst fucking *day*."

She has been in a state a lot, lately. First worried about job applications, then interviews. Then her thesis defense. Her defense was today, he remembers. "How'd it go?" he asks. "What happened?"

She tells him the defense was fine. A breeze, actually. But after, when she picked up Ava from day care, hoping to celebrate—ice cream, was the plan, they were going to go out for ice cream—her car broke down at a stoplight. She relays the whole scene for him. How the light had turned green and she'd shifted into first, but then the engine had died, and the car behind her leaned on its horn, and she tried the engine again and it flickered to life for a second but then failed, then again and again, so the traffic lined up behind her started passing her on the right, the drivers pausing to give her dirty looks while she tried and failed and tried and failed to start the engine.

She is making a skit, trying to play the scene for laughs, exaggerating the looks the other drivers gave her as they passed, exaggerating, too, the handsomeness of the AAA service man who answered her call, extolling his merits, how prompt and how helpful, how kind he was to Ava. "Really," she says, "if there's a service to bring a man with jumper cables to the rescue, happy to help even in the rain, why not also add a grocery service, a handsome man in a truck showing up with exactly what you need for dinner, just a phone call away. At that point," she says, "no one would really need a husband." But Ben can see through her, can tell she is just papering over—that in fact she is tired of having these problems with her car, tired of the whole mess she's made of her life.

On cue, she confirms his suspicions. "I mean," she says, "It's like I can't get away with *anything*. I get through my defense no problem, I'm happy for once, I try to celebrate, and then the car breaks down. It's like I couldn't have a good day if I tried. It's like a fucking *conspiracy*."

So he says, in an effort to help: "It could be worse, you could live in the Sudan, I heard this story on the news today about these roving militia groups sweeping into villages."

"And burning them down," Sammy says. "I just heard that. But I was making dinner and sort of missed it. Were they burning the *villagers*?" she asks. "Or the houses?"

"I think the villagers *themselves*," Ben says. "But I'm not sure."

"Jesus," she says. "You're right. Okay, I'm done feeling bad for myself."

"Glad I could help."

"You just can't let me have anything, can you?"

"I try to keep people in line," he says. "Talk them down from the ledge of self-pity. It's a public service I like to offer."

"You're an unsung hero. You're like the Mother Teresa of the Upper East Side."

"I'm not going to lie," he says. "It's not easy. I suffer." At first he had been trying to make Sammy feel better, but he could never stay there for long—something swerved in him, always, whenever there was an earnest moment between them. Now he is back where he likes to be: in a state of playful irony. In talking about his suffering, he is taking a little stab at himself, his privilege, but he is also taking a little stab at her—for he knows she suffers quite a bit, suffers from regret, disappointment, longing. Why am I like this? he wonders. With Sammy, with the Cat Lady, with everyone. Why? And then answers himself: It's my nature. I can't help it. He is in the wrong profession; some flaw in him, some barrier, will always stop him just short of true feeling.

Then again, he considers, maybe that barrier is part of it all. What makes it possible to keep going.

After they hang up, Ben goes back to the business of making his dinner, but finds his will is gone. The whole point of living in New York is so you never have to face a moment like this, chopping a carrot alone in a kitchen. He looks over at the stove, the scallion simmering in oil in the stock pot, and then turns the burner off. Then picks up the phone and orders takeout.

He feels defeated. Something has passed him by.

2007-2008

Somehow Sammy finishes, then publishes, several chapters on Emily Dickinson's poems. Completes and defends her dissertation. And on the basis of this work, gets a job in The City of No Importance, at a satellite of her current flagship campus, just two hours west. So she packs herself and Ava off to the city. Finds an apartment. Finds a pre-school. Then spends the summer wondering how to be a real adult. Or if not that, how to fool everyone into thinking she's an adult.

Ava starts pre-school the same week Sammy starts her new job. They have never been apart, not in any kind of extended, daily arrangement—in grad school, Sammy only dropped Ava off at daycare for three or four hours at a time, three days a week. And so now, in addition to learning to navigate their new environments, they must learn how to be without each other.

It isn't going so great. It is Monday of the second week of school, and Ava has yet to adjust. They are standing on the front steps of the school, working through a tense negotiation. "I'll be back," Sammy says. "You know I always come back, right after nap."

"Don't leave me!" Ava sobs. She jumps up and down, reaching up at Sammy, clamoring. Her dark hair, which is a mess of curls, bounces, and Sammy bends down to kiss it, settle it. "Remember what we talked about?" Sammy says. They had talked, many times that weekend, about going to school, and saying goodbye at the door, like they are supposed to. Sammy is not supposed to set foot in the classroom, according to the school's protocol, which advises parents to say goodbye to their children at the front entrance with curt, cheerful waves. But Sammy hasn't managed this yet. All last week, she walked Ava to her class and then, because Ava insisted, walked into the classroom and helped with settling Ava's coat and backpack on their designated hooks. "Please," Sammy says. Plaintively. She doesn't want to go back inside. Mostly because she is afraid of Ava's teacher, Miss Henri.

Miss Henri is a retired elementary school gym instructor and part-time professional clown. She is short and broad-shouldered, and her silver hair is shorn close to her scalp. She wears the same thing every single day: a gray sweat suit with spotless white sneakers. Her accessories are a pair of black-framed glasses, and a whistle around her neck.

Miss Henri runs her classroom with a military precision Sammy finds terrifying, but with which the other children seem perfectly fine. After all the children arrive, Miss Henri blows a short burst into her whistle, and all the children stop what they are doing and fall quiet. Another burst, and they line up in a row in front of Miss Henri, tallest to shortest. "Circle time," says Miss Henri, and all the children arrange themselves on the classroom's circular rug, legs crossed, hands folded in their laps.

Sammy knows this because all last week, she sat with Ava in the corner of the room for the first hour of class, trying to quell Ava's sobs. She'd get Ava settled down, and try to break away, but Ava would cling to her neck, wrap her legs around Sammy's waist. All through circle time—while Miss Henri went through a daily routine with a large easel, indicating with a pointer the day's date, time of sunrise and sunset, and weather forecast—Ava clung to Sammy, her little arms wrapped around Sammy's neck, fingernails dug into her skin.

On Friday, she had promised Miss Henri not to enter the room again. So she tries to get Ava to walk through the doors on her own. "I have to leave now," she says. "I have to go to work."

"Just walk me to the room?" Ava says.

"Okay, fine," Sammy says. "But that's it." She pulls open the door, walks Ava to her class.

But then the crying starts again.

Sitting in the corner, avoiding Miss Henri's smoldering stares, Sammy wonders why Ava is like this. Every other kid seems fine, happy to be at school. What exactly is the fucking problem? She does a quick round of math in her head. So far, she and Ava have spent ninety percent of their waking hours together, with the remaining ten devoted to Sammy's work. Now the ratio is more or less flipped. Because this, apparently, is what it means to be an adult. A big girl. But what if, Sammy asks herself, she doesn't want to be a big girl? What then?

The next day, a new little boy joins the class. He arrives on Tuesday morning just after Ava and Sammy, carried in by his mother—a pretty young woman whose hair is obscured by a floral headscarf. The boy is uncommonly small, short and skinny, with dark hair and enormous brown eyes. He is wearing a striped shirt and overalls, leather sandals. Sammy likes him immediately—something about his expression, which is quietly stunned. Miss Henri greets the boy and announces to the class that they have a new student. "His name is Wissam," she says. And adds, with an uncommon enthusiasm, "He's from *Iraq*!" Miss Henri proceeds to draw a vague outline of North America on the whiteboard, and then indicates their city with a star at its center. Then she draws a bunch of waves, and a shapeless blob to the right of them, indicating, Sammy guesses, the entirety of Europe and the Middle East. Here's Iraq, she says, making an X on the mass of land. "Wissam is a brave little boy. He travelled all the way across the ocean." She draws an arrow arching over the ocean. Then she draws a shark in the water, to emphasize the boy's bravery.

But Wissam is not brave, not particularly. When his mother tries to set him on the ground, he clings to her. His eyes are wild. He screams.

Wissam and his mother make their way to the corner, too, so now it is the four of them lingering through circle time. Wissam's mother doesn't speak English, so Sammy tries to establish a friendly rapport with smiles and gestures. Little shrugs and eye rolls. What they seem to be communicating is: They both want to get the hell out of there, they both have work to do; yet, neither one of them wants to leave, because it is too difficult. They seem to acknowledge to one another their shared weakness, the blame they bear in this situation, and yet also, their helplessness—they can do nothing about it.

This happens day after day. The longer they sit in the corner each morning, the more frustrated Miss Henri becomes. She makes a series of increasingly passive aggressive remarks, along the lines of: *If we just had two more friends in our circle it would be complete.* But Ava lingers, as does Wissam.

The way Miss Henri finally gets Ava and Wissam to join the class is with an activity she refers to as Creative Movement. Three times a day she holds movement sessions, which consist of turning on Beyoncé videos and lining the kids in front of the television like a row of back-up dancers. Ava and Wissam love Creative Movement and so as soon as Miss Henri removes the red tablecloth that is draped over the television, they leap up from their mothers' laps and join the class. This is, Sammy knows, her cue to leave the room, but she is often so mesmerized by Creative Movement she lingers at the door, half-in, half-out.

In the first phase of Creative Movement, the kids watch an entire video straight through. Then they watch it again, and

Miss Henri freezes the frame at certain key moments, playing and deconstructing and replaying particular dance moves, moves she has given names to: Feel It, Kneel It, Shove It, Deal It. The kids practice and memorize these moves, then string them together as Miss Henri calls them out. Then they run through the video again, trying to keep up. They trip over their own feet, fall over laughing. Sammy finally leaves for work and spends the rest of the day with Beyoncé songs running through her head.

Her first semester, she teaches two sections of a course called American Lit II, which she subtitles: White Males from Whitman to Franzen. There are thirty-five kids in each class. On the first day, she goes around asking everyone's name and major, hoping for English, but all of the students seem to have pledged allegiance to majors relating directly to job placement. Business. Nursing. Computer Science. And something Sammy has never heard of before: Music Management. After the third student names this as his major, she asks: "What is Music Management?"

"It's like, the management of music?" says one of the Music Management majors. His hair is hanging in his face and she can't see his eyes. Can't tell if he's sincerely trying to answer the question, or just fucking with her.

In the first weeks, in an effort to learn and remember her students' names, Sammy keeps going around the room, soliciting answers to certain softball questions: What is your favorite band, favorite movie, favorite book? The kids have strong opinions about bands and movies, but very few can identify a favorite book. "I don't really read," many of them say. One kid volunteers: "I haven't read for the past two years because my eyes hurt too much."

"Oh," she says.

"Because of the sand," says the kid.

"Oh?" she says. Leadingly.

"I've been in *Iraq*."

"*Oh.*" Tumblers click into place and a door swings open in Sammy's mind. Suddenly this kid makes sense. He is frighteningly large, absolutely enormous, and holds himself with uncommonly good posture. He projects, simultaneously, a sense of aggression and restraint. His mouth is always hanging open. A soldier.

"What's your name again?" she asks.

"Kevin Funkhauser. But I go by Kev."

"Okay, Kev. Well I hope you can read now. I hope we can find a book you like."

"All due respect, Ma'am," he says. "I doubt it."

After class Sammy goes to her office and shuts the door and tries to work on her Dickinson book, the book that will secure her tenure and enable her to continue to feed her daughter. This is basically how she thinks of her work, how she thinks of everything: work equals food equals kid. The stakes are high and she tries to be productive. Tries to write something innovative and serious. But the Beyoncé songs from Creative Movement are still running through her head, so when she reads Dickinson it is with a strangely upbeat cadence, every line glossed over with uncharacteristic bravado.

> *I heard a Fly buzz - when I died -*
> *The Stillness in the Room*
> *Was like the Stillness in the Air –*
> *Between the Heavens of Storm,*
> *Bitch.*

At the end of the day, when Sammy picks up her daughter, she finds her sitting underneath the crafts table with Wissam. Miss Henri informs Sammy that Ava and Wissam like to sit together under the table playing all afternoon, if not exactly with each other, at least side by side. Wissam pushes cars around and Ava manipulates two small plastic dogs through the traffic. "It's their thing," says Miss Henri. "I don't like it, I'd prefer them to stay with the group, but it keeps them happy."

When Sammy bends down to peek under the table and tell Ava it's time to go home, Ava motions for her to join them under the table. Sammy drops to her stomach and army crawls under. "Look out," says Ava, and runs the dogs up Sammy's arm. "Broom, broom," says Wissam, and runs his cars up her other arm. Then the dogs and cars run through her hair and collide and explode: Psh, Psh, Psh.

"Everyone died," says Ava.

"Well," Sammy says. "Good. Because it's time to go."

In the evenings, Ava insists that Sammy go to YouTube and play the Beyoncé videos from Creative Movement, insists she learn the whole curriculum. So she does. She sets up the laptop and finds the Beyoncé songs and follows Ava's instructions. Ava teaches her a handful of moves: Twirl It, Drop It, Work It, Bump It, Hop It, and Jump It. Then various combinations thereof. Drop It and Work It, Bump It and Jump It, Twirl It and Hop It, Jump It and Drop It, Work It and Work It. Ava shouts the moves like a square dance caller, faster and faster until Sammy falls over.

"Uh-oh," says Ava. "Uh-oh, uh-oh."

Of course, Sammy calls Ben and tells him about everything: Kev and the Music Management majors, Beyoncé and Miss Henri, Beyoncé and Emily Dickinson. And then Wissam. She goes on and on about Wissam. "I feel like I'm watching some sort of pageant," she says. "This little Iraqi boy and little American girl hiding away because their love isn't, like, sanctioned or whatever. Their countries are at war, they don't even speak the same language, but love, you know, love is all that matters. It's like the entire American/Middle Eastern conflict hidden under the table. It's like Romeo and Juliet under there, I'm telling you. It's intense."

"You might not want to make that comparison," he says. "I mean, we know how that one ends."

"Right," she says. "Right. We need a comedy here."

"Or maybe you don't have to keep reading into everything. Turning your life into a morality play."

"Gimme a second here," she says. "Maybe, maybe *Midsummer Night's Dream*?"

"*All's Well That Ends Well*," says Ben. "Is what you're going for."

Which is true. He's right. That's what she wants.

In the fall parent-teacher conference Miss Henri tells Sammy that Ava is insecure. There's all that clinging in the morning. And then she still requires transition objects to ease the separation, which she is supposed to have outgrown by now. Ava's particular transition objects are two plastic dogs she brings from home, Franz and Franz, each small enough to be obscured in her clenched palm. She walks around all day with her fists shut tight, the dogs stifled inside.

"Oh, right," Sammy says. "The dogs. I can't really, it's hard for me to explain how important those are for her."

"She won't participate in activities," says Miss Henri, pushing her glasses high onto the brim of her nose with one finger. "Because her hands are occupied with those animals."

"Right."

"No art," says Miss Henri. "No Music. No snack. No building blocks." She is counting these things out on her fingers. Everything, with Miss Henri, has an accompanying gesture. "No writing and no puzzles."

"Oh," Sammy says. Suddenly she appreciates the problem. How, if you're holding onto something, you can't participate in the world around you. The solution is clear—Ava should put the dogs down—but it is also, as a solution, unimaginable. She loves the dogs so much.

"Maybe she can," Sammy falters. "Maybe she can hold both dogs in one hand while she does things with the other."

"In my experience," says Miss Henri, "when something is holding you down, a bad habit or a negative partner or whatever, the only solution is to put it in a box."

Sammy imagines Ava putting Franz and Franz in a box. Carrying the box around.

"To the left," says Miss Henri, swiping her finger.

After a beat or two, comprehension breaks across Sammy's face. The Beyoncé lyric. "Oh!" she says. "Right. A box to the left."

"You get me?" says Miss Henri.

"I get you." So the challenge is: Ava must learn to think of Franz and Franz as boyfriends whose persons and belongings are being evicted. Kicked to the curb, as it were.

"Miss Independent," adds Miss Henri, "is what we're going for." She does a little dance from the video.

"Right," Sammy says. "Okay, good." She is feeling pumped. She's going to help her daughter break the cycle of a dependent relationship. And in the process, help herself. She walks out of the classroom feeling buoyant. Like the Beyoncé lessons she's been taking, her newfound Beyoncé literacy, is going to change her life. All this time she's been shunning pop culture, burying her head in books, but now she gets it. Beyoncé is doing for people now what books used to do. Showing people how to live. How to deal. How to win.

The first chance she gets, Sammy calls Ben to talk through this little revelation. Though by the time she gets him on the phone, the feeling is gone. "I think I felt what it was like to be Beyoncé," she says, "for like twenty minutes. It's totally gone now, but while it lasted, I mean at the time it was amazing. I was ready to take care of business. Be a grown up. Get shit done. You know, what the kids say—I was ready to, like, crush it."

"I think the problem you're struggling with," says Ben, "is that basically you're the photonegative of Beyoncé."

Which is true, she admits. He's cut to the heart of it. Nailed it again.

The year carries on, then closes with a bit of drama. About two months before the end of the term, Wissam stops coming to school. Ava no longer has a playmate—she just plays under the table by herself. Keeps asking Sammy where Wissam is, why he left. But Sammy doesn't know—she never gets an explanation. She feels a pang of guilt, partly to blame. She should have tried harder, she thinks. Been more welcoming. She should have asked Wissam's mother out for coffee, at least.

"Ava put all her eggs in one basket," Sammy tells Ben. "And now the basket has disappeared—we have no fucking idea where it went."

"She'll make a new friend," he says.

"I don't think so. Another boy tried to crawl under the table with her, and she bit him."

"Maybe Wassim's mother," Ben muses, "is a terrorist."

"Oh, please."

"Think about it. A family from Iraq? Disappears suddenly?"

"This is exactly the kind of thing," Sammy says, "that's perpetuating this awful war. This is *exactly* the kind of thinking. I'm surprised at you, frankly. Frankly, I can't believe you just said that."

"Sammy," he says. "I was just fucking with you."

"Oh."

"You're turning into a real shrew. You're hardening into, like, one of those witch faces people make out of shriveled apples. Your two topics of conversation are the news, and children."

Sammy bends forward and places her head on the table, which she does when she is despondent. More and more these days. "I know," she says.

"What are your good qualities again?" Ben asks. "Remind me."

Her brain is working furiously, but she can't think of anything. She feels as if a bell will go off at any moment and if she doesn't think of something before it sounds, she will lose Ben forever.

Finally, at what feels like the last second, she thinks of something. "I'm consistent," she says. And Ben laughs, a single, loud bark. She can still make him laugh, she thinks. At least once in a while.

"I know you won't change," he says, "I know you're just going to keep doing what you're doing, but I'm just telling you it would be better for you and Ava if you stopped reading all of the world's conflicts into your daily lives. Ava is Ava," he says. "You're you. You're not little American avatars for our global socioeconomic crisis."

"I'm just trying to make sense of things."

"You're making metaphors. I get it. It's what you do."

"Exactly," she says. "Thank you. You, you understand me."

"The problem is, if everything's a metaphor, then nothing is real. Nothing is what it is."

She doesn't know what to say to that.

"I think the danger is, then, you're not really being with your daughter, as a person, you're set back and viewing it all like a play. And that's, that's going to be a problem. It's going to sneak up on you."

"I thought you didn't give advice to patients," she says. "I thought you just let them obsess. Then made observations so they could, you know, come to their own conclusions."

"You're not my patient," he says. There is a pause in which Sammy thinks he means she is better than a patient, closer to him, more valuable. But then he says, "You couldn't afford me."

More and more, it feels to Sammy that she is in the middle of a love triangle, except without the love, exactly. Or rather, with a different configuration of love than in the usual triangle. She loves Ava. And loves Ben. But Ava and Ben have never met, and do not love each other. In fact, often they don't seem to like each other at all.

"When are you going to be done talking to Uncle Ben?" Ava is always asking. Tugging on the leg of Sammy's pants. Wanting attention.

"In a minute," she says. "Can I just have, like, a single minute?"

"But you're *always* talking to him," says Ava.

Which probably seems true, Sammy has to admit.

To Ava, Uncle Ben is an abstraction. Just a voice coming through the phone. Sammy realizes this, but never so pointedly as one night when she is cooking dinner, and Ava asks: "What are we having?"

"Uncle Ben's," she says. "And chicken."

Ava is oddly quiet for a stretch. For which Sammy is grateful, because she is trying to slice a chicken breast into strips without touching it, struggling with the knife and fork. Once she gets the meat in the skillet she starts looking for the rice, which has disappeared from the counter. She turns and sees Ava scrutinizing the orange box. "This is Uncle Ben?" she asks, gazing at the picture of Frank Brown, the black chef from New Orleans.

"That's not *Uncle Ben*, Uncle Ben," Sammy says. "It's a different Uncle Ben. This is Uncle *Ben's*, actually."

"Right," says Ava. "Uncle Benz."

Sammy regards Frank Brown, in his dapper tuxedo, and compares him to Uncle Ben. They do share a certain dignified air. But otherwise, physically, there's nothing further from the independently-wealthy Manhattanite, the Rubinesque psychiatrist she counts as her best friend, nothing further from this.

And certainly, Ben doesn't want much to do with Ava. He'll listen to Sammy talk about Ava for a while, but it's never long before he redirects her conversation, or cuts her off entirely. "Sams," he'll say. And he doesn't even need to say the rest. She gets it. She's doing it again.

But occasionally Ben does something that surprises Sammy. Like when he sends Ava presents—once a box of stuffed dogs, once a video game player, once a monogrammed piggy bank. These presents arrive in observance of no particular holiday or occasion. Just random offerings, whose purchase and shipment Ben probably tasks to his secretary. But still, Sammy thinks, he is kind. Or has kindness in him.

Then, this too: on the eve of the 2008 election, the housing bubble bursts, the entire economy collapses, and people lose their houses and retirement savings and their jobs. Sammy feels sorry for the people she sees on the news—people who have worked hard and saved carefully, people who did the right thing and have somehow ended up with nothing. She feels sorry for them, and worried for the country. And yet, mixed in with this, a sense of relief. The guilt that has been hanging over her these past few years—for not saving towards retirement, for putting her money toward rent instead of a mortgage—has suddenly vanished. Because if she had been doing those things, she would have wound up in the same place she is now, possibly even worse.

"The good news is," she tells Ben, "I didn't lose a single penny in the market." And Ben tells her, offhandedly, that so far he's lost about a million dollars.

"Seriously?" she asks.

"A little more," he says.

"Good grief." What she says now instead of *Holy shit*. Because of Ava, who is always listening.

"Ava's college fund is pretty wiped," says Ben.

"What?" Sammy says. Unaware he had established one.

"Don't worry," he tells her. "It'll come back."

It is Ben's nature to be furtive in his generosity, Sammy comes to believe. He is often cold in person, judgmental. Sometimes hurtful. But then, when she isn't looking, when she's distracted with some problem or other, he will offer her something. A bit of tenderness she wasn't expecting. A word, a glance. There's some code governing it all. What Ben allows and doesn't allow. What he gives and receives. Wants and doesn't want. She has given up hope of ever cracking it, but then again, she doesn't stop trying. She is the only one, as far as she knows, who still bothers.

Sometimes Sammy imagines combining the two loves of her life. Imagines visiting the city with Ava. Walking her to all the places she and Ben visited together. She imagines Ben happy. Pulling a coin from his pocket to give to Ava, so she might toss it in a fountain. Imagines him putting Ava up on his shoulders, pointing at various wonders. Imagines the three of them making their way through the Central Park Zoo, riding the carousel. She imagines walking together past a balloon vendor, Ben buying Ava a red balloon and her carrying it proudly through the park. Then losing hold of it. She imagines the three of them with their heads flung back, watching this bright balloon whisked into the sky, soaring beyond the treetops, smaller, smaller, and even this would be wonderful, this lost balloon, in the swiftness of its flight, in its yearning to be free.

Some part of Sammy is waiting for Ben to suggest she bring Ava along to the city. But he doesn't. Because he does not aspire to be happy in this particular way. Because he is not that kind of boy.

2009

One night Ben is checking his email in bed and sees something from Kurtz. He almost never hears from Kurtz these days and wonders what will happen when he opens the message. He clicks on it and flinches, as if expecting some burst of light and noise.

But there is only a link, in Cyrillic script—it looks like spam. He clicks on it anyway. His browser opens to the website of a Russian newspaper. Some article about Dmitry Medvedev, the puppet president serving as Putin's stand-in. He can read none of it, so studies the accompanying photo. Medvedev is pictured walking down a hallway—a grand, gilded hallway with a high ceiling, a giant chandelier overhead, the floor and walls tiled in marble. Medvedev is walking along, at the head of a cluster of men. Ben can find nothing of significance, wonders why Kurtz sent him the link. He is about to give up, go back to work, when suddenly one of the figures in the background catches his eye. A slight, bald man in a steely gray suit. His body turned at an angle, slender as a blade. His head is cast downward and his face is obscured, except for a crescent of his profile. What catches Ben's eye, particularly, is the chin—the spear-like chin. Boris. Ben rummages for his phone and calls Kurtz, who answers right away. "What the fuck am I looking at?" Ben asks. "Is that who I think it is?"

Kurtz laughs. His manic, villainous laugh. "He's all up in the fucking *Kremlin*."

"I *told* you," Ben says. "I told you he couldn't be trusted." Ben is unconcerned with whatever Boris may or may not have been doing for Russia all those years, from inside the Clinton White House. Just happy. Happy to have been right.

"Well," Kurtz says. "Congratulations, I guess."

"Holy shit," Ben says, the gravity of the situation finally settling on him.

"Holy shit is right," says Kurtz. "Holy fucking shit."

Then Kurtz has to go. He is still at the office, he says, even though it's ten-thirty at night. He never sleeps, or rather, as he puts it, *those fuckers won't let me sleep for a single fucking second*. He hangs up. Ben considers the possibility—probability, in fact—that Kurtz is back to using cocaine. How could he not be?

Ben calls Sammy to gloat. Sends her the link, gets her on the phone. "Is that who I think it is?" she says.

"Bingo," says Ben.

"Holy fucking shit," she says. "Oh my God. You should tell someone! Like, the FBI. Or Kurtz! You should call Kurtz!"

"Who do you think sent it to me?"

"Oh, right," she says. "Of course he did. My head is just, it's just spinning. I mean, this is crazy, right? This is huge. Do you think, so you think he was spying the whole time?"

"Maybe," Ben says. "Who knows. But more important, I'm thinking of dusting off that novel. Changing it to more of a spy thriller."

"Right. That seems important at a time like this."

"Think of the book deal. And the movie rights."

"Who's going to play him?" Sammy wonders. "Who's going to play *Kurtz*?!"

"The real question," he says, "is who could possibly play me."

"No one," she says. "No one could ever, ever get you right."

Later, Ben digs through his closet, in search of the novel he never finished. When he finds the manuscript in a plastic storage box he is struck by how old the font is, the quality of the printing. Even the paper seems rougher and more primitive than paper is now.

He reads a few pages, wincing. The prose is better than he expected it to be. What pains him, instead, is how obvious his intentions were. He had thought, at the time, he was being sly, conveying meaning in a way that wasn't immediately obvious to the reader. He thought the way he portrayed himself was subtle—he had made himself the narrator, the best friend of the interesting person, Carroway to Kurtz's Gatsby. But he had imbued himself with too much wisdom and nobility. Now it is plain to see what he thought of himself.

It *is* funny, though, what he had done to Boris. At the end of the novel, after the Clinton character had taken the White House, Boris had been carted away from the inaugural ball by FBI agents. Exposed as a spy. Held in federal prison for three years, then extradited in an exchange for three Americans detained by the Kremlin. Ben had made this part up—it was total fantasy—though in retrospect it seemed like the best part of the book. He had described Boris, struggling against the FBI agents who held him by the arms, as "manic, jerking, wild-eyed as Andy Kauffman, spewing threats in rapid Russian. He had completely lost his mind." It wasn't bad. And in the end, he had to give himself credit—his instincts had been good, he hadn't been that far off.

He sets the manuscript down. Then picks it back up. He flips from the back to the front, stopping now and then to read a passage. Kurtz yelling into his briefcase phone, threatening to kill someone. Kurtz drunk at a party, falling into a pool. He keeps flipping, some instinct guiding him. There's something he wants to find, though he doesn't quite know what. He is nearly back to the very beginning—Kurtz casing Manchester, plucking up Clinton signs and tossing them in dumpster—when he finds it: The scene where he and Kurtz and Boris walk into a sandwich shop. He had placed Sammy behind the counter, neck bent, head inclined toward a delicate little volume of poetry. She was holding a book open with one hand, her little finger extended daintily—imagery he had stolen from a Fragonard painting. When the boys had walked into the shop, she had looked up from her book and placed it on the counter, an old clothbound volume of Keats. Then they had ordered, and the girl—he refers to Sammy only as "the girl"— had gone to work slicing a lump of roast beef. The narrator had observed this closely, and compared the way her neck was first bent to the book, then over the meat on the slicer. The passage was meant to suggest there were still beautiful things in the world, delicate things, but they were being trampled. There were still girls dreaming of poetry in the world, but they were being made to fill orders, satisfy other hungers. They were being crushed.

He plucks this page from the manuscript, folds it. Shuts it away in the drawer of his nightstand.

Yes, his instinct had been good. He hadn't been that far off.

2009

One winter evening, Sammy is taking Ava to her basketball practice, and loses her hold of the ball, which starts rolling down the street. She starts to chase after the ball, worried it will veer into traffic and cause an accident. Snow is on the ground and the roads are slick. She slips and falls backwards, hard. She sits by the side of the road for a few seconds, trying to collect herself. She calls for Ava. Wants to make sure she isn't too close to the road. "Ava!" she calls again. She gets to her feet. Turns around. There is Ava right behind her, with a stunned look on her face. Sammy wonders what Ava is staring at so oddly. She follows Ava's gaze, down to her own hand. Her keys are hanging from her palm. Just dangling, as if suspended by some magic. Then Sammy sees the trick. That in fact the entire blade of her car key has gone through her hand. She must have fallen on it. The fat plastic head of the key is flush against her palm. She crouches down and then sits in the street—right on the cold, wet street. Then the pain comes, which is startling. At first it is local to the hand but then it seems to take over her entire body. Sammy is making strange noises from deep in the back of her throat. Ava is standing over her, confused. Traffic is rushing past and Sammy wraps her arm—the good arm, as she already thinks of it—around Ava's legs to prevent her from stepping backwards into the street. Some instinct tells Sammy she needs to get up, needs to move, but she can't. Several people are walking past on the other side of the street, kind of staring, and Sammy wants to call out

381

for help but something stops her. Not only can she not move, she cannot speak. Perhaps it is shock. People keep walking by, staring, but she calls out to none of them. She is reduced to a pinpoint of pain. There is no logic to it, there is no plan, no narrative, no future and no past. She is just in it.

Again some instinct propels her forward and she tries to stand. But when she moves her hand, the fat head of the key snaps off, leaving the blade stuck behind in her palm. I need to drive to the ER, she thinks. But then realizes she can't—her key is stuck in her hand.

Sammy sits back down and slumps over onto her side. Now she is lying in the street. She starts shuddering and wonders—without words, if this is possible—if she is having a seizure. Ava starts crying. People just keep walking by. The people who live across from her, college kids, pull into their driveway and stop for a second and look at her—she is maybe twenty feet away—but they don't do anything, just disappear into their house. Again, Sammy doesn't know why she can't call to them. Something has gone wrong in her brain and she cannot form words.

Clusters of people walk by and Sammy tries to implore them with her eyes. Finally she hears a car pull over, a door open. Then she sees a pair of boots coming toward her. Thank God, she thinks. When she looks up she sees it is Wissam's mother, who she hasn't seen in a year. The mother kneels down and looks at Sammy, puts her hand on her shoulder. She seems to understand instinctively what is happening. She helps Sammy up and settle her in the car, then helps Ava into the back, next to Wissam, and they all drive to the emergency room. Wissam's mother keeps Ava with her in the waiting room while the ER doctors tend to Sammy. She sits through an odd consultation, wherein one doctor comes and looks at the hand and frowns and says something like, "Huh, this is a new one." Then calls over another doctor who does the same thing. Eventually there are five or six people standing around Sammy in a horseshoe, deliberating. One of the doctors looks at Sammy's face and says: "Has anyone given her anything? Has anyone done vitals?" And the consensus is: No. Suddenly there is a flurry of activity. They are hooking Sammy to an IV, injecting morphine. They wonder whether aloud whether to just pull the blade out with tweezers and see what happens, or whether to wait for the hand surgeon to arrive. The hand is so swollen at this point the blade has completely disappeared—Sammy's flesh has swollen around and over it, and there is just a dent in her palm where the blade is buried. Someone looks into this hole with a light and says he can see the tip of the blade, says he thinks he might be able to get to it. Someone else overrules him, says to wait for the surgeon, to prepare Sammy for surgery. "I can't," she spits out. "My daughter." These are the first words she's spoken. Thus far she's gotten by with nods and shakes of the head. "There's no one to watch my daughter," she says, less to the doctors than to herself. She hasn't fully appreciated this situation until now. If something happens to her, something worse than this, there would be no one to watch Ava. She is alone. She hasn't made any friends at work. Doesn't know any of her neighbors. She doesn't have Wissam's mother's phone number, doesn't even know her name. She has always just thought of her as Mrs. Wissam.

The doctors consent to give a try with the tweezers. Sammy watches the young doctor's face as he works. He grimaces. Grunts several times. Sticks the tip of his tongue out the side of his mouth, like a child concentrating on staying in the lines while coloring. The young doctor works the tweezers down and around. At last he gets ahold of the blade and pulls it from her hand. When it slides out her vision explodes with green and yellow bursts of light. Then her hand is pumped so full of saline it swells to approximately the size of a softball.

After, Wissam's mother drives Sammy and Ava to the drug store, then home. Sammy keeps apologizing for all the trouble. "I'm so sorry, I'm so sorry," she keeps saying. Every minute or so. "It's okay," Wissam's mother keeps saying. "We are happy to help." After about the fifth round of this, Wissam's mother looks at Sammy quizzically, shakes her head. Whatever is wrong with Sammy is wrong with this whole country. "Of course I stop," she says. "You would stop for me."

"Of course," Sammy says. Though she wonders later, if she were driving with Ava in the car and saw someone lying in the street, would she?

Delivered home, Sammy gets out of the car, then opens the back door to retrieve Ava. She sees that Ava and Wissam, both belted in their seats, are holding hands, and are leaning toward each other, so that Ava's head is resting on top of Wissam's, and her curls, which have by now grown long, halfway down her back, are shielding them like a curtain. However improbably, they look content. Happy, even. This crazy, stupid accident has reunited them at last. Sammy hasn't seen Ava like this since the last time she and Wissam were together at school.

Sammy doesn't talk to Ben until the night after the accident, by which time the swelling in her hand has downgraded to the baseball range, and she has made a little comedy of it. Her hand is a minor issue, in the story she tells Ben—instead, her focus is on Wissam and his mother, the coincidence of finding them again. "It was unbelievable," she tells him. "After all this time, suddenly there they were, like a mirage, like out of the desert they come walking, except it's March in Missouri, instead of sand it's snow, but you know, whatever."

The way she tells it, it's as if the accident is a mere preamble to this story of international intrigue. The Iraqi boy and the American girl, smitten with each other, then torn apart, then coming back together by some accident of fate. "The drama!" But Ben is unmoved by this part of the story. "How's the range of motion in your hand?" he asks, sounding like a doctor. She always forgets he's a doctor.

"Undetermined," she says. "It's all swaddled up."

"Which hand is it?"

"Right."

"Isn't that the hand," he asks, "you use to flip people off?"

"It is."

"This is a serious blow to your freedom of expression."

Then Sammy tells him what she considers to be the worst part of the whole ridiculous affair. After she got home from the ER and put Ava to bed, she couldn't sleep because her hand was so swollen and throbbing painfully. So she went out to the living room and lay on the couch with a bunch of pillows all around her—she had been instructed to keep the hand elevated. Then, to distract herself, she had turned on the television, which she never watched except for the news, due to a self-imposed exile from mass media—she believed that the world, and its display of itself on television, was a poison, one that would prevent her from having interesting thoughts, in original language. Sammy rambles on, musing to Ben about the fact that somehow, despite not watching television, she still hears about various shows, and even gains a working knowledge of their characters and plots. It's like these narratives, she says, whatever narratives happen each year to capture the public imagination, are in the ether. First it was a show about mobsters, then a show about ad executives, then several shows about housewives and then maybe housewives married to mobsters, unless she was getting things mixed up. "Who knows," she says. "It doesn't matter I guess. The point is, to be alive in this country is to be adrift in these various narratives, whether you want to or not."

"Sammy," Ben says. "Focus."

"Right," she says. "Sorry." She tells him how she found the remote and pressed the red button and the screen filled with *Late Night with David Letterman*, and she was transported to those long-ago nights with her father. It was as if nothing had changed. Dave was still talking to Paul Shaffer. The fact that they were still there and had been there all this time—*lo all these years* was how she thought of it—troubled her. Probably because it meant her father had been watching all that time by himself in an empty house. She sat for a while absorbed in this troubled feeling. Watching Dave and Paul. Then Dave and his guest, a giggling young movie star in a short white dress, very blonde, her mouth painted red. She watched Dave and this young actress, and continued to descend into a dark mood, feeling like she had gotten nowhere in life, none of the places she'd intended to go. That despite going off to school and getting a doctorate and then a teaching job, despite having a kid of her own, here she was watching David Letterman again. Only no longer young. No longer the young, bright, giggling thing. All the promise was gone. Schopenhauer came to mind—the inevitable relationship between desire and pain, between striving and disappointment.

"And then?" he says.

He sounds a little annoyed. Sammy supposes she's been especially distracted, wandering all over the place. She tries to rein it in. "There I am," she says, "watching Letterman, thinking deeply about life and all of its disappointments, how all human action leads to disappointment, and lo and behold I see something flicker in my peripheral vision. So I turn my head. I turn my head and what do I see? A mouse. A fucking mouse is sitting on the pillow right next to my head—just sitting there, watching David Letterman, with its nose twitching. A mouse!" She tells him how for maybe two seconds she just stared at it. Time unfolded, expanded, an infinite amount of time. In this expanse of time it was as if she rose up out of herself and saw herself from above, lying on the couch, with her hand swollen to the size of a softball, watching David Letterman, sharing a pillow with a mouse. She saw the whole moment in all of its absurdity. Ridiculous! Then she came back to herself and freaked out, sat up screaming.

She tries to play this little scene for laughs. Perhaps because this episode contains a sad truth about herself, one she wants to conceal. It's like everything she'd ever run away from has followed her, or worse, she's become it without realizing.

"Sams," he says. And just the way he says her name troubles her. She is always alert to his mood, tracking its every fickle turn. Nothing unsettles her so much as a joke that fails to land.

"I just don't find any of this funny," he says. "And I don't think you should either."

"I'm fine," she says. "It's no big deal."

"What if something worse happened to you?" he says. "You're all by yourself down there. You don't have anybody. You don't have any money."

"I'm *fine*. It's not a big deal."

"Don't you think you're getting to a point," he says. Falters. He's trying to be gentle, diplomatic. He's hesitant for the first time she can remember. "Don't you think you ought to find some sort of safety net, some kind of, I don't know, security? And if you can't find it there, don't you think you should maybe come back east? Your dad's here," he says. "I mean, at least you'd have family."

"Right," she says.

"And I'm here too. I'm always here for you."

"Right. Of course."

This is all she's ever wanted. For years she's been waiting for Ben to take her seriously, her new life with her daughter—she's been waiting for him to notice her burden and take pity on her. Offer some sort of care. Say something nice to her that isn't a joke.

But now that he's done it, she can't stand it.

"I'm fine," she says. "I'm just, I'm just a normal person. There's absolutely no difference between me and everyone else here, pretty much everyone's life is hanging by a thread. *You're* the anomaly, actually. This is just, this is just what life is like for most people. It's perilous. It's fraught. One slip on the ice and just about anyone's whole life could fall apart."

"I don't think that's true," he says. "I think most people have more resources than you, of one kind or another. They've got more to latch onto."

Her whole body flushes with shame—she is about to cry. "I gotta go," she says. "Letterman's coming on and the mouse, you know. The mouse and I have plans."

2010

It's a Thursday night, and Ben is watching *The Tonight Show*.

Something has gone wrong with his usual routine. He had put in a full day at the office, come home. Then called for a massage. The therapist was a young woman who had been visiting for several months, now—once a week or so. They had worked out an understanding. Ben was happy with the arrangement, and the girl seemed to be, too. But tonight she has done something new, something Ben doesn't like—she falls asleep afterwards. Her back is turned to Ben, her long, dark hair sprawled across the pillow. I'll let her sleep a little, Ben thinks at first. She works hard, must be tired. But an hour goes by, and she is still sleeping. Ben wants, urgently, to be alone. Should he wake her? How awful would that be?

He turns on the television, edges up the volume. Jay Leno has been replaced by Conan O'Brien, to Ben's mother's great relief. But there's trouble—the network has decided to bring Leno back. Conan is delivering one of his last monologues, wringing his hands. He always looks sort of embarrassed to be alive, but now, with this latest news, particularly so.

Then the show cuts to commercial, and Ben drifts into his nightly visitation with Johnny Carson. They talk about his day. Nothing special, Ben says. And Johnny seems satisfied. Ready to wrap up, sign off. But then he notices something. "Wait," says

Johnny. "Is that? What's that lump there next to you? Is that a young woman I see?"

"She fell asleep," Ben says.

"So how did you manage to lure this one in?"

"She's a massage therapist," Ben says. "Half the work was done for me."

"So you're letting her sleep over," Johnny says. "That's new."

"I'm not, really. I have cab fare ready." Ben mumbles this, because he is lighting a cigarette. But Johnny never fails to understand him.

"Why not just let her sleep?"

"Because I'm an asshole."

"Why is it you're so desperate to get rid of her?" Johnny asks. "She's a nice-looking girl. That hair. I'd kill for that hair." The audience laughs.

"I have a routine I like to keep."

"Well," says Johnny. "You're going to die alone."

"Speaking of which," Ben says. "I read something interesting the other day. Do you remember when you had Truman Capote on?"

"Like I could forget?"

"Did you know, did you know your ex-wife is going to end up as the custodian of his ashes?"

"Which ex-wife?"

"I don't know. Joanne. Joanna. One of those. She was friends with Capote and somehow ended up with his ashes."

"What year is this?" says Johnny.

"We're still in the early seventies," says Ben. "Judging from the set. And your jacket."

"So you're asking me if I'm aware my wife will end up as the benefactress of Truman Capote's ashes? How could I be? He's not even dead yet."

"True. I just thought you'd find it interesting."

"You're just avoiding talking about yourself."

Really, Johnny Carson runs an excellent interview, Ben has to admit. He sighs. Drags on his cigarette. He tries to think of what to say, something that will satisfy Johnny without revealing too much. Just enough to get him off the hook.

As if on cue, Ben's phone rings.

"You should take that," Johnny says.

"Do you mind?"

"Are you kidding? I can't wait to get out of here."

And the lights go out on Johnny.

Ben answers the phone. "Hi, Ma," he says.

"Did I wake you?"

"Of course not," he says. "You know exactly what I'm doing."

"I don't know anything about tonight's guests," she says. "I've completely fallen out of touch with popular culture."

"Me neither. But that's not such a bad thing."

"Well, maybe at my age," she says. "But you're too young. You should still be out there in the arena. Slaying the bulls and whatnot."

"Eh," he says. "Overrated."

She waits a beat, one of her calculated pauses. "I just don't like how you're alone all the time, Benny. It makes me feel bad. I feel all gray and swampy inside."

"I'm not lonely, Ma." He looks over at the girl. Still lost to sleep, so much so her mouth is open.

"But you *will* be. One day it will just hit you."

"I'm good," he says. "To be honest, I think I take after Dad. All he ever wanted was peace and quiet."

"Don't say that," she tells him. "He was so unhappy."

"Not when he was alone," he says.

"Benny," she says. "You have to make an effort with this.

This is really the only thing in the *world* that bothers me. I've made my peace with everything else." She says this in an overly-earnest tone that lets him know she is joking. But not really.

Conan comes back on, and they fall quiet, clear to the end of *The Tonight Show*. Then his mother offers a final thought. "In his early years, Benny, just remember, Schopenhauer didn't think people should have pets."

"Okay," he says.

"He thought it was cruel to the animal. And beneath human dignity to look after a dog."

"Okay."

"I'm just saying."

"Don't get a pet."

"No. That's not what I'm saying. What I want to say to you is, later in life, guess who never went anywhere without his poodle?"

"I don't know," Ben says. "Groucho Marx."

"Don't be a smartass," she tells him. "You see what I mean."

"Fine," he says. "I'll get a poodle."

"You need a *companion*," she says. She launches into her old complaints about his father, how cold he was. And talks about how happy she is now, with her boyfriend. Asleep right there beside her. "He never watches late night. He's asleep by nine. Up at five-thirty."

Ben doesn't want to hear about any of this. His mother's blissful domestic life with her new boyfriend, their sleeping schedule. "I gotta go," he tells her.

"Just promise me you'll think about it," she says.

He hangs up.

Finally, he can't stand it any longer—he shakes the girl's shoulder. "I'm guessing you have to work in the morning," he says to her. Making it seem like he's looking out for her, thinking of her needs.

394

The girl gets dressed, gathers her things, clears out. And Ben is alone again. Relieved.

And yet, he can't sleep. He is troubled by the notion that something is unfinished, off-course. It feels as if his life hasn't quite started, or hasn't been made official in some way. What is this feeling? He can't see it, can't quite feel its edges. He can barely even sense it. But yes, he must admit, it is there.

2011

So much of their life together plays out in restaurants. This is where Ben is happiest, most relaxed. Where he is most likely to talk. He needs to be distracted, slightly, in order to talk, and nothing distracts him like watching people mill about, come and go. Ben and Sammy sit together in booths for long hours, making their way through appetizers, then meals, then coffee, then pie, then more coffee. Two, sometimes three groups of people will sit down next to them, eat their meals and go. If there were a soundtrack to their lives, it would be the dull roar of a crowded diner, a dozen conversations happening at once, food sizzling on the grill and in the fryer, coffee brewing, waiters hollering to cooks, plates being set down, ice water tumbling from pitchers, the clink of spoons against coffee mugs.

One night in early spring, Ben takes Sammy to one of his favorite places: El Quixote, the iconic Spanish restaurant decorated all over with windmills, with tilting little madmen. They are hardly settled in their booth before they find themselves in one of those scenarios only possible in New York. At first they are quiet, scanning their menus, holding hands across the table, as is their custom when they first reunite, some instinct propelling them to touch. But the mood is ruined by two women in the booth behind them talking loudly about pubic hair. "I didn't *know*," one woman says. "I was *married*, I wasn't following what was going on. The last I heard we were still leaving, like, a *strip*. You just kind of trimmed things up and called it a *day*."

"Nope, nope," says her friend. "It's all gone now."

"Seriously?"

"Totally serious."

"Oh my *God*," says the woman. "When did this happen? I had no idea. I mean, I've been out there. I've been out there with the strip and I thought it was okay."

"All gone," says her friend.

"Isn't that, like, kind of creepy? I mean, don't men feel like they're fucking a little girl?"

"I don't know," says the friend. "I don't make the rules."

"Oh my *God*. I can't believe this."

"Just go get a wax. It's no big deal."

"How much is it?"

"I don't know. Twenty bucks."

"Twenty bucks? I have to pay twenty bucks a month now for this?"

"More like every other week," says the friend.

"Are you fucking *kidding* me?"

"That's life, sister. Just add it to the list of things you need to do."

"Who has that kind of *time*?" says the woman.

"It takes five seconds. Boom. Done." She makes a ripping noise.

"Jesus. *God*."

Ben gives Sammy a wide-eyed look—an expression he reserves for occasions when people are making public fools of themselves and he doesn't want to comment, yet does want to comment. Sammy can't look at him, and yet can't resist. Every time she looks at him, she starts snickering. She puts her hands over her face.

"Can't you just leave, like, a *little* strip?" says the woman. "Just a short one?"

"I tried that," says the friend. "But it just looked like Hitler."

The women move on, started talking about the kitchen remodel of a mutual friend. Nightmare, is a word they keep using. But Ben and Sammy can't move on. They are still thinking about Hitler.

"Mein Kampf," says Ben, in a Hitler voice. And they both start laughing, thinking of this little talking Hitler mustache of pubic hair.

"Go ahead," he says. "Do your thing. Make a theory." Sammy can never let a moment like this go by without indulging in some kind of cultural critique. It's like she's a perpetual guest on *Dick Cavett*.

"None of this is funny at all," she says, though she is still laughing. She takes out her phone and frantically starts punching buttons. "There's this book I read," she says. "Or to be completely honest, there's this book *review* I read." She scrolls and swipes. Then she reads: "In this Foucauldian system, individuals are responsible for learning and living up to a code of dominant norms, for making themselves compliant with the ever-changing ideals of masculinity or femininity, constantly evaluating their success or failure to comply with increasingly-exacting societal mandates." Ben turns his hand into a puppet and all the time she is talking, works it frantically. He does this sometimes, when she gets too serious, when she's being an academic.

"So, what we're witnessing here," she says, setting her phone back on the table with a thwack, "is the willing reinforcement of the police state by females themselves, females living under the male hegemonic, you know, system." The puppet is still going, so she slaps at his hand.

"The state has declared," he says, working the hand again but now using the voice of Hitler, "that all women must be swept clean!"

"This really isn't funny," she says. "It's exactly this kind of thing that leads to tyranny." This had all started out as a joke, but she is getting worked up now. "I mean, we essentially have two classes of women, now, the shaved and the unshaved."

"Isn't it shaven?" Ben asks.

"I don't know," she says. Frowns.

"Isn't shaven the past participle?"

She shrugs.

"You're not prepared to give a verdict here?" he says. "*All of her pubic hair is shaved*, versus *All of her pubic hair is shaven?*"

She shushes him, even though the women beside them are now loudly talking about a reality show, and also obviously no one in New York cares what anyone at the next table thinks of them.

"People ask me these kinds of questions all the time," Sammy confesses. "But I don't really know." She is an English professor, she says, with only an intuitive grasp on grammar. The rules are as much a mystery to her as anyone else.

"Aren't you, like, the last person standing guard over these customs?"

"Well, yes."

"Shouldn't you at least keep a little primer handy? In case there's some kind of grammar emergency that needs settling?"

"Probably," she says. "But instead I've been getting away with a sort of 'language is evolving' defense. Like, *Language is a living thing. Who am I to tie it down?* That way I don't actually have to know how anything actually works. I can just *look* like I know how it's supposed to work, but I've decided to be magnanimous about other people's errors. It's a win-win. All I really have to do is uphold the image of being the kind of person who discreetly possesses, but declines to enforce certain codes."

"This is one of those times," Ben says, "one time among a great many, that I'm grateful you didn't go into engineering."

Their food arrives. He has ordered a lobster dish, because his doctor has recommended he eat more seafood. Though perhaps, he considers, this wasn't quite what the doctor meant—the lobster is smothered in some kind of cream sauce. "I went with the fish," he says, rubbing his hands together, "so I can have dessert later." He is large enough at this point that it is difficult for him to fit comfortably in a booth. Sammy is aware of his latest blood pressure reading, but almost never says anything to him about what he eats, the rules he keeps breaking. "I just worry about you," is the most she'll say. What she says now, in fact.

They start eating. Ben is wholly distracted, intent on the little object of his desire, a bit of meat stuck in a claw, and doesn't notice when a drop of cream sauce gets stuck in his beard. But then Sammy reaches over to pinch the sauce between her thumb and forefinger. He thinks nothing of it at the time, but will later look back on that moment, remembering how comfortable they were, how close, thinking how much affection there was between them. How they were married, more or less. Or as close as either of them would ever get.

The next night, the final night of that same trip, Sammy learns more about Ben in one sitting than she ever expected to know, and all because of a decorative quirk at the deli they happen to stop at.

They have been out walking in the snow, one of Sammy's favorite things. One of Ben's, too. An affinity they share. They have been walking for a while and are cold, so seek out the warmth of a narrow, nondescript deli. There is a row of booths along one wall, all of them empty, practically a miracle in the city. They settle in, peel off their coats, inspect the placemats in front of them. Paradise Deli, they say, in sky blue lettering, a vaguely Arabic font. In the center of the menu is a picture of the owner, Yousef, with a message of greeting printed underneath: Welcome to Paradise! All around his head, pictures of food float about, as if ideas he is conjuring: hummus plates, gyros, little triangles of baklava. The menu is filled with endearing misspellings: chickin, cheezes, samwich.

Absentmindedly, Sammy flips over the placemat and finds printed on its back a list of questions. A banner stretches across the top: Conversation Starters! For the Most Memorable Meal of Your Life!

"This seems hard to turn down," she says, turns Ben's menu over for him.

"Okay," he says. "I'm game."

Just then Yousef himself comes over and nods. Sammy is afraid they won't come back to the questions, that Ben will take this interruption as an opportunity to squirrel away. But their encounter with Yousef is brief. "Just coffee," Ben says. Yousef nods again, disappears, and they are back to it.

The questions start out easy, the kind they have already covered, albeit so long ago, they have forgotten the answers by now. Or at least, there is no harm going over them again. *First Pet?* is the first question, and Sammy reminds Ben of her father's perpetual series of basset hounds named Lou Grant. Ben seems not to register the name, so Sammy reminds him of Mary Tyler Moore's famously cranky boss. Played by Ed Asner, Scrooge to Mary's Tiny Tim. "We must have watched every single episode of *Mary Tyler Moore*," she tells Ben, "ten times. It was the only sitcom he could tolerate. That and *Taxi*."

"Louie DePalma," says Ben. He makes the vengeful little noise Danny DeVito's character used to make. She is surprised he knows it. She always assumed Ben grew up sitting in front of a concert piano, a Wimbledon match.

"Did you have a pet?" she asks. She can't remember.

"No. My mother didn't want animals in the house."

"Right," Sammy says. "She didn't need a pet. Because she had you."

"Yes!" he says. Slapping the table. A rare bit of enthusiasm. "Exactly."

Yousef comes with their coffee, then disappears again. He is the most discreet and efficient waiter they have ever had. Sammy begins to feel that something unusual is happening, something extraordinary. They are in some kind of dreamscape, maybe.

They move down the list to Favorite Movie. Which for Ben, despite his affinity for Welles, is *Dr. Zhivago*. Something Sammy already knows—a bit of trivia she would have answered correctly, in a match.

"You?" he asks.

"I can't think," Sammy says. Her mind goes blank whenever she is asked this sort of question. "I don't know." She grasps for something equally grand—an epic from one of her college film classes. Probably, in the past, she told Ben her favorite movie was *Ghandi*. Or *Bridge Over the River Kwai*. Or *Lawrence of Arabia*. Or *The Godfather*. But here she can only come up with her true favorite, the movie she and her father used to watch, a hundred times if they saw it once. "Blazing Saddles," she says. Embarrassed. Dime Western to his Russian classic.

But he only laughs. It's all okay. For some reason, everything here seems okay.

First Crush is the next, and Ben admits to falling head over heels for his third-grade classmate's mother. A woman named Rebecca Black, who dressed like an old Hollywood movie star. "She was elegance itself," he says. "Grace Kelly." He describes her tea-length dresses and kitten heels. The seams in her stockings. Her pillbox hats with little veils that pulled down over her face. "I was smitten," he says.

Then it is her turn, and Sammy actually blushes, because her first crush is so embarrassing to admit. "Scott Hamilton," she says, covering her face. "The figure skater."

"Jesus!" he says. Laughs.

"I just loved him. I loved watching him on the ice. And then later, in the interviews, he was so nice."

"I suppose you could do worse," he says. And then, in a rare bit of graciousness: "But he'd be lucky to have you."

They move on to *Celebrity Crush*. Elizabeth Taylor for Ben—the eyes alone. Which Sammy already knew. And for Sammy, it's obvious, a running joke between her and Ben: Peter Jennings, the late ABC news anchor. She has always loved him. For years she had hoped he would be there for her always, to narrate life's burdens in a way that lightened them. She had even imagined him at her hospital bedside, ushering her into death. "Here we go now," he'd say. "The pain is gone, and there's just a bit of brightness ahead, if you look up to your left. There you go, easy now, easy as the heavens bear you away."

But then Peter Jennings had up and died. Far too young. And who had ushered him, she wondered, who had eased his pain at the end? Sometimes this troubled her.

They go through more: *Favorite Book, First Car, Favorite Song, Favorite Food, Favorite Place.* Yousef appearing now and then to refill their coffee. Unobtrusive, nearly silent.

First "Date," the list says, toward the bottom. And they wonder aloud why *Date* is in quotes. "I wonder if it means sex," Ben says.

"Maybe."

"Well?" he asks. "Should we?" This, they have never talked about.

Sammy is too embarrassed to tell the truth—she never told Ben he was her first. She makes something up. Prom night. A friend from concert band, a trumpet player. No big deal. Just to try it, just to see.

"High school, too," he says. "Summer camp. In a tent."

He goes on to describe a hushed encounter with a girl from Canada, in a different group—someone he didn't know but locked eyes with across a campfire. He had noticed the girl slipping away from the group, into the woods, and followed her. "It was all very hushed," he said. "I never even found out her name."

Ben describes then, haltingly, while staring out the window at the snow, how he came back the next summer, hoping to find the girl again, but she wasn't there. What he found instead was the girl's picture sort of enshrined in the mess hall—she had drowned the previous year, just after Ben left for home. Just days after their encounter.

"Oh my god!" Sammy says. "That's so awful!" She is seized with the feeling that she has finally learned what makes Ben the way he is. Now she knows that this young girl's death is at the root of Ben's loneliness, is the reason he has never had a real relationship. "This just, this just explains so much! I mean, you lost your first love! No wonder! Suddenly it all makes sense!" She has one palm on top of the other, and is pressing them to her chest, as if about to perform CPR on herself. Like the force of this revelation has stopped her heart.

But then Ben bursts out laughing. "I was just bullshitting," he says. "I mean, it was true about the camp. But she wasn't a mystery, and she didn't die. Her name was Rachel Wallace. We went to camp together for years. Then we went to off to college. Lost touch. Never saw each other again. I looked her up once. She's a pediatric nephrologist in Toronto." He laughs again. "I had you," he says. "You have to admit."

"You *fucker*!"

"Sorry. It's just this list. It's a bit much."

"Your heart is crooked," she tells him. She is angry. And yet still sad somehow. She can't quite shift gears. Even though he was just messing with her, the feeling is still there—that some tragic loss defines him, lives at his core. Something to do with his father, perhaps. By all accounts a cold and difficult man, a man who never really loved. "It's like you can only get so far without, I don't know, shitting on everything."

He only shrugs. This is the best he can do.

Then they are at the very end. The biggest question of all, the best for last: *First Love.*

"Ava," Sammy says. Curtly. She is still a bit flustered.

"That doesn't count."

"But it's all I have," she says. The notion of Ava tugs at her. What am I even doing here? she wonders. Why do I keep coming here, going through the motions of this tortured dance? I should be with the person I love, who loves me in return. My little whirlwind. My curious girl.

But then Ben pulls her back in, like he always does. "Well, my dear," he says, in his most gallant voice. More Welles than Rosenberg. "I probably shouldn't tell you this, but my first love is you."

"Stop bullshitting," she says. They are clear of whatever sincerity passed between them, back to being skeptics, ball busters. Though she is blushing slightly—some small part of her must believe him.

Ben pulls his wallet from his coat, fishes out a twenty, tosses it on the table. The gesture that saves him every time—overpaying for everything. Settling the bill so he can slip away, move on.

Then they are outside walking again, the snow falling faster now, flakes accumulating on their heads and shoulders, their eyelashes. Sammy sees a dark figure in a thin raincoat shuffling toward them, just a thin raincoat left open over an old, misshapen suit. He shuffles closer, lift his face as they pass. The man has one of those faces, large and square, heavily-lined, like a map of sorrow. And his eyes. Big and dark, with a weary, pained expression. He looks for all the world like W.H. Auden.

Only then does Sammy realize not another living soul had come into the deli the whole time they were there. It was as if they were set apart for that moment in time, as if the rest of the world had hidden itself away. It was peculiar, in the city, to be alone for so long. It really was like a dream.

What the menu said was true, she thinks, already wrapping up this encounter in special paper, tucking it away in her mind. Making a myth of it. *The most memorable meal of your life!* She will open it later to see it again. She will turn it this way and that under a bright light, inspecting its facets, its color and clarity, taking note of its flaws, assessing the nature and quality of their friendship. Then she will wrap it back up. Then unwrap it again. A little gift she will keep giving herself.

It really was paradise, she will think later. If only for a moment.

2011

The next time Ben and Sammy see each other, it is summer. Sammy comes north to visit Ben, though not in the city—in a resort town in Maine, where the Rosenbergs have their beach house. The house is a classic New England cottage—cedar shakes, white trim—perched on a rocky bluff, overlooking the ocean. Sammy has been here before, many times, though not since Ava was born. It's been eight years, maybe nine, something like that.

They are in town, having dinner at a restaurant on the cove—one of those places with a back deck that extends into a dock, so that people can cross the cove in their boats, dock them, and stroll on up to dinner. Ben and Sammy are seated on the deck, just finished with dinner, killing their second bottle of wine. They are watching a couple disembark from their skiff. The couple is dressed alike, in khakis and polo shirts, sweaters tied around their necks, boat shoes, straight off the pages of an L.L. Bean catalog. The man is red-faced, with a large beer gut bulging over his pants, belted low on the hips. The woman is tiny, with a smart bob and large sunglasses, one of those Joan Didion types, so slight she could blow away. And yet somehow it takes a woman like that to anchor this kind of man, this kind of life; all the wives Sammy sees here, the wives of these rich older guys, are built like birds.

Ben and Sammy are talking about Anthony Weiner, the New York congressman who has just resigned after disgracing himself in the most salacious possible way, snapping pictures of himself and texting them to a handful of younger women. Sammy doesn't want to talk about him, has been avoiding this bit of news—which is hard to do, since it is everywhere, on the front pages of all the papers, and running continuously on cable, even network news. But she supposes it is inevitable, dissecting this scandal that has consumed the culture; she supposes they should congratulate themselves for waiting all through dinner to go after it.

"My favorite part," Ben says, "is watching the networks try to explain the content of the photos without saying *dick pic*."

"Oh, God," she says.

"*Man bulge* was my favorite. With *erect member* running a close second."

She is laughing a little bit now, though trying not to. "I wonder how many producers were huddled around that copy," she says. "Trying to solve this little linguistic crisis."

"*Inflated sex organ* was another," he tells her. "Like it was a Macy's parade balloon."

She laughs fully now, covers her face with her hands. "That's just awful."

"If I'd been in charge," he says, "it would have been *cock tent*."

"That's good. It's a good visual. It gets at the, you know, the essential choreography of the situation with the boxer shorts. I haven't actually seen it, mind you, but I've heard about it."

"How have you not seen it? Are you living in a cave?"

"I can't believe I'm saying this," Sammy says, "but I haven't watched any of the coverage. Ava is always in the room, so I turn it off. And even if she isn't, I just, I don't know. I just don't want to watch. It makes me feel bad. I get all flustered. I just don't want to participate in anyone else's humiliation."

"Well," he says, "you're entirely alone."

"I don't think so," she says. "I think there are other people who, you know, don't want to be a part of all that, all that mocking and finger pointing."

"What else is there?" he asks.

"That's a good question," she says. And she wonders: What else is there? "I'm going to have to think about that one."

They are quiet for a moment, content, looking out at the water. Then all at once Ben shifts in his chair. Turns toward Sammy, his back to the water. "Oh God," he says. "Hide me. It's Art Garfunkel." He covers his face with his hand.

Sammy sweeps her eye over the landscape—just a beautiful sunset, boats at dock bobbing on the water. Toursists milling about. "What?" she says. Leans toward him.

"An old friend. Just keep talking to me. Make something up. Pretend you have the Senate floor and can list all of your grievances."

"Okay," she says. "Finally." She is still scanning the tourists, trying to spot the person Ben is hoping to avoid. "It's difficult to know where to start. I mean, we have so many problems before us."

"That's never stopped you before," he says.

She laughs, inclines her head toward Ben. Hoping that, with their heads angled down, they might close themselves off to the rest of the world. That it will pass them by.

But a few seconds later she can sense someone approaching the table. She keeps talking—gesturing wildly with her hands, recreating a conversation she had with a student who kept referring to Truman Coyote—and can only see the figure from the corner of her eye. She can only see his clothes—an ensemble of white linen, the shirt unbuttoned halfway down his chest, the sleeves rolled, his pants secured by a braided belt. He is standing with his hands in his pockets. There is a little too much leisure, here, she thinks.

Finally, the man interrupts. "Ben?" he says.

Ben and Sammy turn to the man, and that's when she sees that it really is Art Garfunkel. Or seems to be. His hair is the overwhelming thing—frizzy and blonde, standing on end. But there's also the icy blue eyes. The handsome, boyish face.

"Hey!" Ben says. Stands, offers his hand. Meanwhile Sammy's mind works through some calculations. This man standing before her, she realizes, can't be Art Garfunkel, because he looks exactly like the Art Garfunkel from the cover of the *Sounds of Silence* album. 1966. The math doesn't come out.

But now she is being introduced. "This is Sammy," Ben says, and she is shaking Art Garfunkel's hand. He fixes his eyes on her. "Pleasure," he says. She moves to withdraw her hand but he holds onto it. "It's so very nice to meet you," he says. A beat passes where they hold one another's gaze. It has been so long since a man has looked at Sammy this way, she is momentarily confused. Then something clicks, a pilot light ignites in her brain, and she realizes: Oh, this. This old game.

Then it is all unfolding in exactly the way Ben hoped to avoid. Art Garfunkel—of course this isn't his real name, but if Ben said what it was, Sammy missed it—is pulling up a chair, and then the waitress is coming over, and then a bit later, a different waitress approaches with a bottle of wine and a glass, and she is serving Art Garfunkel, and he is asking her to bring two more glasses. "They let me store my own wine here," he explains to Ben. "This is a Burgundy. '83. A great year."

"If you're into that sort of thing," Ben says.

So they are locked in for a glass of wine. The waitress comes back and pours a glass for Sammy, which she swirls while waiting for Ben to be served. Art Garfunkel is studying her and she is nervous. She waits for Ben to drink, then takes a sip.

"What are you tasting?" Art Garfunkel asks, leaning toward her a bit.

Sammy struggles to put it into words, but fails. All she can think to say is, "Dirt."

Ben smirks, but Art Garfunkel is earnest, excited. "Soil," he says. "You're absolutely right. This soil is so rich, with this type of Burgundy. You're a natural."

They go through the bottle, Art Garfunkel paying extravagant attention to Sammy the whole time, asking her where she works, what she teaches, who her favorite poets are. He throws a few quotes at her to see if she can identify them, which she does— she has no trouble. Ben is impatient, swirling his wine, bobbing his leg up and down. At one point Art Garfunkel says: "One must have a mind of winter." And Sammy continues, "And to have been cold a long time." And Ben breaks in, exasperated: "Well you don't need a weatherman to know which way the wind blows."

"Okay, fine," Art says. "Enough poetry." He moves on, edging toward the future. He asks Sammy if she's ever been to Shakespeare in the Park. Whether she would like to go—they should all go this year! Then they can go for a sail. Does Sammy like to sail? Does she like the blues, jazz? Because, Art Garfunkel says, he is the director of a sound archive, specializing in preserving the earliest jazz and blues recordings in existence. And if she wants to, she can visit the archive, hear some early recordings of Howlin' Wolf, Robert Johnson...

Sammy answers all of Art Garfunkel's questions, a bit too enthusiastically, actually—it has been so long since anyone paid this kind of attention to her. She can sense Ben's mood darkening. At one point, while Art Garfunkel describes the climate-controlled Brooklyn warehouse in which he stores his priceless records, she sees that Ben is staring into his wine glass, frowning, intent on something. She leans forward and sees that a tiny fly is struggling in his wine. She can see its wings beating madly. There passes a moment when Sammy believes they are both considering the same thing: the fragility of life, and yet its resilience, its profound and enduring instinct for survival. But then no, maybe Ben isn't thinking that: he tilts his head back and in one swift gulp swallows the rest of the wine.

"It's good to see you," Ben says abruptly, "but we're running late."

Then they all stand, shake hands. Art Garfunkel invites them to go sailing the next time Sammy is in the city. Then Ben puts his arm around Sammy in a proprietary manner, and leads her away.

"Who was that?" Sammy asks, when they are out of earshot. "How do you know him?"

"We went to high school together," says Ben. "He's insufferable."

"He didn't seem so bad," she ventures.

"Just stay away from him."

"That shouldn't be a problem."

"He'll contact you. I guarantee. Next thing you know, he'll suddenly have a meeting in Kansas City. He'll send you an email saying he's in town."

"I'm not too worried about it," she says.

"He's always trying to take things from other people. He doesn't have a game of his own. Just taking other people's shit. That's his thing."

"Oh." A moment passes when Sammy considers whether she qualifies as someone else's shit.

"He's a billionaire," Ben adds, sourly.

"Oh," Sammy says.

"People get weird when they get into the high millions, low billions. It's hard to explain."

"I wouldn't know," she says. "I mean, I'm still keeping track of frequent flyer miles, here." A long list of petty difficulties springs to mind. "I have this little card I use at the grocery store, for discounts, and you can also use it for five cents off a tank of gas, I mean, there's a considerable loss of dignity going on."

Ben waves her complaints away. He is still in such a bad mood. "Just stay away from him," he says.

They decide to take the long way home, walking through town instead of along the shoreline. The streets are milling with tourists. The town they are in, Ogunquit, is popular with gay couples—in fact the majority of couples Sammy sees holding hands are gay. When she first started coming here, back in the early nineties, before AZT was released, the town had been full of dying men, couples taking what must have been their last vacations together. She remembers seeing lots of wheel chairs, men pushing around their dying lovers. The sick men were so emaciated they could only be described as skeletal. All of them wore long pants and sweaters, and had blankets draped over their laps. They were cold even in summer.

Now everyone is healthy again. The mood is festive. Couples are everywhere, buoyant and happy. Gay marriage has just been approved in New York and Sammy sees several couples wearing sets of t-shirts—some that say Just Married on the backs, some that say Groom & Groom. There are so many tourists in the streets that it is difficult to navigate the town's historic center, a cluster of old shops, some of them selling the finer things, like homemade jams and soaps, candles, Irish knit sweaters, but most of them selling garbage. In one storefront Sammy sees a t-shirt with a cartoon lobster stuck in a trap, its eyes bulging, and beneath it, the caption: Trapped in Maine. In another she sees a coffee mug, something she considers buying for Ben, a simple graphic modeled after the ubiquitous I Love NY logo, but instead of NY it says I Love ME. She points these things out in the windows, charmed, though Ben only rolls his eyes.

They pass through town, then up a scenic drive with a view of the water. When they are almost to Ben's cottage they pass a gay couple taking a selfie, with the ocean as a backdrop. As they pass by one of the men—the younger one, dressed in a neon pink polo shirt and white pants, his bleached hair spiked with gel—calls out to them. "Yoo-hoo!" he says. "Can you take our picture?" His voice is high, loud, excited. Ben's face takes on a beleaguered expression—he hates people who can't keep their happiness to themselves.

Ben approaches, takes the phone. "Just press here, love," says the man in the pink shirt. Ben steps back, gets the couple in frame. "Smile," he says. The man in the pink shirt is already smiling—his teeth so white they are startling—but the other man, who is much older, and more soberly dressed, in khakis and a white button down, a blue blazer with brass buttons, is stoic. Ben snaps a few pictures, hands back the phone.

"We're on our honeymoon!" says the man in the pink shirt. "Isn't it wonderful?"

"Congratulations," Sammy says. She likes this man, or feels sorry for him—he is willing to be happy, when everyone else, even the man he has just married, doesn't seem to have the heart.

The men are hardly out of earshot—in fact, Sammy fears, still able to hear them—when Ben says: "If I had to spend the rest of my life with that man, I'd shoot myself."

"Oh," she says, "he wasn't so bad."

"He actually used the word *yoo-hoo*. In earnest."

"He's just happy. He just got married!"

"I suppose," Ben says, "one of those problems will solve the other."

They arrive at the cottage, which Sammy has always loved. She has always thought of it as a middle ground between the life she knew growing up, and the life Ben is accustomed to. The furnishings at the cottage are all castoffs, factory-rejects from the Rosenbergs' place in the city. The beds and chairs are large and ornate, overstuffed, with legs and arms elaborately turned and tapered, unlike the sleek lines of their city home. All the plates and mugs are mismatched, chipped. The silverware is light and dull, the towels and linens are threadbare. Even the shoes Ben keeps there, his old leather loafers, are falling apart, collapsed outward at the edges, scuffed, the lining worn through at the heels.

The cottage has been, for the most part, under the care and custody of the Rosenberg men. Ben's father had been the one who purchased and appointed it, who loved it, who drove up for the weekends, even when the rest of the family wanted to stay behind in New York. The home's décor plays on two themes—the sea, and hunting. Its walls are wood paneled and decorated with anchors, swaths of netting in which starfish and buoys are ensnared. All along the mantle, and lining the shelves and windowsills, there are green glass bottles encased in rope net, sand dollars, little wooden seagull statues. On the walls of every room there are large paintings depicting hunts of various kinds—geese in flight at the top of one canvas, hunters at the bottom, their guns raised. On another, a pointer with his nose stuck into a shrub, his tail sticking up. In the living room there's an enormous oil painting of an English foxhunt, with lords on horseback, their dogs running, and at the far end of the canvas, a desperate looking fox, airborne, its mouth open, a frantic look in its eye.

Now the father is gone, and Ben is the only one who comes to the cottage. Three or four times a year. It is falling into disrepair, he has often complained to Sammy, and he should sell it. His mother wants him to, keeps asking him to clear it out, turn it over to a realtor. But he can't quite let it go. Sammy thinks this has to do with the way the cottage remains unchanged—in the way, she supposes, the whole purpose and function of summer homes is to stay constant through the years, to remind the people who inhabit them of the people they used to be. There is something seductive about it. Even she can feel it, and she's not even part of the family.

They go through their routine, changing into pajamas, washing their faces and brushing their teeth. Ben pours himself a scotch, three fingers in a coffee mug, and gathers up his cigarettes and ashtray. They make their way to the master bedroom, the best room in the house, with a king bed facing a wall of windows—a pristine view of the water, though what they usually do is push the TV and its stand in front of the bed and watch that, instead of the ocean. Which is a sin, Sammy always thinks. A mortal sin they keep committing. Then repenting. Then committing again.

They haven't had sex in years, since way before Ava, but still it is their custom to share a bed, to sleep side by side. They lie in bed and watch TV for a while, nothing special, nothing new. It isn't long before Sammy is asleep. She sleeps better with Ben, falls into it more deeply, than she ever can at home. Sometimes when she wakes with him—she wakes every night at three, these past few years—it occurs to her how completely she was out, how deeply surrendered, and she feels embarrassed. A bit ashamed. *Excuse me, that wasn't like me*, is the phrase that goes through her head. *That was out of character*.

This night, though, she wakes early, because a violent storm is coming up off the water—lightning claps, and then thunder rolls in right behind it. The wind is furious, assaulting the house, the rain driving against the windows. "Jesus!" she cries, sitting up. She is disoriented in the dark—the power has gone out.

Ben is sitting up, too. "Christ," he says.

"That lightning scared me half to death."

"I think I had a small heart attack," he says, holding his chest.

The wind gusts again and they feel themselves sprayed with water. "The windows!" she cries. They have left the windows open, to catch the air off the ocean. One of life's little pleasures. They bound toward them. The windows are the kind that turn in and out by cranks, a whole row of them. She starts on one end, he on the other. But before they get to the middle, another gust comes and blows the screens right out of the two center windows. They go flying out, land on the bed.

"Jesus Christ!" she cries.

"Goddamn," he says.

They finish cranking the windows closed, laughing. By the time they are finished, they are both soaked.

Ben fumbles his way toward the bathroom. She hears him peeing, in trickles and bursts. She knows this happens to men as they get older but doesn't know why. She doesn't know very much about men, actually. He returns from the bathroom with a flashlight and two towels. She takes a towel and wipes off her face, her hair. They remove the screens from the bed and climb back in. He props the flashlight between them, pointed at the ceiling. It is as if they are kids at camp, telling ghost stories.

But they don't talk for a while. They lie there considering the storm, which is beautiful, if viewed in a certain way. In the flashes of lightning Sammy can see the ocean churning, and yes, she thinks, it is beautiful. It is sublime.

There is a family photo on the bedside table next to Sammy, in a silver frame that catches and reflects all the light in the room. Sammy picks it up, studies it. It is a picture of Ben, about three years old, lying on top of his father, in a lounge chair on the beach. The father is youngish and handsome, with a full head of curly silver hair. His body is still trim and muscular—he looks quite a bit like Charlie Chaplin, Sammy realizes, not the tramp but the real Chaplin. Ben, curly-haired and cute, is asleep on his father's chest, and his father is shielding him from the sun with an open newspaper. There he is, Sammy thinks, my best friend, the love of my life, asleep in the shadow of the daily news.

Ben's father has turned toward the camera—towards Ben's mother, no doubt—with a stern expression. As if he has been rudely interrupted. Sammy recognizes this look. It is the look of a man who, beleaguered with child care, has found a pocket of happiness, a moment of quiet in which he is actually able to relax and read the paper, and he doesn't want to be bothered.

"So young," Sammy says. "So handsome."

"I was pretty cute," he says.

"I was talking about your father."

"Well he was handsome," Ben says. "Handsome, but miserable. Look. He never smiled."

"It's still a great picture," she ventures. "I mean, it's honest."

"I suppose."

"I mean, what I'm finding out is, it's all crap. Every day is just, it's just one bullshit thing after another. But then you look back and, I don't know. Somehow all that misery, you have all these fond feelings."

"I guess," he says.

She puts the picture back in its place and stares at it for a while. The storm is dying down and the rain is gentler now, pleasant. She is settling down, thinking about letting herself fall asleep, when Ben turns toward her, pulls her into a hug. She rolls toward him, buries her face in his chest. "You're the only person who knows me," he says. Then, after a bit. "What if you move to New York? What if we're each other's family, each other's misery."

She's been through this before. The memory of that night at the Carlyle, all those years ago, is still so close to the surface. Come to New York, why don't you. She won't fall for it again.

"You're just saying that because of Art Garfunkel," she says. "You don't want anyone else talking to me. You're jealous."

What he says next shocks her. "You're right. I want you all to myself."

She lets a moment pass. Then asks, "How would it work?" So quiet she almost can't hear herself. Why is she doing this to herself?

"My apartment is huge. And I'm hardly ever there. I mean, you could move right in."

"I guess. But I mean, I'd have to get a job."

"So get a job," he says.

"And Ava." How can she even begin to describe Ava, her funny little sidekick, her quiet little companion? Ben knows almost nothing about Ava, none of the real things—the trouble Ava has at school, the loneliness, the bit with the dogs. Sammy has mentioned these things here and there, but mostly in a joking way—she has kept the painful truth of these matters to herself. He doesn't understand, couldn't possibly understand. She says all she can think to say. "I don't know what we'd do about school."

"There are schools in New York," Ben says. They are pressed so tightly together they can't actually see each other. His face is buried in her hair, hers in his chest. She can hardly breathe. Suddenly she is on the verge of crying.

Then, she can't help it, she is actually crying, the idea of changing her life, of being spirited away, is so desperately tempting. She is shaking and sniffling.

"It's okay," he says. Strokes her hair.

"I know," she says.

"Just think about it."

"Okay."

And she does. Practically all night, long after he falls asleep and starts snoring. She thinks about it the next day, though neither of them mentions it. And the day after that, while she travels back to Manchester. On the one hand, it's an absurd idea, two old friends—two old friends, and a little girl—making a family. Though on the other hand, what difference does it make? They love each other. Seem to need each other. But then again, would it last? He is so fickle, so cold sometimes. Just because he loves her one minute doesn't mean he will love her the next—there have been times when a single glance from him has just sliced her in half. She thinks about what happened between him and Meg—how one day he just looked at her and hated her guts. And if he looked at her one day, Sammy thinks, and decides he wants her to leave, then what? It's not like she could just get another job—almost no one is hiring in her field. This is just something he can't appreciate, can't understand, because he has always had money. He just doesn't get it. Everything has always been so easy for him. He can buy himself out of anything. He doesn't even know what he's asking. Then again, she thinks, doesn't love require, in whatever form it takes, a leap of faith? Some kind of risk? She keeps going back and forth, back and forth. Trying to calculate the likelihood of things working out between them. She is like an insurance adjuster, a Vegas fixer, someone trying to work out the odds. But no matter how she does the math, which formulas or algorithms or chart she uses, at the heart of it is always this moment, this mystery, this X to be solved for, her favorite memory, that moment in bed, holding each other in the center of the storm. She doesn't quite know what it meant. She doesn't quite know what it means.

2011

A week later, back in New York, Ben is in bed on his computer and an email from Sammy pops up. He opens it and sees that she has forwarded him a message from Art Garfunkel. *Hello!* it reads. *Perhaps you might remember that we shared a glass of Burgundy in Ogunquit, Maine a few days ago. I'm writing because as it happens, my work with the archive is bringing me down to Kansas City. I hope to procure some rare recordings, have some barbeque, and visit Charlie Parker's grave. Maybe even have a conversation about poetry! If any of this sounds interesting to you, please let me know when you're free....*

Ben calls Sammy right away. "That *fucker*," he says.

She laughs. "You were right."

"I was *so* right. Don't you dare answer him. Just delete it. Delete it right now."

"Well, I'm not going to just *delete* it."

"You'd better not meet up with him."

"I'm kind of curious," she says. "I have to admit."

Ben thinks how to properly summarize Art Garfunkel's character, calls up a story from high school. "This is the kind of guy," he says, "for his eighteenth birthday, his father took him hunting in Arkansas." He pauses for dramatic effect, lights a cigarette.

"Okay," Sammy says. "So?"

"So," he says, his cigarette bobbing. "The deal with the

hunting was, they went up in helicopters. And shot down at groups of wild boar. With AK-47s."

"*Jesus*," Sammy says.

"He's the kind of guy, even way back then, who was saying shit like, *You can always put a price on a car, but you can't put a price on an experience*."

"I suppose that is kind of stomach-turning."

"Trust me," he says. "You don't want to be one of this guy's experiences."

"But it's so *boring* out here," she complains. "I mean, going to visit a gravesite would be, like, the highlight of my life."

The feeling Ben used to have around Sammy—of wanting to protect her, yet also wanting to harm her, slap her like an obstinate child, because she is so naïve, always so many steps behind—flares up in him. He is filled with bright rage.

"Just so you know," he says, hoping to sink in a little dagger, "where all that money comes from, his father owns Bartleby."

"I have no idea what that is. Except for, like, a Melville character."

"Super conservative propaganda media outlet. It's like the news FOX News watches when it goes home at night."

"Oh. Yeesh."

"Funny he didn't mention that."

"Right," she says. "I guess he wouldn't."

They say goodbye, and Ben takes up his computer. When Sammy's email came in, he had been working, trying to decide which online CME course to take—something he'd put off too long and needed to take care of. He was finally getting down to it, reviewing the courses, feeling good about himself, productive. But now, instead of going back to his work, he is typing in Art Garfunkel's name, tracking him all over the web. He finds a handful of puff pieces on the sound archive. Pictures of Art at various benefits he'd sponsored and attended. There was even an article in *People*, picturing Art with an old, supposedly important musician displaced by Hurricane Katrina. Art had built a new house for the musician—in fact he had paid for a whole block of houses. Blah, blah, blah. What gets to Ben the most is Art Garfunkel's smile, which is the same in every picture. His signature expression is to turn up just one corner of his mouth, so he appears to be agreeable, but also somehow superior, too cool to smile fully. It's a smile that says: *I'm footing the bill for this whole thing, but really, it's okay, don't make a fuss. Well, okay, if you insist.*

Ben can't remember the last time he felt this angry about anything—can hardly remember feeling angry at all, these last many years. He keeps clicking, keeps reading, until he realizes he has finished an entire bottle of wine.

He is finally feeling something, and what he is feeling is desperation.

He slaps his computer closed, tells Johnny Carson his problems, which can be summarized in a single line. "I think I fucked up," he says, and passes out.

Meanwhile, Sammy takes another look at Art Garfunkel's email. She imagines the possibilities—the jazz, the barbeque, Charlie Parker's gravesite. But mostly what she imagines is Ben—how crazy it would make him.

She spends a minute or two thinking of these things, then snaps out of it. She is acting like a teenager, she realizes. A teenager hoping to make a boy jealous by going out with another boy. She deletes the email, closes her computer. "I have a Ph.D.," she says aloud. Just to remind herself. "I'm thirty-seven years old."

431

2011

Three months later, Sammy flies to Manchester at semester break, like always, and spends a few days with her father. Then she leaves Ava in his care so she can visit Ben in the city. Whenever she comes to town Ben clears his schedule, and they go out to movies and restaurants, to the museums. They spend large swaths of time sitting around his apartment watching television and eating takeout—sometimes they don't leave the apartment all day. This particular trip, though, the first thing Sammy asks to do is ride down to Zuccotti Park, so she can see it for herself. There isn't any point, Ben tells her, because all the tents have been confiscated and the park cleared. But still she wants to go—wants to return to The City of No Importance as a person who had been there. When they arrive, she sees that indeed the park is nothing special, just a patch of concrete punctuated by trees and benches, people in suits walking through. She experiences a strange dissonance, some kind of reverberation between the imagery she'd seen on television and the park itself. The park itself is smaller than she imagined, and the degree of difference between the two creates a sense of shame in her, at having made a bad calculation. Her understanding of the world is flawed. And if this is true in this one particular instance with the park, she reasons, perhaps it is also true about all kinds of things.

"This park makes me feel sort of depressed," she tells Ben, and he suggests they eat—this is pretty much his solution to everything. He takes her to a restaurant that was once, decades ago, a bank. The hostess leads them to the back room, and they follow her through a giant metal door that had once sealed off the bank's vault. They sit in that room like valuable commodities, precious holdings, ordering vast sums of food and wine. Every few minutes a hand reaches in front of Sammy to retrieve an empty plate, then replaces it with something new: Caviar, bacon-wrapped dates, a wheel of brie baked into a pastry puff, a dozen scallops sizzling in a cast-iron pan. Soon she is too full to go on and sits chewing on the sprigs of parsley and curlicues of radish that come on the side of each plate—even the garnishes here are beautiful, bright as jewelry. She and Ben pass the time talking about nothing in particular: His work, her work, the news. They talk and drink until her head spins. She watches Ben swallow an entire plate of oysters, tilting his head back with such gusto that it makes her dizzy. It is wrong, some part of her feels, to eat and drink so much, to be so wasteful, so gluttonous, while other people are just barely scraping by. But then again she is so drunk, so full, these thoughts just pass through her head. When they finally stand to leave, she can barely walk, and has to steady herself against Ben.

All through that trip, she wonders how to bring it up to him again, this prospect he mentioned back at the beach house, of moving to New York, living together. She worries about it for three days, and is so distracted that Ben keeps asking what's wrong. Finally, on their last night, she resolves herself to bring it up.

They are sitting around the apartment watching television, and Sammy is flipping through the paper looking at ads for matinees—wanting, essentially, to trade in the screen they are already watching for a bigger one. Whenever she visits Ben, she aspires to see films in limited release, films that won't make it to the Midwest, usually documentaries about suffering. "Oh, I heard about this one," she says, pointing to an ad. A group of small children are picking through a giant mound of trash. "That looks great," he says, then points to an ad for an action movie, its hero pictured dangling from a cliff. "Though personally I think we should see this." This was always happening—she'd mention a documentary, but he'd argue for an action movie, and they'd go back and forth, each tugging an end of the rope, what they should watch versus what they secretly really wanted to watch, back and forth, all the way down the elevator and out into the street, through a series of twists and turns, until inevitably, just as they arrived at the ticket counter, Sammy would give up, and they'd spend their evening watching spies evade security systems, dangling from ropes and diving through laser beams, they'd watch cars crash into each other and plummet over bridges, their bodies would tremble in the wake of bright explosions, they'd stuff their faces with buttered popcorn, they'd lick their fingers clean of oil and salt then plunge them into the bucket again, they'd pass a giant soda back and forth, sucking it through a shared straw, and they were happy.

"Well," she says now. "Okay. I guess I can catch that documentary some other time." She wants the night to go well. Wants them to enjoy the movie, then come home with takeout, which they'll eat in bed. That's when she'll ask him.

He goes off to find his shoes and coat. Sammy continues flipping through the paper. She feels happy. Completely at home. She feels more at home here, it occurs to her, than anywhere else in the world.

Then the buzzer rings, and she gets up to answer the door. A young girl, maybe twenty, is standing there, with a very large case of some kind resting next to her. She is tiny, maybe five two, and beautiful—with long black hair and a full mouth, painted bright red. Her breasts are so large Sammy can see their shape, even underneath the down parka she wears.

"I'm here for Ben?" says the girl. She looks a bit shy, sort of confused.

437

"Oh," Sammy says.

Just then Ben comes out, buttoning his jacket, and when he sees the girl, he falters. Checks his watch.

"Evita," he says. "Hi." He looks stunned. Uncomfortable. Sammy has never seen him look this way in all their years together.

"I'm sorry," he says. "I called to cancel."

"They didn't tell me," she says. "I'm sorry."

"Here, here. Let me pay you." He pulls out his wallet, starts counting out bills.

"You know what?" Sammy said. "I was just going to a movie. Do your thing. Don't let me interrupt."

"No, no," Ben says. "Let me just settle this. Just wait one second."

But she is already down the hall. She takes the stairs, runs down a few flights. Then gets on the elevator. Descends to the lobby, races out into the street. She doesn't want him to catch up to her. Doesn't want him to see her. She is crying, a little. *Right under my nose*, is the phrase that keeps going through her mind. As if she were Ben's mother, as if he were living under her roof.

She walks to the documentary and sits alone in the small theater, watching a group of children picking through piles of trash in a dump outside of Calcutta. She tries to focus on the tragic poverty unfolding in front of her, but she can't, she isn't that kind of person. Instead she is the kind of person who sits replaying the scene of her most recent humiliation. Thinking about that girl, how young she was. Her hair and makeup. And those breasts—those gigantic breasts. Sammy doesn't credit herself with many abilities—doesn't consider herself particularly savvy—but about one thing she is sure: She can read people, tell when they've been caught in the middle of something. She has a special gift for sensing these things. He's been sleeping with this girl. Probably many more like her.

Then she thinks: Well, so? What did I expect? She tries to figure out why she is so angry. It's not like any promises were made between them. It's not as if he ever swore to forsake all others. What bothers her, she decides, is that this girl, this massage therapist, has *revealed something* about Ben, about his relationships with other people. It's the fact that he *summons* people, if and when he desires them. That's what's bothering her, she decides.

That and how young the girl was. And those giant breasts.

And the fact that she considered, even for a second, bringing Ava up to live with him. Ultimately she is mad at herself, she decides, for being so stupid.

Sammy sits and tries to remember what she and Ben were like when they first met, when she was eighteen and he was twenty-three. He'd come sweeping into the sandwich shop with Kurtz and Boris, and she had singled him out in an instant. Partly because of his towering height, partly because of his clothes, the air of formality about him. Kurtz and Boris still looked and acted like college students, but Ben looked like a man of the world, in dark pants and a white dress shirt, a long black coat with a plaid scarf, wingtips, even a fedora. He had taken her breath away.

Back then Ben's plan was to finish his novel—the great American political novel—then med school, then a psych residency, after which he would work in city hospitals, treating the people who needed it most, the schizophrenics and the suicidally depressed, the drug addicted and homeless and destitute. He had no interest, he claimed, in sitting in a fancy office listening to rich people cry about their problems. As for Sammy, she had wanted to write, too. Stories and poems telling the tales of the orphaned and destitute— she had wanted to be Dickens, basically. But neither of them had followed through. Ben had chosen the path cleared for him by his mother, and Sammy, well, the best she could say for herself was that she was teaching other people's books to students who had no desire to read them. There was no denying it anymore: they had fumbled, they had fucked everything up.

When she got back to the apartment Ben was in bed—*his mother's bed*, was how she thought of it, smugly—watching cable news, smoking a cigarette. Sammy stood at the edge of the room and stared at him. His beard had grown so long that it blended seamlessly with the tuft of chest hair emerging from under his silk robe. She thought of a picture she'd seen of Orson Welles in a smoking jacket and wondered how it was he'd died—a heart attack, maybe, or a car crash or drugs, she couldn't remember. But at the end, around the era of the smoking jacket, you certainly couldn't say it was a surprise. You couldn't say you hadn't seen it coming.

She climbs in bed beside him. Even now, when she is angry with him, because it is such an old habit, because they are, in so many respects, like a married couple. They are silent for a while, trading his cigarette back and forth, watching reports of the latest suicide bombing in Iraq. Then a commercial comes on—again!—for an erectile dysfunction pill. A man and a much younger woman are pictured on a yacht, laughing. An announcer says something about being the man you were meant to be. Then, in a lower voice, something hurried about an erection lasting more than four hours.

"How was your *massage*?" Sammy asks.

"Not exactly the best," he says. Then he tells her how he's been procuring the services of this particular massage therapist for a few months now and has always enjoyed her company. But tonight, things had gone badly—he just couldn't get into it. "She tried everything," Ben said. "All the tricks she could think of. But it just wasn't happening."

"That's a shame," Sammy says.

"Poor girl. It's got to be sort of humiliating to be in that position. To be working so hard and failing so completely."

"Right," she says. Suddenly feeling sympathy with that young girl. Trying and trying to please Ben. Failing and failing.

"She offered to give me another hour for free," he says. And so that Sammy could appreciate the magnitude of what he was saying, elaborates: "An hourly rate employee offered me an hour *for free*."

"Sounds like she has feelings for you," Sammy says. And so that he could appreciate the magnitude of what she was saying, elaborates. "I mean, that sounds like true love."

"Some of us have to take what we can get," Ben says.

"Give me a break."

"I blame you, of course. You're so judgmental."

"Psh," she says. "I'm not your problem. Your problem is, this isn't what people are supposed to do. This isn't what people do at all, and you know it."

"They certainly do. Maybe not in Missouri, but they do here."

"Maybe some. But that doesn't mean it's okay."

"My balls are crawling inside me as we speak," he says. "You're like the ocean in January."

"But it's never going to be okay. What you're doing, it's never going to be authentic, or like, meaningful. You're never going to love anybody."

"At least I'm having sex," he says. And leaves unsaid: "Which you aren't." But still she feels it, this little stab at her life. Her pathetic life.

"I's not a big deal," he adds. "It's just sex. It's a basic trading of commodities." He is lighting a new cigarette, holding it between his lips, and so the next bit comes out as a mumble: "Supply and demand. Econ 101."

"People aren't commodities," she says.

"Sure they are. My patients come to me for something, and

I give it to them, and they give me something. The same with your students. We're all just trading resources here."

"You're talking like people are walking around with, like, price tags hanging from their collars."

"They pretty much are," he says.

"Jesus! You're turning into, like, *Harry Lime*!" She fumbles for the speech in *The Third Man*, with Orson Welles up in the Ferris wheel looking down at the tiny crowd, trying to justify the fact that he'd diluted medicine to make a profit, killing people in the process of lining his pockets. She fucks the speech up, mostly, though she gets at the general idea. "Would you really give a damn," she says, in her best imitation of Ben, as Orson Welles, as Harry Lime, "if one of those dots down there stopped moving, forever?"

Then comes a rant in which Sammy picks apart the ways in which Ben's money has ruined him. Has taken away the hunger that drives most people out of their homes and into the streets, where they encounter other people and come to know them, to work with them and care for them, to love them, to which Ben replies that Sammy, whose hunger has driven her into the streets her entire life, has never managed to forge a meaningful relationship with anyone but him. They continue to slice at one other, quick and sharp, back and forth, trading twenty years of pent up confessions and accusations, Sammy calling Ben a spoiled fucking brat, and Ben calling Sammy a sanctimonious martyr, a self-pitying pain in the ass whose whining no one, no one in the world would put up with other than him. They do this until they are both queasy and Sammy finally asks, softly, whether maybe they aren't two people who have always meant well, but who have tragically and somewhat sympathetically failed to make the most of themselves. She wonders if maybe instead they are just villains. Common villains.

Then comes a long silence, after which Ben notes: "You're no fun anymore." He starts working the remote, flipping through channels so fast he can't possibly tell what it is he's moving past.

"Well," Sammy says. "I guess we're not doing each other any good."

"It's true," he says. "You'd be better off without me."

Sammy thinks, for a moment, that he is conceding a point, admitting to his fault in the matter, the flaws in his character. But then he says, "It's better when you don't have to keep comparing your life to a life that's so, well," he gestures with the remote, sweeps his arm across the room, toward the window, his view of the park. "Different."

A notion forms in her mind that he might be saying what he is actually saying. That he could be so smug, so cold.

"People do better when they sort of stay within their means," he says.

"Oh," she says. "Okay. Wow." She stares down at her lap. "That's helpful." She is going for sarcasm but it comes out deflated. Repentant, almost.

She sinks down in the bed, turns her back, takes up a pillow, hugs it. She is waiting for him to touch her shoulder, turn off the television, something, but he just keeps watching TV, flipping through channels. A few minutes pass. Then she says—spontaneously, as if the thought came from someone else and she was merely voicing it: *I wish I never met you.*

The next morning, Sammy flies to Manchester, then returns with her daughter to the City of No Importance, resumes her routine. Every night she thinks of calling Ben, but doesn't want to break first. She feels her integrity is at stake, the integrity of every relatively poor person locked in a service relationship with a rich person.

A few weeks go by, during which Sammy sees each of her personal struggles in a new light. Her car, for instance—her Toyota Tercel, which shudders to life when she turns the ignition and stutters down the road, often shaking to a halt at stoplights. She has named the car Marcel, Marcel the Tercel, because she likes to think that invoking Marcel Proust's French haughtiness and refinement in the context of this truly shitty, broken-down car will lift her spirits. She likes to think it is still possible to be Marcel, internally, while driving a 1988 Toyota Tercel. Somewhere deep inside she is in Paris, relaxing on a bed topped with silk pillows, is her point, even though she is technically driving around Missouri in a rusted hatchback with a Blue Book value of two-hundred dollars. But in fact, this is a private joke that doesn't go very far, it does nothing to make her feel better when the car breaks down in the middle of the road, and over the years she has begun to feel less and less like Marcel Proust internally and more and more that Marcel the Tercel represents her, speaks to certain truths about her—that she is out of date and falling apart, that she is common, done for, that she is broke. Sammy hates, particularly, the moments she and her daughter spend in the drop-off line at school each morning, hates when Marcel collapses in a spasm, when she has to wave the other cars around her as she struggles to start him again, hates watching her daughter slip out the door and walk hunched under the weight of her backpack, not looking at any of the other kids as they emerge from their parents' Audis and BMWs. Sammy doesn't know why she feels she deserves better, doesn't know why she has always felt she had been born in the wrong place and time, to the wrong set of parents. Manchester, New Hampshire as she had known it was full of people clad in white denim, smoking Marlboros, drinking cans of Budweiser, blasting classic rock from their aging Camaros, basically an endless George Thorogood concert, and even from a young age she'd turned away from them, kept to herself. All that reading had done her in, she supposes now, all those books written about beauty. She wants beauty around her, dignity, she is mad for it, has spent her life running after it, running after Ben. There is something small in her, she realizes, something petty and covetous. Whenever she sees a bit of beauty, she sits thinking about how to get it, spinning and spinning the idea of that beautiful thing, like a squirrel frantically turning a nut in its paws.

Is this what it's always been about, with Ben? All these years, has she just been after some unattainable measure of beauty?

For a couple of weeks after the fight, Sammy develops a new appreciation for Marcel. She sees Marcel's problems as the types of problems real people—this is the phrase she is using, *real people*—deal with. She begins to see other cars on the road as garish perversions, sickening displays of wealth. She imagines Ben making fun of her car, and she imagines herself defending it, sometimes, in fact, losing herself so completely in these imagined arguments that she recites her lines out loud. *Like you'd know*, she spits, and Ava says from the back seat: *Know what?*

Sammy starts to see The City of No Importance, for the first time, as maybe having some importance, maybe having, in fact, more importance than New York itself. All the names you see in the paper, she imagines telling Ben. All the kids who join the Army and go off to war, all the kids sent home in body bags, all the kids hobbling around on prosthetics—you know where they're from? Right here, she says, in her mind. Right fucking here. All through those punishing weeks of winter she is fighting with Ben in her head. Which is ridiculous, she knows. But talking with him is a habit of mind. It is how she knows she's alive.

Finally Ben does call, but strangely, it's no longer what she wants. The first time—she's driving home after school with Ava and her phone is packed away in her bag—he calls but doesn't leave a message. Later that evening, she goes to call him back, pulls up his name on her phone but then just…looks at it. Backs out. Puts the phone down. Tomorrow, she thinks. But she doesn't call the next day, either. Some instinct is guiding her, something new, something she can't yet identify.

He tries again a few days later. This time it is late in the evening, and she is in bed, grading papers and watching television. When her phone lights up, she just stares at it. Lets it go to voicemail. A minute later she listens to his message. "Hey, Sams," he says. Sounding meek. Like he's about to apologize, or confess something. But then he says: "I just saw a dog on TV who could walk on its hind legs while carrying a tray full of glasses across a room. Somehow." She'd seen it, too, on *The Late Show*, and wished Ava had been awake—it was pretty impressive, for a dog. "And anyway, I just, well, it reminded me of you."

She laughs out loud. Because it's funny. Because it hurts.

He tries again, on St. Patrick's Day. May the road rise to meet you, he texts. And it would be so easy, she thinks, so easy to fall back into it. May the wind be always at your back, she could write—the line is already written for her. But then, her thumb hovering over the keys on her phone, she can't.

Finally something shifts, and Sammy no longer sees herself as someone having an argument with her best friend; she becomes someone who has lost that friend, someone who is now alone. Alone and faced with the prospect of making something of her diminished life. The anger recedes and the grief sets in. When she thinks of Ben, and all the time they spent together, it's not a living thing—it's a dissection. She has a memory of Ben and thinks: Anatomy 101. Their life together is dead on the table in front of her, and the only work left to do is to dissect it.

One afternoon, on one of the last days of the spring semester, she is sitting in the lounge, watching everyone ball up the remains of their lunches, pack up their briefcases and bags, and finds that she can't get up from her chair. It is like this lately, in those first weeks of spring, when she is just facing the prospect of being alone—like a force is working against her. One by one her colleagues carry themselves away with their chattering, until she is left in the room with only the Shakespearean, who seems to be taking an unreasonably long time finishing his soup, one of those packages of noodles in a Styrofoam cup. He keeps shaking the cup in his hand and examining its contents, frowning, then tilting the cup to his mouth. Sammy worries he is about to say something to her. He is the senior-most member of her department and is rumored to wield great power, and so she is afraid of talking around him, of exposing herself as a fool. She's said nothing to him in three years—she didn't even manage to offer her condolences when his wife died the previous winter. But she has studied him in his grief. His wife had been a real Véra Nabokov, the kind to pack his meals, launder and iron his clothes, type his papers, tie his tie, open his umbrella. When she died there had been a few whispered jokes by some of the feminists about how the Shakespearean would continue to function without her. He was going to have to hire a graduate student, they said, to pick him up and drive him to class, to answer his emails and do his grocery shopping. But of course in the end the jokes weren't funny, because how the Shakespearean functioned now was this: He rode a bicycle to campus and arrived with his hair windblown to hell; he wore the same clothes for a week straight; he carried around messy stacks of papers in his arms and often trailed sheets behind him like some kind of ancient Hansel; he brought instant soup for his lunch; he sat in silence in the lounge, sunk in his armchair, listening to the dialogue of their colleagues but no longer participating in it.

Now here they are in the lounge, just the two of them, the Shakespearean tilting the last of his noodles to his mouth, slurping. He smacks his lips, lowers his cup. Then he says, without quite looking at Sammy: "You look these days as though you lost your best friend." His voice is hollowed out by age, ghostly. The words he speaks sound like they have blown through a dark forest in winter. Sammy hears them and bursts like a pipe. Covers her face with her hands, surrenders to a moment of ugly, guttural sobbing.

"I did!" she cries, sounding more incredulous than grieved. As if the worst of things is, it's all such a fucking cliché.

"People will tell you it gets better in time," he says. "But in my experience, it does not."

She is still covering her face, still crying, though silently now. She can't bear to look at the Shakespearean but feels the need to explain something to him. She wonders how to put it, how to make him understand. "He was my Falstaff," she finally says.

"Ah," he says. "Your sweet creature of bombast."

"Yes. My huge hill of flesh."

She uncovers her face. The Shakespearean crumples the Styrofoam cup in his speckled hand. He is so old and weak he seems to have trouble even doing that. He tosses the cup toward the garbage can but it bounces on the rim and falls to the floor. He bends to retrieve it. "Oof," he says. He straightens up and gives it another toss into the can. Then he shuffles past, tipping an imaginary hat. They belong to the same club now.

Sammy sits and watches the clock on the wall, watches the minute hand creep toward the hour when her class will start. The shame of having burst into tears in front of the Shakespearean is still burning through her. She watches as the hand clicks past the hour, three minutes, four. She imagines her students, two flights up, their heads bent toward their phones, their thumbs typing madly. Perhaps a small cluster of them might actually be talking to each other—or yelling, more like, young people are so loud. She imagines a growing giddiness coming over them, a collective wisdom coalescing in the room: *If the prof is more than five minutes late we get to leave*, someone is saying. *I thought it was ten*, answers another. And the first says: *It used to be ten, but it's five now.* She is making a little story again, something to tell Ben. *These kids have doubled the value they place on their time, though they do half as much with it.*

She wonders when she will stop talking to Ben in her head, when she will stop arranging the minutiae of her existence into little anecdotes. *Pull yourself together,* she thinks. *Once more unto the breach.* She pushes herself out of her chair and walks up stairs. But instead of going to class, she walks out of the building, walks all the way home.

When she arrives, she finds a letter in the mailbox. From Ben, whose handwriting is so messy she's amazed the post office was able to decipher it. Anger flickers through her—he is always so careless. But then again, she thinks, he sent her a letter, an actual letter. No one does that anymore.

She lets herself in the house, stands in the living room, opens the envelope. There is just a single sheet of paper inside. It is not a letter, but a page from a longer manuscript—the upper-right hand corner is numbered 47. The printing is faint, the paper thin and slightly yellowed. She reads a few sentences, gathers that this is Ben's failed novel.

He is so tired, it reads, and hungry and lonely, so worn out from months on the road, and the café is so warm and brightly lit, that he has the feeling, watching this girl make his sandwich, her head inclined toward her work, that he is home at last, that they aren't strangers, that she is happy to see him, that if he came up behind her and rested his head along the curve of her neck, she would let him, because she has been waiting for him all day, because she loves him.

In the margin beside this passage he has written: From the moment I saw you.

She sits on the couch, sets the paper down beside her. Picks it up, reads it again. She has the urge to call Ben and almost does. But then, no. She won't. Something has happened in her body; an aversion has developed, an allergy. Ben is like a food that poisoned her. No matter how hungry she is, no matter how good it looks, she won't touch it again.

2012

It's the cat lady again. Crying in Ben's office. She has lately taken to using antique handkerchiefs—with little cats embroidered in the corners—to help manage her grief. There is almost always a delicate handkerchief in her hand, which she fondles or crumples, depending on mood. At the moment she is pressing the handkerchief over her eyes.

"I think he died of *grief*," she says. Sobs.

Ben had gotten her over the death of Ramone, and she'd been doing better for a while. In recent months she had even considered getting a new cat, though *not*, she always insisted, holding up a finger, *not* a replacement for Ramone. But then, just as things were improving, her remaining cat, Reggie, had died. Quite out of nowhere, as she phrased it.

"This is just," he tells her. He fumbles for something to say. Part of life, would be his normal advice, but they've already gone through that together. "Absurd," is what he says, quietly.

There passes a moment where the cat lady looks up, a bit stunned. Ben thinks he is in trouble—she will report him to someone. Because he has failed to console. Because he is taking her money, and yet can't seem to hold himself back from mocking her.

But that's not it. The look she gives him is one of stunned gratitude. "It *is* absurd," she says. "He was perfectly fine one day, and gone the next. It's just *absurd*!"

Ben is especially compassionate for the remainder of their

time together, leaning into her interpretation of his comment. Though privately he is wondering whether he has crossed some kind of threshold; maybe he can't do this kind of work anymore.

He sees the cat lady out, and then it is, thank God, time for his afternoon walk.

He's on his way to the park, lost in the bustle of pedestrian traffic, when he hears his name called out. "Yo, Rosenberg!"

He turns and sees Kurtz sitting at an outdoor table at a café, reading the newspaper. "Kurtz!" he says. Kurtz stands, and they hug.

"What's up, my man?" Kurtz says. "You fat fuck!"

"What are you doing here?" Ben asks.

"I left Washington, man," Kurtz says. "Got lured away by McKinley."

Ben nods as if he knows what that is. He sort of does— some kind of investment capital firm with business overseas, oil companies, that kind of thing. "What do you do for them?"

"Dude," Kurtz said. "Officially, I assess their political risk in foreign countries, but mostly I just cash their fucking checks." Kurtz's is a mess: his eyes bloodshot, his nose red. "Two million a year."

"Jesus," Ben says. In a way, that's more money than he has. Though in another way, it isn't, not even close.

"You were right all along," Kurtz says. "Politics doesn't fucking matter. It doesn't fucking matter at all. All that matters is money. Money is the true lingua franca. Everybody speaks money."

Ben winces. This is exactly what he'd argued to Kurtz, all those years ago, and Kurtz had fought him off, defended the ideals of democracy, the great civilizations of the past. They'd gone back and forth about it. Now, finally, Kurtz was declaring Ben the winner. But he doesn't want to win—he's never been so unhappy to be right.

"And anyway, my mother got sick," Kurtz says, bitterly. "She got sick and didn't have any security. All those years working for the Kennedys and then, well, what did it get her?"

Ben doesn't know what to say.

"She fucking broke her back cleaning other people's shit," he says. "And wound up with fucking nothing."

"I'm sorry," Ben says.

"So now here I am," he says. "Cashing in."

Then a blonde girl, quite young, possibly still in college, approaches the table and sits down. Ben stares at her for a moment, bewildered. She is disheveled, her hair a mess and her makeup smudged beneath her eyes. They probably just woke up. "This is Katie," Kurtz says, and give Ben a thumbs up. "Everybody speaks money," he says again, and laughs, and the girl laughs. And Ben laughs, but it is only a reflex. In truth, he is stunned. Punched in the gut. He tells Kurtz he's late for something, then walks off.

Ben heads for the park, because the park always makes him feel better. It is fall, a chill in the air, the leaves still clinging to the trees, though barely. People are running, walking their dogs. He sees a group of school children walking two by two, holding hands.

He sits on a bench and stretches out his legs, crosses his feet at the ankles. He sits stewing in this latest news: that the last true believer in the sanctity of democracy, his former best friend, has been knocked off his horse by the knights of capitalism. He is so bothered by this that he feels nauseous. He needs someone to take some of the burden, to receive his thoughts and observations. He needs Sammy. Like so many other times in the last few months— almost a year, now, he can hardly believe—he takes out his phone thinking he might send a text, something coy, like: You'll never guess who I just ran into. He scrolls through their old texts and registers, once again, something he has found curious since their split. All those years, he had always thought of Sammy as needy, a mouth to feed. But when he looks over their texts now, he sees that nearly always, he was the one to start things. Just around every morning at nine, when he was walking to work, he'd send her something. He weighs the urge to try again, against the last thing she said to him: *I wish I never met you.* He considers the possibility that by keeping in touch with her all those years, what he was really doing was ruining her life. He had kept her close for so long. And never quite knew why he was doing it. Only that, he couldn't stop.

He puts the phone down. Tries to shake Kurtz and Sammy out of his head. Really, he reminds himself, there are all kinds of things he should be doing instead, like keeping on top of his profession. He opens the journal he has brought with him, one of his trade publications. Scans through a few studies, then flips through the notices in the back. The VA is hiring, he sees, and thinks: Of course they are. All that PTSD. All those suicides. The long wait times, the bureaucracy. Jesus. What a mess.

He sets the journal aside, folds his hands in his lap, regards the scene in front of him. Then closes his eyes for a minute and just listens. Conversations pass him by—two women discussing their boss—*I know, I know!* one of them says—and a mother and her young son, negotiating—*It isn't time for the party*, the mother says. *We can go when it's time.* He opens his eyes and sees a nun in full habit drifting past, her black dress billowing behind her. Not long after she passes, a bearded, lumberjack of a man walks by, juggling. Ben feels content for a moment. In love with the whole city. But just after this feeling comes another—he can't experience pleasure these days without, right on its heels, a pang in his chest. Something is wrong and it won't go away.

A gust of wind swirls through the park and his journal flaps open, its pages rippling, and settles back to the ad he saw before, for the VA—it seems to be flagging him down. The feeling he gets, once again, is that old cliché about city life, how people keep walking past someone fallen in the street, thinking someone else will stop: *Someone should really do something about that.*

But it keeps coming to him. That night, the next day, the day after that. Something has snagged on a nail, and is unravelling. *Someone should really do something about that.*

Six months later, Ben has left his practice and is working at the VA.

The job is much as he expected. Too many patients, inadequate staff. Crappy facilities—flickering fluorescent lights everywhere, cinder block walls, linoleum floors. The computers are a nightmare, the phones. The hours are long, the patients often hostile. *You work for me, Jack*, is the feeling he gets from them, *and you're doing a shitty job*. Almost every patient he sees now has an axe to grind, is upset about the wait time. Almost everyone is suffering from anxiety and depression. In many cases severe. He checks people into the hospital now on a regular basis. These aren't false alarms, cries for help. He has already lost several patients to suicide.

It doesn't make sense, what he's doing—working so hard, when he doesn't even need the money. He wonders how long it will last, how many years he'll keep going. All he knows is that for the moment, a sense of urgency compels him: He gets right out of bed in the morning. It has never been easy for him to wake up, especially if it is still dark. He has always had a mantra—that if he is awake before the sun, something is terribly wrong. Well, something is terribly wrong, he supposes. But not in the way he thought. Something is wrong in the world, and it's his job to help fix it.

Ben's favorite part of the job is the group therapy session he runs on Friday afternoons. Mostly men, mostly combat vets. Generally, the men fall into two camps. Either the military is still central to their identity—fatigues, buzz cuts—or they have turned away completely, styled themselves according to a single principal: they do whatever they weren't allowed to do while in service. Their clothes are baggy, unkempt, and their hair and beards are long.

Ben's favorite patient is different, in a category of her own. She calls herself Minerva, though her benefits are filed under the name Jeff Jones. Minerva is a glorious reproduction of Marilyn Monroe—the white halter dresses and fur stole, patent leather heels, a red mouth with a mole painted just above it. She has been coming to the group for as long as he's been there—in fact even before that. She is the group's longest ranking member and considers herself its leader. Every time someone new shows up, Minerva takes it upon herself to do the introductions, going around the room summarizing the other vets and their basic circumstances and issues. *This is Brian, Iraq and Afghanistan, PTSD, rage issues, wife left him, can't stop lifting weights. And this is Joe...* She speaks in a delicate falsetto, at odds with the trauma she describes. It works, somehow. The other vets seem to like her, enjoy her performance. She brings something to the room the vets didn't know they needed, is the way Ben has come to think of it. The possibility of reinvention, perhaps. The possibility of grace.

Minerva always introduces herself last. "I'm Minerva," she says, touching her manicured nails to her stuffed breasts. "Formerly Jeff Jones, three tours, Iraq and Afghanistan, responsible for the death of forty-three civilians. Which is why I had to kill Jeff Jones, you understand. He had to be killed."

There's a lot going on with Minerva, and the rest of the group. Nightmares. Rages. Disassociation. Loss of control—many of the patients feel like they could *lose their shit* at any moment. "How am I supposed to walk around," his patients ask, "show up to work, go to the grocery store, when I can lose control any second? How am I supposed to take care of my kids?"

Ben keeps offering the same strategies. Breathing. Meditation. Routines. Exercise. Medication. "It works," he tells them. "It's not perfect, but in time, it works."

His job is to be steady. To keep saying the same things. He thinks of the Benedictines he studied in college, how he always thought they were crazy, because they believed that by staying in one place, and repeating the same prayers over and over, they could save the world. Well, now here he is, muttering the same things over and over, trying to save the world.

One night after group, Minerva follows Ben all the way back to his office. She can never quite let him go—she always holds him for an extra minute or two, chatting about her plans, trying to get him to come along to concerts, galleries, pop-up restaurants. Tonight she tells him about a one-woman show she's putting on: *Minerva: Unplugged.* "It's off-Broadway," she says. "Actually, it's in my apartment. But it's a start." She hands him a flyer—a sketched self-portrait, with a butterfly perched on the part of her hairline. "One weekend only," she says. "Miss it, and you miss it."

He says he'll try to come.

"I knew I could count on you, Big Daddy," she says. She calls him that. At first he discouraged it, but now he lets her. He pretty much lets her get away with whatever she wants.

"Good night," he says.

"Toodles," she says. And saunters away, a bit wobbly on her heels. Ben has the feeling he might never see her again. He has this feeling every week. Minerva is hanging by a thread.

At home that night, Ben is cooking dinner for himself, peeling a carrot. He has the TV on, CNN. It's the top of the hour, and the anchor announces the date. He is stunned when he hears it. He had known Sammy's birthday was coming up, but has been so busy it escaped him. He doesn't give himself time to think about it—just picks up the phone and taps her name. Then there is that second before it connects. He thinks of what he'll say. Surely she can't still be mad, he thinks. She'll be glad to hear from him.

Then a robot is telling him the number he has dialed is no longer in service.

He is stunned. Sammy has changed her number. To send him a message, no doubt, in case he ever decided to call. She doesn't want to hear from him.

He tries to picture her on the phone with her service carrier, requesting a new number—how angry she must have been to do such a thing. He remembers Kurtz writing down her number in his address book, remembers leaving his card for her that first night, after the ball. Having each other's number, keeping in touch, has been the guiding principal of their life together. Though they haven't spoken in months—a bit over a year, actually, come to think of it—there was the sense, for Ben, that something was still alive—just aging, maybe even improving, like whiskey in a barrel. There was always the sense they would tap back into it someday. Everything he has done this past year, he admits, he has imagined presenting to Sammy one day, as evidence of his self-improvement. He has imagined the triumphant moment he tells her about his new work. About Minerva. The purpose he feels. He has gone out into the streets and encountered people and come to know them, like Sammy said. He is a new man.

But she doesn't want to hear it, apparently. He thinks of what Minerva always says: *I had to kill Jeff Jones, you understand. He had to be killed.* And wonders if getting rid of him was, for Sammy, a matter of survival.

III.

Boy meets girl, catches girl, loses girl.

But it doesn't matter, because it's just a game, a game they shouldn't have spent so much time playing. They have been called inside. There are other things to tend to, work and family, the business of their lives. So they get to it.

The boy gets up in the morning and goes to work, comes home at night. And the same for the girl. They do this again and again, until they can't remember who won the game, or whether they were even keeping score. They work until the game is obscured by time, until they forget its rules and even its object. They work until they can't even remember what it was, a game or a dream.

2012-2017

Then a long time passes, and Ben and Sammy don't have anything to do with each other.

Sammy sets her mind to the tasks and people in front of her. She does her work, cares for her daughter. Suddenly she is all-in: The room parent at Ava's school, the one organizing the Halloween parties and raffle ticket sales. She goes on all the field trips, to the pumpkin patch and cider mill, the dairy farm, the art museum. She is there for all of it, documenting everything with pictures and notes, though not because she wishes to turn them into snide anecdotes about life in the Midwest. But because, after all, this is her life.

During these initial months, Sammy does something she never considered before: She makes an appointment with a therapist, a woman in the phone book who advertises herself as a family counselor. The therapist's office is a small space in the middle of a suburban strip mall, just a spare room with two chairs and small table between them. When Sammy arrives, the therapist is already sitting in her chair, her hands folded in her lap. "Welcome," she says, and Sammy nearly turns away and runs back to her car. Something about the therapist makes her nervous. The woman is wearing a flowing, flowered dress, and has long, silver hair parted in the middle. Pale blue eyes. A smile on her face that says: *I am one with myself and the world.* She looks like she has been wandering the earth since Woodstock.

Sammy sits across from the woman and fidgets. Her eyes dart around the room.

"What brings you here today?" the therapist asks. Her voice is tranquil to the point it is unsettling.

"I'm not here for me," Sammy explains, waving her hand a little, pushing the notion away. "I suppose I'm just looking for strategies. Strategies to help my daughter. She's a little." Sammy falters. "She's a little lonely. Not making friends at school. And the situation has sort of, well, gotten out of hand a little. She keeps pretending to be a dog, is the problem."

"I see," says the therapist. "How old is she?"

"Eight."

"And what were you like at eight?" asks the therapist. Sammy winces. This isn't what she's here for, not at all. The fact that she was the same at Ava's age—lonely, silent—has been troubling Sammy this whole time. She doesn't want to be the source of this particular spring. But here she is. "Were you the same?"

"I was a little quiet," she says. "But that was different. That was understandable because, well." She trails off.

"Because?"

"Because that was the year my mother died."

Jesus! She's only been here a minute and already, this.

"I see," says the therapist. She seems pleased with herself. As if she's beaten some sort of personal record. Death of mother in under sixty seconds.

And so begins a series of four sessions in which Sammy comes in to talk about Ava, but winds up talking about herself. One session, she tries to talk about Ava's only friend, Wissam, gone with the wind. "She had this one good friend," Sammy says. "They were really, it's hard to explain. They got each other. They had their own language. But then he sort of disappeared."

"And what about your friendships?" the therapist asked.

At the end of the fourth session, Sammy breaks up with the therapist. "I really don't need help," she says, frustrated. "All I want from this arrangement is a little help with how to help my daughter, and we keep talking about all this other shit. Pardon me for saying."

"I understand," says the therapist. "Let me ask you just one more question about yourself, if you don't mind, and then we'll leave it. I'm just curious, when your mother died, how did your father handle it?"

Sammy thinks for a minute. Stares at the ceiling. Lets out all the air in her lungs in a rush. "Well," she finally concludes, "we got a dog, I guess."

They sit for a moment in a profoundly awkward silence.

"Have you ever considered," asks the therapist, "getting a dog?"

Sammy frowns. No, is the answer to that particular question. It has never even crossed her mind.

"It might not be the worst idea in the world. You might try it."

Suddenly Sammy is buoyant, lifted up by the notion of a dog. She practically jumps out of her chair, she is so excited. "That's all I was looking for," she says. "All I wanted was one little piece of concrete advice. Thank you. Thank you!"

"You're welcome." The therapist stands, and they hug it out.

That very day, Sammy picks Ava up from school and they go straight to the shelter. They walk down the row of dogs, all of them jumping and howling in their cages, stopping once to interact with a bulldog, once with a terrier, once with a lab. Then, toward the end of the row, slumped in a cage, her head resting on her paws, they encounter some kind of spotted basset hound/beagle mix. Her ears are unbelievably long. They ripple down the sides of her face and pool on the floor of the cage. She lifts her head a little at the sight of Sammy and Ava, then sets it back down. She isn't one to get her hopes up.

"This one," Sammy tells the attendant. The attendant unlocks the dog's cage and scoops her out, delivers her into Ava's outstretched arms. The dog looks bewildered. She looks up at Sammy as if wanting some kind of explanation.

"It wasn't me," Sammy says. "You can't prove anything."

At home, Lou the Fifth sniffs around the perimeter of the living room, then circles the braided oval rug a few times, then settles herself down right in the middle of it. Sammy heads off to the kitchen to make dinner. When she looks back toward the living room, she sees that Ava has stretched out next to Lou the Fifth on the rug, and has draped her arm around her. Their heads are pressed together. They are looking at each other like: Where have you been all my life?

In the following months, she finishes her book on Emily Dickinson, places it with a press. Gets tenure. Then applies for jobs closer to home. She winds up landing a job in Amherst, right where Emily Dickinson lived and worked, and starts a new life there. The kids are smarter at her new school, which is nice, though she finds she misses her old students, the first-generation ones, the ones who were hungry. On the whole, though, things are better. Ava is in a good public school. And they are closer to Sammy's father, so close he can drive down on the weekends, still in the old Buick, for Ava's soccer games. Sammy is living more or less the kind of life she lived growing up—if a bit better. She and Ava are renting a carriage house behind an old mansion, one of those stone houses with a red tile roof. Sammy feels she has struck a good balance. While it is true that horses used to be stabled in the house she lives in, it is also true that she is living on an estate.

Eventually, all those years she spent with Ben, when she couldn't get through even a single day without some kind of contact with him, seem like a dream. An illness she had. Something she has gotten over. Most of the time, when she thinks of him, she is happy to be rid of him.

Then again, she sometimes thinks, none of this is quite right. She studies narratives for a living, and has never read a story like this, a story where two characters spend so many years together and then, suddenly, nothing—they erase each other. Sometimes, three of four times a year maybe, she falls into little reveries, wondering about Ben, what it all meant, how it could end the way it did. Wondering if he ever thinks of her. But then she pulls herself out of it.

This isn't a book, Ben used to say to her. Whenever she got carried away. Whenever she thought she knew how something would turn out. Grow up, he sometimes added. This isn't a book.

Then it is 2016, and Hillary Clinton is running for president, and suddenly memories of Ben are impossible to avoid. The months leading up to Clinton's nomination seem linked to those months twenty years earlier, in some opposite yet integral way, the way a photograph relates to its negative. Sammy can't watch a campaign event without thinking of its predecessor. Tonight, for instance—the second night of the Democratic Convention. She remembers watching all those years ago with her father. Now she is more or less forcing her daughter to watch, thinking it will be good for a girl Ava's age—she is thirteen already—to see the first woman nominated by a major political party. "This is important," she keeps telling Ava. "I know you might not think it is, but it is. It totally is."

"I know," Ava says.

It's the night of Bill Clinton's big speech—he is going to talk about his wife, going to give the country a sense of what she's really like, what she really cares about. Sammy's father has driven down from Manchester, and they are making a little party of it. He and Ava and Lou Grant V are sitting on the couch. Sammy monitors this little scene from the kitchen, where she is making popcorn, standing at the stove waiting for the oil to heat, waiting for that first kernel to pop. She keeps looking from the stove to the living room, impatient, nervous for some reason—she doesn't want to miss Bill Clinton's arrival on stage. Sammy has the strange feeling, watching her daughter and father and the dog sit on the couch, in front of the television, that she is watching herself, all those years ago. The older she gets, the more frequently this happens: she feels she can see forward and backward in the same moment. Everything is layered. Everything echoes, resonates.

Clinton keeps everyone waiting, as usual, and Sammy has more than enough time to make the popcorn. She dumps it in a bowl, cranks some salt over it, carries it out to the couch, sits next to her father. Ava and Sammy's father are telling jokes. Sammy has missed the setup but arrives just in time for the punchline. "Buddy," Ava says. "I don't know how you got here, but I stepped on a duck."

The father laughs. And Ava, who has managed to deliver the punchline without cracking a smile, breaks too. At the same moment, and in just the same way, they both bring their hands to their mouths. A family gesture, Sammy supposes. They are guarded, tentative in their joy.

Finally, Bill Clinton comes out on stage, and the crowd erupts in cheers. Sammy is shocked at how thin he has grown. His eyes are bulging, and his head appears too big for his body. Clinton stands taking in the applause for a long moment. Something he's still good at. Still loves, Sammy can tell.

Then Bill Clinton begins his speech. "In the spring of 1971," he says, "I met a girl."

And the crowd goes wild.

Bill Clinton goes on talking about how he came to know Hillary Rodham back at Yale Law School. About the first few times they saw each other, in classrooms and at the library. How they stood in line together to register for classes. Then went on their first date—a walk through the art museum. It is a sweet story, a meet cute. Not at all what Sammy was expecting. The last thing, in fact. It's been so long since the Clintons tried to look like a normal couple, since that time in Manchester, that 60 Minutes interview. Ever since Clinton took office, every aspect of their lives has been sniffed out by bloodhounds, printed in the papers, looped endlessly on cable news, and none of it was sweet, none of it had to do with love. But the love story, or lack of a love story, doesn't matter anymore, Sammy has been thinking lately, because Hillary Clinton is running against a dangerous man, someone who might very well get us all killed. This is basically what she expected Bill Clinton to come out and say. That now isn't the time for games. That he and Hillary aren't playing around anymore, they're not trying to pass themselves off as regular, middle-class people from Arkansas. Nor do you want us to, because that shit's over, all of that American Pie bullshit is dead, a stupid dream from which we were rudely awakened in 2001. Shit is real now. ISIS, Al-Qaeda. The total collapse of the housing market we're still recovering from all these years later. Not to mention we're still fighting the forever war, and probably always will be. So who do you want driving this bus, this bus careening through the flames of hell? Don't you want this woman, who was Secretary of State, don't you want this bitch, as so many of you call her, don't you want this bad bitch at the wheel, instead of that lunatic, that petulant monster? I sure as hell fucking do, I can tell you that.

Or something along those lines. That's what Sammy was expecting to hear.

But what Bill Clinton ends up saying is something sweet. A simple story. Two kids eyeing each other across a room. Falling in love. Because that's how it always starts. No matter the wild turns that come later, the soaring highs and crushing lows, the obsession, the boredom, the fortune, the devastation, no matter what, Sammy thinks, that's how it always starts. That's how lives are altered. Boy meets girl. Boy meets girl. Boy meets girl.

Later, after her father has gone home and Ava is off to bed, Sammy can't stop thinking of Ben. He must have watched the speech—she is sure of this—and she wonders if it made him think of her, too. She considers calling him. Or maybe just texting. She pulls up the app, types his name in. A dialogue bubble pops up on her phone. *I met a girl*, she types. Thinking it somehow encapsulates everything she wants to say. But then she loses her nerve. Deletes it. Backs out of the app.

Then on that long, crazy night in November, when Hillary Clinton loses the election, Sammy finds herself thinking of Ben again. What is he doing right now? she wonders. What would he say, if he were here? She considers calling, but is too stunned. Queasy. The world has lost its mind.

Then comes the night of the inaugural ball, which she both does and does not want to watch—a feeling something akin to watching an accident. All night she goes back and forth—yes, no, yes, no—and finally turns on the TV.

The ball is in a different building than the one she attended years ago, though things look much the same. She watches for a few minutes. The new president and his wife are dancing to a simpering version of Frank Sinatra's "My Way." They have somehow made the song into a duet, a man and a woman singing over each other, each claiming personal victory. Which doesn't make any sense, when you think about it. *Who's running this thing?* she wonders. It looks like the kind of entertainment you'd expect to find on a cruise ship. It's as if all the bad taste in the world has gathered together in a single room.

The camera pulls back, scanning the crowd, and Sammy notices the most salient difference between the ball, as it is happening now, and the ball back then—everyone in the audience is holding up a cell phone. The room is flecked with hundreds of rectangles of blue light.

Ah, the phone. For better or worse, the place where people store and even carry out their lives. She picks up her own. The screen lights up with a picture of her and Ava, their heads pressed together. One side of the screen is cracked in a pattern that encircles the left side of her face, creating the effect of dramatic crow's feet— the left side of her face looks twenty years older than the right. It won't be long, she understands now, before that time arrives. Twenty years will pass by in a moment.

She thinks of the night of the ball, how young she was, how naïve, how everything was new to her. She remembers feeling dizzy, seasick—everything made her so nervous. But it was exciting, too. She runs through the whole thing, the way Lara Gardner had organized her transformation, then the ball itself, getting lost, crying in the bathroom, the drive back to Charlottesville, the diner. She lands, finally, on those few hours she spent in bed with Ben, curled against him, the first time she had ever felt close to anyone. She is surprised to realize it doesn't hurt to remember this. The pain is gone. She is able to think of Ben, and all those years she spent loving him, without the flush of embarrassment she usually feels. No one is at fault, it seems, no one is to blame. All that time they spent together, they were both just doing their best. They hardly knew what they were doing. They were just kids.

2017

Friday group is almost over. They are going around the circle, talking about the trouble they had during the week, though in some cases, too, there is good news. One of the vets says he landed a job in an IT department, is excited to start working, to have a reason to get out of bed in the morning. Another, who is working now as a fireman, has taught his first yoga class. Hot yoga is his tribe, he says. His people, his thing. All the shit, all the shit from the war and the fire department, it all melts away on the mat. Some of the vets nod, interested, while the others are skeptical—it can be hard to listen to someone who thinks he's figured it all out.

Ben is going over the parting routine, telling the circle about new services at the hospital, when he hears, softly at first, a trudging—footsteps approaching down the hallway. A man shuffles in and takes a seat in the circle. He is broad, stocky, wearing a gray sweat suit. His hair is shorn close to the scalp.

"Welcome," Ben says. "We're just wrapping up."

This is a new patient, someone Ben doesn't recognize, though something about him is familiar. Then Ben sees it, in the eyes: this broad, squat, acne-scarred, buzz-cut veteran is, or was, Minerva. Is Jeff Jones, apparently.

In the past year, Minerva has been unraveling. Has missed group some weeks, and when she has shown up, has had a cracked façade. The shoes were the first to go—all of a sudden Marilyn Monroe was wearing Nikes instead of stilettos. Then the clothes started to taper. From glamorous dresses to more practical ones—simple ones that pulled over the head and floated freely. Then another downshift, into blouses and slacks, until finally one week, she appeared in a purple bathrobe and pajama set. The false eyelashes were gone. Her makeup was simple, just some lipstick and shadow. But tonight is something else entirely. The wig is gone, the last of the makeup. It marks the first time Jeff Jones has appeared.

"I'm Jeff," he says. "I'm just stopping in to say hello." Jeff's voice is lower than Minerva's, though still has a delicate quality at odds with his muscular build. He is so soft-spoken, the other vets lean forward in their chairs.

"How are you feeling this week?" Ben asks. His standard question.

"I'm okay," Jeff says. "Just tired."

"Are you getting any sleep?" Ben asks.

"Enough," Jeff says. "I'm fine."

Jeff is so different from Minerva. Shy. Deflecting attention. Unwilling to elaborate.

"Well, we're happy to see you," says Ben. "We're here if you want to talk."

"Not really," Jeff says. "I know the hour is up. I just wanted to say hello."

Then one of the vets, a kid with a head injury who is slow to catch on to almost everything, says, "Holy shit! It's Minerva!"

Jeff smiles—just a slight lift of his mouth in the left corner. There's a twinkle in his eye, but only for a second.

The session wraps and Ben waits for Jeff to approach. But he doesn't. He is bent down, tying his shoe. Then he is talking to some of the other vets. Ben lingers, waits until Jeff is free.

"Do you have anything going on this weekend?" he asks.

Though he never once attended one of Minerva's events, he is interested now. He wonders how *Minerva: Unplugged* turned out. The self-portrait show. The burlesque dancing hour. The acoustic showcase. "Any shows? Any revivals?"

"No," says Jeff Jones, softly. "I'm taking a break from all that." Then he does the most startling thing he has ever done—he waves goodbye, and walks away from Ben.

Ben watches Jeff disappear down the hallway, and considers the possibilities. There's a chance that, despite appearances, this could be a good thing—maybe Jeff Jones feels safe to exist again. Has forgiven himself. Is making his first tentative steps in the world.

Or it could be a bad thing.

Most likely it's a bad thing.

Later that night, troubled, still thinking of Jeff Jones, Ben climbs into bed and unpacks his dinner from its plastic bag, settles the cartons around himself. Everything as usual, just as he likes it. He turns on the TV and is faced with a spectacle—throngs of people in formal wear, crammed in a giant room, chatting in little circles of three and four, holding drinks, throwing their heads back, laughing. Somehow he'd forgotten. It's the night of the inaugural ball.

He watches for a few minutes, watches the new president and his slender wife dance to a cover of Frank Sinatra's "My Way." They are tentative together, awkward. The wife looks like a contestant at a pageant, nervous, tortured in her movements. Twirl, is the direction she's given, and she twirls, though it looks perfunctory, like the definition of a twirl in the dictionary. There is no joy in it. No joy in the music, a sappy cover, something you'd hear while on hold with the cable company. As if all the world's bad taste, he thinks, has come together in the same room.

He is disgusted. He pats the covers around him for the remote, hoping it will spring up.

Then his phone lights up.

Ben doesn't recognize the number, though his phone tells him the caller is not far away, somewhere in Western Massachusetts. Where Sammy is, he knows—he still keeps track of her. Something in his chest tightens. She must be watching the same thing, must be thinking of him, too. He knows that she is closer now, and if he picks up, they will fall back into it. He stares at the phone for a few seconds. Wonders what to do.

An image flashes through his mind, a memory—his very first glimpse of Sammy. She was behind the counter at that old sandwich shop, her hair pulled back. A loose strand had fallen across her face and, as she looked up and saw him, she had moved to brush it away with the back of her wrist. This image, recreated all these years later, is still so intense it is visceral—it stirs something in him. The feeling now is the same as it was then. What he had wanted, in that moment, was to reach out and brush away the strand of hair that had fallen across her face—to do that, himself. The same feeling surges through him again, a rush of warmth, tenderness.

And he picks up the phone.